A Falcon Flies

A Falcon Flies

by

James Boschert

Fireship Press
www.FireshipPress.com

A Falcon Flies by James Boschert

ISBN-13: 978-1-61179-285-0 (Paperback)
ISBN-978-1-61179-286-7 (e-book)

BISAC Subject Headings:
FIC014000FICTION / Historical
FIC032000FICTION / War & Military
FIC031020FICTION / Thrillers / Historical

Editing: Chris Paige

Cover Illustration by Christine Horner

Address all correspondence to:
Fireship Press, LLC
P.O. Box 68412
Tucson, AZ 85737
Or visit our website at:
www.FireshipPress.com

Dedication

This book is dedicated to Danielle.

Acknowledgements

To Chris Paige for all the hard work editing and Christine Horner for the cover.

Rubayat of Omar Khayyam; Persian Miniatures	By Liber Press
Dungeon Fire and Sword; The Knights Templars	John Robinson
The Castles of the Assassins	Peter Willey
The Assassins	Bernard Lewis
The Legendary Cuisine of Persia	Margaret Shaida
The Valleys of the Assassins	Freya Stark
A Fool of God [Poems of Baba Tahir	E. Heron Allen
The Dream of the Poem	Peter Cole
A Short History of the Ismailis	Farhad Daftary
The Templars	Barbara Frale
Saracen Faris	David Nicolle Ph.D Christa Hook
The Illustrated RUMI	Phillip Dunn, Manuella Dunn Mascetti. R.A. Nicholson

Translations

Atabeg Military Seljuk chief or governor
Barbari Long, flat, corrugated bread
Bātinīs Assassins, or 'Assassins
Bazaari Men from the bazaar
Chai Khane Tea house
Chash Subservient "Yes"
Doogh A drink made of yogurt
Ferengi Foreigner
F*ida'i* Assassin
Genab "Sir"
Ghilim A mat woven of goat hair or wool
Gorban Lord
Gorban e Shoma "Worship to you"
Hakim Physician
In Shah'Allah "If Allah wills it"
Khanom Madame
Kharagi Foreigner, Outsider
Khoda Hafez "God protect"
Lasiq Novice
Maast Yogurt
Madrassa College, school
Maidan Public square in a town or village
Masjid Mosque
Nan Flat bread
Nizirite Member of the Niziri Ismaili people
Oustez Egyptian 'Sir '
Rafiq Senior member of assassins

Rais Headman
Salaamed To bow and call for *salaam*: "Peace"
Samiran Rud Samiran river valley
Sarvan Captain
Shah Rud Valley of the king
Syce Groom
Tar Earliest twelve-stringed guitar
Taroff Debt of gratitude
Timsar Military rank of general
Zor Khane Working house, or gymnasium

Part I

Discoveries and Dangers

The falcon now with rapid wing soars through the azure sky,
Below a scene magnificent bursts on its piercing eye;
Proud Carmel rears his grassy peak, bedecked with varied flowers,
His woody plumage proudly nods, o'er Acre's snowy towers:
Behind—he views Naplouse's hills, that shew a winding road,
Which leads to fam'd Jerusalem, the city lov'd of God.

—from *Poems,* compiled by Hadler

Chapter 1

Acre 1177 AD

A figure dressed as a monk and hooded against the pattering rain made his way along the muddy street towards the doorway of a large stone house, where sleepy guards loitered on the steps, talking to one another. They became alert as the figure approached. It was just past midnight, and the sound of singing could be heard as the monks attended midnight mass in the chapel of Saint Jean, two streets away.

"Who goes?" one of the guards demanded, his spear slanting towards the silent figure at it stopped in front of them.

"Brother Jonathan, to see the Bishop," the cowled man stated in a sharp tone.

"Ahem, Brother, please wait," the other guard said more respectfully, and knocked on the heavy wooden door.

A sleepy voice answered from within, whereupon the guard opened the door, which creaked on its iron hinges. He spoke to someone inside, then gestured to the monk to enter.

Brother Jonathan brushed past the guards without even acknowledging them, and waited for the door to close behind.

A Falcon Flies

A servant waved for Brother Jonathan to follow and led the way along silent corridors. He carried a rushlight that flickered in the draughts. The shadows thrown up by the light galloped towards them, dancing like lively phantoms on the cold stone walls as the servant and monk passed, imitating their forms in grotesque shapes, then merging into the darkness behind them.

Eventually they arrived at a small hallway illuminated by guttering torches in sconces along the walls. The servant, who had not said a word the entire time, knocked on the door, opened it, then announced the monk in a low tone to someone inside.

He stepped back to make way for Brother Jonathan then pulled the door closed with a creak of leather hinges and a click of the latch. The monk moved a couple of paces into a room brightly lit by candles; clearly the bishop did not stint himself for expensive beeswax. Jonathan bowed obsequiously to the man seated behind a large desk strewn with paper rolls and ink pots. He was bundled up in woolen clothes and wore a fur-lined cloak. The embers of a fire still glowed in a corner fireplace, emitting a little heat into the stone room.

"Who are you?" the bishop demanded.

"I, er... I am Brother Jonathan; you sent for me, Your Eminence," Jonathan stuttered. He wiped his nose with the sleeve of his cowl, his eyes looking at the floor.

"Ah yes, so I did." The bishop put down a quill and waved Jonathan to a seat in front of him. Jonathan hurriedly sat down and for the first time looked up at the bishop.

The Bishop looked tired, with dark shadows under his eyes. He was a thin man with a tight, humorless mouth and an aquiline nose. Dark, deep-set eyes regarded Jonathan with suspicion; at the sight of his worn sleeves and not very clean habit, the grim mouth tightened.

"I understand that you know a knight by the name of Sir Talon. Is that correct?"

"Er, yes, My Lord. I sailed to Constantinople with him and Sir Guy de Veres last year."

"I have seen your report; in fact I have it here." The bishop waved at the thick pile of papers in front of him. "The report makes it clear that you disapproved of much that took place; and while you did not say much about Sir Guy himself, you seem to have found Sir Talon wanting in his behavior, and excessive in his contact with the Byzantine citizens."

"I... I did not find Sir Talon a pious man, My Lord; that along with his close attachment to the Greeks was... offensive. They err on the side of heresy, but he seemed to find them more to his liking than prayers and attendance upon God's work. His confessions were, to put it mildly... sparse."

"You are aware that he is now back in Acre and has somehow accumulated in a very short period of time a great deal of wealth, including ships, which he obtained perhaps... in Constantinople?"

"I am aware, Sir. He has three ships, and reputedly much treasure. He has a large house in the city, and from what I can see he pays mere lip service to the Order of Templars, for whom they say he still works. I do not know if he is in fact a Templar!"

"Indeed, he is not, and I find it strange that he should have become rich so quickly," the bishop mused. "I doubt it was done honestly. But there is something more important, and it is why I have asked you to come."

He leaned forward, his dark, hooded eyes boring into Jonathan's. "It would seem that Sir Talon is here under somewhat false pretenses."

Jonathan sat up; the bishop had his full attention now. "What do you mean, My Lord?"

"I have received a document of impeccable origins from the bishop of Albi, who informs me that Sir Talon is wanted in Languedoc for witchcraft," the bishop announced. He watched the emotions crossing the thin features of the man in front of him, and knew that he had chosen well.

"I am charging you, Brother Jonathan, to find out all you can about this... this knight. There are many rumors. I wish to know if he is attending mass regularly, with whom he spends his time, and what he does at night. Everything is to be reported to me, and only me. Do you understand?"

Jonathan gulped. "Yes, My Lord. I understand. But... if I am to make enquiries of this nature I will need help to keep watch and so forth, and I may be questioned. What am I to tell anyone who asks?"

"You may inform any inquisitive colleagues that I have given you a special mission, and should they have questions they need to come to me. I think that will cool their interest. Speak to the head servant and ask him to find you a place in this house where you can go to work."

He leaned back in his tall-backed chair. "I need not tell you the gravity of these charges, Brother. This depraved man, who sins against God, does not have the protection of the Templars, for he is not yet a full brother of that Order. Word of this investigation must not get about, or that Order might well find some way to protect him. He is not without friends, and Sir Guy carries great influence with the Grand Master, and even the king."

Jonathan blinked, but nodded and wiped his dripping nose. "I shall be discreet, My Lord."

"Remember that while the Holy Church can benefit from this, so can you," the bishop said, and narrowly observed the look of gratification and greed that flitted across the monk's face. Nodding almost imperceptibly, he said, "You may go," and waved the monk towards the door.

Jonathan stood up and bowed low to the bishop, who paid him no attention; then he hurried to open the door and go back along the long dark corridors and to exit into the night.

*****

Talon rolled over on the soft bed to stare blearily across the room at the woman who stood by the window. Early morning sunlight poured in through the opened shutters, lighting the heavy drapes and throwing her naked form into sharp relief. The clangor of bells from the nearby church of Saint George was beginning to make his head ache. The bright light made him squint, but he could still appreciate the halo of russet hair that flowed over her finely shaped back.

As though sensing his gaze she turned, revealing full breasts, a flat belly and a light bush of hair at the junction of her long thighs. She came towards him, reaching for a cover on a nearby chair as she did so. She threw it over her shoulders but did not close the front.

The woman walked towards him with a smile that told him she enjoyed his gaze and reached out a hand to caress his bearded cheek. "You were on form last night, my handsome knight, despite the skinful of wine you brought with you." She licked her lips in a manner that threatened to arouse him all over again, but then she frowned and said with a laugh in her voice, "Now you must go. My confessor will be here before very long."

"Your confessor?" Talon asked stupidly.

"Why yes. Brother Martin... do you know him?"

Talon's eyes opened wide and he scrambled out of the bed. He knew and liked Brother Martin, but this was not the place to be found in by a man of the church, no matter how well they liked one another.

"Susannah, I apologize, I should have left long ago!" he said as he struggled into his loose trousers, then almost fell back onto the bed to drag on his calf-length boots. His eyes searched for the rest of his clothing, strewn over the chairs and floor of the spacious chamber. Susannah picked up his sword and its belt and handed them to him.

"No matter, Talon, it was a good evening; you were in fine spirits and your sword was as sharp as ever." She grinned at him mischievously as she helped him with his overshirt. "Go out the back way; it will be better. The servants will not talk... if they know what is good for them. Do not fear my confession, as it will be vague, and I suspect that Brother Martin will not know how to deal with it.

Talon grinned and kissed her on the lips, reliving for an instant the chaotic coupling of the night before, then stepped out of the upstairs room to walk gingerly along the passage and out onto the rear balcony of the house. He could hear the clatter of pots and pans in the kitchen below and the loud talk of servants as they went about their business.

It would be preferable, he thought, if he weren't seen leaving the widow Lady Geoffrey's house in the early hours of Matins. He carried his sword, belt and cloak in one hand as he quietly made his way down the stairs. A maidservant at the bottom of the stairs was just about to come up; she made way for him with a knowing smile and a brief curtsy, then he was past and stepping out of the garden gate, leaving the house and the evening behind.

He had come to like Susannah during the last few months, and wondered if his feelings for her might be progressing to another level. She was intelligent and carried a title; with their combined wealth, who knew?

He shook his head to clear the cobwebs as he made his way to his own house, situated on Bertram's street, only a short walk from the Templar stronghold of the city of Acre.

*****

Two days later, as the dawn lightened the eastern sky the city of Acre awoke. Those who were of religious orders, such as the Templars and the churchmen, prepared for the services of Lauds at the various churches and chapels dotted about the city. Bells began to ring, creating a discordant cacophony. Guards on the walls yawned, and apprentices crawled out of their primitive beds in attics or stables, rubbing the sleep out of their eyes.

At one street intersection a man hunched in his cloak and stared across the road at a doorway further down the street. He was cold and slapped his arms against his chest in an attempt to keep warm. The beginning of activity along the street made him sidle deeper into the stone wall crevice he had found for himself the night before.

From the window of his bedroom Talon caught sight of the movement and quickly slid back into the darkness of his room to avoid being spotted. He hastened to descend the stairs and slipped out into the street through the back garden. Today he would follow his shadow.

Talon had noticed the night before that someone was following him. It was unsettling, as it could be that Assassins were here in Acre with a score to settle. He needed to know why he was being followed and where the man had come from; rather than confronting him and perhaps having to injure or even kill the man before he knew what was going on, he would see where the fellow went. He had little trouble picking his watcher out as the man walked along the streets in the general direction of the western part of the city.

Top Talon's surprise the man stopped at the gates of a well known building, where he was admitted after rapping on the wood. The man murmured to someone just inside the gates and then glanced behind him briefly to check the street, but Talon had dodged out of sight. Talon stayed where he was, watching the Bishop's palace for a few long minutes, then made his way home in a thoughtful mood.

Why was the Bishop having him watched? He kept very much to himself in his newly built and spacious house. His needs were taken care of by a housekeeper and several servants, which allowed him privacy, and, compared to his first stay in Acre, comfort. Aside from the occasional foray to an inn with his captains and their crews, and those rare visits to Susannah, he could not be faulted for debauchery or lechery, unlike most of the inactive and bored knights in this city.

He resolved to find out as soon as he could, but it would have to wait until nightfall, when the man might come again. The streets were already filling up with laborers, shopkeepers, and peddlers preparing their stalls for another day. The market place over on the south side would be open already, and much of the pedestrian traffic was making its way in that direction. Servants, maids and cooks went to buy what they could for their households, while others went there either with wares to sell or in the hope of finding some form of work.

He passed beggars crying for alms with outstretched dirty hands, squatting in corners alongside the filth of the street. Small boys pushed past, shouting to one another as they ran errands, Apprentices walked in groups, eying him warily because of his manner of dress. Talon wore flowing robes which at a distance made him resemble a Saracen, a mode of dress that was no longer unusual in the Holy Land among those Franks who appreciated the fact that the loose cotton was cooler to wear than the tight, restrictive woolen clothing the Frankish people normally wore. Some of the apprentices glanced at him from under their brows and made remarks in low tones. None, however, attempted to accost him; most of them had noticed the way he carried himself, and if the long curved sword at his side was not warning enough, some even noticed the scar along Talon's jaw, barely hidden by his light colored beard, and the slight menace it gave to his features. Especially now, with the scowl brought on by his thoughts, Talon was not someone who looked like he should be trifled with.

There were few knights on the streets at this time of day; they would be slow to rise, having spent the night carousing in the many ale houses in the city. The only knights who would be about would be those of the Orders who had risen before the dawn to make their obeisance to God in the chapels.

He ignored the apprentices and hurried on to reach his house and thump on the heavy wooden door. While he waited for Samuel to come and open it he glanced around him. The street was possibly a little cleaner than others, but it still had piles of rubbish moldering in corners, and even at this early hour dogs were nosing around in the heaps of rags and offal rotting in the open. There was a beggar squatting at a corner at the end of the street who raised his hand in acknowledgement, and Talon nodded to him.

Talon had an affinity for beggars; they were not seen by most people, but they saw and heard a great deal. He helped this one with the odd coin and food from his kitchen, and in repayment was kept informed as to what that worthy saw and heard from his kin. He would talk to him again later in the day about the watcher.

The smell of fresh baking wafted to him and his mouth watered as he realized that he was hungry and eager for breakfast. He turned as he heard footsteps; the small grill in the middle of the door slid open with a snap and Samuel peered out at him, his aged eyes watchful.

"Open up, Samuel."

"Good morning, Sir Talon," Samuel replied in his rasping voice as he hurried to open the stout door for his master. Talon entered.

"God be praised, it is a nice day again, Sir Talon," Samuel said, his tone neutral as he shut the door with a clatter. Talon merely nodded; the day would be another hot one. Samuel limped after him as he made his way down the short passage to the courtyard of the substantial house he now called home. He gave a brief look around, took in the work being done at the stables and the bustle at the kitchen doors. His household was wide awake, and those who noticed him acknowledged him with ducked heads or curtsies along with smiles.

"Sergeant Max is waiting for you in the dining chamber, Sir Talon," Samuel wheezed as he hastened after Talon; he was an old Templar Sergeant who had survived many years of service in the Order and now served out his old age as a doorkeeper and watchman for Talon.

"Thank you, Samuel," Talon said.

"God bless, Sir," the old man said as he watched Talon head for the dining room.

Max Bauersdorf, Sergeant of Templars, was seated at a large table in the middle of the room which had been piled with food for breakfast. The usual heavy fare of the Franks was absent; in its stead was a light meal of baked pigeons and a roasted fish caught the day before. Next to the meat was a loaf of fresh baked bread and some vegetables that came from the garden of the house. There was even a bowl of grapes from his young vines, which had appealed to him when he bought the house. They reminded him of his stay in Constantinople with Alexios's family. The cook's husband tended to the garden, and to save the grapes from the migratory birds he had picked bunches a week ago when they were at their peak and had coated the stem with beeswax to retain their freshness.

Talon's cook, Sateen, rose at dawn every day and went to the market find the best fruits, vegetables and fresh meat for this house. He considered her a rare find. Her family came from the region near Tiberius, and could rightly claim to have been in the country for generations. Her sharp tongue kept the other servants in line, and the shopkeepers respected her enough to ask fair prices for their wares.

"Hello, Max, God be with you," Talon said as he slid onto a chair and hefted a large jug, from which he poured clean water into a beaker. Max observed him quietly; his grizzled and scarred face registered mild disapproval.

"God be with you, Talon. I shall not ask you where you have been today as you missed Lauds, but there was some concern about your absence."

This was as close as Max would come to a rebuke. Talon nodded acknowledgement of the implied telling off. He and Max had been comrades for many years now, and knew each other well. Max, while a Sergeant in the Order of Templars, worked for Talon under an arrangement made with Sir Guy de Veres, Knight of the Order. Max might not approve of Talon's occasional nightly forays, but he would not reproach him, as Talon was discreet and did not often go out on the town. In this particular case he was mistaken, and Talon intended to inform him of what he had discovered.

Their friendship went back to the time when Talon had left this very city in chains bound for his home in the Languedoc near the town of Albi. They had had many adventures since, and had been on the verge of poverty before they lives had changed when Sir

Guy de Veres had taken them to Constantinople. After more adventures, they had returned with not one but three ships, and much wealth.

"I was out following someone who spent most of last night watching this house."

Max's raised eyebrows indicated his surprise. "Did you find out who it was?"

"No, but he made straight for the Bishop's house when he left; I followed him there. Who in that house would have an interest in me?"

Max shrugged, "I do not know, but I can make some enquiries among the people at the Temple keep. Eat your breakfast. We might be needed there, as I hear that Sir Guy might arrive today."

Talon's eyes lit up. "He is coming to Acre? I wonder where he has been this time? It is many months since we saw him last."

"I heard that he was down in Gaza recently. But I doubt he would have news of the Al Fayoum," Max said. He was a typical Sergeant of the Order and seemed to know what was going on everywhere within the domains of the Templar Order.

"What was he doing down there?" asked Talon through a mouthful of bread and meat.

Max ran a hand over the stubble of his cropped graying hair and then down to scratch his bearded cheek as he eyed Talon. His weathered face showed affection and concern.

"The word is that there is something going on, and the Bedu' are nervous. They are like birds of prey, those people. They sense when there is something about to happen. You know Sir Guy; he listens carefully to everything. I am surprised that he did not ask you to go down there with him."

"He did ask me to go south about a month ago, but I was busy with Guy and his ship. They were just returning from Constantinople and there were important letters to be collected from the emperor and sent on to Jerusalem, remember?"

Max nodded. "I recall. Nigel is still out there somewhere, and so is Henry. Guy has gone off to see to his precious ship and will be with us later in the day."

Talon smiled at the comment. All three of his captains lavished great care upon their ships and crews, Guy probably more than the others.

He continued to chew thoughtfully on some bread and goat's cheese. "We have not done badly, when you consider how difficult the Genoese have been. Our contracts with Alexios and the Kalothesos family have made us all wealthy, and now General Mavrazomes wants us to trade for him too. Even that crusty old senator, Alexios's father, is pleased with us."

Max chuckled. "You know perfectly well that he likes you, Talon. It is also clear the Genoese do not like us. But our good friends in Constantinople take care of us every time we send a ship there. Guy mentioned that Theodora was asking after you." He grinned at the flush that rose on Talon's neck, then continued.

"Every time one of our ships goes out I pray to God to protect our men, as we have more enemies than anyone has a right to. Why, some of the ships' captains in this very harbor would burn us down to the water level at the first opportunity, they are so jealous of our success. It could it be that jealousy is behind this watcher of yours, Talon," Max remarked thoughtfully.

"And that is not including the Egyptians, if they knew where to find us," Talon responded with a wry grin. "Max, I have no idea, but why would it involve the Bishop?" He shook his head.

"You are wealthy enough to go back to Languedoc, purchase a lot of land and own a castle, Talon. Or you could pay off the Church for your sins and get married to some noble daughter with vast estates. Why do you stay here in this land that is in constant turmoil?"

"I cannot really tell you, Max. God has ordained it perhaps, but I simply do not know. In any case, why do you stay?" he countered. "You could have left a long time ago. You too are now wealthy and could go back to those frozen old mountains you have talked about in the past."

"I do not know any better than yourself, but I wish you would take some thought to your standing. Your wealth will not protect you if you are denounced for bedding widows and such like, Talon. The bishop here is a pious man."

"He is a sanctimonious old hypocrite who has his own mistress," Talon remarked with some annoyance. "But I know how these things work, Max, I shall be discreet."

"Simply be very careful, Talon. The man watching you came from the bishop's house. Envy and jealousy can destroy anyone. You are envied for your wealth and the men you now command at sea. Soon you will command men on the land. It won't be long before they need you for that too."

They finished breakfast and Max went off to talk with Guy, one of their ship captains, while Talon decided to sweat it out with some energetic weapons exercise.

*****

The man who had been watching Talon's house was ushered into a small spare room with a rack of rolled papers in one corner and only a table and chair as other furniture. The person seated on the chair was a monk, thin and pale from lack of sun and a mean diet. He was reading a large document, which he laid down when the visitor entered. Brother Jonathan had moved into the Bishop's residence in order to maintain some secrecy and to be able to report speedily to the Bishop himself.

"I thought you would have been back before now," said Brother Jonathan in a thin, sharp tone. His look was peevish.

"I and my companion watched all night, but no one left the building, Brother. I have nothing to tell at this time."

Jonathan gave an impatient flick of his bony fingers. "I want you to keep watching him. He consorts with the Jews; I want to know why. And it is known that he visits a woman. Keep following him."

*****

Later in the day another monk knocked on the door and called out Jonathan's name before he stepped into the room. He remarked the table with a few papers on it, and the otherwise empty chamber. Brother Martin wondered where Jonathan might be, and decided to wait a few minutes in case he came back. He had come over to the Bishop's house to find Jonathan because the abbot wanted to know why he was absent from the services. Idly drifting about the room, his glance fell on one of the papers, half hidden under the others. He saw a name which caught his interest. He glanced nervously at the open doorway, then quickly shifted the paper so he could see better. It was scripted in Latin, so he had no trouble reading it, and what he saw made him gasp with surprise. Thoughtfully, he replaced the paper.

At that moment there was a small sound at the entrance, and Jonathan entered the chamber. He nodded to Martin and asked, "What brings you here, Brother?" His glance went to the papers on his table, then flicked back to Martin, registering suspicion.

"I was sent to find you by the Abbot. He wants to know what you are doing. You have not been seen in either the scriptorium or in the chapel for days now."

"The Bishop has given me some work to do," Jonathan said. His tone was not welcoming, but Martin knew that Jonathan disliked familiarity, so he dismissed it as normal. He was perturbed enough to forget discretion.

"Brother Jonathan, you are conducting some kind of investigation for the Bishop. Is this true?"

Brother Jonathan stared back at him with his intense blue eyes. "Word has come to the Bishop that there is a charge of witchcraft placed against a person in this city. Papers arrived a week ago."

Martin looked incredulous, “Can you tell me who it is?”

Jonathan looked shifty and refused to look at Martin. “Let us just say it is someone we know, and I am charged to find out more before a court is convened.”

“Is it Sir Talon?” Martin blurted it out before he could stop himself.

Jonathan placed both hands flat on the table and glared at the young monk before him. “You have been going through these papers!” he accused Martin.

“I... I came to see you but... but when you were not here I could not help but see... ” Martin stammered. He flinched under the ferocious glare Jonathan sent him.

“Have a care, Martin,” he grated. “You could be severely punished for interfering.”

“But why, Brother? Sir Talon has never shown the slightest sign of being involved in the dark arts,” Martin insisted. He had paled at the intensity of Jonathan’s stare and the implied consequences of his actions.

“The Bishop has commanded it, and I shall pursue his orders to the letter. Anything that we find will be recorded, and we shall see what comes of it. Witchcraft is a very serious crime.”

“I would stake my life that Tal... Sir Talon has done nothing of the kind, and I am disappointed that you should in any way think ill of him, Brother.”

Jonathan’s stare was cold and unpleasant. “We shall see, Brother Martin. If this charge is proved to be true then not even the Templars can prevent an enquiry. In the meantime, had you not better go off to the scriptorium? You will be late, and you know that Brother Peters dislikes that. You would do well to forget you ever heard of this too, Brother Martin.” He picked up his paper and began to read, pretending to ignore Martin.

Martin opened his mouth to say something, then thought better of it. He turned and left the room, closing the door behind him with care. He was pensive the entire time he spent in the scriptorium, doing little more than etching a single line of gilt letters the entire morning. Finally he asked to be excused, pleading a headache. Brother Peter, who was a hard task master, reluctantly gave permission for him to go for a walk, admonishing him to pay better attention to his work the following day.

*****

Having practiced with his bow for a good half hour and then another hour of hard work in the yard hacking at a pole with his blade, Talon was drenched in sweat, clad only in his loose pants and boots, having cast off his shirt. He paused to catch his breath and rub his upper arm, which still ached from an old wound, when he became aware that Samuel was approaching with Brother Martin in tow.

Talon stopped what he was doing and greeted Matin with a friendly smile and an offer to be seated on a bench nearby. He sent Samuel off to bring fresh cool water and fruit.

“What brings you to my house, Brother Martin? I do not see enough of you these days,” he said.

Brother Martin gave a wan smile and said, “Gods blessings, Talon. I hope I find you well?”

“Very well, Brother. How may I help you?” Talon noted that Martin lacked his usual cheerful manner and appeared to be preoccupied.

“I have come... to tell you something, Talon,” he hesitated and fumbled with his rosary with ink-stained fingers, stared at the ground with a frown on his young features for a few moments, then glanced back up at Talon almost guiltily.

“I... I think you are in danger and... ” he stopped and looked down again, fidgeting with his rosary.

“What are you trying to say, Brother?” Talon prompted. Martin exuded unease.

“Did you... were you ever accused of witchcraft in Languedoc, Talon?” Martin blurted out.

Talon stared at him hard for a long moment as he digested what he had just heard, then he placed both hands on his knees and looked up at the sky. He had an unpleasant feeling in the pit of his stomach, and suddenly the sweat on his body felt cold and clammy even in the heat of the day.

"Who has been saying this?" he asked in a low voice.

"Brother Jonathan has been told to investigate you by the Bishop because of news from that region that has come to him. It is a serious charge, Talon!" Martin said. His tone was agitated and he was clearly very embarrassed.

Talon hesitated as he wondered if he could even trust Martin. Finally he spoke. "Well over four years ago, an accusation was made by a man who called himself a priest but who was trying to steal my father's rightful inheritance. It is utterly untrue, a completely false and malicious accusation, but it was made by a man of the church, and of course I was not given the opportunity to refute it," he told Martin.

"I believe you, Talon; I have known you for well over two years now, and have never had any reason to suspect anything of this kind," he crossed himself, " but it is a hard accusation to refute, and if the Bishop is involved then it is very serious indeed. Brother Jonathan has, I am sure, many good qualities, but he also has a certain... er, vindictiveness in his character as well."

Talon gave a wry smile."I know, Martin, it is a serious charge but utterly false. In front of God I can tell you that, as could Max, who was there at the time. But there might be other reasons for pursuing this accusation. I wonder..." Talon began.

They were interrupted by a commotion in the street outside. The bells, which had been silent for a couple of hours, began to ring again, but this time there was an urgency that told them that either ships had been sighted or there was an enemy army at the gates. Before long there was banging at the doors of his house and Samuel hobbled over to open them. One of the servant boys came running into the yard.

"Sir Talon, Sir Talon!" the boy yelled.

"What is it, Daniel?" Talon asked, wiping the cold sweat from his brow with a rag.

"There are ships sighted out to sea and everyone thinks they might be pirates!" Daniel said, barely able to contain his excitement.

Talon stared at him. "Calm down, boy! Do you know anything else?"

"No, Sir. But there is a lot of shouting. God protect us!" Daniel said, crossing himself.

Talon turned to Brother Martin and said, "You came here with good intent, Martin. I thank you for that, because you took a risk. We should find out what all the commotion is about, then later we can perhaps talk more about this?"

Brother Marin nodded. "I agree, Talon. I shall not say anything, but beware. God protect." He stood up and hastened out of the open gateway into the now crowded street.

Talon stared after him for a long moment, then shook his head and hastened to don his shirt and his outer robe. "Has Max or Guy come back yet?" he asked Daniel.

"No Sir," the boy replied.

Talon shrugged. Perhaps they were already on their way to the harbor. He took his sword and told Daniel to inform Max, if he came by, that he would be at the South Tower gate. He remembered to snatch his cloak off a peg on his way out.

It was only a few minutes fast walk for him to arrive at the gates, which opened onto the harbor itself. He paused to look up at the large archway with its heavy portcullis, which could be dropped in front of the main wooden portals. He was admitted to the inner yard by the guards, who knew him well, and from there he hurried up a series of stone steps towards the battlements that overlooked the southwestern part of the harbor. This gave him a good view of both the harbor and the sea to the west, where he assumed the ships had been sighted.

He discovered a large and growing crowd of men and even women milling about and chattering excitedly while staring and pointing out to sea. Among the crowd was a mixed group of Knights Templar and some Hospitaliers in their flowing robes. Along with a fair number of their Sergeants, loiterers and guards, they crowded the edge of the battlements.

Men who knew him nodded and made way for him as he shouldered through the press of humanity to the battlements. He stared out to sea towards where they were all pointing. Far off in the distance, he could make out the shapes of three sails that indicated ships. A blustery wind blowing directly from the west had turned the sea choppy, creating white caps on the waves. One of the ships was well in front of the other two and seemed even at this distance to be running from the others.

There was something familiar about it. It was difficult to make out the details of the ship at this distance, but it was clear that the three boats were under full sail, their hulls rising and falling, their bows tossing spray high into the air as they ran into the choppy waves. He wiped his eyes to see better and glanced to his left at the harbor a hundred feet below.

The fortress dominated the port of Acre and Acco bay, which curved in a great crescent to the south of the city. Just on the outside of the bay was a peaked rock known as the Tower of Flies, which served as a beacon at night to the ships' captains as they sailed towards the fortified town. He gazed down at the hive of activity below, the workers seemingly oblivious to the excitement on the battlements. Sea gulls wheeled and screamed as they competed for the offal and scraps tossed over the side from the numerous ships in the pool of the harbor. The sky was azure blue but the blustery wind swirled briefly and pulled at his cloak, bringing with it not only the tang of salt water but the stink of the filth that the ships' crews dumped overboard, which was never fully cleansed by the tide.

Some of the ships were anchored out in the basin waiting their turn to be unloaded, while others disgorged their cargoes onto the stone wharfs. Gangs of slaves driven under the lashes of their overseers hurried from ship to ship, where they were put to work unloading the vital cargoes of goods that had come from the distant lands of the Franks, Constantinople, and even Genoa and Venice, the new great merchant cities of the Christian world.

He watched the two larger ships belonging to the Order of the Templars, recently arrived, which were unloading men and horses. The men seemed weak and exhausted from their trying journey from Aigues Mortes, the port on the south estuary of the Rhone near Provence. Those men and knights who had survived the journey staggered onto the quays carrying their bundles of possessions and equipment. They were herded into groups by waiting sergeants from the nearby Templar fortress. After the surviving horses had been unloaded, the men began to stagger after their new comrades along the stone quay towards the Templar keep, which dominated the city to the north. They would be indoctrinated into the ways of the military orders in the Holy Land, and before long they would be sent to man one of the many castles owned by the Order. Some of the arrivals were too sick to walk and were carried in litters by other men.

Talon had observed laden ships arriving almost every week to disgorge their cargoes of fighting men or equipment and horses that had travelled from the western countries. He knew all too well that, depending on the journey, some arrived in good health while others arrived in pitiable condition. The storms of the Mediterranean in the late autumn and early winter months took a regular toll of merchant ships and military vessels, making no distinction between the two. The sea was full of hazards, ranging from storms to pirates and predatory merchants, seeking to make a quick profit out of the those ships less able to defend themselves. While the Templar fleets were for the most part immune to these depredations, the length of the journey took its toll. And there were always bold or foolish captains gambling on an easy profit who took long chances to run the gauntlet of Egyptian pirates or predatory Venetian or Genoese galleys.

He turned his attention back to the ships out to sea. Now he could see clearly that the vessel coming towards them at great speed was a galley and his interest quickened. Just then Max called out and shouldered his way towards Talon, who turned to greet him. Accompanying Max was Guy, the captain of the ship belonging to Talon anchored in the harbor.

"Well met again, Max, and greetings, Guy," Talon said.

"Greetings, Sir Talon. God protect you." Guy stood almost a head higher than most of the other people on the battlements, so he could see clearly what was taking place out at sea.

"What is going on, Talon?" Max asked.

"I suspect we are seeing Henry making a grand entrance. Is that not our banner?"

Guy and Max darted their looks westward.

"By God, I think you are right, Sir Talon. But the wind is directly in our faces; it is hard to tell," Guy said in a low tone. "But yes... that is your pendant, I could swear it."

He was referring to the banner that was Talon's coat of arms. A shield with one side azure blue within which lay a ship; on the other side of the diagonal was a red background with a lion's claw in its middle.

"Does it look as though he needs help? Should we not be sailing out to meet him?" Max asked, his voice full of concern.

"There is little we can do for him at this time except to pray," Guy said. "But Henry is one of the best sailors in the Middle Sea and I am sure he has the heels on these two."

"All the same, I shall be very happy when he finally enters the harbor and is safe with us," Talon said.

"My prayers are with yours, Talon," Max said.

If only, if only I were a sailor,
If only somebody'd give me a boat,
I would furl my sails each evening
In the blue harbor of your eyes.

— Adab.com

Chapter 2

Plans for the Future

By now it was clear to all watching that the leading ship was being chased by two smaller galleys. The pendants on the following ships displayed green with indistinct gold markings. Everyone knew what that meant. These were Arab corsairs, and they were hunting the ship in front.

Despite the strong wind all the ships were using their oars; the blades flashed in the sunlight as they rose and fell in rapid unison. Talon felt a prickle of apprehension: it would be a close thing. He glanced up at the tower to the north of where they stood. He noticed activity around the mangonel catapults perched up there. Squatting like some giant insect, just fifty feet away at the same level as he was standing, was a huge Trebuchet towards which men were now running. Once the enemy came within range these armaments would be put into action. Talon knew that the chances of a missile from one of these machines actually hitting one of the enemy ships was very remote, but it might act as a deterrent.

The three ships were drawing near. The galley that Henry was sailing was a dromon, one deck of oarsmen and two sails, which gave it more speed than either of the following ships; but still they were near enough to give Talon concern. He knew Henry was good but the atmosphere on the battlements was tense. If anything went wrong, a sail lost to the wind or a stay snapped there would be nothing they could do to help him. Talon could now make out figures on the deck of his ship and the activity as Henry used every inch of canvas and all his powers of seamanship to tease the very best out of his ship.

It made a handsome sight as its long hull slid through the dark waters, the oars flashing up and down in perfect harmony. Its prow dug deep into the waves and tossed the spray as far back as the rear deck, where Talon could now see a figure he assumed to be Henry directing the activity of the crew.

"Henry will be enjoying this," Max remarked with a glance at Talon. Guy chuckled and Talon nodded; he could almost see Henry laughing with the excitement of the chase. His ship was now pointing directly towards the twin towers at the entrance to the Acre harbor, but not far behind were the slim, menacing shapes of the pursuing Saracen ships. Both were being sailed with skill by men who knew what they were about. Neither of the ships' captains seemed to be daunted by their proximity to the massive fortifications of the city and ran their ships forward with courage and determination in a bold attempt to apprehend the ship they were pursuing. Talon had to admire their audacity and wondered where they were from.

He was startled out of his contemplation by a shout, followed by huge crash off to his right, and then a rock the size of a horse's head whirled high into the air. It rose rapidly in a long arc and then quickly became very small as it began its descent towards the sea, into which it plunged, raising a great spout of water high into the air. He was not surprised that the rock landed nowhere near the two enemy boats. Nonetheless there was a great cheer from the onlookers on the wall with much gratuitous advice and encouragement to aim the next one better.

The crew of the trebuchet, using levers, heaved and hauled the massive machine around while an engineer gesticulated and pointed out where to position it. Others ran to seize another huge rock and trundle it over, then with a great heave placed it onto the platform.

Now there were loud crashes and thumps from above as the mangonels placed in the towers went into action and smaller rocks were launched into the air. Their progress was followed with more cheers as these projectiles, better aimed, began to plunge into the water in front of the enemy boats. Meanwhile the leading ship had almost gained the protection of the harbor towers, as more rocks from the engines placed along the seaward harbor wall were fired over his vessel towards the Saracens.

Another loud shout followed by a huge recoiling crash deafened the ears of the spectators, and the trebuchet tossed another rock out to sea. Its progress was followed with keen interest by the people on the battlements. This time it landed in the sea between the two enemy boats, again throwing a huge pillar of water high into the air. There were more shouts of excitement.

"Had that one struck it would have sunk one of those ships immediately!" Guy remarked with glee, as the onlookers cheered noisily.

"Look! I think they have decided they cannot succeed. They are pulling away," Max said, pointing.

"Now would be the time to strike one of them with a rock, while they are slowed," Guy observed to his companions.

Others were also aware of this opportunity. The enemy ships were slowing and turning. Even so, they maneuvered quickly, and to the frustration of the men on the battlements the crew of the trebuchet seemed slow to take advantage of the changed situation. There were shouts of, "Hurry! They are at our mercy! In God's name, why do you not hurry!" from all around as the crew frantically hauled the arm down in order to place a boulder in its cradle.

The shouts and mockery from their audience must have disturbed the concentration of the crew, for the stone was badly placed and when the lever was pulled to release it the rock flew in a twisting motion and fell far short of the two ships, which, having spun almost on their keels, began to speed away. The failed efforts of the trebuchet crew met with jeers and catcalls from all sides. Chagrined and chastened, they secured the armament and left the spectators to remain on the battlements, watching the enemy ships recede into the distance. The mangonels in the towers continued to shoot rocks after them, but it was not long before the ships were well out of range and finally these too stopped.

“Come on,” Talon said as he turned to leave. “Excitement over, we have to greet Henry.”

They hurried through the crowd and ran down the stone steps towards the Templar Quay where they could watch Henry's arrival.

Despite its speedy entrance the ship would have to wait in the middle of the harbor for its turn at the crowded quay before it could unload its cargo. Talon knew full well what it was carrying: iron, leather and cloth, and perhaps some salt. These were the supplies that were in constant demand by the Templars, Hospitaliers, and other orders. He wondered how successful Henry had been in obtaining the vital commodity salt, which was something everyone needed. The ship was quite different from most of the other heavy cargo ships that now surrounded it. This was a sleek battle galley and it drew much appreciative comment from people who were watching nearby. Even at rest in the harbor it presented a menacing aspect.

There were other, slower ships in the harbor, including the disliked Venetians and Genoese merchant ships that brought their own cargos of precious salt ingots from all over the sea board. These merchants also carried wheat and many other basic supplies that the Christian armies needed urgently in order to maintain their presence in the Kingdom of Jerusalem and the state of Tripoli. It had now been many decades since the first Crusade, but the sporadic wars never stopped, as one king after another tried to consolidate his hold; meanwhile, the Holy Military Orders expanded their influence over the land, at the same time building huge castles to prevent the Turks from overrunning the remoter parts of the kingdom.

The three men hurried through the small gate that gave onto the crowded quayside and watched as Henry skillfully slid the ship into its allotted place among the other boats. Some of the great Templar three-masted ships towered over it, but none could match its slim, predatory appearance. The oars of the galley flashed in the sunlight as they dipped and rose, pulling the long, sleek shape forward to lay it almost alongside the other galley belonging to Talon, and then at some unheard command the rowers made the water foam as they reversed their stroke; the water boiled briefly and the ship came to a full stop. The sail had already been furled. The anchor stones were dropped with a splash fore and aft and the galley was suddenly still. Talon watched critically as these maneuvers were completed, pleased that Henry had made his entrance well. Now he noticed that there was much activity on deck as Henry and his men prepared to receive him. Talon was expected aboard.

"I swear the heat of this land wears me thin," Guy exclaimed as they walked along the quay to wait for the boat from the galley to pick them up.

"The last time I looked, I could swear that you are not so thin, Guy," Max said with a grin.

"Bullocks balls to you too, Max. Look at him; does the heat never bother him?" Guy gestured towards Talon.

Max laughed. "I don't think I have very seen Talon worry about the heat of this country, Guy. But then, you are a Northern man and you prefer the cold anyway."

Max was dressed in the dark clothing of a Sergeant of Templars, while Guy was wearing a mixture of wool and cotton. His doublet and hose were already damp with sweat in this early summer heat. Talon wondered why, after all this time, his friends did not adopt the loose, light clothing worn by such as himself, but Guy was adamant about not looking like a Saracen, so he suffered.

"That I do, Max. Now Constantinople is my kind of climate!" Guy grinned at them both as he mopped his red, sweating face and pushed his damp blond hair back off his forehead with a rag.

"We all know why you want to go back there, Guy, and it isn't the climate," Max rejoined.

"Come along, you two old men. Midsummer is past, and I still hear complaints about the heat! We shall greet Henry and then feast with him at my house this evening," Talon said, as he boarded the transport boat and beckoned to his companions.

As they crossed the water, the three men gazed at the ship that had brought them to Acre from Egypt almost three years ago. It now belonged to Talon, and Henry was the ship's Master. Of the two other ships that also belonged to Talon, the one already in harbor was commanded by Guy, while the third was commanded by their other captain, Nigel; but he was off trading in Constantinople and would not be back for many weeks. Guy's ship was awaiting a new cargo, which Talon had planned to ship to the port of Paphos situated on the north coast of Cyprus, which was part of the Byzantine empire.

Henry's ship was not unlike those of the Byzantium's navy that were well known for speed and maneuverability. Guy's ship, however, although it was a galley, was Genoese built; and whenever he saw it Talon savored a feeling of satisfaction over how it had come into his possession.

The galley had been taken off the very man who had helped betray Talon and Max in the port of Alexandria, those long years ago when they were trying to reach the Kingdom of Jerusalem, and where their companion Montague had died. Talon considered it only justice that he now owned the ship and his men sailed it to trade across the seas.

As they clambered aboard the new arrival Henry was at the ship's side to greet them. He gave a shout of joy.

"Sir Talon, Guy, Max! Greetings! God be praised, we have arrived intact and we have a full cargo to unload!"

"Well met, Henry! Praise God that you made it safely. That was a grand entrance you made there. I would have preferred more discretion," Talon said with a grin, as he climbed onto the deck of the busy ship. They embraced with feeling. Henry slapped him on the back with his calloused hand and with a huge grin on his bearded face.

"By God, I am glad to be here, Talon," Henry roared with laughter. "Those bastards were lying in wait three days from here. I was confident we could lose them, but they caught up with us during the night. There is much to tell, but you will be glad to know our cargo is in good condition and we shall profit from the voyage."

Talon grinned back. "I am most relieved to see you and the men, Henry, but it is a bonus to hear your words as well. I thank God that you have safely arrived, and profitably, too."

Guy climbed over the side, bellowed a greeting and embraced Henry, then waved at the men on the main deck. Many of them paused from their work and cheered their arrival. Some of them had escaped on this same ship out of Egypt with them; they owed their lives to Talon and Max for having had them released from their chains as galley slaves.

Talon still found it a little odd that many of them had volunteered to stay on the captured ships and sail them for him. However, he had made them all wealthy men in the intervening years. They could not have done as well ashore in the doubtful existence in the army or the life in the city.

"Welcome aboard, my friends," Henry said as he embraced Guy and Max in turn. "How long is it that we have been gone?"

"I think it is almost three months."

"God be praised. We arrived in Aigues Mortes in June, delivered your letters, then sailed back, initially under the protection of a fleet of Templar ships."

"Seems that you beat the fleet back to the city,"said Talon.

"Well, you know how well those lumbering old tubs sail! We survived two storms, one as we made our way around the toe of Sicily, which was when we lost the fleet, but I made sure we did not come too close to that land, as it is still a nest of pirates, and those Normans of Sicily are not to be trusted. Even with my crew of cutthroats I do not wish to tempt fate." He grinned.

Talon looked around him. There were signs that the ship had weathered some hard seas, but there seemed to be no broken spars or shredded sheets, so he nodded and asked, "And the cargo?"

"It took some water, but we baled it out quickly and I do not think there was much loss, especially as we brought mostly hides and iron core with some armor. The salt ingots we picked up gave me some concern, but we managed to protect them from the worst. I followed your instructions and did not bring beef."

"Good. We have seen how it spoils on a long voyage. If we buy it from the islands and salt it properly it keeps, but otherwise it is not worth the cost," Talon remarked.

"You do not seem to have suffered too badly, thank the Lord," Guy said, inspecting the mast and looking up at the furled sails.

"We lost one man overboard and could do nothing for him. God protect his soul," Henry said crossing himself.

"That was a small price to pay for all that distance and the hardships to go with it," Max said. "All the same, it is always sad to lose a good man. Who was it?"

"Edmondson, remember him? One of my best steersmen! It was the darkest of nights, a running sea, and a freak wave just came at us aboard and swept him away. It was very quick and we could not turn back in those seas," Henry said. "May God have mercy on his soul." They all crossed themselves.

"If he had family we will try to send them help," Talon said.

"I shall see to it," Max informed him.

He added for the benefit of the other two, "I have heard that Sir Guy de Veres will be here tonight, Sir Talon. We are commanded to see him as soon as he arrives."

"Very well, Max. Henry, God be praised you are here. I shall leave you with Guy to see to the unloading; and then you must come to the house, where we can talk more, and you shall feast on good food for a change. You and your crew shall have a well earned rest after you have unloaded the ship and we have paid them all their earnings. I dare say they will try to wreck the city by dawn. Inform them that I shall not be pleased to hear of damage to property or rapine."

Henry grinned and nodded. "I shall pass the word, Sir Talon."

They spent another two hours on board, examining the cargo and going over the manifest with Henry; then Talon and Max were rowed back to the Templar quay, leaving Henry and Guy to complete arrangements for unloading the ship and taking care of the hundred and one tasks that were required to close the ship down for a period of time.

The men cheered when Talon supervised the payment in silver and gold coin for their period at sea. Most of them would go ashore and get mightily drunk for days on end but they would come back to his ships when summoned as they knew Talon by now as a fair man and his captains were among the best.

His own particular summons came for Talon to report to the Templar keep, as Sir Guy had arrived and wanted to see him.

He left the house accompanied by Max. They were both now dressed in chain mail and wore the insignia of the Templars. Talon was at this time an associate knight, but Max had been a Sergeant of Templars for many years and proudly wore his dark surcoat, contrasting sharply with the white of Talon's, which had a red cross sewn onto the left breast.

Talon also wore a small turban with a round pointed helmet similar to the style favored by the Saracen, which made him stand out among the other knights whenever there was a gathering. More and more of the knights who had spent many years in the service were following his example, however, so it went for the most part unremarked, although there were always some who eyed him askance, or scowled.

They were admitted by the guards through a small postern gate cut into the wood of the main entrance, and they proceeded up a slope towards the living quarters of the garrison commander.

They were met at the door by Claude, Sir Guy's Sergeant, who grinned at them by way of welcome. They clasped hands and embraced.

"It has been many months since we saw you last," Max said.

"Sir Guy likes to move about," Claude responded with a wry grin, then he waved them inside before shutting the door and following them.

Sir Guy de Veres greeted them both with a smile of pleasure as they were ushered into the garrison commander's chamber. The evenings were becoming cooler, so there was a small fire burning well in the large stone fireplace, near which were placed chairs for guests. Sir Stephen, the Master of the Templars in Acre, rose from his desk and greeted them by name. They all knew one another.

Talon and Sir Guy embraced, and then they all seated themselves at a thick wooden table where food had been placed. They were bid to eat and drink, although there was only water in the pitchers. The Templars did not drink wine. As long as he had known them, Talon had never seen either man drink anything but water. Sir Guy had told him on an aside with a wry smile that if an Arab decided to offer wine he would not be able to refuse as that would have been insulting to their hospitality .

The conversation was initially all about Henry's race to safety that morning. Sir Guy listened with some amusement as the story was recounted and laughed outright at the derisive comments made about the luckless trebuchet crew. Sir Stephen defended them stoutly for a while, but even he had to admit ruefully that they could have done better. Eventually the conversation came around to the purpose of Sir Guy's visit.

"I have been in the south of the Kingdom of Jerusalem with the knights of Gaza, Talon," he said, wiping his lips with a linen cloth and then taking some water. He looked tired, and he had aged in the years since Talon first met him. The gray on his temples was extending to the rest of his short cropped hair, and his well trimmed beard was very gray; some teeth were gone too. However, despite the sun creases on his weathered face, his blue eyes were youthful and as keen as ever.

Talon knew that Sir Guy de Veres filled a special role in the Templar Order. He was fluent in Arabic had the authority to move around the kingdom at will, keeping his finger on the pulse of things, and this had proved very valuable in the past. He was highly respected by everyone in the Order, but also by many in even higher places near to the throne. Talon admired this man whose knowledge of the country and its neighbors was even greater than his own.

"How is it in the Sultanate of Egypt, Sir?" Talon asked politely as he cleaned and put away his knife. A pear looked appetizing, so he reached for it and took a bite.

Sir Guy glanced at Sir Stephan, then sat back and rested his elbows on the arms of his chair while he contemplated Talon and Max over his steepled fingers, a gesture by now quite familiar to Talon. It signaled a change of direction in the conversation.

"The Sultanate of Egypt is quiet... almost too quiet. The Sultan, Salah Ed Din, is well aware of our king Baldwin's affliction, the leprosy, of that we can be sure; but we do not know what is going on in that country. Your ships now ply the seas in all directions, including Alexandria. Have you not heard anything?" he asked, looking directly at Talon.

Talon shifted in his chair. "My ships have not been in that area for some time now, Sir Guy. As you know, we left in somewhat of a hurry that one time, and since then my captains have only occasionally traded there for salt, figs and dates. It has always been a hazardous enterprise, because neither the Venetians nor Genoese would hesitate to denounce my men if they knew we were there. They are jealous of our trade in the salt and gold markets."

Max interjected. "Talon's ships have been plying the north of the Middle Sea for most of the last few months, since we obtained trading rights with Constantinople. It is difficult enough to do even that, what with the harsh restrictions the Genoese try to impose upon anyone who competes with them."

"Hmm, if I am not mistaken, Talon, you have nonetheless done well since you undertook that enterprise, isn't that so?" Sir Stephen said dryly.

Talon looked him straight in the eye. "You also know that I have served the Templar Order well because of it, providing a speedy means of transport for you and Sir Guy as well as for secret missives and letters on several occasions to Constantinople and once even to Rome. Has there been some complaint regarding my situation, Sir Stephen?" he asked, trying to keep his tone from sounding sharp. His knowledge of the spy sent to watch him was behind his remark.

Sir Guy smiled at him and lifted his hand in a placating manner. "No, Talon, no indeed. However, rumor does have it that you are bored, and it seems you have little to do these days."

Talon glanced at Max, who scowled at the table. Someone, it would never have been Max, had obviously mentioned the fact that he spent some time with a woman; or he might have been seen in one of the drinking places. Not for the first time he marveled at how fast news travelled and how efficient Sir Guy's intelligence system was.

Sir Guy gave a chuckle and leaned forward. "Talon, you are one of my most trusted people and our friendship is of much value to me. Indeed, both you and Max have proved to be invaluable on more than one occasion, which is why I think it is time to discuss a matter of some importance and perhaps get you out of Acre for a while."

Talon and Max glanced at one another. Talon sat up. "What is it that you need from me, Sir Guy?"

"The Templars have castles ranging widely across this land, from Gaza all the way north to Syria," Sir Guy said quietly. "While I was down in Gaza recently, word came to me that there have been some curious incidents taking place in the far north."

"What kind of incidents, Sir?" Max asked, his scarred face displaying interest.

"Incidents... of the 'Assassin kind," Sir Guy said slowly. He looked hard at the two men.

Talon felt his pulse leap. The last time he had encountered the 'Assassins of Rashid Ed Din it had been violent and could have gone either way but he had inflicted serious casualties and they would not be about to forgive him.

Sir Guy continued. "I leave for the north with Claude here to a fortress called Darbsak. We leave in two days and I want you to come with me, Talon. If anyone can, you will be able to divine what is going on. My suspicion is that Sinan Rashid Ed Din is involved, perhaps even the 'Assassins from Persia, but I cannot be sure."

"I should go with you, Sir Guy," Max said.

Talon looked Max with a half grin on his face at Max's tone, but Sir Guy gave him a puzzled look.

"Someone has to look after Sir Talon, and I am his Sergeant," Max said defensively.

"I thought he could look after himself better than most," Sir Guy said with a smile. Even Sir Stephan chuckled at that.

Talon placed his hand on his friend's shoulder and gripped it, affection in his eyes."Max, while I would like nothing better than to have you with us, you know as well as I do that with two ships in the harbor I will need you to keep an eye on both the vessels and the crews. Neither Henry nor Guy are much at book keeping. There is a great deal of preparation to be done for their next voyages, and I would feel much more secure if you would see to it while I am gone," he told him.

Max nodded reluctantly. "You are right of course, Talon, but... well, I shall stay if you do not think you will be gone for long."

"At most three weeks, Max," Sir Guy said. "It is agreed then, Gentlemen? Talon, we leave in two days' time."

*****

Later that evening,having finished with the welcome feast for Henry and his crew, and then put a drunken Henry to bed, Talon sat down with Guy and Max to discuss their situation.

"Why does Sir Guy need you to go north, Talon?" Guy asked.

"Because of the Templars relationship with the 'Assassins, who are governed by a man called Sinan Rashid Ed Din, also known as the School Teacher, although to my mind he is more of a wizard. It is very sensitive, Guy. The 'Assassins pay the Templars a tithe and the Templars in turn offer them protection from the Turks. But... Sinan is a difficult man to deal with, and Sir Guy wants a second pair of eyes to view the situation.

"Talon knows these people better than even Sir Guy," Max remarked.

Guy gave them both an odd look, "How so?"

"I should not be gone for very long, Guy," Talon said, evading the question. "With Max to help you, your ship should be made ready to sail for Paphos in Cyprus to collect a salt cargo, I hear that there is sugar cane to be had. See if you can load some of the extract. These Military Orders feed their people nothing but bread and corned beef, so their appetite for salt is almost insatiable."

"When should I sail?" Guy asked him.

"I think that you and Henry should go out with your ships at the same time. After that incident today it will be safer for all, and few would be rash enough to attempt to attack such ships if you are together," Talon said.

Guy nodded agreement. "That makes sense."

"If I am not back within three weeks, then Max will decide the time for you to make sail. Make sure that you leave with a good crew and hasten back as fast as you can. The salt market prices here are going up, as supplies are running low. But I see the possibility of sugar being valuable too. Not even the Venetians have been able to lock that market up. As Cyprus belongs to the Emperor of Byzantium we have the documents to allow us to trade there whereas they do not."

"Keeping the crew should not be a problem Talon. Men vie for a place on your ships since we came back from Constantinople."

Talon nodded acknowledgement then said, "I need you to do something else while you are in Paphos, Guy."

"Anything, Talon."

I shall prepare papers, which you will take with you, along with some gold. I have received a grant to buy land on the island. I want you to find out what can be obtained. There are salt marshes there and I would like to own some of that. There is also land in the mountains with good access to the sea that I would like to have. Find out where the cane is grown and see if we can buy some of that too."

Guy looked at him and Max with a curious expression. "Are you planning to live there, Talon?" he asked.

"It might be a safe haven one day for all of us, Guy. The land outside this city is all taken by the great nobles, but there could be some available on that island, as it is still Byzantine. Alexios told me that he could help with letters to enable me to acquire some. I need some men whom I trust to have a look."

Guy nodded. "Always thinking ahead, eh, Talon. Of course Henry and I shall do this for you."

"Then God speed and may he protect you and the crews; the seas are still dangerous."

"Those Saracen ships have probably intercepted more ships than we know, and although I have scant sympathy for the Venetians or those treacherous Genoese, it is becoming a problem," Max stated. The others nodded their agreement.

"Then make sure our crews are well armed." Talon said.

They talked deep into the night, discussing the events of the day and trying to peer into the future, but finally the candles guttered and began to go out. Talon bade his friends good night and then walked out into the yard. The night sky was a blaze of light, which would unfortunately make his last task of the day more difficult.

*****

The watcher propped himself against the wall of the corner house and stared up at the candlelit windows in the house across the street. He wished he were in bed; however, the coin he had been paid would keep him in wine and beer for many evenings to come, so he endured the cold and the boredom as the night advanced and the city slept. He would have much to report because of all the activity that had gone on, so he was content to simply watch for anyone leaving at a late hour.

He did not hear the shadow that came up behind him and it was too late to resist when a hand as hard as iron went over his mouth to stop his involuntary scream of agony as the knife went into his back. His struggles were violent, but only for a few seconds before he went limp; he was dead before he slid to the ground. The figure who had killed him picked up the body, heaved it over its shoulder, then walked off into the night.

*****

The next day when the watcher's companion came looking for him, he was not at the agreed meeting place. The watcher looked for him, but another full day would pass before he decided to inform the thin monk with the staring blue eyes. Brother Jonathan looked displeased and told him to take over the night watch until his companion showed up again; and although that man obeyed, he was concerned. He had survived in the twilight world of theft and cut-throats long enough to heed his instincts. The fact that his companion had disappeared worried him. It was on the second night of his watch that he felt a blade slide across his throat and heard a voice whisper in his ear. "Do not stay here; it is dangerous, and you might not see the dawn. Your friend was not so lucky. Do you understand?"

He had heard no movement at all. He gasped and nodded his head, then he began to shake.

"Leave. Do not come back and do not turn around as you go," the voice whispered and the knife was removed. He listened hard but again heard nothing whatsoever to tell him whether the phantom behind him remained there or not. The hair on the back of his neck rose and he almost wet his pantaloons.

He all but ran down the street past the house he had been watching and headed for a tavern where he could get a bottle and get safely drunk. He glanced back when he was a hundred paces down the street, but the night gave nothing away, still and dark. All the more terrifying for that, and because it was difficult to tell whether he had just had a nightmare or not. The thin line of pain along his throat, however, told him he had not been dreaming.

Talon watched him go knowing that Jonathan would not easily find another man to do the task once this one had talked. Fear rather than death could do the work better, he reasoned.

A band of fierce barbarians from the hills
Rush'd like a torrent down upon the vale
Sweeping our flocks and herds. The shepherds fled.
I alone with bended bow and quiver full of arrows,
Hovered about the enemy, and mark'd
The road he took.

—John Ross, *The Book of Scottish Poems*

Chapter 3

Assassins and Templars

Talon stared out into the night and wondered for the hundredth time who was out there in the desert this cool, dark, moonless night, and what they might be doing. The darkness was changing to a lighter form of gray as the first streaks of dawn glowed in the east. A light wind keened over the walls and cooled his impassive, bearded face.

He was resting his arms on the battlements of one of the two square gatehouse towers while he thought about the situation. Standing nearby were two other men, a crossbow archer and a sentry with a pike. They gave him respectful space while he stared out into the desert. He was dressed much as any other Templar, but instead of the standard heavy chain hauberk he wore a fine chain mail shirt that having taken it off a man who no longer had need of it in a sea battle the year before. It was made of small, tight links that were of much higher quality than the normal hauberk made by Frankish armorers.

He wore an overshirt of much patched, and now none too clean, coarse white linen cloth. On his left breast was sewn the standard red cross. Like many of his brothers at arms here at the keep, he wore a loose turban wrapped around his head, half-covering his round helmet, its long end hung over his shoulder. He wore scuffed horsehide boots that had known better days. From the rough cut leather belt on his left hip hung a fine, well tempered, slightly curved sword held in a battered scabbard, not the regulation weapon his fellow knights used. This was a sword for a horseman.

They had been in this crusader castle called Darbsak for two days now. He had arrived with Sir Guy de Veres, his sergeant Claude, and some other knights of the Temple after an overland journey of well over two weeks.

This stark fortress was situated one full day's ride northeast of another much larger castle called Baghras. They were in the state of Antioch, far north of Acre and the Kingdom of Jerusalem. This was a small, mean outpost that had been built to control one of the main caravan routes that came south from Armenia. It was situated almost as far north as the Templars' influence extended.

They were here at the request of the Captain of Templars in this castle because, he said, there had been a strange series of events that had disturbed him, and he needed help with a prisoner he had captured.

Sir Guy still slept in the tower reserved for visitors, but Talon had requested to be woken should there be any kind of disturbance during the night. This was why he was now peering into the desert, listening hard for any noise that might mean an assault about to take place. The sentry and bowman had heard some movement out there and had called him.

*****

Soon after their arrival, he and Sir Guy had interrogated the prisoner, a youth who had been captured during an aborted raid on a small caravan en route to the castle. Only a sortie and determined counter-attack by the knights of the castle had chased them off. This boy had not been so lucky; he had been skewered in the leg by the lance of one of the charging knights.

Talon had become very attentive as soon as they entered the cell behind the two guards, but had allowed Sir Guy, who spoke good Arabic, to interrogate the prisoner without saying anything himself.

He instinctively moved back into the shadows cast by the guttering torch in its sconce on the wall, and made sure that the prisoner did not get a good look at his face. The last thing he wanted was to be recognized by one of the former students of the infamous Sinan, if this was one of his killers and not one from Persia. But it turned out that the boy was not from Persia; he spoke no Farsi. To Talon's surprise Sir Guy discovered that the ragged but proud young man was one of the Ismaili 'Assassins from the region; their strongholds were just south of this fortress and the other Templar castles, and as such formed a potentially dangerous wedge between Antioch and the principality of Tripoli. The mountainous country inhabited by the 'Assassins of Sinan Rashid ed Din was not far off; merely two days ride at most. The boy had trained under the tutelage of Raffiki, loyal followers of the Old Man of the Mountain, as Rashid ed Din had become known.

*****

He now lay on a pallet; a sheen of sweat on his dark face. He was in obvious pain from his suppurating wound, but nonetheless he controlled himself well and stared back defiantly at his captors with eyes full of hate. Neither Sir Guy nor Talon had any intention of torturing the boy and had made sure that the jailers treated him carefully. Talon did not think the boy could escape with a leg wound like this, but nonetheless, in a low voice he told the men to check the boy's clothing carefully.

To their astonishment they found a knife hidden in his undergarments. Talon nodded to Sir Guy, and then took the knife and looked it over. It was a cheap but deadly blade, good enough to take down the unwary and allow an escape; it had the boy's name scratched on the handle, Hussein.

Talon placed it in his sash and Sir Guy continued his interrogation.

They ascertained that Rashid Ed Din was looking for ways to enrich himself at the expense of the pilgrims and caravans that came from the north heading for Jerusalem. Talon was dissatisfied. He suspected that there was something else. The 'Assassins took what they needed in tithes and protection money from their own and rarely infringed upon the Templars' property or the pilgrims. Perhaps this was one of those occasions, but it was unlike them to resort to banditry.

Despite Sir Guy's persistent questioning the prisoner would say nothing more. Talon waited until Sir Guy had given up, and then reached a decision. He moved forward, leaned over the boy, and whispered into his ear in Arabic. The boy, already pale with pain, drew back suddenly as though he had seen a snake. He moaned and shook his head. Talon gave a meaningful nod.

"I shall give you an hour to think about it, and then I shall expect some answers," he told the terrified boy.

Both he and Sir Guy left the boy in the darkness of the cell and went out to the main yard.

"What in God's name did you say to him, Talon?" asked Sir Guy, clearly puzzled.

"I told him that I was going to cut him a thousand times until he died," said Talon in a matter of fact manner.

Sir Guy looked at him aghast. "Do you really mean to?" he asked.

"No, but he does not know that," responded Talon. "We should give him time to think about it, however. Have you eaten yet, Sir?"

"You are a cold man, Talon," said Sir Guy, shaking his head. "But now that you mention it, I am hungry, and we might as well eat."

They came back an hour or so later to find the prisoner hanging from one of the bars in his cell. He was almost naked; he had used his clothes to fashion a rope and then kicked himself back off the pallet.

They cut him down and then left the cell, telling the jailer to clean up the corpse and cover it.

"Well, what do you think of that, Talon?" Sir Guy sounded irritated that his interrogation had been cut short.

"He took me seriously, Sir Guy, and now I am sure he had something to hide. We should post extra guards in case this castle is a target, as I think it is," said Talon.

*****

This was why he now stood in the early dawn hours on the stone flags of the parapet at the highest point in the castle, staring out at the eastern desert. He was furious with himself for not having judged the situation better; at the same time he knew that they could have tortured the boy all night long and learned little more, but even a small amount of information might have helped with this puzzle. The boy had been trained to endure great pain and welcome death, and he had had not wanted to blurt out the truth during torture, so he had taken the only way out left open to him. Now at least there was a clue, and it pointed to their castle. The boy.

If there was to be an attack on the castle Talon was sure it would come by stealth and not by direct assault; but how, he wondered, would that be accomplished? There were nearly twenty knights in this small outpost; with their retainers, Sergeants and other servants, they numbered about sixty men under arms who could defend the walls against all but the most determined assault.

No, they would find another way in. But why did they want to take this castle? He surmised that it might be a little too close to the 'Assassin castles in the region and was interrupting their activities. Also he had heard that the Old Man of the Mountains was getting somewhat tired of paying tribute to the Knights Templar.

Perhaps Sinar was going to try his luck at taking one of the outposts the Templars possessed to teach them a lesson? Talon stood and watched in silence with the two men at arms for company.

Dawn came quickly here in the low mountains of western Syria, and the sun soon bathed the stony fields and sparse orchards below the battlements with a bright light. Talon saw a motion in the distance along the road to the north. The sentries noticed too and one pointed.

"There! I see something. Do you see it, Sir?" he asked Talon.

Talon nodded. "I see it."

Coming along the road they could see a procession of people walking slowly, accompanied by some animals. It was unclear yet who they might be and what their intentions were, so he continued to watch them warily.

The brightening sky revealed a column of between forty and fifty people, some on foot, some of them leading donkeys, and there were even several horses. Many of the people were bent over, carrying what looked to be loads of wood and other bundles of possessions on their backs. Others seemed to be monks, as they wore hoods, while others still were women, also hooded, who carried their possessions on their shoulders or loaded onto the backs of the donkeys. They looked like pilgrims, as this was the route taken by the more courageous, or foolhardy, on the cruel hard road to the holy city Jerusalem still many weeks to the south.

They looked ragged and very much done in. It would be at least another half hour before they reached the gates. Then surely they would want to be permitted entrance to avail themselves of the fresh water of the well and some food the knights might spare them. Talon told the men to watch carefully to make sure they were indeed pilgrims while he went down to wake Sir Guy and get some breakfast.

He called over to Claude, who was down in the yard, half dressed and talking to the blacksmith. Claude looked up and waved.

Talon woke Sir Guy by pulling the leather curtain of his cell open and nudging his leader with his boot. Sir Guy came awake instantly and bade him a sleepy good morning.

"Did you not sleep, Talon?"

"I was called by the sentries, who thought they heard something; instead we have company of the pilgrim sort."

"Who?"

"A column of pilgrims are making their way here. I imagine they must have camped out in the desert last night. That must have been what the sentries heard on the wind. There is something... "

"What are you thinking, Talon?"

"Oh, nothing, Sir, I must be tired, that is all."

Sir Guy nodded and Talon went off to wake others of the group who had come to the castle with them. He heard the rest of the castle rousing as he did so. The pumping of the bellows for the blacksmith's forge and the clang of a hammer on metal was loud in the still, clear air of the morning.

The smell of new baked bread came to him, making him remember his hunger as he took the worn stone stairs down to the main hall where the rest of the knights would soon gather for prayers and then the brief, silent meal that would follow.

Most of the knights were up and about already, some wearing their chain hauberks, as they would be on duty, while others in light working clothes were carrying out their daily tasks. Talon paused at the top of the stairs as he came out of the tower and stared down at the activity taking place in the yard.

Horses were being taken to the forge for re-shoeing. Sergeants were checking swords and other weaponry, and retainers were busy running errands. It had all the bustle of a busy Templar castle waking up for another day of duty. While the knights might for the most part maintain a dignified silence during their morning activities, the retainers showed no such restraint. The yard was becoming noisy with the clatter and murmur of the men. There were no women in the castle; the Rules of the Order forbade their presence in a Templar stronghold of this kind.

Talon surveyed the bustle y in the main yard and low buildings along the walls with practiced eyes. Everything seemed normal. Nonetheless some of the uneasiness of the night before remained, and Talon, who had come to trust his senses, went to breakfast in a thoughtful mood.

The Castellan, a huge man, as large as Claude, with a massive beard and cropped head, met him as he joined the others for breakfast.

"Talon, what do you think of the prisoner and his death?" he asked somewhat caustically.

"He was an 'Assassin, Sir; he would have withstood torture one way or the other. I think he told me more with his death than we would have learned by torture."

"What do you mean?"

The man stared curiously at Talon. Like all the others he knew little of Talon, who accompanied Sir Guy on some of his missions, but there were many rumors and tales about this quiet young man. He was not quite a full Templar; he was very rich and owned ships; Sir Guy liked it that way, as it gave Talon freedom to move around and test the wind, as Sir Guy liked to put it. Nonetheless he dressed much like the others and spent a considerable amount of time with the Templar Order.

"He chose to die rather than reveal anything to me by word or deed. That could be very important if only I could fathom it," Talon said. Then, as an afterthought, "Do you know of the pilgrims?"

"Yes, I have given instructions for them to be allowed entrance."

Talon nodded and took his bread and gruel with him to an empty table. He sat alone for a few minutes until Sir Guy came over with a mug of water and a huge chunk of bread. Claude entered the cavernous room, glanced their way, then followed him and sat down with a sigh.

"Another hot day, I think. This is not the same stuff we used to eat in Constantinople, eh Sir Talon?"

"No indeed, Claude. But much better for that black soul of yours, I am sure of it!" Talon murmured with a grin.

Claude gave a rumbling laugh and began to eat. He and Talon went back a couple of years now, and the banter was part of their friendship. They sat listening to the muted sounds coming from the kitchens and the clink and rattle of the men at the tables eating. Talon found it almost suffocating to be in the hall. He found the proximity of unwashed men and fetid air unpleasant. He was becoming used to it but would never like it, he decided. He instinctively preferred the outdoors and the clean crisp air of the desert above all.

He thought about the pilgrims. There were women among them and monks, but something was missing. His mind wrestled with it for a few more minutes, and then he realized: there were no children. Unusual for there to be no children; some pilgrims bred along the long road from Europe, so children young and older were a common sight among them. Many older children became men and women over the time of the journey. Why were there no children?

He gave a start. "Sir Guy, Claude, I am going for my bow. Arm yourselves very quickly and tell the others to hasten to do so too. I think I have my answer. We must hurry!"

Sir Guy and Claude heard the urgency in his voice and reacted. They both trusted Talon of all people to know what he was about. They both stood up and Claude called to the men nearby to get up and follow Sir Guy. His roar of alarm shook everyone into action. Men scrambled to their feet and rushed off to arm themselves.

"Alarm! Alarm! Arm yourselves and hurry! Follow me outside!" Sir Guy shouted to the assembly.

Talon raced along the corridors to his cell and seized his bow and quiver. He hoped that he was right about his instincts. He would never hear the end of it if he were wrong!

He ran up the stone stairs to the entrance that gave him a clear view of the gateway of the castle. To his consternation the gates were open and already a large number of the pilgrims were inside. He gazed intently at the quiet group that had already come into the courtyard.

They remained a loose group, but there was no conversation, which he found chillingly ominous; none of the usual noise and chatter that would have accompanied the arrival of a group of tired but relieved people who had just been given along the route. He stared at them hard, the hair on the back of his neck rising and a hard lump growing in his stomach. The monks' heads were still covered; a small group was heading purposefully for the gate tower. Talon decided to take a chance.

"Stop those men!" he shouted, pointing at the four men making their way towards the men at arms by the gate. There was a surprised silence as many eyes turned his way, and then the men in monks' habits began to run straight at the gate men.

With one smooth motion Talon knocked an arrow and sent it speeding toward the forward man. At forty yards it caught him full in the back and sent him sprawling in the dust almost at the feet of the stunned men at arms holding the gates open. Talon knew he could not do anything for the men at the gate now.

"To Arms! To Arms!" he yelled at the top of his voice.

The newcomers were suddenly everywhere, daggers out; in spite of Talon's cry the surprise was almost complete. Retainers and others in the castle yard who were anywhere near the group were swiftly dispatched by flashing daggers. There were shouts of surprise and fear followed by scuffles, then shrieks of agony as men were stabbed to death.

Seven men began to sprint towards the stairs, straight for him. Talon shot down two of them, then found himself joined by Sir Guy, Sergeant Claude brandishing a sword in one hand and a mace in the other, and other men. They charged down the stairs, roaring battle cries, leaving Talon to continue to shoot his arrows at any targets he could find.

The high ground gave his an archer's advantage, but it meant that he could do little about the gates. He shouted at Sir Guy and pointed urgently at the people pouring in. It was imperative to seize back control of the gates and stop the remaining 'Assassins from getting in.

He saw a 'woman' use a knife skillfully on one of the luckless Sergeants. The man went down with a look of utter shock on his face, clutching at the intestines that roiled out of his slit belly.

Talon shot the disguised man down before he could stoop to finish his victim off. Then the remaining knights came boiling out of the main hall brandishing spears, swords, maces, and in one case a huge axe. They were outnumbered but better armed and certainly had nothing to lose. The fight became a ferocious melee as men hacked savagely at one another, shrieking and roaring as they killed or maimed each other.

No quarter was given and none expected. Talon could see small groups of retainers and Sergeants facing off against clusters of 'Assassins all around the yard now, some at the entrance to towers and others at the top of stairways.

Talon leapt down into the fight below. He had seen many of the unwelcome visitors spreading away from the fight in the middle of the yard towards the buildings. Heaven alone knew what mischief they could do if they were not stopped.

The overriding importance for the moment, however, was the gate house. Whoever controlled that could dominate the yard and the battle. He saw the bowman who had been on the tower fighting for his life, and then shortly thrown dead from the battlements.

He charged after Sir Guy. Passing an uneven fight between three of the 'Assassins and Claude, dressed only in his kilt, Talon all but decapitated one of the opponents, leaving Claude to hack one man to death with his huge sword and crush the head of the third with his mace. Clause shouted his thanks and chased after Talon as he raced away.

The shouts and screams continued as the battle spread all over the castle yard then into the towers and the buildings. Talon was confronted by a youth with a sword who shouted a challenge and came straight at him.

Dodging sideways he flicked his blade at the point coming at him and deflected it past his shoulder. The youth spitted himself on Talon's blade. Talon had to stamp on the writhing man's chest to release his sword.

He spun around and blocked another slashing attack with his blade; the metal rang in a high-pitched tone, but then he struck hard at the exposed neck. The man screamed in agony and disappeared in the churned up dust. Talon knew he had to hurry. The knot of fear in his stomach was growing. If those men could hold onto the gate house, who knew how many more would be able to make their entrance.

Sir Guy and his yelling, bloody men had made it to the gates but were being fought off savagely by the press of men trying to enter the castle, and Talon could see that at least one of the towers was in the hands of the 'Assassins. If he could get into the other one he might be able to reach the mechanism for the portcullis. He shouted at Sir Guy, who looked up and was almost killed then and there as his opponent lunged. With a flick of his arm Sir Guy deflected the sword of his opponent, and Claude, who had just caught up, hacked the 'Assassin down.

Sir Guy quickly saw what needed to be done and pointed at the tower to the right of their group. Talon nodded and led the way. He still held his bow in his left hand and had no shield, but neither did his opponents. For the sake of their disguise, they were for the most part lightly armed. He closed on two men who came at him, and found that he had to work very hard to deal with their concerted attack. He managed to wound one and took a cut on his forearm in return.

Then he attacked ferociously and drove them back with his stabbing and flickering blade. Just as he was going to take one of the now worried looking men down, Sir Guy and his men broke out of their stalemate and charged past him. The two men Talon had been fighting simply disappeared under the hacking, yelling knights.

Roaring "Deus Lo Volte!" they rushed the doorway only to find their way blocked by a spearman, who held them all at bay in the narrow entrance. Looking quickly behind him to make sure he was safe and nodding to Claude, who seemed to have become his body guard, Talon fitted an arrow to his bow and sent one thumping into the man's chest. He fell back without a sound, clutching the arrow protruding from him.

The two knights in front of Talon almost fell over themselves as they charged into the space. Talon was right behind them, and then they were pounding up the stone stairs, trampling the body of the man Talon had just downed. They stumbled over the edge of the stair top and were met by four more 'Assassins, who cut one knight down the moment he showed his head.

Talon and the other knight fell back out of the way of the slashing and stabbing swords. Talon fired another arrow from his cramped position in the stairwell and took one of the yelling men in the throat. He died choking, falling back among his surprised companions.

This gave Talon and the knight the chance to charge up the remaining four stairs and gain a foothold on the wooden floor space. It was cramped here; the winch for the portcullis took up most of the space available, so the 'Assassins were almost on top of each other as they fought.

Talon slung the bow over his shoulder, and now he and the knight held their swords with both hands, one on the blade, and stabbed and hammered with them as they pressed their opponents back. The 'Assassins were nimble and fast as snakes, but Talon evened the odds by stabbing upwards with his blade into the belly of the nearest one. The man fell back with a shriek of agony, tumbled over the winch, and then rolled onto the floor.

The remaining two backed off, shocked and bewildered at the quick reduction of their numbers and now uncertain of themselves. Pitched battles of this kind were a new experience and they could not control the outcome the way they would have liked.

"Come on!" Talon bellowed. "It's time to finish this!" Seizing the opportunity Talon and the knight attacked with renewed fury and literally battered the 'Assassins' guards down. The two youths were overpowered by the ferocity of the attack and fell to the floor to be stabbed to death.

But as Talon straightened up he saw the knight fall to his knees on the floor holding his groin, a grimace of agony on his face. He sat back on his haunches looking down at himself as blood poured over his fingers. The 'Assassin who had taken a blade in the stomach had stabbed upwards as the knight stood over him. The youth died with a smile on his face.

Talon could think of nothing to do to help his comrade. Instead he strode over to the winch and hacked at the thick rope that went out of the opening in the wall and held the portcullis. On the third stroke the rope was severed, the part attached to the iron portcullis whipped through the opening, and there was a crash that shook the tower, followed by screams from below.

What men are those, despite of scars,
Who facing flashing scimitars,
Defend the Cross in Holy Wars?

—"The Templars", *Poems* by David Barker and John Edward

Chapter 4

Knowledge

Talon peered out of the arrow slot down on the chaos below. Men had been crushed by the large wood and iron portcullis as it fell. Their mangled corpses and the portcullis itself now provided an effective barrier against the ones outside, who hacked futilely at its frame with their swords, cursing and yelling in Arabic. He even heard Farsi being shouted, which confirmed his fears.

Breathing heavily, Talon turned and checked each one of the 'Assassins on the floor, ensuring they were dead, and then went to the knight sitting against the winch. His was sitting in a puddle of blood, his legs straight out in front of him. He clutched at his groin, from which poured his life's blood. His face was already ashen under his tan and his dirty beard. He spoke to Talon in a whisper.

"Shrive me, Brother, for I am wounded to death."

Talon nodded. He held the man by the shoulders and recited the verses of the prayers. The man confessed in barely a whisper, then leaned back as though very tired and died with barely a tremor. Talon closed his eyes and stood up. There was still much to do for the living, and his help was needed.

As he did so, Sir Guy shouted up the stairs. "Talon, are you safe? Nicely done with the portcullis!"

Talon ran down the stairs to join him. "The others are all dead, Sir Guy. If you will hold these men off I shall continue to use my bow from the tower top."

Sir Guy nodded. "Go to, Talon. We can deal with any counter attacks from here."

Talon turned and ran back up the full stairway to the top of the tower. He warily poked his head over the top of the stairs, half expecting to find others there, but the parapet was empty. He quickly stood up and then crept to where he could observe the other tower. Three of the invaders were peering over their side, shouting down at their companions on either side of the gate.

Standing up fast Talon loosed an arrow that transfixed one of the men, and then before the other two could react another arrow flew. It drove into the shoulder of the second man, who shouted with pain and abruptly sat down. The third man disappeared from sight.

Then Talon turned his attention to the men on the outside crowded into the gate well. They soon realized that they were in a trap and the only way out was to flee the area, or the archer above would slay them until he ran out of arrows. Shouting threats and imprecations they prudently ran back from the walls of the castle until they were well out of range. Talon then turned his attention to the men in the yard. The battle now favored the surviving Knights and their retainers. They had formed into several solid gangs who charged around the yard attacking any 'Assassins who still had any fight left in them.

The fights were brief but savage; the knights were not in the mood to waste time and simply overwhelmed the opposition. The main body of Knights had been reduced from twenty to less than twelve. They spared no one, and finished off the wounded as they went by. Their armor and clothes were covered in blood and their weapons gory; they looked like butchers who had gone mad in an abattoir. Blood was staining the dust in the yard.

Sir Guy quickly sent some of his own men up onto the battlements to secure the high ground and then, accompanied by Claude and Talon, who had joined them, strode toward the Captain of the Templars and a small group of knights. They had paused to take stock of the situation.

There were bodies everywhere; they hurried past men of both sides dying or groaning in their agony. The Captain turned at their approach and stared at them. He too was covered in blood: his weapon arm was red from the blade he held all the way up to his shoulder; even his face was smeared with it and his beard matted. It was not his blood. There was an insane look in his eyes and of those nearby, exhausted but triumphant, and willing to do more killing if the need existed.

"Captain, we owe the fact that we are still alive to Talon," said Sir Guy.

The Captain nodded. "How did you know?" he asked.

"There were no children," said Talon.

The men thought about this and then nodded agreement. It made sense to them.

"You saved our lives with your quick action," said the Captain. "But there are still numbers of them all over the castle; we do not know how many."

"That is correct. We will have to pry them out one by one. It will not be easy. They do not know how to surrender. Death is a welcome friend to them."

"How do you suggest we go about it, Talon?" Sir Guy asked.

"I need to interrogate at least a couple, but that may be harder than we think. For the rest of the day the men should never go anywhere unless in pairs, and perhaps threes, for the hidden men will attack from any place without warning."

There was new respect in the eyes of the Captain when he asked the next question. "How do you know so much of these people?"

"I suggest that we ask questions of Talon later when we have dealt with the enemy, Captain," Sir Guy interjected. "I for one want to sleep in my bed with both eyes shut, not waiting for a dagger in the night."

"You are right, Sir Guy," said the Captain. He turned to his men and began to issue orders. The fighting in the yard had died out and the men were going round killing the remaining wounded. He called over to them and told them to bring two captives to Talon before continuing the search for the hidden Assassins.

Two of the wounded 'Assassins were carried to where Talon stood in the middle of the yard with Sir Guy. Having dumped their prisoners unceremoniously and none too gently on the bloody ground, the knights went off to help their own wounded.

The two young men on the ground were weak from their injuries but still defiant. Talon went up to one of them and without warning slapped him very hard on the face, knocking him flat on his back. The wounded youth gave a startled cry of pain. Talon stooped and very quickly searched the groaning youth. He turned up a knife, just as he expected, and stood back, allowing the angry young man to lie back and glare up at him.

"Why did you attack this castle?" Talon asked quietly.

There was only the glare in response while the youth clutched at his wounded chest.

"I know it was Simon Rashid Ed Din who sent you, and I respect your courage, but you will tell me why you were sent," said Talon ominously. There was silence.

"Are you *Fida'i* or *Rafiqi*?" he asked in Arabic.

There was a startled look from the pair of youths on the ground. Then one spoke to the other in Farsi. "How does this Ferengi know of the *Fida'i,* or the *Rafiqi* for that matter?"

"I do not know, but he speaks Arabic very well for a *Ferengi*."

"I also speak Farsi; I am a *Fida'i* from Alamut," said Talon, very quietly this time.

They stared up at him speechless.

"You should not have attacked this castle, but I will let you and your companions live if you tell me why you attacked us. You must tell me quickly, as the Knights Templar are thirsty for blood and want to kill you all."

"I am dead anyway," said one of the youths. "We were told to take this castle in revenge for the attack on one of the caravans by your Duke Raymond, may his soul burn in hell." He gasped with the pain in his chest and lay back. There was blood on his lips and he was very pale.

Talon knelt by his side. "Have you come from Persia? Did you come from Samiran?" he was referring to the great castle of the 'Assassins situated at the entrance to the Alborz Mountains, in far away Persia.

The youth nodded, as did his companion, who had a bad gash in his leg and on his right arm.

"Is Timsar Esphandiary here in Syria?"

Again the surprised looks. But the youth with the chest wound was going fast. Talon lifted his head and asked Sir Guy for some water. One of the nearby retainers brought over a skin and Talon allowed some drops to wet the parched lips of the dying youth.

"Your bravery will be remembered. What is your name?" he said.

"Kemal. Tell me, what is your name, Templar?" the youth whispered.

"Talon, I am Talon," he told them.

"Are you the one that killed the lion when only a boy at Samiran?" There was genuine surprise in his weak voice.

"I am that one."

"They still speak of the Ferengi Tal'on who killed the lion," whispered the youth, then his body racked in Talon's arms and he died. Talon closed his eyes and laid him back on the bloody ground, covering his face with his head cloth in respect.

He stood up and went to the other youth.

"Let me bind up your wounds without fear," he said.

"It is Allah's will that my companion should die. We are *Fida'i*, Tal'on—Kemal, you and I. What are you doing fighting for the *Ferengi* as a Templar? I will not fight you now."

"First let me bind your wounds, and then we must call your companions and ask them to surrender. I shall ask for quarter and try to send you back to Simon Rashid Ed Din or...is it to the General?"

"It is to the General; he is near Allepo with the Master of the Syrian Ismaili."

Talon's heart began to pump violently but there was no time to dwell upon the one thing that he wanted to ask most. There was the clash of steel and more shouts as the Templars, their Sergeants and retainers hunted down the remaining 'Assassins.

Talon quickly gave Sir Guy the gist of what had been said and told him, "Sir Guy, I think we can do ourselves some good if we do not massacre these people. You should know that we and they both hate the Seljuks and the son of Nur Ed Din."

Sir Guy nodded agreement. He shouted for the Captain of the Templars, telling some of the men to run and fetch the Captain and to ask him to pause in his searching while Talon tried to get the 'Assassins' out with words rather than by force.

"I have to have real assurance that they will not be killed if they do come out," Talon told Sir Guy.

"I shall be the guarantor of this, Talon, if you really believe this to be the answer."

"If we miss even one of them he will wreak havoc with the survivors during the night, Sir. That I can promise. It will be easier for all of us to get them to leave of their own free will."

Sir Guy saw the sense of that, and then they waited impatiently for the Captain to arrive. He eventually came striding out of one of the towers.

"Well, it is going to be very hot work prying these people out of the nooks and crannies of the castle," he agreed. "They certainly know how to fight, and to die," he added as an afterthought. "What do you want of me, Sir Guy?" He glanced down at the living prisoner and the dead youth.

"Talon thinks he can talk them out of there, Captain. He spoke to these two and they are from Persia. The rest come from both

Persia and from Syria. It would do us no harm at all to let these people go as a sign of respect and to gain their allegiance if not their friendship."

"Do you really believe this?" the Captain asked him forcefully, glancing at Talon as he did so.

"Captain, I have come to trust Talon in these things and one day I shall explain why," said Sir Guy, standing his ground.

"Very well then. I shall command the men to assemble out here where we can take a roll call, and then Sir Talon can try to get them all out."

"Thank you Captain," said Sir Guy.

The Captain bellowed orders that were quickly relayed to the houses and buildings where the hunt continued. Slowly men in small groups filed out and assembled in the yard. The men on the battlements remained where they were.

It was a disheveled and very bloody group of men who assembled in front of the Captain and Talon. They murmured angrily when told what was wanted and were not a little skeptical. They had felt the hard edge of these phantoms from outside and didn't really believe that it would be possible to achieve what Talon wanted.

Talon, who had been binding up the wounds of the youth on the ground next to him, spoke to him.

"I shall help you to stand and then we must go to the buildings one by one and call them out. Can you do this? Will you do this? Also, what is your name?" He spoke in Farsi so that none of the assembly could understand. The Templars had a few men who spoke some Arabic, but no one who spoke Farsi.

"Do as you will, Ta'lon. My name is Mehmed. Yes, I shall speak to them," the youth said.

Talon asked the Captain to provide two men who would support the wounded youth and then they headed for the nearest building.

At the entrance they stopped and Mehmed called out loudly in spite of his pain. Although his wounds were now bound up they were not insignificant and he had lost a lot of blood.

He called to his companions, telling them that he had been spared by another one such as themselves.

"This man with me is called Tal'on. He is a *Fida'i* and is one of us although he is a Frans and now a Templar. He will protect you and make sure we can all leave the castle safely if you come out now. We have his word and that of his chieftain."

The whole castle was eerily silent after he had spoken. Even the men in the yard grouped with the Templars were quiet, waiting tensely for whatever might happen.

There was a slight sound within the building. Talon tightened his grip on his sword and the two men holding Mehmed upright looked fearful. But they all relaxed a little as a youth much the same age as Mehmed, dressed in the remnants of a monk's habit, came cautiously to the door. He was armed with a sword and looked very wary. He called out to Mehmed.

"What have they done to you that you are now calling for us to come out and die in the sun, Mehmed?"

"This is Ta'lon, killer of the Lion in Samiran, who has spared me. He is a *Fida'i* just like you or I, Mahmud. Remember the tales of the Frank who slew the lion when only a boy? This is he. I trust him as no other."

Mehmed had called this out loudly to ensure that any other listening would hear and think about it.

Slowly, very slowly, the 'Assassins came out of the buildings; one by one they came towards the small group standing by the entrance to the main hall. They did not give up their weapons nor did they say very much. They looked warily over towards the glowering Knights clustered in the middle of the yard, but on the whole they concentrated their attention upon Talon.

Many were the questions thrown at him in Farsi by the Persian survivors, who then explained to their Syrian counterparts the story of his time with the 'Assassins in Alamut.

Talon heard it all but said nothing and finally Mehmed asked him, "You have said nothing, Ta'lon, I have kept my word. Are you going to have us all killed now?"

Talon looked him in the eye. "My word is my life, 'Assassin. I shall personally escort you away from the castle. Are they all here?"

"I think so," Mehmed said. He talked rapidly and forcefully with the others, demanding to know whether there might be someone still hidden; most looked around and told him that they were sure that they were all there were left. There were fifteen in all.

Talon beckoned to the men gathered in front of him. In Farsi he tersely told the startled men to lift Mehmed and carry him, as he was sorely wounded. The two retainers who had been supporting him thankfully walked quickly off to join their fellows among the Templar contingent. Talon then asked the youths to follow him.

Walking in front of the 'Assassins, he led the way to stand in front of the equally surprised Templars.

"I shall lead them out of the castle, Sir Guy, with your permission," he said to a bemused knight and his Captain.

"Can we trust them not to kill you when you go out with them, Talon?"

"No, but I gave my word that we would not kill them, and now I must keep it."

Sir Guy looked hard at the 'Assassins. "Very well, may God protect you."

The knights stood aside and watched while Talon led the hesitant group of ragged youths towards the gate.

There he told them to wait while the portcullis was reattached to its rope and then winched up out of the way. This was going to take time, so he told them they could take their dead with them or they would be interred outside the castle walls within one day as per the proscribed rules of Islam. They nodded acceptance.

The while they squatted in the bloodstained dust Talon was subjected to a barrage of questions. The Persians all knew of the legend of his fight with the lion. Few knew of his involvement with the killing of Ahmand or his uncle those long years ago, for which Talon was grateful. He started asking questions of his own.

"How was the General Esphandiary?"

Still the mightiest warrior that ever lived, they bragged.

"What of Reza...does he still live?" Talon held his breath at this point.

"The Reza of fame, who had saved the life of the Master?"

Talon nodded.

"He has not been seen for many years," one of them said.

"He is somewhere in the south with the Master's sister."

Talon's heart began to thump very loudly in his chest. He spoke very carefully. "The Agha Khan had only one sister, as far as I know."

"He *has* only one sister and she is living somewhere in the south," the leader of the group of young men told him.

"What is her name?"

"Why, it is Rav'an. If you had been in Samiran you should know this, as she grew up there they say, around about the time you were there."

Talon had to stare at the ground. "Yes, I know," he whispered almost to himself.

Work on the portcullis was finally finished and the winch turned by two burly men in the tower. Talon watchfully herded his new acquaintances out of the castle.

"Please convey my deepest respect to the Timsar Esphandiary and tell him that this was the wrong castle. He should punish Lord Raymond in the manner that he would normally use, if indeed Lord Raymond deserved it," he told the man who led them out. "Tell me, where is the General?"

"He is in Aleppo," was the reply.

Taking care not to seem too interested Talon managed to obtain a fairly detailed understanding as to where the youths would be going, and ascertained that would also be the place where the general would be staying.

The youths came up to him one by one. "*Khoda Haffez, Genab Agha,*"—God Protect, honored Sir—they said in unison, clasping his hand between their two. His onetime enemies were almost ready to embrace him. But he would not permit it. His own mind was racked with a different kind of emotion; he barely noticed them anymore. But he mustered himself and bade "*Khoda Haffez*" to each as they came to him and clasped their hands in his. They had been trying to kill each other only half an hour ago but fate had changed things for all of them.

The youths were barely gone when the fearful retainers hurriedly closed the main gates with a loud crash of wood and iron on stone.

Talon was left alone in the archway of the gate to ponder what he had heard.

Rav'an was alive? How could this be? His mind was ready to explode and his heart was thumping so hard he could hardly breathe. He sat down abruptly on one of the steps leading to the tower nearby and put his head in his hands. How could this be? He had lived for nearly six years with nothing inside him to be called hope and now fate had come and laughed in his face.

She was alive! He could not believe it! And yet these men had told him so to his face, innocently with no guile, that she lived. His mind was in such turmoil that he did not notice Sir Guy when he came up and stood in front of him until that man asked him if he were all right.

Talon stood up shakily. "Yes, I am all right, Sir Guy."

"For a moment there I thought you might be wounded, my boy. God be praised, but that was a close thing," said Sir Guy with concern in his voice.

They were interrupted by the Captain, who marched up, still covered in dried blood, to clap Talon on the shoulder and exclaim, "I have never seen the like of what we saw today. What kind of hold do you have over these people?" he glared at Talon as though he would tear the answer out of him.

"Talon was a prisoner of the Saracen at one time, Captain. He speaks their language, which is Persian."

"It would seem this is a man of many talents. I saw him fighting, and then he took care of the portcullis. Now he speaks to them as though they are his brothers. In God's good name, I am bound to say that I am grateful, Talon, but I understand little of how it came about!"

Talon shook his head and gave a bleak smile. "There is no need to be concerned, Sir. It was chance and a lot of God's help that saved the day."

Luckily Talon did not have to answer too many questions, as for the rest of the day the entire company of men were tasked with cleaning up the wreckage of the battle. They had to clear the grounds, bury the dead and look to the wounded. The sad truth was that while they had survived the attack by the 'Assassins, the company of men was now badly depleted. Many of the retainers who had been neither armed nor protected by armor had been killed in the first few minutes of the battle.

Sir Guy told the Captain that he would be leaving on the next day and would ensure that replacements were sent north as soon as possible. In the meantime, they would have to manage somehow to give the illusion to any marauding bands of Seljuks or Arabs that they were an impregnable stronghold.

Pass on from the name,
and look closer at the source.
The source will show you what you seek.
Leave the form behind.

—Rumi

Chapter 5

Usama and News

Their work done Sir Guy and his men left the survivors to fend for themselves and left to go back to Acre. The journey was uneventful until they encountered a small caravan of the Saracen.

The approaching horsemen stopped abruptly, once they realized it was a Templar group in front of them. Talon and Sir Guy watched the way they hastily organized themselves to present the mounted warriors to the front. It was all done smoothly, as though the Arabs had rehearsed this maneuver before. Sir Guy, keeping a wary eye on the group, said in a low voice,"We should see if we can avoid a fight, Talon. It is not why we are here."

Talon nodded but said nothing.

"They look as though they are going to attack, Sir Guy," said another knight.

Talon glanced back at the man. He was a newly arrived Templar, and therefore new to this kind of situation, probably fearing the worst.

"That would be foolish," he said, "for we are more than they are and better armed."

"That never stopped them before!" was the laconic murmur from Claude nearby.

Talon had to agree. He knew that within the 'Saracen' population there were many different peoples, and while some would go to great pains to avoid a fight with such as the Templars, there were others who deemed it necessary to do so at every opportunity.

"Perhaps we can talk them out of it?" he suggested to Sir Guy.

"Very well, Talon. Go and see if they will let us pass without a fight. But keep your shield up, just in case some hothead tries to win glory at your expense."

Without further discussion, Talon walked his horse forward alone towards the horsemen arrayed to their front. He kept his lance high. He stopped about twenty yards before them and called out in Arabic.

"Salam Aliekum! We come in peace."

He could see the surprise among the swarthy men; it was clear they had not expected a Frans to speak to them in their tongue. He could now clearly distinguish the warriors from others who appeared to be merchants. This seemed like a strong escort for mere merchants, he thought to himself.

A man rode forward on a spirited horse that danced as it walked as though it would rather be running, but he held it in check with a quiet but firm hand. It was clear that he was a very good horseman. He was armed with the usual slender lance, held in his right hand with its point in the air, its haft seated in his stirrup. There was the familiar curved sword at his side. His round metal shield was carried casually on his left forearm, low but ready.

Talon and the warrior eyed one another warily.

"Aliekum Salaam, Templar. What is your name and why are you on this road?"

"Like you we are merely travelers going from one place to another... and in peace." responded Talon.

"You are not men of peace, Templar," retorted the warrior.

"What is your name, Sir?" asked Talon politely, ignoring the barb.

The warrior hesitated but then answered, "I am Salem bin Mahmud ibn Nur."

He stated his pedigree with such obvious pride that, although Talon did not know the family ties, he realized this man was a noble and quite possibly related to Nur Ed Din himself, the former Sultan of Damascus. The man was young, a few years younger than Talon. Then the young man asked,"To whom am I talking?"

"I am Talon de Gilles, Templar," replied Talon briefly. "Greetings, Salem. We would pass without a fight, as we have no quarrel with you or the people you are escorting."

As he said this he became aware that another man was approaching on horseback. This man was obviously not a warrior; by his rich clothes Talon judged him to be a wealthy merchant.

The man rode up slowly and addressed his companion.

"I thought I heard you both speaking our language. Does this frengi then speak in our tongue?"

"He does, my Lord, and, it seems, fluently," answered Salem politely, but he kept his eyes on Talon.

"This is my Lord Usama ibn Munquidh, whom we are escorting to Aleppo to meet with our overlord As-Salith Ismail al-Malik, who is there for the winter. My Lord, this is Talon de Gilles. Frans Templar."

Having finished the introductions, Salem sat still, watching. Talon did not want his own interest to show too much, so he bowed in the saddle and spoke respectfully.

"My Lord Usama. I am honored to meet you. I have heard much of you. You are a recorder of events, a poet and a scholar."

Usama inclined his head, looking pleased with the complement.

"And you, Sir, know our language well. Where did you learn it?

"Here and there, my Lord," Talon responded evasively, "I was just telling your noble bodyguard that we would pass in peace and do not wish harm upon you."

Usama nodded, then peered past Talon towards the tight group of Templars a hundred yards away.

"If I am not mistaken, that is Sir Guy over there among your people. We have met before, and then I was impressed with his knowledge of our language. Few among you Templar warriors seem to care to speak our tongue," he added.

Talon turned in his saddle and beckoned to Sir Guy to come and meet with Usama. Sir Guy rode up and immediately recognized the man. They greeted each other elaborately and clasped hands. It was clear that they had a mutual respect for one another. Talon and Salem listened with interest to the exchange.

Very quickly the encounter altered from one of wary hostility to one of congeniality, so much so that to the surprise of both Talon and Salem, Usama invited them to camp with him that night at a place the Templars had passed half an hour earlier. It was well situated, near to a stream with wide meadows to either side of the water for the horses to graze. Here a comfortable camp could be made.

"It has been some time since we had the opportunity to talk and bring ourselves up to date on items of interest, Sir Guy!" Usama exclaimed.

"Indeed, it has been many years, Sir," Sir Guy responded gravely, a smile on his lips.

"The last time was when I was praying, and one of your knights kept insisting that I pray directly to the east!"

"I remember, Sir. He was new and did not know all he might have of your faith," Sir Guy said with a straight face.

Usama and Sir Guy, now deep in conversation, led the way back towards the location. Talon rode alongside Salem, who, despite his reserve, was clearly curious and wanted to talk.

"I have never ridden along side a Templar before, Talon. We usually charge in to fight whenever we encounter your knights."

"Have you done so often, my Lord?" enquired Talon, he was careful to keep his tone respectful.

The young man sent him an uncertain glance.

"In fact I have not; this is the first time," he confessed.

"Your answer is honest and therefore the better in the eyes of Allah," said Talon. "We may be enemies, but we are also much alike, and it does none of us any harm to share our thoughts with one another from time to time."

Salem nodded as though he could comprehend some of what Talon had meant, and then he looked at the horse Talon rode.

"That is a good animal, and not like those that the Frans ride into battle."

"This is merely the horse I ride when traveling around the country. He is also an excellent mount to have for a game of polo," said Talon.

"But your animal is one to be proud of. He is magnificent!"

Within a minute the two were discussing ponies and their relative merits. It lightened the mood and allowed the men riding behind to sense that the ice had been broken.

Their discussion continued until they come to the stream, whereupon, as though by some unspoken decision, each group took a camping position on either side of the shallow rippling water. There was a wide field that could be used for good grazing for the horses that all could use.

Covering the low hills to their east were many old olive trees that had not been tended for a long time, as the fruit was strewn all over the grass. Talon and Salem, also by unspoken agreement, seemed to be the men elected to organize their respective camps. They met on the side of the river occupied by the Egyptian caravan as the huge red sun perched on the crests of the distant mountains to the west.

"We should post sentries for both our sakes," suggested Talon tactfully. Salem agreed readily. It was becoming clear to Talon that the young man took his duties very seriously but was inexperienced, and once he had overcome his initial distrust of the Templars he was observing them carefully as they set up their camp along the lines of all Templar horse lines and tented camps. Talon smiled inwardly; the young man would see that there was no chance of surprising these men at night.

Salem had another reason to meet with Talon. It was to invite him and Sir Guy to dine with Usama in the merchant's tent at sunset. When Talon passed the word to Sir Guy he agreed readily; and thus after prayers, when the knights made Vespers and the men on the other side of the river prostrated themselves in prayer, the two men crossed the shallow stream and made their way past the watchful sentries towards the warm orange glow of their host's tent.

They were greeted by a servant at the entrance, who proffered a copper bowl of water for them to wash their hands in, and then a linen cloth with which to dry them.

Usama was sitting cross-legged on a fine traveling carpet around which were the modest but well cared for possessions that he traveled with. He rose to his feet and greeted them politely, bowing and touching his heart and forehead to honor his guests. Both Talon and Sir Guy responded in kind, much to the pleasure of their host, who said, "Sir Guy, I am delighted to see you have survived the vicissitudes of your profession, although I do detect a little more gray about your temples than the last time we met!" His eyes twinkled.

Sir Guy laughed ruefully. "You are an observant man, Sir. I hope that I have become more wise with the aging."

"I had thought that among you barbarian Frans there was only one who spoke our language, and that was you. But I learn from my young escort Salem that the knight with you also speaks our language, and very well at that."

"Indeed, my friend, Talon does speak the language of the Arab," said Sir Guy easily, "but you will have to find out from him where and how he learned it."

Usama looked at Talon reflectively, but decided instead to let it go for the moment and instead said, "Please, I beg of you to partake of my miserly hospitality for this evening, so we can at least enjoy each other's company."

They seated themselves, and just as they did so Salem came into the tent. He bowed respectfully to Usama; the two knights, who remained seated, acknowledged his presence with nods.

Usama waved him to sit also, then offered honey cakes and other sweetmeats that were on copper plates placed in the middle of an elaborately designed carpet. The conversation started a little slowly; although enemies officially, the men were agreed that this evening was a time of truce, and all four were determined to enjoy the chance to gain more understanding of each other's culture.

The offerings were hardly miserly: the mouth-watering smell of roasting mutton wafted in from outside on the light evening breeze, and the small cakes and nuts on the copper platter were of very high quality, a delight to the knights'. They had been subjected to the normal food the Templars ate the world over: corned beef, thin stew and hard bread, with little in the way of variation.

Usama asked in Arabic, glancing at Talon as he did so, "Well, Sir Guy, you are further north than usual. May I ask what business brings you so far away from the 'Kingdom of Jerusalem'?" He used the Arab name, Al Kuds.

"We came to do business with the Count of Tirol, and then had an incident with the 'Assassins at Darbsaks," Sir Guy replied.

"Ah, those people! The Batinas from hell! May God curse them for the murdering heretics that they are! They put fear into all men!" exclaimed Usama, and Salem looked apprehensively at the entrance to the tent.

"The Batinas can come upon a man as he lies with his woman and kill him right next to her without her even knowing of it until the next day," said Usama.

"I have heard that they can come to him in his bed and leave a dagger on his pillow to teach him a lesson," said Salem.

Sir Guy glanced at Talon as though to say, *Be careful here*; but the two men they faced were well launched into recounting a list of horror tales about the depredations of the accursed 'Assassins.

"We think that this time Rashid Ed Din was trying to take one of our castles for his own, as his men almost overcome our garrison with trickery," Sir Guy said during a pause.

Usama said, "It is foolish to underestimate that man. He is the master of some ten castles that I have heard of to the north, up there where you have been, and while it is his men, the Batinas, who murder, he himself is a learned man of great personal presence."

"Have you ever met him?" asked Talon.

"Your young friend speaks our language as well as you do," remarked Usama with a smile, obviously pleased.

"I would guess that he speaks it better than I, my friend." said Sir Guy.

"Your people are for the most part barbarians, Sir Guy. But then I meet you and your friend here, who have learned our language and perhaps a little of our ways, and I am forced to change my thinking somewhat."

He took a pinch of something between two fingers of his right hand and sniffed it. It made him sneeze but he seemed to enjoy it.

He wiped his moist eyes and was about to say something when the servants entered the tent, bringing with them supper. Usama sneezed again.

Talon was amazed and wondered where the copper and brass trays could have come from. It did not seem that they could be packed away so well for a journey such as the poet took, but there they were, with a mound of rice on the one tray and many succulent pieces of mutton on the other. The aroma made his mouth water in anticipation. Water from the stream was poured into silver beakers for drinking, while an aromatic tea was served in small porcelain cups.

Usama seemed to want to impress his guests, because he spoke to the lead servant, who nodded and left the tent, to return with a stone jar from which he poured red wine into more beakers and handed down to the seated company.

Both Talon and Sir Guy paid many flowery complements to Usama for the plentitude of the feast.

Usama encouraged them to eat more and watched the two knights to see if their manners were appropriate to the occasion. Both men used their right hands to eat, never letting food touch their left, and ensured that their feet were kept out of sight, not presenting the soles of their feet to anyone in the tent.

He seemed pleased with the good manners of his guests, and as the evening progressed he regaled them with observations and anecdotes of his travels up the Palestinian coastline and his experiences with the Christian armies and with the Templar Order itself. He was keen to make comparisons between the two civilizations.

"Sir Guy, have you ever been wounded?" he asked with a sly wink at Salem.

"I have indeed, but not severely. Why do you ask?" replied the knight.

"How did you ever survive the wounds? Did you have one of the people called a 'leeeech' work on your wound?"

Sir Guy looked sheepish. "I did for a while, but he nearly killed me. Luckily I knew of a physician from Egypt who came and took care of me."

They all laughed at that, because each man knew of the dreadful reputation the Christian 'leeches' had.

"I have had occasion to witness a most incredible incident involving a 'leech' in one of the hospitals, I think it may have been your St John's in Jerusalem. He wanted to show off his skills to me. He showed me a man with a festering wound in his leg. It was clear that the corruption had set in and he could not live much longer without having it amputated. The man was in a high fever, and looked as though he was ready to go to his God.

"The 'leech' and I agreed upon that fact at least, but the madman then said to me, 'See now how we treat that which is evil and corrupts the soul, Master Usama.'

"He called over to a burly man standing near the doorway and told him to bring his axe. The man came over and the 'leech' ordered him to lop off the offending leg to save the man's soul.

"The man swung his axe and the bad part of the leg fell off, but the wounded man shrieked and then died from the shock of it and the blood he lost. Do you know what the 'leech' then said to me?" asked Usama, sounding incredulous, his eyes wide.

Everyone looked back at him questioningly.

"He told me that the man was obviously destined for heaven now that he had disposed of the bad leg, and when he got to heaven he would find a new one waiting for him there!"

Usama then laughed merrily, took another pinch of some dust from a tiny pot and sneezed, then continued laughing and sneezing until the tears dribbled down his cheeks.

Talon and Sir Guy laughed too, but more at the lugubrious image Usama presented than at the incident he had recited. Both warriors were more frightened of the notorious 'leeches' than of death itself.

The talk turned to politics and the events that were taking place in the area of Syria, the Kingdom of Jerusalem, and Egypt.

"Do you come from the kingdom of Egypt, Sir? Sir Guy asked with care.

"I do indeed, and am heartily glad to be out of there for the time being," said Usama.

"Why would that be, good host?" asked Talon with interest.

"That young upstart Salah Ed Din, the nephew of Nur Ed Din, is turning the place upon its head, and now there is conflict between the Shia' and the Sunni followers he has brought to the kingdom. It was once the Fatamid empire, you know, and a great one at that, but it is no longer. He intends to convert its citizenry to the full Sunni faith and dispose of the heretical Shia' once and for all! He will find it hard to do, as there are many underground sects still there waiting to rebel.

"It is always the problem of our people, Sir Guy. Do you suffer from heretics the way we do?" he asked.

Sir Guy smiled and shook his head. "We suffer from other problems than an excess of heretics, Sir. Our problems stem more often from adventuring nobles who do not respect the truces that we have between us, " he said ruefully.

"Ah yes, the last was broken by that thrice cursed Reynald de Châtillon, was it not? God damn him!"

"I fear so, Sir. He is a greedy man and would not honor any agreement between our peoples if it got in the way of his profit."

"That is a sad thing for both of us, Sir Guy, because I am sure that there is much room for understanding and friendship between our peoples."

"I would agree with you, my Lord, were it not for the fact that we both want to live in exactly the same country," said Sir Guy with a wry smile.

"I still think there is room for us all, but while you have people like this Reynald, and we have our hot heads too—" he glanced with a smile at Salem—"I see little future beyond the truces we have between us."

It was now dusk outside, and the servants came in to light candles, which bathed the tent in a warm glow. The light gleamed off the copper bowls and silver plates.

Talon asked, "How did you leave the Egyptians, Sir? Is there much unrest since the last drought? I had heard that the Nile did not rise to the needed levels this year and the crops failed."

"You are well informed Sir Talon," said Usama with a sharp glance at Talon. "If I did not know better, I would say that you learned your Arabic in Egypt." He shot another keen look at Talon, then continued.

"But you are right. Crops have failed, and that is one of the reasons I left. The mobs in Cairo and Alexandria are getting unpleasant, and the prices for rice and bread are becoming impossible. The Sultan is well and has demonstrated his leadership against his enemies, both at home and abroad. He has won some battles in the south of Egypt, somewhere in the upper Nile against the Nubians, but that is not a huge accomplishment.

Still, it has placed him in a position where the people respect him and he can do no wrong... however, with the failed crops and starvation looming up and down the Nile, and in particular in that new city Cairo, he might have to do something to prove he can do even better."

"And what would that be?" probed Sir Guy.

"We all know that when things are not going well at home, an adventure abroad often works to take people's minds off their problems," said Usama taking another pinch of the dust and giving off an ecstatic sneeze.

Sir Guy and Talon looked at one another. There was a message here.

Usama suddenly changed the subject. "But there are some things that we, the Chosen people, could not live with, Sir Guy, and that is this thing you Frans call Feuda'lar?" he mispronounced the word.

"Feudal Law, Sir?" interjected Talon. "Why is that?"

"You must understand that all laws are promulgated with the approval of God, and therefore the Princes of our lands have absolute power; and this is ordained by God, so your laws could not work for us."

"Our laws?" Sir Guy said surprised. "The Feudal laws stem from the time when a man was of a tribe and could go to his chieftain and obtain redress for a wrong done to him by another. How do you find that wrong, Sir?"

"Ours permit that too, within the guidelines of Sharia and the laws of the Koran; but what is outrageous is that among you Frans a peasant! a man of no rank whatsoever, can petition his lord and even the king and demand a hearing!" Usama sounded genuinely shocked.

Talon glanced at Sir Guy, who was having trouble suppressing a grin.

"That is right, Oustez. He may petition the king himself if there has been a wrong done to him by his Lord and obtain redress. Why do you think this is so bad?" Sir Guy asked.

"Because each man is born to his heritage and should not presume to lift himself above it, other than that God should intervene and uplift him."

"But Sir, your princes take what they want, when they want, and often leave chaos in their wake. Should there not be laws to govern them too?" said Talon

Usama looked piercingly at Talon. "It is clear you do not know our ways, Sir Talon, even if you speak our language well. A prince or Sultan is above the common man and hence should not be governed by any law but that of God. No, we could not live with your Feuda'law. It would bring chaos and anarchy!"

"Do you intend to visit with His Highness Ismail al-Malik while in Aleppo?" Sir Guy asked in an attempt to change the subject.

"Why yes, I do, although I hear he is not well," replied Usama. "He is very young, and I doubt that his regents will protect him from Salah Ed Din when the time comes to do so."

"How do you mean, Sir? When the time comes to do so.... Do you mean that Salah Ed Din intends to take Aleppo and Damascus from him?"

"I do not doubt it!" said Usama and took another pinch of the dust. He sneezed happily and blew his nose on a napkin; his eyes were streaming again.

*****

Later that night Sir Guy and Talon discussed the evening. They were seated in Sir Guy's much less grand tent with only a candle to light the interior. The night was well advanced, but neither of them was tired. The dark shadows jumped and shifted on the canvas walls of the tent as the candle flickered in the light breeze from outside. They had no fear of being overheard. Claude had been asked to stand guard while they talked.

"Do you think what I am thinking? Is Usama saying that Salah Ed Din is about to invade the Kingdom of Jerusalem?" asked Sir Guy

"Indeed I do, Sir Guy. Our King Baldwin is sick with the leprosy, everyone knows this, and most unlikely to be able to lead his men in battle. Would you not agree that this would be a good time for a... visit from Egypt?" Talon returned thoughtfully.

"You served the Sultan before you escaped, Talon. Do you think he is ready to attack the Kingdom?"

"He has Egypt under his control just now, Sir. I know that his brother owns the Yemin, but that was just an investment in case Nur Ed Din decided to take back Egypt. However Nur Ed Din is now dead. With unrest in the country due to the poor harvest, a sultan could promise his people much plunder and high standing in God's eyes if they could wrest the city of Jerusalem from the Christians. He has many enemies, not least because he is a Kurd, and hence is not loved by either the Arabs or the Turkish tribes, who distrust him, even if they do respect him thus far. If he fails to demonstrate his ability to defeat the Christians, he could be in difficulty with his so-called allies. I think it is only a matter of time, Sir Guy."

"The information we heard tonight will be of huge value to the King when he hears of it. This, Talon, is why I travel so much. Usama probably beggared himself tonight with that display of food and drink. I suspect from what he has told us that he holds no love for Salah Ed Din. It is up to us to do with this information as we see fit, and I am sure he knows that. I hope he does not have too far to go beyond Aleppo."

"They will hear him sneezing long before he gets there, Sir Guy," Talon remarked with a laugh." I suppose that dust contained some spices to make him sneeze like that!"

Sir Guy grinned, but then said, "I will want you to come with me to Jerusalem, Talon. It is high time you met with the Grand Master. He has been asking about you."

Feathered their thoughts, their feet in wings were light,
Swiftly they marched, yet were not tired thereby,
Form willing minds make heaviest burdens light;
Jerusalem behold, appeared in sight,
Jerusalem they view, they see, they spy;
Jerusalem with merry noise they greet,
With joyful shouts and acclamations sweet.

—Tusso's *Jerusalem*

Chapter 6

Jerusalem

Sir Guy de Veres decided that they should ride directly to Jerusalem instead of returning Acre. He sent several of his knights off to that city with letters from himself and Talon, and Claude went with them to recover from his wound.

Talon wrote to Max, informing him of the warning passed along by Usama, and entrusting him with the trading operation until he could get back to Acre himself. He was perfectly comfortable doing so, as his trust in Max was absolute. In the letter he also asked Max to keep an ear to the ground on the subject of Brother Jonathan's investigations. This was not going to go away, particularly with a fanatic like Jonathan trying to chase the charges down.

He bade Claude farewell as he gave him the letter, and told him to go to his house where the servants could care for him and Max would make sure that a Jewish physician attended to him. Talon did not want Claude to become a victim of the leeches in Acre.

"I look forward to seeing you again in Acre, Sir Talon," the Sergeant said in his gruff manner as they clasped hands.

The knights sent upon their way, Sir Guy made haste to reach Jerusalem as soon as possible.

They pushed on past the Sea of Galilee, and Talon remembered his childhood visits as they rode along its western shores. They spent the night at the small Templar post located just to the south of the Count of Tripoli's large fortress on the midwestern point of the lake, overlooking the small town of Tiberius. Sir Guy did not want to draw too much attention to himself, so they bypassed that town. Talon enjoyed the cool breeze that came off the lake; it brought a welcome relief from the still fierce October sun. It seemed very peaceful here, with the fishing boats and the light that danced on the rippling waters of the lake.

Their approach to the city of Jerusalem was from the northeast and Talon was struck by its grandeur. This city rose high above them, resting upon the highest point of a jumbled mass of sun-burnt hills. Talon was impressed by the fortifications and the well built towers, but also by the sense of its turbulent and long history. They joined the traffic of carts, camels, donkeys and pedestrians interspersed with the occasional group of armed men that made its way towards the high, sand-colored walls and towers of David's Gate.

Once they arrived within the walls, Sir Guy informed Talon that he had to try to obtain an interview with the Grand Master and pass along the news they had garnered from Osama the Poet. It was a matter of some urgency.

Before he left he advised Talon to obtain a small house within the city so that they could move about with ease and not have to enter and leave the main gates to the Temple garrison. He eventually found a small plain house squeezed in between a group of others along a narrow street near to St Peter's church not far from Zion's Gate. As he wanted no company it suited him well allowing him and Sir Guy could come and go as they pleased without attracting much attention from the locals.

The next day Talon and Sir Guy strode along the narrow streets that led from Herod's gate via the church of the Holy Sepulcher along the crowded Via Dolorosa east towards the castle of Jerusalem. They were on their way to meet with the Grand master of the Templars, Odo de Saint Amand who had asked for Talon to be presented. Sir Guy had passed along the information but as usual it had not seemed to sink in. He shook his head as he mentioned this, and Talon realized that for all his intelligence gathering Sir Guy still ran into difficulties with his own people.

The Church of the Holy Sepulcher was covered with scaffolding as the restoration, initiated nearly seventy years ago, was still under way. The Christian Kings wanted this to be the center of the Christian world. There were those who said that the king wanted this church to rival the Church of Saint Sophia in Constantinople, but that would have been absurd. To Talon's mind, nothing could match the grandeur of the Hagia Sophia. Its soaring pillars, domes and magnificent frescoes depicting scenes of the Trinity and the saints was a jewel in the crown of Christianity.

The Christian kingdoms of Palestine lacked the wealth, the skilled craftsmen, and the materials to compete with the riches of the Byzantium empire, Talon knew that for certain. He and Sir Guy had traveled to Constantinople only last year as emissaries. Talon was fairly sure that King Baldwin III, known as a modest man, had just wanted the resting place of Jesus to be built into a worthy place of worship. His son Baldwin IV was continuing the work.

They were on their way to the Temple of the Mount barracks, which was Odo's headquarters and where the Templar garrison was housed. Despite the fact that they were both clad in mail with the distinctive white overcoat and the red cross sewn onto the left breast, it was hard going down the narrow, crowded streets.

Vendors were hawking their wares on every corner and from stands placed in the middle of the street itself, shouting in many different languages at passersby. Along with the yells to clear the way from the laboring porters as they staggered along under impossibly heavy looking loads, and the cries and screams of children of every age, Talon was hard put not put his hands over his ears. The hot sun cooked the filth in the streets to a noisome stew of revolting stinks that seemed to get worse the deeper they went into the center of the city.

They wandered into the market area to, as Sir Guy put it, gawk like any other pilgrims at the churches of fame, the splendid structures that remained after the siege, as well as those now being built by slaves under Christian supervision. The work going on to restore the holy sites since the first Crusade relieved the city of its Moslem masters was continuing at a fair pace, with most of the effort going into restoring the damaged battlements and the Church of the Holy Sepulcher.

Talon, however, had learnt that Sir Guy rarely did anything on pure impulse. He guessed that they were here to take the measure of the mood on street.

Wares were on display, ranging from mutton, already with a sheen on the meat and almost black with flies; fruit; and even some live chickens and ducks. Trapped hares from the hills and other creatures of a less recognizable nature hung, smelling ripe, in the still warm sun of the October day. Salted strips of fish from Tiberius and the Mediterranean Sea hung on hooks over poles by the stalls, and there was much of the bustle that accompanies a peaceful world. War seemed a long way off from Jerusalem on this sunny day.

Sir Guy's Arabic was excellent, as was Talon's; they could often linger near a group of people and listen. The men would glance contemptuously at them from time to time, never knowing that the two Templars understood them well. Talon was amused, as this was something he had learned elsewhere, to hide in plain sight. But now was no time for standing still; they must take in impressions as they moved through the crush of pedestrians and merchants.

Being dressed as Knights of the Templar Order they stood out, and even men at arms from noble houses stood aside respectfully, if resentfully, for the Templars. Talon drew curious glances for his unusual form of dress. His fine chain mail shirt with its long sleeves was not part of the usual uniform seen on a Templar, nor was the turban on his head, which he favored for its practicality and comfort, having learned a long time ago that this kept his head cooler than the cumbersome helmet he wore only to protect his head in battle.

The press of people grew denser as they approached the main market place. Here there were stalls where cloth of many bright colors was on sale, but Talon noted that there was not much in the way of fine silk of the kind he had seen so often in the streets of Byzantium. Jerusalem was a poor city by comparison. The heat from the early autumn sun was still capable of being uncomfortable between the walls of the narrow streets, and there was little in the way of a breeze to refresh the foul air. The babble of many voices, the stink of rubbish, offal and the unwashed laborers who shouldered by, along with the beggars and lepers on almost every street corner, made Talon think, not for the first time, how nice it would be to be out in the clean air of the desert.

Despite all this he was enjoying himself. He could hear a multitude of languages, from Arabic and the Yiddish of Jewish traders from northern Europe to the dialects of Kurdish, Turkish, and other tribal dialects of the Bedouin; then there were their own Christian monks who talked in bastardized derivatives of the Greek and Latin languages which had once been prominent here. It amused him to understand the Arabic conversation of the vendors—not all of it complimentary as the Templars walked by.

After one especially rich insult was murmured at their passing, Sir Guy explained as they continued on.

"When this city was sacked, Moslems were killed by their thousands. Now, many years later, there is a kind of unspoken truce, dictated by the necessity of having to survive, regardless of whosoever rules for today. But they don't like us."

Talon's keen eye noticed Jews; they too were to be seen in the streets, although very few in number.

"Does that include the Jews of this city, Sir Guy?"

"Yes, Talon. They too were massacred by the army of the first Crusade, who made no distinction when they sacked the city. Most of the Jews took refuge in a synagogue and were burned to death inside. We Templars were not present for that first assault, for Sir Hughes de Payen came later, or we might have been able to bring some sanity to the madness that overcame the first crusaders."

"Why did they massacre the people of the city, Sir Guy?"

"Because they were mad with hunger and disease! They were not about to share with the hated Saracen, nor anyone else for that matter, what they considered they had earned by hardship, famine and death. As far as they were concerned, it was all to be theirs for the taking. You should know, Talon, that few of the crusaders who came to this land came here for religious reasons. It was plunder for the common men and lands for the wealthy."

Now, a generation later, Jews could be seen in their coarse dark robes of dark linen, reciting their prayers or hurrying along the streets talking to no one, as though they were in another dimension from the world of bustle and common people.

Talon listened carefully to Sir Guy, but kept half an ear open to the babble of voices, distinguishing the Frankish peasantry from that of the Arab community. They were often dressed in much the same clothing, but it was clear to his ears who were Moslem and who were Christian among the people of the streets.

Sir Guy changed the topic to the pending meeting with the commander of the Knights Templar, Lord Odo, and what Talon should say when they met. It was to be his first interview with the Grand Master and Sir Guy wanted it to go smoothly.

Just as they came near a fruit stall, Talon's sharp eye caught a flicker of movement, and he noticed a small, thin boy dressed in filthy rags stealing a bunch of figs. The boy almost got away with it, but the alert vendor noticed and ran around the back of the stall and caught the boy just as he was about to make off with his booty. The owner was yelling abuse and threats in Arabic as to what punishment would befall the struggling brat. He cuffed him viciously and shouted at the now tearful boy, whom he shook by the arm as though he wanted to tear it off.

Talon nudged Sir Guy, who was in the middle of his instructions and quite unaware of the incident, then he moved to where he could see more. It was clear that the man wanted to make an example of the boy.

"I shall see you hung for a thief at the gates this very day! The Fran patrol shall come to collect you. You know how they deal with thieves. You goat's dung! At the very least you shall have your hand cut off as punishment!"

Although tears were sliding down his cheeks the boy stood up to the man and said bravely, "I am hungry, Oh Master, have mercy. Merciful Allah will bless you for your kindness! It is to feed my sick father, who has nothing; you can spare some figs."

It was of no avail, and a crowd gathered, sensing entertainment. Their sympathies were divided between the ragged boy and the irate stall owner, so a noisy discussion was developing in several languages as to what should be done.

"A likely story indeed! You are nothing but a common thief! Where is the patrol?" the stall owner called out to no one in particular.

Talon, observing the situation, watched the boy as he faced the shop keeper and noticed that although he was ragged and thin he was trying hard to hide his fear. The punishment would be out of all proportion to the crime. But the boy made no excuses once he realized his fate was sealed. Talon made a decision. He elbowed his way through the crowd, who parted as soon as they saw it was a Templar and gave him a small space around the stall. Its owner and the boy looked up at him as he arrived.

"God's blessings upon you! What did he steal, Hajj?" Talon asked respectfully of the stall owner, who sported a beard, although Talon was sure he had never been anywhere near Mecca. His greeting was respectful enough to make the man turn to him with his mouth open. He displayed several rotting teeth in an uneven line. Few had heard a Templar speak Arabic before, but then for him to be addressed as Hajj was a genuine surprise to all the listeners nearby. There was a short silence before the stall owner recovered himself and shook the boy by the arm.

"He wanted to steal this sack of fruit from me, my Lord!" he exclaimed, indicating a small sack that lay nearby.

"If it is the sack that you are pointing to, then I believe you are mistaken," stated Sir Guy with an amused look on his face. There was a murmur of surprise. Two Templars speaking Arabic was very unusual. This time the shop owner was silent. He looked warily from one to the other of the two imposing men standing in front of him.

"I believe he was trying for the figs on the top of the stall," Talon said. "I shall pay you for them, and some extra for your trouble; you shall drop your charges and give the figs to me."

There was a smothered laugh from Sir Guy and another murmur from the crowd, who were enjoying the interchange; someone snickered. Then the crowd began to laugh, and some even to jeer at the stall owner, telling him to accept the payment and let the boy go.

The stall owner, realizing that he was not going to get anything more out of the incident, hesitated, then nodded reluctant acceptance. He released the boy, pushing him hard so that Talon had to reach out an arm to prevent him from falling. Suspecting the lad might dash off, he decided to hold onto the boy with one hand; then, turning, he took a few coppers from his pouch and tossed them to the stall owner. The man seized the coins, which represented far more than the of figs were worth, and touched his forehead respectfully.

"May Allah bless you for your generosity, Oustez," he muttered.

"May his blessing be upon you for being so merciful; indeed, you are a Hajj," said Talon softly.

The stall owner, much mollified, grinned back through his bad teeth and bowed again, then handed over the small bunch of figs.

Still holding the filthy boy by the arm, Talon moved off with Sir Guy. The crowd dispersed, casting many curious glances at the three of them. When they came to a street intersection, Talon released the boy and handed the figs to him.

"Is Allah so unkind that he makes you so poor that you must steal?" he asked the boy.

The skinny lad looked up at him with huge eyes. "My father is very sick and we are starving," he replied in bad Arabic. He wiped his nose with a dirty hand.

Talon looked at him. Clearly Arabic was not the boy's native tongue. He tried Farsi. "Where are you from?" The boy looked surprised and replied carefully in broken Farsi.

"We are Kurds, from Mosul; we were attacked by one of your Christian Lords in the north and our caravan destroyed. My father was taken prisoner, but he was so ill they left us to die, and we came to Jerusalem."

Talon stared at the boy. "You are lucky he was not killed. How have you lived since you came here?"

The boy shrugged. "I steal. Sometimes I run errands."

"I do not think you make a good thief. What is your name?" Talon asked.

"It is Dar'an, and I am the son of Hindrîn Ed Kareman, who was a rich merchant until your bandit lords in the north destroyed him," the boy replied with an edge to his voice.

Talon turned to Sir Guy, who had been watching the interchange with interest. "He tells me he is a Kurd and his father owned a caravan that was attacked by a lord in the north. I would wager it was Reynald of Châtillon, or someone like him."

"I would agree, Talon. There are rumors that he has broken the truce yet again. He is greedy and ambitious, that man. What are you going to do with this boy?"

"I should give him some coins and send him on his way, but I could do with an urchin to clean my equipment. Would that be acceptable to you, Sir Guy?"

"You can't go around collecting every waif and urchin you come across, Talon," Sir Guy laughed. "But if you really want to have a slave to help you, it's your choice."

"Do you like horses, Dar'an?" Talon asked, looking down at the boy.

Dar'an drew himself up proudly. "I am a Kurd, your Lordship." It was said with all the dignity the thin frame could muster. Talon was reminded of another young boy in a different time who had faced his fate clothed in little else but his pride.

"Report to the Temple of the Mount in the morning; be somewhat cleaner, and ask for Talon. The guard will call me to come and collect you. In the meantime, Khoda Hafez. God Protect, and no more stealing." He dropped several coppers into the surprised boy's hand and smiled. "If you do not come I shall know you are a liar and that you are not what you say. If you come, there is work."

The startled expression on the face of the boy, then the frown of anger at the suggestion that he was a thief, was all Talon needed to see. The boy turned and, head held high, stalked off.

There was an amused chuckle from Sir Guy, and he cocked an eye at Talon as they moved forward through the thinning throng.

"What has happened to make the iron Talon go soft on a thieving Kurd?" he asked.

"Perhaps I remember what happened to me at that age, Sir Guy. I too had no friends and was in a strange world that was not interested in whether I lived or died."

Sir Guy nodded and held his peace.

Finally they reached the main castle where Lord Eudes de St. Amand, or Odo, as he was affectionately known by his knights, was billeted. This was also where King had his royal apartments, and where his mother and sister lived. The fortification doubled as the stronghold for the Templars and the royal family, dominating the city below.

Talon knew that Odo was widely respected, both as the Grand Master of the Templars and as a steady leader, very loyal to the king. He knew too that Odo's men loved him and would follow him anywhere.

They were admitted through the wide gates of the castle by the king's sentries, and then Sir Guy unerringly took them along dark, narrow corridors, much cooler than the baking streets of Jerusalem, and up the stairs to the Master's chambers. At the door they were greeted by one of the secretaries. The harassed man snapped that Odo had left word that he was in the palace with the King, and that they should join him there as soon as possible.

Sir Guy lead the way swiftly along the open stone corridors and then along some gloomy stone passages until they were standing on the balcony overlooking the gardens of the King's palace. These were spacious but not extensive; however, there was a lot of color among the larches, lemon trees, and tall shrubs that dotted the garden. There was also one of the fountains that had been repaired by Arab engineers after the destruction of Jerusalem. Talon compared it to the huge fountains he remembered from Isfahan in distant Persia and Constantinople and found it wanting. Still, it was water in a dry land, and it was making a small music among the green trees. But its sound was almost drowned by the noise of many people in animated conversation and the strains of some reedy music being played in the background.

People in Jerusalem who were part of the King's entourage wore bright clothing. Multi-colored cloaks vied with bright green, blue and yellow dresses worn by ladies of rank. Lords and knights from all over the kingdom paraded with their wives or mistresses, giving space to the King and his immediate advisors. Knights were now beginning to wear their emblems and family crests on their Surcoats as part of the new style that had come over from France. There were very few wearing the light flowing cotton robes of the Arab people, and even fewer people wore the silk sheaths Talon had seen on the women in Constantinople other than on those of the royal family. Instead, many people present wore wool, in which they sweated. The stuffy air of the courtyard was made worse by the smell of unwashed bodies.

Talon noted that the king seemed young, a mere boy in fact. The King's father had died suddenly, and the Kingdom of Jerusalem had been thrust upon the young Baldwin prematurely. Now he was sixteen and could rule as he pleased—or more likely as his advisers pleased, Sir Guy had dryly informed Talon during one of their discussions.

Sir Guy pointed out Lord Odo standing near the King. Talon also observed a stocky man with a cropped head and a full beard clad in Templar uniform standing next to several richly dressed men who appeared to be of some distinction.

"That man at the King's elbow is Count Raymond III of Tripoli, who probably knows more about the Saracen than anyone here today. Rumor has it that he even has an uneasy relationship with Rashid El Din, but lately things appear to have gone sour between them. The other, yes, that one with red hair and the pose, is Reynald de Châtillon. He was released not long ago by the Syrians from the dungeons in the castle of Aleppo, along with Joscelin of Courtenay. They were there for many years; it is a wonder they survived! That is Joscelin over there, that dark ugly fellow standing off to the right, talking to one of the lords in waiting. He is now the Seneschal of the kingdom. It is hard to believe how quickly he has regained his position of power after so long an absence!

"There is no love lost between any of those three men, but I would trust Tripoli before the other two. Reynald and Joscelin have already attacked caravans in defiance of the truce made by the king's father. Tripoli knows the Saracen mind and plays by their rules, so they respect him, and his territory is seldom bothered by raiding bands."

"I have heard of My Lord Raymond, and somewhat of Reynald de Châtillon. Isn't he the one who sailed down to attack Medina?" Talon asked.

"Yes. None of the men who went with him came back. Reynald has led a charmed life. God must be reserving a special fate for him. Why the Arabs let him live after that is anyone's guess. I suppose they thought they could get a ransom of some kind."

"Who is the woman with the King?" asked Talon.

"I believe that is Sibylla, the King's sister; and the man in attendance upon her is Sir Guy de Lusignan, a knight of no real consequence, but because he is with Sibylla he is able to put on airs and strut."

Talon glanced at Sir Guy. It was not often that his mentor allowed any contempt for other men to show.

Odo happened to glance up and saw the two men leaning on the balustrade of the veranda. He waved them to come down. Sir Guy lifted his hand in acknowledgement and led the way along the veranda to the steps leading down to the garden.

Sir Guy opened a path before them through the crowd by his mere presence as a Templar, so Talon had but to follow and listen to the murmurs of the people they passed. Some were respectful and others were barely civil. It would seem that the Templars were not entirely popular even among Christians, he thought to himself. Suddenly they were before the King. Sir Guy knelt on one knee and Talon followed suit. King Baldwin IV was talking to Raymond, but he turned when he noticed the two knights kneeling in front of him.

He turned his head towards Odo de St Amand hovering nearby and said, "Do I know these knights, Odo?"

"You know of Sir Guy de Veres, my Liege, but the other you do not know, Sire. They are two of my best men. Sir Guy de Veres here," he indicated Sir Guy with his hand, "and Sir Talon de Gilles both speak fluent Arabic and other languages."

The young King looked interested. "Indeed, few of us Christians speak the language of the Saracen. Where have you learned this?" He indicated with his hand that they should stand.

Sir Guy replied, "I have been in the Kingdom of Jerusalem for many years, Sire, and have found it useful to know the language of the Arab people. Sir Talon here has learned it in the same manner."

King Baldwin looked at Odo. "I wish for one of one of these men to accompany me on my journey to the south, Odo. They can help me learn more of the activities of the ruler of Egypt, Saladin, is that his name?"

"Salah Ed Din. Yes, Sire, he is the nephew of Nur Ed Din, who ruled Damascus until quite recently," said Sir Guy, his tone respectful.

Odo looked at Sir Guy and Talon. "Which of you should go south with the King, Sir Guy?"

"Sire, it should be Sir Talon here. He is familiar with the Egyptians and can advise the King well," Sir Guy murmured.

"Very well then, it is decided," the King said, and then he turned away to talk to a bishop who was trying to attract his attention.

Talon was struck by the pallor on the face of Baldwin and the lifeless seeming mouth. But the eyes were alive and intelligent. He knew the king was afflicted with the dread disease of leprosy and instinctively felt somewhat repelled, but at the same time he was drawn to the young man who refused to give in to the inevitable and continued with his rule despite the hardship of the disease.

Odo and his two knights were left alone in a small quiet area while the King moved off.

"So you are the famous Talon de Gilles that Guy is always talking about!" Odo said to Talon.

Talon looked abashed. "Sir, I am he, but I doubt I am famous."

"Few of us have lived as you have in the midst of the enemy and survived, young man. If we live among them at all it is usually as did Reynald and Joscelin here... as prisoners in a dungeon." He gave a short bark of laughter. "Not that everyone here is glad to see them back. As for us Templars, when we are captured we do not come back—ever.

"Have you not been with the Templars for several years now, Sir Talon? Where have you kept him, Sir Guy?"

"Sir, Talon spent last year as a guest of the Emperor Manuel in Constantinople, and distinguished himself in the disastrous battle of Myriokephalon. Then he returned, and has been to several of our castles. We were most recently at Darbsak together, as I mentioned in my report. He works for me in the capacity of a gatherer of information, among other duties."

"You're the one who came from Egypt with a ship, are you not?" Odo chuckled. "And now Sir Guy reports that you have three ships at your disposal! I should like to hear more about this one day, Sir Talon."

The man Sir Guy had pointed out as Raymond, Count of Tripoli sauntered over, his cloak billowing about him. He was of medium height, not as tall as Talon but lean, and he looked strong. His fine clothes indicated wealth, but not ostentation. Talon was struck by his angular face.

The nose was aquiline, and although the mouth was wide the lips were firm and his jaw determined. His complexion was swarthy and his hair dark, which set him apart from the lighter Franks in the room. Talon knew he was of Languedoc nobility, which accounted for the dark good looks.

There was no mistaking the bearing of this man; he held himself upright with his shoulders drawn back. He nodded his head in recognition of Lord Odo and Sir Guy, then turned his dark piercing eyes on Talon as though assessing him.

"Who do we have here with you, Lord Odo and Sir Guy?" he asked. "Did I hear you mention that this knight speaks the Arabic?"

Odo bowed, as did Talon and Sir Guy.

"Indeed Sire, both men are fluent in the Arabic, and Sir Guy tells me that young Talon de Gilles here speaks Persian," Odo said with a friendly smile. It was obvious he liked the Count.

The Count looked interested. "Now where would one learn that language in Palestine?" he asked.

"I learned it in Persia, my Lord," said Talon.

"Ah... and you lived to tell the tale, eh?" said the Count with a gleam in his eye. "In the north there are people known as the Hashashini, otherwise known as the 'Assassins by us Franks. I hear they also speak Persian, and that their Master lives in the mountains of Persia many leagues away from here." He was looking hard at Talon as he spoke.

It was Sir Guy who intervened, "That is correct, Sire. Talon was captured as a boy and taken to the castle of the Master, where he was trained in their arts."

"So the rumor is true," said the Count with satisfaction. "You were Sir Hughes de Gilles' boy. We might be distantly related, as I am from the Saint Gilles family. And now you are a Templar knight. Indeed, this is passing strange but very interesting. Do you think you know the minds of our enemies, young man?"

"I am not fully a Templar, although I work with Sir Guy. I would not be so bold as to say I knew their minds, Sire, but I know their ways and much of how they think."

At that moment William, the Bishop of Tyre, came up, and after giving a curt bow to the Count spoke in a peremptory manner to Odo.

"Sir Odo de Saint Amand, I wish to talk to you. It has come to my attention that your knights have violated the edicts placed upon the people of the city of Acre. The Church has the right..." His voice faded as Lord Odo led him away, accompanied by Sir Guy.

There was a brief silence as the Count contemplated the Bishop's departure with a sardonic smile on his lips; then he turned back to Talon.

"I dare say the good Bishop is complaining yet again that the Order of Templars is violating the mandate of the Pope. We have more interesting things to discuss. Let us walk through the gardens, young Knight. I wish to hear what you might think of our relations with our neighbors."

They walked away from the crowd and the music to a corner of the gardens, where they were out of sight of the King and his entourage. The Count stopped pacing and turned to give Talon a speculative stare.

"How much do you know of the people who are the King's advisors, Sir Talon?" he asked abruptly.

"Very little, Sire; I do not frequent the places of high office. I do not even know the names of these Lords, other than those whom Sir Guy pointed out to me when we arrived, including yourself," he added politely.

"What did he say of me?" asked the Count with that same sardonic smile.

"He said that you were one of the few whom he would trust, Sir. That you were also one of the few lords who knew the Arabic and understood the Saracen better than even he."

"Did he now! Well, Sir Guy and I go back some time. It interests me to see that he has found a protégé such as yourself. But you should know this if you are to go south with the King: he has no good advisors, and those who would give him good advice are not permitted too close to him."

"Why is that, Sir? Are you not close to the King?" asked Talon without thinking and feeling a little naïve.

The Count glared at him then gave a short bark of laughter.

"I am condemned by events that I could not control. Lord Miles de Milly was killed by the 'Assassins, who are directed from Syria by Rashid al Din Sinan, of that I am sure; but it was I who was blamed, because I know those people.

"He offended someone in a high place, so he was murdered by those Batinis of Rashid's, and gold probably changed hands. His widow is now being chased by that scorpion, Reynald de Châtillon. She would be a fine prize for him, as he is deeply in debt and her lands are many. He is putting out rumors that it was I who had her husband killed. Indeed, Miles probably deserved to die, but I would not dirty my hands with that kind of thing.

"The other offal eater, Joscelin, has been made Seneschal of the kingdom. Others who could advise the King well are pushed aside."

"How do you know so much about the 'Assassins, Sir?"

"Because we are neighbors, and they sometimes share useful intelligence with us, as their enemy is our enemy. Nur Ed Din before he died swore to exterminate them. His son al-Malik al Salih is of the same persuasion. Besides, I have to deal with them in order to survive. That is an irony, as they murdered my father, Raymond II. There are always wheels within wheels.

"The Templars extract two thousand gold pieces each year from Rashid Ed Din as tribute. Did you know that? They are the most cunning of people, and useful allies, but not to be trusted. Why, Rashid has even convinced that naïve idiot the Bishop William that they want to convert to Christianity. Pshaw! They simply want our protection against the Seljuk Sunnis, who are their mortal enemies, so they will say anything."

Talon nodded his head. Indeed he knew of Rashid, having first encountered some of his men while he was a slave in Egypt, and then again very recently.

The Count faced Talon and said abruptly, "And are you what they think you are, Sir Talon? Or are you one of the Batinis, sent perhaps... to kill our King?"

It was said so unexpectedly that Talon gaped at him. "I... I don't know what you mean, Sire," he stammered.

"I know these people; they have infinite patience, and you would have been a perfect prize for them to train. How did you survive unless they had a purpose for you? Do you think their training was for nothing?" the Count grated. He had his hand on his sword and was tensely watching Talon as he spoke.

Talon breathed deeply, then he looked the Count straight in the eye.

"You are right, my Lord, I was trained, and trained well, but I was trained for something quite different. I was trained and schooled to kill the Master! The attempt failed because his sister prevented me. I then killed his uncle, who had tried to use me to take power from the Agha Khan. The Master's sister pleaded for my freedom and he granted it. That was many years ago, Sir."

He stared unflinchingly into the suspicious eyes of the frowning count for long seconds, until Raymond finally seemed to relax.

"This is an incredible story, and I do not know that I believe you, but perhaps I do." He turned away as though thinking, and then quickly turned back to face Talon.

"Then I have a mission, no, a request for you over and above that of the Templar Order for whom you now work."

"What is that, Sir?"

"The King is brave and determined to keep the Kingdom of Jerusalem from falling into the hands of the Saracen. He is, however, young; and although his life is going to be short because of the foul leprosy that afflicts him, he is possibly in danger from more than Saracen enemies. I do not want to have his chance of being a wise King cut short by the ambitions of those whom I despise.

"I charge you, Talon, to protect him while he is in the south and to bring him back safely. Do this and you will find me a good friend." He looked hard at Talon, who realized that there was something being left unsaid. If he should fail, for whatever reason, the count might have a friend who, if paid well, would send his 'Assassins after Talon.

He knelt in front of the Count and, holding his sword by the hilt in front of him, he said, "I need no encouragement, nor threats, Sir. I shall do as you ask and give my life for the King should it be necessary."

The count gave him a wintry smile. "Good! Rise, Sir Talon de Gilles, I am sure that you will."

He continued, but this time in Arabic. "The King has asked you to go south with him. What do you know of the ruler of Egypt?"

Once he had overcome his surprise Talon responded. "Salah Ed Din, the Sultan? I know that he was related to Nur Ed Din, Sire. His nephew, I believe. They are a powerful Kurdish family who control much of Syria and some of Mesopotamia and even the Yemen, which his brother conquered for him a year or so ago.

"I know too that he was thrust into power because his uncle Shirkuh died suddenly, poisoned they say, and Salah al Din was appointed by the Caliph Al-Adid to be the ruler of the country. They did not think he would last very long, as he was young and untried, but so far he has survived attacks from outside the country by the Crusaders and conspiracies from within. He looks as though he will be able to survive for a while longer. The Ayyubid brothers are resilient and united."

The Count nodded vigorously, "That's right, Talon. More than that, his uncle Nur Ed Din wanted the Kingdom of Egypt for himself before he died, and now his son would like it as well, which could be a useful piece of news if we could only just exploit it. Which one to make an alliance with, that is the question?

"On the other hand, if they agree to settle their differences then we are caught between two powerful enemies who can attack us simultaneously if they wish, and then Jerusalem really will be in peril," the count added, his tone pensive.

"You might be right, Sir, but I think that Salah al Din will not be willing to cede the ownership of Egypt to Damascus so quickly. Since the death of Nur Ed Din he grows in power almost by the month. It is more likely that he will try to make an attempt on the Kingdom of Jerusalem by himself. He might try for Damascus first, of course."

"Why do you say that?"

"Because he has been very successful in taming the people of Egypt who were Ismaili and of the Shia' Fatimid persuasion before he took power. Now he is imposing Sunni laws and there is little opposition. Not only that, he has led expeditions into Africa, where he has won battles. He is now viewed by his people as a wise leader and a good general. Recently Sir Guy and I met with an interesting man who gave us to know that there is discontent within Egypt because of drought and impending famine. It is very likely that the sultan will send or lead an expedition our way to take the Egyptian peoples' minds off of their woes."

Raymond's eyes widened at the news, but he held his tongue and allowed Talon to continue.

"Also, my Lord, why would he submit to a young boy, As-Salith Ismail al-Malik in Damascus, and give all that up? I am sure he is now turning his attention to our Kingdom, as witness the raids that have become more and more frequent, raids he himself has led against us. It has always been a Holy War to retake the city Al Kuds back from us. To them it is a sacred mission, a Jihad, and the man who succeeded would be great indeed. Sal Ed Din would want that glory for himself. The time is not too far off when he will make a bid for that power, Sire."

The Count regarded Talon with interest. He pulled at his beard.

"You are probably right, Talon. You seem to understand the situation in this region better than most. I like your reasoning. That is why I wish we could persuade the King not to go anywhere near Egypt at this time. My spies tell me that there are preparations being made to form a large army in Cairo. We seem to agree on our Sultan's ambitions. I think it is too late for any kind of truce. Where else other than here would he come, if he can bring a large enough army?"

"Only to Jerusalem. Can you not manage to convince the King of the danger, my Lord?"

The Count stamped his foot with frustration and scowled, "My enemies are all around and will not let me spend time alone with the King. He is so innocent that he believes his idiot friends Joscelin and that snake Reynald who tell him that Egypt is supine and no threat to us."

He sighed. "Go you with him then and protect him, Sir Talon. He likes the Templars, and fortunately for you, so does Reynald. I have to go back to Tiberius for the time being, but I shall come back to Jerusalem within two weeks. If you need me, send a message to me. Take care of him, Talon. I suspect few could do it better."

The count turned and strode away, leaving Talon staring after him and wondering.

A week later news came of a huge army that was moving through the Sinai desert.

It was almost as though fate had listened in on the conversation between the Raymond and Talon. The Egyptians were heading for the fortress of Gaza.

We are as pieces of chess engaged in victory and defeat:
our victory and defeat is from thee,
O thou whose qualities are comely!

—Rumi

Chapter 7

An Army Leaves for Gaza

Frantic preparations were underway in Jerusalem, for all the knights and barons who were part of the King's army were to depart for war.

The King's entourage left Jerusalem on a bright and sunny November day. It had taken far longer than anyone had intended to complete preparations for the journey. Despite the urgency, the king delayed the departure until he had received the blessings of Bishop William in the chapel, followed by a fanfare of trumpets. He was waved off by an apprehensive but gaudily dressed crowd of notables' families and church officials. The common people lined the streets and cheered as he rode in splendor through the city to leave by David's Gate.

Lord Odo said to Talon sardonically that it had taken that long for the small army to get organized because the King, was encumbered by two of the biggest idiots ever to hang off a King's belt: Reynald de Châtillon and Joscelin.

Lord Odo had decided to come with the king in spite of an urgent call from the north, for he considered it his duty to be with the king time of war. There were few other Templars left in the city, as even Sir Guy had been taken away with the force that went north, but before he left he gave Talon one of the Destriers from the stables. "You might need this animal," Sir Guy said with his half smile before he bade Talon God speed.

Talon missed the company of Max. He also missed Sir Guy's dry observations of life around them and hoped that he would see him when he returned.

Despite his ability to rule, the King was considered an invalid, thus Sir Reynald de Châtillon came along as the army commander, and Joscelin, because he was the King's Seneschal. Lord Odo was clearly unhappy with this situation but could say nothing other than to grumble. "Both men have sat on their arses in a Saracen prison for years! How does that make them useful generals today?"

None of his men felt that it was a safe question to answer.

The army was further encumbered with slow moving baggage trains, most of which belonged to the two most senior lords. Eventually the impatient King abandoned them and, taking his Lords and knights with him, made his way south at a brisk pace for horse and men towards Hebron, the first stop, where there was a Templar stronghold. His final destination was Gaza, but he wanted to visit the shrine of Abraham before he turned west.

He also wanted to check his defenses here in case of an incursion by Salah Ed Din, who, it was rumored, was preparing to move in this direction. No one knew quite where he was, nor when he might make his move towards the heart of the kingdom, but the young king wanted to be prepared.

Talon accompanied Odo, as a bodyguard to the king. Apart from himself and Lord Odo, there were only two other Templars in the whole army. They rode just behind the King along with the other knights who composed his private army, numbering about three hundred and seventy mounted knights and almost two thousand foot soldiers.

The days were still warm but it was nearing winter, so it was not unbearable. The land was greener than usual, having had the benefit of some rain in October that had laid a light blanket of green over the otherwise stony countryside, making for pleasant traveling. Talon, now free of the stenches of Jerusalem's streets, delighted in the dry clean scent of the air.

Talon noted that there were nowhere near the same number of farms and vineyards south of Jerusalem as there were to the north and west on the side nearest the river Jordan. Here the country was almost barren, with rocky hills softened only by the light mantle of green. The road was stony, and the army, although small, churned up a lot of dust as it moved. Herds of goats and sheep roamed the countryside in large flocks tended by ragged herders, men and boys, who regarded the army with alarm and hastened away over the hills with their flocks when they realized that it was a Christian army on the march.

Talon watched the scouts ahead of the party dourly. He was not satisfied that they were doing their job as well as they should. In his opinion they should have been much further forward than they were. He turned his attention to the men around him.

The Lords closest to the king were indeed men of high rank. Apart from Lord Odo de St Armand, Reynald de Châtillon and Joscelin, there were Baldwin of Ibelin—who shared Raymond of Tripoli's dislike for Reynald and Joselin—and Reginald of Sidon. These men were in constant attendance upon the king as they rode south. He regretted that Lord Raymond of Tripoli was not amongst them. Despite the man's caustic behavior Talon had come to respect him in the very short time he had met him.

During the ride Talon made the acquaintance of the knights who followed Baldwin, and at one time the King himself expressed a wish to talk to him by leaning back in his saddle and calling him by name.

"Talon de Gilles, Templar, I would talk to you. Come and ride near to me."

It was impossible to refuse an order of this kind, so Talon, with a glance at Lord Odo, who nodded approval, nudged his horse closer.

Baldwin knew a little of Talon's past, as Lord Odo had told him of some of it, but he was interested in knowing more.

Talon was careful not to tell the whole story, for he knew from past experience that there were consequences when people did not understand the compromises that survival demanded. However, he politely answered the King's questions. Talon knew from Sir Guy that Baldwin IV, despite the disfigurement of his disease, was an intelligent young man who was curious about his enemies and very interested in the land he governed.

"Tell me, Sir Talon, now that Nur Ed Din is dead, will Salah Ed Din make a bid for the kingdom of Syria? Can Nur Ed Din's son fend him off?"

"I would think it likely that Salah Ed Din will eventually move to take Damascus, my Liege. He is ambitious, but far and away his greatest ambition is to take back the kingdom of Jerusalem."

"How so? Are we not too strong for him, with Templars and Hospitaliers in well located castles both to the south and north of the city? How I wish that they would not bicker so!" he added as an afterthought.

Talon nodded. It was well known throughout the kingdom that the Grand Masters of the Hospitaliers and the Templars were barely on speaking terms. Sir Odo de St Armand and Gerard Jobert, the Grand Master of the Hospitaliers, had had a falling out over the last campaign against Egypt, which had ended in disaster. The Templars, having refused to go on that ill-conceived and badly executed campaign, were now blamed by the Hospitaliers for having left them in the lurch, thereby causing their defeat.

"My liege, we are strong, but their numbers are vast. We are few, and any loss is hard for us, while they have huge regions from which they can replenish their losses."

"Ah, but our few are so well trained that we are almost invincible, are we not?"

Talon temporized. "You are right, my Lord, but we should not be reckless with our resources, as their loss will surely harm us."

Sir Guy had said often enough that the Grand Masters seemed to agree with the King and would happily send a few hundred Knights crashing into a much larger army of Saracens and hope to drive all before them. Sir Guy, who understood that time was on the side of the Saracen, lamented this reckless attitude. He had told Talon that he felt sure that their enemy would learn one day how to deal with them, and then the small kingdom would be in trouble. The King seemed not to notice Talon's guardedness and they conversed on other matters. He was particularly interested in knowing more of the up and coming Salah Ed Din.

Talon told him what he knew, which was considerable, and thereby gained the company of the King until they saw in the distance the castle of Castilian Saint Abraham, or Hebron, as the Jews had named it. The crusader Godfrey de Bouillon had renamed it in honor of the patriarch Abraham.

The small army had made good progress and arrived in Hebron after one day of fairly determined riding. It was evening when they came to the gates, which were thrown open upon their arrival to allow the king a triumphal entry. The young King dismissed the objections raised by his nobles that the baggage train would not get there until the following day and insisted on being billeted in the fort without ceremony.

Talon saw that the town that clustered about the castle was small by comparison to Jerusalem, but he knew that it was famous because the bones of Abraham were supposed to be buried here in a shrine that all three of the religions respected. That made it a very holy place. Talon knew it was known as "Ibrahim al-Khalil" or Ibrahim the Friend to the Arabs.

The King went into the converted mosque, now a church, and gave thanks for his safe arrival and prayed with his men.

They stayed only one night and then headed almost due west towards the castle of Bethgibelin. As it was only half a day's ride, the king decided to linger in Saint Abraham and leave at mid day.

This had Lord Odo in a towering rage, as he was sure that Reynald de Châtillon had influenced this decision. He sought Talon out and ranted on about the stupidity of Reynald and his second Joscelin.

"For all we know the Egyptians are beyond Gaza even now, and we are dawdling here in this place! I cannot persuade the King to listen!" he raged.

They arrived just before sunset, so they had a good sighting of the huge castle still under construction. Odo told Talon that Bethgibelin was within easy riding of Gaza and was strategically placed as one of the three main castles between the border of the kingdom of Jerusalem and Egypt, thus it was valued. He was still seething with anger at the King's advisers.

Talon noticed that there was extensive construction going on as they rode through the gates. He was impressed with the tools being used; the masons even had a squirrel cage powering a crane for lifting the huge stones into place. The two slaves in the cage looked worn out. There were many slaves building the fortifications and improving upon them under the supervision of men with long whips who gave them no respite, even at this late hour.

The Hospitaliers commander in charge of the castle greeted the King warmly and whisked him away with his lords in attendance, while the troops had to find what accommodation they could for the night in the castle and the surrounding village.

Talon noted that he and his two other Templar companions were treated civilly but very coolly. But for the fact that they came with the King, Talon was sure that they would have been ejected from the castle without ceremony. As it was, they had to share a dank cell with little in the way of comfort.

They barely saw the King that night except at evening mass. Vigils was a grand affair because the King was present, so every Hospitalier knight and sergeant in the area was present, crowding the naves and aisles and even standing outside the chapel, listening while the words of the order and homage to the King were pronounced.

Because Talon and his companions were part of the King's guard they too were expected to be present. The Master of the castle led the service; Talon again received icy looks from the Hospitaliers during the ceremony, but he ignored them and focused on the words of the service.

His mind went back to the time he had been sworn in as an auxiliary member of the Templar Knighthood. Sir Guy had told Talon that he did not expect him to become a full Templar Knight, as his usefulness depended upon his being able to move among the Arab community; the restrictions of the full Order would have prevented that. Sir Guy had finally been able to have Talon accepted.

Nevertheless the ceremony had been intimidating. He recalled the chapel within the walls of the Templar stronghold hard against the ancient temple of Solomon, the solemn and menacing group of knights standing around him, his name being called by a voice behind him.

The chapter Master had asked if anyone present had any objections to Talon as a candidate, After which had followed an intense interrogation during which Sir Guy, his sponsor, had defended him.

He had been obliged to swear to the assembled knights an oath of absolute obedience, and to defend Jerusalem the holy city. This, he was informed, was part of the Rule that the Templars lived by and died by. Other aspects of the Rules were recited to him while he knelt in front of the altar.

He had recited his obligations and commitments to the Order and to God, trying not to forget the manner and presentation that was obligatory for a Knight at this level. The ceremony that followed he was forbidden to discuss with others outside the Order; this also held true for the revelations that came once he was pronounced a Knight Templar. Later he had spent the night either prostrated or on his knees, praying before the altar.

The two long candles on either side of the stone had spent themselves in the early dawn of the vigil. Not having eaten the evening before, he had been light-headed with hunger and tired from the tension of the initiation.

As the first shafts of dawn had filtered through the high windows of the chapel he had been gazing at the Virgin Mary off to the right of the main nave. It had seemed to him that she smiled, and he had wondered why. A voice in his head had seemed to say, "Enter unto our kingdom when you are ready, Talon; there is time."

He was still musing over this memory when the service in the Hospitalier Chapel came to an end and the King walked by, accompanied by the Master of the castle, his Lords, and Odo.

The night passed uneventfully with the king presiding over the high table and the assembled Hospitaliers, who pointedly excluded the Templars from any conversation. Odo sulked and fretted over time lost, while Reynald and Joscelin flattered the king and their host. The other knights were placed in two long rows below the dais. Talon went to bed wondering at how leisurely this expedition was becoming. There seemed to be no sense of urgency, although he knew that the reports they had received in Jerusalem indicated a huge army of Egyptians was on the march.

The next morning the king and his small army rode out of the castle and set off for Gaza. As the army wound its way out of the gates, Talon could not help comparing it to the mighty army of the Greeks just before the ill fated battle of Myriokephalon. This army was but a fraction of that one, and no where nearly as well equipped or trained. The horsemen were a colorful hodgepodge of shields, emblems and banners, each trying to out shine the others. Talon could not find fault with their horses; the Destriers they rode were magnificent, but the foot soldiers seemed more a rabble than a serious group of fighting men. There were only a few long bow archers, and there were clearly not enough pikemen to protect them should they encounter an enemy force.

As the day advanced Talon, out of habit, eyed the scouts ahead to see if they were doing their work properly and did not like what he saw. They had become lazy and bunched into a group that moved ever more carelessly, obviously thinking there was no threat. He spurred forward and came alongside Odo.

"My Lord, I must request permission to talk to the scouts and to ride ahead with them for a while. I fear they are lax and need some instruction."

Odo, who was preoccupied and talking to Reynald, only nodded assent and went back to talking with his companion. They were almost quarreling about the role the Count of Tripoli was playing with the king.

Talon waved his fellow Templars along with him. Neither Sir Thierry of Flanders nor Sir Vorhert de Naples wanted to be left with the men who surrounded the King. Although the Templars were a highly respected Order, few of the common knights liked them because of their privileged position in the country. As a result, they had been riding in virtual silence for the duration of the march so far, ignored and excluded by the others. They were visibly relieved as they cantered forward, and Talon explained that he had been watching the scouts and found them inattentive. Both the other knights were seasoned men and Thierry grunted sourly.

"I've been watching them too, Talon. They are lazy and incompetent and most certainly not paying attention."

"Perhaps we will make better front scouts for the King," said the burly Vorhert in his thick accent.

"That should not be hard to do," agreed Talon.

They rode at a steady canter until they came up with the men who composed the light cavalry the King used as his scouts. The knights on their huge Destriers were regarded warily by the leader, who reined up as they came towards them.

Before he addressed the man Talon stared forward. There was nothing immediately alarming, but he noticed that there were low hills in front which would give way to flatter land at a lower altitude.

"You do not appear to be paying much attention," he told the man, who grimaced.

"There is no danger from the Saracen, Sir. They have not been here for long months."

"Then you neither know nor respect our enemy," snapped Talon. There was a growl of agreement from Thierry and Vorhert behind him.

The three knights must have presented an imposing front to the scouts, for they did not answer back, and their leader issued a curt order for them to spread out and get more forward of the column that was not far behind.

Talon made a point of riding with the leader, who was mounted on a spirited horse that looked like an Arab of mixed breed, possibly bought from a Bedouin, or perhaps the spoils of war.

They said little as they trotted the next few miles and crossed a low dip between hills. The road, if it could be called that, wound up the slope of a medium sized hill in front of them. They cantered up the slope and breasted the crest together. The other scouts were off to the right and left, but they were not yet on the crest.

Suddenly Talon reined in very sharply, as did the scout leader beside him. The two other knights who had been right behind them pulled their horses up with a quiet curse.

"What by the Lord are you doing, Talon?" rasped Thierry.

Talon was backing his horse sharply, waving them back until all four of them were below the crest line again.

"There is something ahead of us, stop talking!"

The men muttered but fell silent as they watched, while Talon on his larger horse eased his mount forward till he could see just see over the crest but would be out of sight himself. He had seen a plume of dust ahead, and his instincts had made him react the way he had. He shaded his eyes to see more clearly. Despite the heat he felt a chill.

He let out an exclamation of surprise.

"Was there to be a reception for the King so soon?" he asked his companions.

The scout eased forward to see for himself, followed cautiously by the knights, and they too let out exclamations of surprise.

"I do not think so, Sir, and where did the camels come from?"

Talon shaded his eyes again. What he saw was more than just a plume: it was a veritable wall of dust that rose into the still, sunlit air. He realized that it was being made by a huge army of men. He continued to watch but said quietly, "This is what I most feared. Salah Ed Din is on the march, and he has come a long way north."

They all looked at one another, appalled.

"You are right, Talon. That is not a friendly army," Thierry said in a very low voice.

"Why did no one report this to anyone?" Vorhert demanded irritably. "We must tell the King immediately!"

"You are right, Vorhert. Please go back and warn the King. We cannot hope to get to Gaza now. The King must move as quickly as possible to Ascalon to seek safety. I want to see a little more of this army and try to estimate the numbers, and then I will join you," Talon said.

Without a word Vorhert wheeled his huge horse and galloped back toward the king half a mile to their rear.

"I see many thousands of cavalry and footmen," Thierry said.

"I see an army of tens of thousands of men," Talon said curtly by way of reply, "Look at the baggage train and the camels they have with them; there have to be many thousands of them alone!"

"But why are they here?"

"That is easy. It is Salah Ed Din, of that I am sure, and he is on the march for Jerusalem."

There was a sharp intake of breath from both men.

"We cannot stop him with what we have," said Talon. "We must take care to protect the King. Ascalon is our only choice!"

They turned their horses and galloped back down the slope towards the milling army and the king.

Lord Odo rode out to meet him.

"What is this I hear of an army of Saracen in front of us, Talon?" There was concern in his voice.

"Indeed there is, Sir, tens of thousands of men. The King must seek shelter in Ascalon, or we will be trapped in these hills."

"Ascalon is north of here. Can we not get to Gaza?"

"His entire army is to our front, Sir, and if we continue it is sure that his scouts will see us and then we will be quickly engaged."

The young king had ridden up and stared at him in disbelief; Talon's heart quailed. For a moment he thought the man would recklessly want to charge the army in front of them and call upon God to ensure victory. Indeed, one of his Lords, Reynald, even suggested this, with a sneer at Talon to imply that he considered retreat cowardly. Lord Odo however was quick to interrupt.

"Only a fool would fight in this type of country, my Lord!" he said with dripping contempt in his voice. "We need the flat space of the plains of Ascalon to help us."

Baldwin was not a fool, and his trust in the Templars was implicit.

"We shall ride hard for the city of Ascalon and try to raise more men to make up an army to deal with this," he said with finality.

Talon gave a sigh of relief and glanced at Odo, who winked.

They began to move briskly north along some tracks that would take them to the main road to Ascalon. They were just about to clear the saddle between two hills when there was a distant shout behind them.

Boiling over the rise that Talon had vacated not long ago came a large cavalry force. Thousands of them streamed over the crest of the hill and began to gallop after the retreating Christians.

Now it became clear to all how serious their situation had suddenly become. They had almost run head-on into a huge army of Saracen; had they not taken the northern route they would have been directly attacked and quickly surrounded by the cavalry now giving chase.

The Christians were a good mile ahead, but now they would have to keep up a fierce gallop to maintain that lead, and they had about eight miles to ride. Fortunately were north of the river Sorek, but they still had to splash furiously across one of its tributaries. The infantry were running hard, knowing that they had to keep up with the cavalry or be surrounded and killed. Many of them seized a stirrup leather and ran alongside a rider; it was the only way they could survive the eight mile dash to safety.

The scouts raced ahead to ensure that there were no further surprises. They were paying a great deal more attention than they had formerly. The four Templars grouped themselves around the King, as he was now their prime responsibility. There was another group of seasoned knights who formed a defensive rear guard, trying to protect the infantry and be ready to fight off the enemy if the king's main group slowed.

Lord Odo called to Thierry to stay with him and the King, and ordered Talon and Vorhert to ride just ahead to ensure that they were not surprised again from that direction. It was clear that his faith in them exceeded his faith in the king's scouts.

They rode stirrup to stirrup at a flat-out gallop over a rise in the road and saw the city of Ascalon ahead of them. The enemy, however, were gaining ground with their lighter, fleeter horses, and were close enough to fire arrows into the backs of the fleeing Christians. Some of the infantry dropped, wounded or dead, to be left where they lay, at the mercy of the oncoming enemy.

Looking over his shoulder, Talon made out that they were being pursued by about a thousand lightly mounted men who were able to outrun the larger horses of the king's men, but they were also much more lightly armed. He managed to get the attention of Lord Odo and pointed to their rear.

"They are only lightly mounted and armed, Sir," he called. "We can join the rear guard and hold them off while the King makes his escape."

It was becoming clear to all that the King and his army would not make the safety of Ascalon unless there was a determined effort to delay the enemy.

Odo waved to the Lords alongside the King and shouted, "Take him to the city and defend him with your lives!"

Lord Joscelin and several of the other lords nodded and, accompanied by the king's guard, raced off.

Lord Reynald reined in and stayed.

"I shall not run from the enemy whom I despise, Odo. I am with you!" he rasped.

Odo may have not liked Reynald, but no one could fault his courage. He nodded and turned to Talon.

"Form a line, Sir Talon. Vorhert, Thierry, go with him, and I shall take up the center with Lord Reynald to add beef to the men there."

Odo reined in his horse and wheeled it to face the group of men following. The leader of the rear guard was a grizzled knight of indeterminate age with a long beard who pulled up when Talon and his two companions galloped back to them.

"Our horses will soon be winded, and the enemy has faster horses, Sir," Talon exclaimed as they hauled their horses alongside. "Lord Odo says we must charge them at least once to delay them, or the King cannot make the gates of Ascalon!"

The man nodded, pointed to the Templars and shouted, "We are with them! Face the enemy!"

The band of men, numbering only a few hundred, wheeled their horses towards the oncoming Saracens.

God of our Craft, enable me
A faithful, worthy Knight to be,
And bring me home at last to Thee
A Templar.

—David Barker and John Edwards, *Poems*

Chapter 8

In Defense of the King

Talon and his Templar companions called out directions to the men to line up and ride knee to knee. Both his companions knew the drill well, but the other knights were unused to the discipline, and the line was very crooked. But Lord Odo with Lord Reynald were in the middle and managed to keep the line from falling apart before they had begun.

They sat in silence as the shouting and screaming men from the Egyptian army reined in their excited horses in the face of the line, now not in retreat but silently waiting for them. The stillness and silence of the knights must have seemed ominous, for the enemy hesitated.

The men on their light horses milled about and sent a few arrows in the direction of the knights, and two of them who seemed to be leaders were shouting at each other and gesticulating furiously at the Franks, but no one seemed in a hurry to ride at them. Sensing their uncertainty Odo raised his lance and shouted.

"Men of the King's army, advance at the trot!" His command was repeated by Talon and his companions further down the line.

Talon prayed that the formation would not immediately disintegrate; to his surprise most of the men tried to keep some semblance of a line, although it wavered in such manner that it would have caused the training sergeants from the Templar Order to have fits. In spite of the tension and coil of fear in his stomach he found himself smiling at that thought. It helped to steady him for the encounter, and the close proximity of his companions calmed him. This was just a drill, he told himself.

Thierry on his left side saw him smiling and grunted. “You like a fight, it would seem, Talon. What in Saint Denis’s good name is there to smile about?”

Talon eased the strap of his shield on his shoulder and replied, “Better to smile at danger than to frown at it, my friend. It confuses the enemy. Stay close.”

There was a short bark of laughter from Vorhert. “I shall try to smile. My teeth rattle so hard that Death himself might be confused.”

Talon and Thierry snorted with amusement despite their own fear, and Talon could have sworn that the couple of knights nearest them in the line giggled. Talon suddenly felt better. He had two of the best on either side of him, and they would do the enemy much damage this day.

“May God be on our side this day, my friends! We shall be doing our duty for God and the King!” he called out.

The enemy was milling about in a dense cluster, only a hundred yards off. Odo raised his lance above his head and shouted as hard as he could, “Deus lo Volt! For God and the King!”

He set his horse into a gallop, and on either side of him the line of Knights leapt forward. Those with spears and lances lowered them, while others raised their swords, the whole line charging flat out at the enemy, screaming their defiance. Talon could hear only the drumming of the horses’ hooves and the mad cries from the knights all around. He too was yelling as they charged across the plain.

The men of Egypt saw the approaching charge and panic gripped them. Riders pointed and yelled warnings, but very few were prepared for the shock as the line of horsemen smashed into them.

Talon knew the Frankish line was not a cohesive solid block of knights and horses, as an attack of trained Templars would have been, but the effect was still devastating. The lightly mounted horsemen went down under the hooves of the huge horses that hammered into them. Talon pierced a man through the side as he tried to turn his horse and flee.

The man fell without a sound, pulling Talon's lance out of his hands. Talon's mount ran straight into the side of the fine horse the man had been riding, throwing it too to the ground. His own horse stumbled, but he managed to haul its head up and they surged forward again.

He found that he still had Thierry and Vorhert almost knee to knee with him, shrieking their war cries and hacking down at any of the enemy they ran into. Vorhert rode alongside a fleeing horseman and sliced the man's arm off as he rode. The wounded man's shriek of agony was drowned out by the shouting and yelling of the maddened knights.

But most of the other knights were dispersed all over the place, hacking and stabbing at the enemy who now tried to fight back. While many of them were trying to break and run, others were beginning to form up into groups that would become a real danger to a solitary knight. Talon realized that the Franks had broken up the pursuit and it was now time to leave, as sooner or later the enemy would regroup and then they would be surrounded, or worse, outflanked.

He raised his sword and screamed at the Franks to pull back. Vorhert and Thierry broke away from his side and began to round up the bloody, yelling knights and point them towards the city. He saw Odo and Reynald doing the same in the distance.

Most turned and followed, but some who had their blood lust roused refused to hear them and continued to try and slaughter as many of the enemy as fell within reach of their bloody weapons. The sound of screaming men and shrieks of wounded horses filled the air all around. The nauseating stink of blood, fear and death permeated the air, making Talon want to gag.

With a regretful glance at these men Talon turned and drove his spurs into the sides of his horse to ride hard back along the road with most of the rear guard. He knew it would not take long for the enemy to get over their surprise and reform. Then whoever remained would be surrounded and killed. They had chosen their death.

The group of exultant Franks, depleted by casualties and absentees, now cantered their tired and winded horses back towards the distant gates of the city. They all knew that their lives depended upon conserving the remaining energy of their mounts; at the same time they still had a very angry force behind them that could still catch them if they were too slow.

Talon glanced behind. Just as he had thought, he could see in the distance that the enemy had indeed recovered from their surprise and were now dealing with those Franks who had foolishly stayed to fight. In the distance he saw a knight pulled off his horse to disappear under the flashing blades of the vengeful Egyptians.

The charge had gained the time the King needed, however; when Talon stared forward over the plain it was clear that the King had made it to the fortified city safely. Now they themselves had less than a mile to go. He shouted to the old knight who had led the group that they should stay together or they would lose more men.

The man nodded. His sword arm was red with blood up to his shoulder and he had a gash in his thigh, but he was still well able to ride. Lord Odo took command and shouted orders. Eventually he was able to pull the laggards together so that the whole group of horsemen was able to trot their weary mounts through the open gates and into the safety of the city. They were cheered by the crowds on the walls who had witnessed the fight, and now the people on the streets were cheering them too.

When Odo came up and clapped him on the back and spoke, Talon could barely hear him, but it sounded like something about the Templars doing their duty for God and the King. Glancing back one final time through the gates as they were closing, Talon saw the enemy horsemen pulling up just out of long bow range, waving their weapons in the air and shouting taunts and challenges at them. He could hear and understand some of them, which made him smile, as they were the elaborate insults that the Arabs were fond of shouting.

There was a shout, then a loud crash of hammering wood as a catapult loosed off a rock that soared over the walls towards the enemy. Talon did not see the effect, but by the cheers on the walls he guessed that it might have done some damage.

Talon saw that ahead was a group of dismounted men who waited for the rear guard. It was the King with a grin of welcome on his distorted face.

"By God, but you did well there, Lord Odo, Lord Reynald and Sir Pandaff. We saw it all. That showed them who we are!"

Sir Pandaff, the old knight who had commanded the rear guard, waved his hand at Talon and his two companions. "God chose to favor us today, my Liege. He gave us some Templars who made all the difference. We would not have done as good a work if we had not been blessed with these soldiers of God to help us."

The king nodded. "Well said, Sir Pandaff. My Templars have the protection of God and we are grateful. You have earned honors for the Order of the Templars, Sirs, and my gratitude. You shall dine this evening at my table."

He was led away by his Lords and a church man of rank. Reynald and Odo were in attendance.

The old knight turned to Talon before they parted to stable their horses. "I am grateful for your help there, Sir. Who are you, that I might remember your name?"

"I am Talon de Gilles, Sir Pandaff. My part was of no great consequence, but it was a good fight!" he grinned.

Pandaff laughed out loud. "By God, yes, it was a good fight, Sir Talon. I commend you and your two companions for your help again."

Thiery and Vorhert were exultant; the fight had clearly wound them both up to the point of recklessness.

"We should have stayed and thrashed them!" Vorhert said boastfully.

"Did you not see what they do to people who are on their own?" Talon almost snarled. "They swarm people and kill them that way! Our only hope will be to stay close together. This was just a skirmish, the real fight is yet to come." He had not meant to sound so harsh, but the battle at Myriokephalon was still fresh in his mind, where the Greek army he had been with had been all but annihilated by the Turks.

His two companions were chastened, and Vorhert spoke. "I will listen to you, Talon. Thierry tells me that you are a knight of much experience. He says that you were in the great battle between the Greeks and the Turk."

Thierry grinned. "Your sergeant Max Bauersdorf has told us of you, Sir Talon. I was in Acre not so long ago. He told us of your deeds in Byzantium."

Talon managed a wry smile. "He is a great warrior himself, my friends, and I wish he were here at our side. He taught me much. Now we should rest, as this is only the beginning."

Talon and his companions managed to beg some stabling for their horses and then sought out some place to rest. The afternoon was well advanced, but they still had time before the evening meal. Talon was tired: the excitement of the chase and the fight had drained him; his limbs were weary and he needed to sleep.

It was as though he had barely put his head to the folded blanket when he was being shaken by a rough hand on his shoulder. He was awake on the instant, and sat up abruptly, making the man who had awakened him take a hasty step back.

"Your honor, Sir Talon. Lord Odo and the King wish to see you. It is very important," said the soldier nervously, standing back from him and eyeing the knife in Talon's hand.

"Where?" Talon asked blearily.

"On the walls, near the gates, Sir."

Talon scrambled to his feet and, taking his sword in its scabbard with his belt over his shoulder, walked swiftly after the messenger. He cast a reluctant glance back at his snoring companions, wishing he were still asleep beside them. His eyes felt gritty with fatigue.

As he climbed the stone steps to the parapet he could see the sun low on the horizon to the west casting a red glow into the lightly clouded sky, its light glittering on the calm sea to the west. He had forgotten in the rush to reach the city that Ascalon was on the coast.

The east was now in shadow but he could still clearly see that the small plain in front of Ascalon was heavily occupied by the Egyptians. Standing on the platform on top of the walls near the gates was a small group of men. They were having a loud argument and there was much gesticulating. He walked over to them, noticing that Lord Odo and the King were there, as were Lord Joscelin and Lord Reynald. Reynald was holding forth, in fact he was almost shouting.

"If we had followed through with the charge today we would have defeated Saladin and his grubby Egyptians totally. Now I say again, we should sortie out and chase them back to Cairo! It would not be hard, and we don't need the Templars or the Hospitaliers to show us how!"

Lord Odo gave out a rude sound and snorted. "We managed to keep them at bay, my Liege. Merely that! Even then the men of your army paid little heed to the call for retreat, and they paid for it with their lives."

"We only retreated because you and your men ran out of steam, Lord Odo!" remarked Joscelin snidely.

Lord Odo whirled upon Joscelin. "My Lord!" He hissed venomously, "While you have been taking your ease in a Saracen dungeon, the Templars have been keeping the Arab armies occupied. Do not presume to suggest that we Templars are not up to the task. It requires the discipline of the Templars, and indeed the Hospitaliers, to defeat an Arab army. They and we alone have the discipline to do this!"

The King tried to mediate.

"My Lords, there is no question as to our making a sally either tonight or tomorrow without considering the chances of success well before hand. My Lord Odo," he said in a conciliatory tone, "how could we send word to reinforcements to come to our aid?"

At this moment Talon, who had been standing respectfully back from the group, stepped forward and touched Lord Odo on the elbow. Odo turned to him and said, "My Liege, here is the knight Sir Talon, who knows the enemy better than most. Perhaps we should hear what he has to say."

Baldwin turned from his conversation with the men around him.

Talon knelt before the king and spoke respectfully.

"What do you ask of me, my Liege?"

"Ah, Sir Talon, rise. Lord Odo mentioned that it was your quick thinking that helped save the day. Once again I must thank you. If we had not listened to you we might this moment be prisoners of the Sultan of Egypt, God help us." He cast a glance at Reynald, who chose not to respond.

"It was nothing more than my duty to you, my Liege," responded Talon simply.

"What do you make of that?" the young king flung out his arm to take in the eastern plain. "Look out there and tell me what we are seeing from your point of view, Sir," he commanded.

Talon stood up and walked the single pace and leaned his hands on the parapet.

The enemy cavalry had set up camp and the glow of many fires lit up the plain. There was the murmuring sound of a large body of men and horses settling down for the night.

"I see many more of the enemy than before, my Liege. But I know that this is definitely not the whole army."

"Why do you say that?" asked Joscelin with surprise, doubt obvious in his voice.

"Because what I saw earlier in the day before we retreated to this city was a very large army, many thousands, no, tens of thousands of men, horses and camels. They are not all here in this place this evening."

He turned to the King.

"Sire, if I am not mistaken, the enemy has only placed this body of men there to keep us bottled up in Ascalon while the main force continues on to Jerusalem."

His words were greeting with total silence; the young king blanched, then stared hard at Talon. Finally he asked, "Are you sure, Sir Talon?"

The men beside him looked shocked and suddenly very concerned. Talon could scarcely believe that they had not thought of this.

"As God is my witness, my Liege. This is just a diversion to keep us here. I do not even think they know it is yourself that they have besieged in this castle. If they did, they would make an all out assault on this city with more of the army. Of a certainty the main army is on its way to Jerusalem. This is Salah Ed Din's chance to make his name in the Islamic world."

Even Lord Odo looked worried now, and tugged at his long straggly beard.

Baldwin was now limping up and down in an agitated manner, and the men who had been with him were conversing in worried tones. For a moment Talon was left alone to contemplate the forces arrayed against them.

It was clear that the enemy considered it sufficient to simply camp on the plain to stop anyone from leaving, for they had not surrounded the city. On the seaward side there was a way out. He was sure, however, that there would be the odd patrol that covered the sides, while the sea kept the rear secure.

He turned to Odo and unceremoniously waved him over to the parapet so that the two stood apart from the others and could talk privately.

"If you are right, Talon, this is a catastrophe," Odo said quietly.

"Sir, we know that there are Templars in Gaza, enough to put up a good fight. With the king's men here we could muster a small army to harass Salah Ed Din, if we could bring those men into the fight."

Odo looked out at the camp fires.

"Talon, Gaza might as well be in France for all the good it can do us while we are trapped here in Ascalon." The frustration was clear in his voice.

"If someone could reach them and tell them what has happened, then we might be able to bring them here, Sir. It is only ten miles."

Odo turned his head toward Talon, his features tense and gaunt in the dusk.

"What are you suggesting, Talon? Who do we have that could do this? All the king's knights are Franks and look the part, by God. Neither could I trust this task to one of the serfs we have, let alone to one of those useless scouts!"

"I could go," said Talon quietly. He held up his hand to stop Odo from exclaiming.

"Sir, please do not raise your voice. Knowledge of what we are talking about could be dangerous for me, even here. Yes I could go. I speak the Arabic, with an Egyptian accent to boot. In the night all men are dark, and I would use wood black to hide my lighter skin and color my beard."

They had not heard the king come up behind them, but they turned quickly when he spoke.

"Sir Talon, I have heard that you knew their ways better than most men, but this is too dangerous!" he protested with a catch in his voice.

Talon shook his head and said in a low voice, "Sire, it must be done or we stand to lose the kingdom by doing nothing!"

The three men, the young King and his Templar knights, faced the plain almost shoulder to shoulder while they discussed the plan in low tones. Finally the young king placed his hand over Talon's resting on the parapet. Talon did not flinch at the touch of a leper. In his agitated state the king was totally unconscious of the gesture.

"Go you then with God's protection and my blessing, Sir Talon," he said softly. "I pray that you will survive to bring us the Templars. You are a very brave man. May God go with you."

"Go with God. I shall pray for your soul in the chapel tonight, Sir Talon," said Odo quietly and placed his hand on Talon's shoulder, gripping him hard.

Talon nodded and without a backward glance he walked away. He went down to his two companions, and there they held a whispered conversation that was at times agitated, as his new friends listened the plan incredulously and then protested its insanity vehemently.

"Max said that you were a brave man, Talon but he did not add that you are also mad," Thierry half-growled at him. Finally they calmed down, as Talon explained how he hoped to accomplish the task.

And you have earned an honored name,
And living one, we trow—
No laurel bathed in human gore
Decks your Masonic brow.

—David Barker

Chapter 9

Ascalon to Gaza

Late that night a postern gate opened on the seaward side of the city to the south of the port walls of Ascalon. In the darkness Talon led a fine Arab horse out onto the sandy banks overlooking the water. The two stood absolutely motionless for long minutes in the dark shadow of the walls, invisible to any casual observer from the beach. They were both listening for any sound that might indicate danger. The horse had belonged to the lead scout for the King; he had willingly parted with her, saying only that Talon should bring her back if he could.

There was a whispered "God speed" from inside the door and it closed with a creak and a soft thud. He heard the iron bolts scraping into place on the other side of the wall. Even though there were men on the battlements above him watching for any movement on the beach or nearby, he felt suddenly very alone.

Despite the darkness Talon could see enough to make his way slowly along the path that led down to the beach. He listened with keen ears for any sound that might differ from the normal surge and splash of the small wavelets as they washed up the sandy beach, but heard nothing other than the cry of a distant seagull.

He was glad that there was no moon tonight. Fortunately the sky was partly overcast, a portent of change in the weather. Looking up he could see the silhouettes of men who were peering down at him or staring off into the distance, straining their eyes to see if there was any danger threatening.

He tugged gently at the reins of the mare and she followed him willingly enough along the path, her hooves making almost no sound in the sand. Talon was now dressed in the manner of a light cavalry warrior from some indeterminate tribe belonging to the Egyptian army: a chain mail shirt with a loose flowing overshirt of light cotton and an old dented breast plate that someone had found. The pantaloons he wore were tucked into calf length boots, while a round shield hung off his left shoulder over his back. On his head and around the lower part of his face he had wound a turban. As a precaution he had also blackened his face and beard, and now in the dark would not be recognizable as a Frank by any casual observer. His bow was in an improvised sheath and a quiver full of arrows hung off his belt on his right side within easy reach. The sword was his own of fine, highly tempered steel.

Reaching the beach he stopped and mounted the horse, then began to walk the animal forward towards the south and Gaza. He was tense and very alert, every instinct wide awake, watching the eastern sand banks for any sign of danger.

He knew that he could not ride along the beach all the way as it would be slow progress, so he tried to think where he could mount the bank and make his way onto the road, where he could move far more rapidly.

There were no alarms raised as he completed the first half mile of his journey, but then he was forced to turn the mare inland because there was a large jumble of rocks that prevented further progress along the beach. He knew that half a mile might not be enough distance to avoid the encampment, but there was no choice now. His heart thumping, he turned the mare up the bank.

The horse scampered up the rise onto the tufted grass of the banks in a flurry of sand. The ground was firmer here; he patted the mare and quietly walked her along the top of the bank, moving slowly ever more inland. As he did so the sound of the sea receded, so he could hear better to his front.

His luck held until he had to cross a small stream of clear water flowing towards the sea. There came a sharp challenge in Arabic. "Halt, who travels at this time of night?"

It was a sentry who stood on the opposite bank about ten feet away from Talon, peering across at him in the darkness.

"Salaam Aliekum, It is only I, by God, Najm al Malik, messenger for the General."

"Aliekum Salaam, but I wish to see more of you before I can allow you to pass," came the nervous response.

"Do not stop me, as I am on urgent business and he will surely hear if I am delayed by a recruit! Allah is your witness that you have done your duty. Now allow me to pass and may God protect you this night," said Talon.

The sentry could see that the man in front of him was well mounted, and he spoke with authority, so he said respectfully, "Peace be with you. You may pass, Najm al Malik. May Allah in his infinite mercy protect you on your mission."

Talon nudged the mare across the stream and raised his hand in salute to the sentry as he went by. He breathed a sigh of relief; the first test had been passed.

Now he could sense that there were many men and horses nearby to his left. Soon he saw camp fires smoldering red in the dark, the men having gone to their rest long ago. He could smell the horses and hoped that the mare he was riding would not neigh and raise the alarm. But apart from a low whicker as they came particularly close to some standing horses she remained silent.

He was challenged once again, but this time it seemed that the sentry could clearly see that the rider was one of the Egyptian army because he called, "Salaam Aliekum. Go with God!"

Talon replied, "Salaam. May Allah protect you," and rode on.

Still heading south by southeast in order to strike the coastal road, he put the mare into a trot that covered the miles. Although the temptation to go swiftly was enormous now that he had the better part of the enemy encampment behind him, Talon knew that it would be a mistake to canter or gallop in the night, as it would only take an injury to the mare's legs and he would be finished.

He had made almost two miles without any further challenges and had gained the road south when his luck ran out. He was trotting the mare at a brisk pace along the road when out of the darkness loomed two men on horseback going the other way.

There was a shout of warning and then the three of them came together abruptly in a tangle. Talon quickly extricated himself in the hope that he could continue, but one of the riders seized his reins.

"Who goes south so early in the morning before sunrise?" the man queried in a gruff voice tinged with suspicion.

"Salaam Aliekum, It is I, Najm al Malik, on a mission to the men who are besieging the Infidels in Gaza. May God damn and destroy them all!"

The men paused and then the first said, "Aliekum Salaam, friend, but did you not know that the men have been pulled back and have gone to join those in front of Ascalon?"

"Why have they been pulled back?" asked Talon, sounding alarmed.

"Why sit in front of a skinny chicken that can wait when the real booty lies in Ascalon, or more probably Jerusalem," said the first again.

"There are not enough men in Gaza to worry the Sultan, so we were ordered to leave them be. They can be dealt with when we come back this way after capturing Jerusalem," said the second with a coarse laugh.

But the first man was still seemed unsatisfied with the answer Talon had given.

"What did you say your name was again?" he asked, suspicion in his voice.

"My name is Najm al Malik, as I just told you," said Talon as calmly as he could, although his pulse was pounding.

"Who sent you? How is it that they did not know the army from Gaza arrived at Ascalon many hours ago?" The first man still held the reins of Talon's mare, but now he edged his horse a little closer as though to get a better look at Talon. Talon said nothing but his blood was racing. His mind was working furiously as to how he would get out of this situation when it was decided for him.

The other man hauled his horse back on its haunches and started in on Talon's other side. He knew that if they came from both sides he could not deal effectively with them. He had to act very quickly, using the advantage of surprise. Without a word he drew his knife and in one lightning fast move buried it in the first man's throat. The man gave a choking gurgle, released the reins of Talon's mare and clutched at his throat as it spurted blood in a dark rush down his chest, before he started to fall off his horse.

Talon drove his spurs into the flanks of the mare and drew his sword in one swift motion. She jumped forward in surprise and rammed the other man's horse in the shoulder, taking it off balance. Talon stood in the stirrups and leaned well forward, bringing the blade down as hard as he could on the startled man's neck. The edge cut deep and his victim fell with barely a sound off his terrified horse. Talon tried desperately to grab the reins of the horse but it danced back out of reach and then galloped off north, following the other horse that had gone the same way.

He looked around quickly to see if there were others nearby, but other than the drumming of the hooves of the fleeing horses there was no sound. Apart from the blood pounding in his ears the night was quiet. He knew that the alarm would soon be sounded in the camp, and he estimated that he still had at least eight more miles to go. The first streaks of dawn were coloring the eastern hills, which made matters worse.

He cleaned and sheathed his sword and put spurs to the mare. Holding her at a steady gallop he pushed her on down the road. It was more clearly defined now and he could avoid the larger holes and rocks on the way. She was in any case an Arab mount, and as such nimble and very sure footed. He realized that despite his apprehension he was enjoying the rhythm of her gallop and rode comfortably deep in the well made wood and leather saddle. The dawn light from the east grew with each stride until the sun was just visible on the edge of the horizon.

They had covered the ground at a rapid pace and were climbing the slope of a low rise, part of the undulating country along he coastline, when he looked back; to the north and somewhat to the east he noticed a plume of dust. He stopped the mare to get a better look and realized with a sinking heart that the chase was on. The riderless horses must have galloped into the camp and there men had found blood on them and perhaps recognized them as belonging to known comrades. Now they were coming after him, having no doubt discovered the bodies of their comrades on the road.

He turned the mare and put spurs to her. She scuttled up the slope and at the top he paused to look back again. In the distance he could see a small group of mounted men riding furiously along the track he had just come.

Again he turned his mare and now he charged down the other side of the rise. The road was dusty and rocky but the nimble-footed mare seemed to relish the running and went willingly. At the bottom of the hill they splashed across a small stream and then galloped up the next rise.

She was laboring a little now, and he knew with a sinking heart that they could not keep up this pace for the remaining distance, whereas the pursuing Egyptians could afford to run their horses into the ground if need be, just so that some caught up with him.

The mare was making good progress up the next slope, but the pace and the incline were beginning to take their toll. Talon sensed that they were in trouble. The enemy horsemen were almost within bow shot now and he could clearly hear their screamed insults and battle cries. They knew he was theirs. He took out his bow and knocked an arrow, then turned in the saddle and loosed it. It arced high into the air and then plunged into the ground just in front of the riders. They did not even pause. An icy fist of fear threatened to take hold but he was determined to go down fighting, so he waited for an opportunity to present itself. He loosed another arrow and had the satisfaction of hearing a choking scream as one of the riders was hit; he did not even wait to see the man fall but returned his attention to the road ahead. At least putting the curve of the hill's crest between him and his pursuers would buy him a little time.

As he cleared the top of the slope he saw something ahead that made him blink. The sun in the east was glinting off something shiny. Then he saw that there were armed men ahead. He felt as though he had lead in his stomach. He had no escape now! Then he noticed that there was a difference. A huge difference! These men were Franks.

Now he could clearly see their tunics and the huge horses they were riding. They were Templars on a patrol. Looking back Talon realized that he had little time to act, and there was a very real danger he would be mistaken for a Turk and slain by the very men he was laboring to reach. He drove his spurs into the bloody sides of the laboring mare and screamed at the men before him.

"I am a Templar from the King! Au Secour! Deus Lo Volt! Deus Lo Volt! Au Secour!"

The men ahead reined in briefly, then with a shout they lowered their lances and started their Destriers into a ponderous gallop towards him. It was a terrifying sight because he could not be sure if they had heard him or were about to spit him on their lances before engaging his pursuers.

It was now a race whether the knights would reach him or the men behind him, as both groups spurred their horse towards each other. But suddenly the mare stumbled and fell forward onto her knees. Talon was tossed over her head to land in a ball on the side of the road. He tucked his head in and rolled on his shoulder, coming to his feet in one motion. He cast about for his bow, but it was well out of reach on the saddle of the mare, so he drew his sword to face back the way he had come. He was determined to go down fighting.

Just as he did so the ground shook and the thunder of hooves rushed towards him from behind. He glanced over his shoulder just in time to see the band of Templar knights charge past and up the rise. They crashed into the lightly mounted enemy, who had been expecting to overtake a single fleeing rider, not encounter a full charge of Templars. It was a slaughter. The knights rode over man and beast as though they were straw. The Egyptians who had pursued Talon went down in a tangle of spitted or crushed men and broken horses. The shrieks of wounded and dying horses and men filled the air. Blood spurted as the knights cut and slashed at the remainder as they went by.

There were very few left, and those were so stunned that they were annihilated by the knights when they came round again and took them from behind. There were neither men nor horses left standing, and the Templars did not seem inclined to take prisoners. Within a few short minutes Talon's pursuers were no more. Men and horses lay dead or dying almost at his feet. No one escaped to flee and pass the word.

Talon, watching mesmerized, was surprised by one of the knights who rode right up to him and pointed his bloody lance at him. He had a sense of déjà vu from a time long past when the same thing had happened. He hurriedly explained who he was.

"I am Sir Talon de Gilles, Templar, and I come from the King!" he shouted up at the knight.

"You don't have to shout! I can hear perfectly well," said the knight irritably. "What was this all about? Why were the Saracens chasing you? And why do you look suspiciously like one yourself?"

"I come from Ascalon. The King is shut up there by the Egyptian army. I was sent to deliver the message to the knights at Gaza, in disguise to get by the Egyptian camp. I speak their tongue, but I was discovered and they came after me. The King needs all the Templars we can muster. The Egyptian army is making a path straight for Jerusalem!"

The knight looked startled. "Eh! What's that you say? Egyptian army heading for Jerusalem? The King is in Ascalon?"

Talon nodded, breathing heavily. He glanced over at the mare; she had come to her feet and was standing with the reins loose. Her head was down and her breath was labored, but otherwise she seemed recovered enough to bear a rider.

By this time the other knights were gathering around and Talon had to repeat himself several times to the incredulous men. These were veterans of many battles and they understood the implications of the news.

"The first thing we need to do is to get back to Gaza and collect all the other knights," remarked the first one, who seemed to be the leader.

He turned to Talon. "I am Sir Parsifal. A part of that Egyptian army came here first, but we had the gates shut, so they camped here for a while and then sort of drifted off. We did not know if they would be back or were diverted to another mission. We were on patrol to find out more. Now we know."

"I think I have heard of this one," said one of the knights, pointing at Talon. "He is the one who speaks the language of the Arabic and is often seen with Sir Guy de Veres."

"Sir Guy de Veres has gone north to see about a problem near Tiberius, but Odo de St Amand is with the King," said Talon. If he had needed to convince them any more this seemed to do it, as few outside the Order would know of both men and their whereabouts.

"Will she take you to Gaza, Sir Talon?" enquired the senior knight with respect in his voice now, indicating the mare.

"I think so, Sir, but I would like to change into Templar attire for the journey back."

There was laughter at this from the tough looking crowd of bearded knights. "We can accommodate you with a change of clothes when we get to Gaza, Sir Talon." Sir Percival said.

After Talon had mounted the mare they set off at a brisk pace.

Gaza turned out to be closer than he had thought. A mere three miles' ride later they arrived. Talon was relieved that the Templars had left no survivors, as they would have alerted the army around Ascalon, and he didn't want that. Surprise was needed for the venture to come.

They were greeted by the other knights in Gaza, who at first thought Talon was a prisoner, but when Sir Parsifal told them who he was there were other knights who remembered seeing him in the company of Sir Guy de Veres, so he was welcomed. He was asked to describe the situation as he knew it to the Master of the Knights in Gaza, Sir Ralf de Montcalm, who acted very quickly once he understood. He told his lieutenants and Sergeants to make all preparations for battle and to be ready to ride out within the hour.

Talon had to tell of his adventure to many inquisitive companions, but at his request they gave him a strong and fractious Destrier to ride and one of the long shields favored by the Templar knights, plus the uniform necessary to dress like the others. Someone found him a helmet of the flat top kind. The leather inside stank of old sweat, but it fit reasonably well.

He begged some food, as he was starving, and received some stale bread, cold mutton, and a chunk of very salty corned beef, which he wolfed down with some brackish water from the city well. He arranged that the mare would be led by one of the Sergeants; Talon was honoring his word and bringing her back to Ascalon and the scout.

There were perhaps eighty knights who took the road towards Ascalon that day, Talon among them. He registered the eight-cornered Black Cross on a white banner that had replaced the original black square on a white background, carried by a nominated Seneschal who was none other than Sir Parsifal. It fluttered proudly in the breeze as they trotted forward through the gates. Talon looked around as they rode out of the city, and wondered how in God's name they could hope to overcome an army of many thousands.

His companion Templars seemed to be content with whatever their fate had to offer, however. They seemed determined to win this contest even if the odds were hundreds to one!

There are two roads on which we go
To other worlds than this—
The One leads down to endless woe,
The other up to bliss.

—David Barker

Chapter 10

To Save A King

The knights Templar, led by Sir Ralf de Montcalm, rode steadily north, following the coastline towards Ascalon. The sun climbed the eastern sky, making men and horses sweat in the early morning heat. The force threw up a dust cloud behind them that concerned Talon; he felt sure that the enemy would notice and have time to prepare for them. He felt the sweat trickling down his neck from the heat and wished he could wear his turban, but in this company of knights that was unthinkable.

The men were silent for the most part, as was the way of the Templars, so that the only sound was the thud of the horses' hooves, the jingle of many bridles, the snort of a horse or the occasional slap of a hand at a persistent fly. They had outriders, seasoned Sergeants, well in advance, who were there to warn of any ambush that might have been placed by the enemy. Talon was impressed with the care that Sir Ralf paid to his front. At every moment Talon expected to see a facing army of Egyptians come to meet them.

Just when Talon estimated that they should be upon the enemy camp, the four outriders stopped and became visibly more cautious. Then, while the others remained, one turned his horse and rode back to the knights.

"The Saracens are just over the rise in front of us, Sir Ralf," he called when he had reined up his fine Arab horse.

Sir Ralf ordered the column to stop; then, indicating that Talon and Sir Parsifal should accompany him, he trotted his huge horse forward to where the other scouts were waiting. They could see Ascalon about one mile ahead, and dotted all over the plain in front of the castle were the enemy tents. It looked as though the camp was still waking up; the Egyptians seemed to be quite unaware of any threat to the south of them.

Sir Ralf turned to his two companions. "If we can charge through them, one might hope that the King and his men would join us to counter-charge together and break the enemy completely before they can recover."

Talon nodded, and Sir Ralf grunted and wiped his brow with his leather glove. "We have the advantage of surprise. They do not seem ready for a fight of any kind, but we should do this quickly," he said.

"Bring the men up and prepare them, Sir Parsifal. Sir Talon, you stay with me."

Parsifal galloped back to the waiting column. After calling out orders he wheeled his horse and brought the knights up the road towards the waiting men.

"We have about a half mile to go before we strike the camp, so we will advance at the trot and hope that they stay focused on the castle and only notice us when it is too late to counter our charge. I pray to God that the people on the walls are awake and realize what is going on," rumbled Sir Ralf to Talon.

They set off in two columns and crested the rise. Talon was tense, convinced that they would be noticed the moment they appeared on the skyline, but still the leisurely activity in the enemy encampment continued.

The Templars had shortened the distance to almost a quarter of a mile before suddenly men began to run about, pointing at the oncoming Templars. A trumpet sounded, and men began to run for their weapons and towards the horse lines. But it was far too late.

On a shouted command Sir Ralf brought the columns of Templars into two straight lines, one behind the other. The maneuver took barely two minutes to execute. Talon found himself in the center with Sir Ralf and Parsifal, knee to knee in the tactic he had learned so well those many years ago in Langue d'Oc. This was the first time he was actually taking part in a real battle with Templars; he found that it demanded concentration and thus took his mind off the impending conflict.

Talon settled his shield strap comfortably across his shoulder, moving the shield forward to where it covered his left shoulder and breast but also gave some protection to Sir Ralf on his left side. He felt a trickle of sweat down his back and his breathing became sharper.

Another shouted command, whereupon the lines of horsemen broke into a steady canter and lances were lowered. Talon could see that panic had struck the immense army before them: hundreds, thousands of men were gesticulating and running in all directions. He could hear nothing but the pounding of his pulse and the loud drumming of the many hooves all around him.

Then there came a shout from Sir Ralf. "Deus Lo Volt!" The shout was taken up by eighty throats and became a roar as the Templars charged into the enemy encampment, their battle cry of "Deus lo Volt!" bellowed by every man.

Talon, watching only his front, skewered one victim on his lowered spear. The man disappeared with a scream under the hooves of his horse, and Talon felt the familiar rotation of the spear towards the rear; he tugged it hard and swung it in an arc over his head so that it was once again pointing forward. He felt a splash of blood on his neck as the point passed over his head.

Many a luckless man was caught in front of the devastating charge. There were few horsemen to confront them.

Suddenly they were through the enemy encampment and almost at the walls of Ascalon. Looking up quickly Talon could see people peering down at them and waving wildly. He could also hear the king's trumpeters within calling the men to arms.

A shouted command from Sir Ralf was taken up by others in the two lines and they hauled their excited horses to a halt, then Sir Ralf ordered the two lines to wheel so that they were facing the enemy again.

Behind them came the welcome blast from several trumpets on the walls and the gates of Ascalon opened. Out poured the King's army, both mounted men and on foot. They roared their welcome to the knights and prepared to follow them back into the fray. Talon strained his eyes for sight of the king, but the only men he recognized were Lord Odo and Reynald de Châtillon, who led the King's army. Of the king there was no sign.

Sir Ralf timed his next charge to the second. Just as the King's army was formed up behind the Templar double line, he gave the order to trot forward.

The trumpets behind sounded again for what Talon fervently hoped would be the order to follow the Templars. Sir Ralf shouted for the knights to charge, and they were off again. Then above the drumming of hooves Talon heard the shouts and yells of defiance from the King's army as it hastened to follow the Templars into the battle.

The enemy leaders had still not managed to organize their men enough to effectively resist the oncoming force. Talon could see some of the braver men trying to rally the less willing, but it was all for nothing as the Templar double line smashed into the milling body of men and horses, cutting a swath of death and destruction as they went.

Again the great shout of "Deus Lo Volt!" issued from every mouth as they struck. The Templars met little resistance to their front, while the King's men swarmed into the gap made behind them and widened it. Their opponents broke and fled; there was nothing they could do to stop this juggernaut which must have chilled the bravest of them as they watched its methodical destruction of their camp.

Once again the Templars were through, and this time they were closely followed by the cheering men of the king's army.

Looking back Talon could see that there was mopping up being done by several hundred of the King's men, but the main body of his small army was still with the Templars.

The two groups of men, the king's army and the Templar knights, paused on the rise overlooking the plain where the jubilant Lord Odo now joined them.

But as they waited, the Templars received word that the king had collapsed. He was now being brought from Ascalon on a litter. It was not long before he arrived, and then despite his condition the young king was full of joy.

"God is on our side today, Templars. I thank you from my heart!" the young king shouted in a reedy voice. "Now we have to continue to find the main Egyptian army. Do we know where it has gone?" he asked the silent lines of men.

"Salah Ed Din has gone up towards Ramla and Lydda north of us, my Liege," called Talon.

"Ah, Sir Talon!" exclaimed the king. "It was you who brought the Templars?"

"He did indeed, Sire," Sir Ralf called over, "although from what I could see it was a near thing." There were chuckles from some of the men around him.

"I shall give thanks for your safety, Sir Talon. You have served me well and I shall not forget," said the King.

Talon bowed in the saddle but said nothing.

The young king stood up from his litter and addressed the army in a clear voice that carried to all.

"For the sake of Jesus Christ and Mary, mother of God, we must catch up with the Sultan's army and place ourselves between them and Jerusalem. Will you come with me?"

There was a concerted roar of assent and approval from those who heard him, taken up by others as his words were passed along. Soon the whole army was shouting and cheering.

Then they began the march. Everyone realized that the situation was dire and this forced march was the last chance for the Christian army to place itself in a position where it could at least maul and delay the Egyptian army before it arrived at the walls of Jerusalem.

The army commanders rode alongside the king's litter and discussed the situation among themselves as the small army moved north. Finally the king, who was exhausted, settled back on his litter and waved them forward. Those on horseback maintained a steady trot, alternated with a canter, to conserve the mounts, as they had at least twenty miles to ride before they came close to Ramla. The footmen kept up as best they could. No one wanted to be left behind to the tender mercies of whomsoever had survived the Templar charges.

As the army continued north, signs of the presence of the invading army and its activities became clear. The sultan had allowed his marauding army, cavalry and footmen alike, freedom to burn and loot wherever they chose. The destruction was absolute: villages and farms had simply been obliterated as the huge army came through. The smoke from the burning ruins got into mens' eyes, and the smell of death tainted the air. The bodies of horses and farm animals lay where they had been felled, alongside those of their former masters. Many of the unfortunate peasants and villagers had died horribly.

Lord Reynald de Châtillon, despite his ugly reputation, knew how to keep the King's men in order. The men shouted with anger and cursed the Saracen out loud at the sights that met them, but he made the commanders who were subordinate to him keep their men from dispersing. Lord Odo was with the Templars in the van of the army; he had quietly congratulated Talon on his safe return and thanked Sir Ralf for being so prompt in coming to the relief of Ascalon.

Looking about him at the destruction he observed dryly, "This serves to bring the anger of our small army to white-hot point. We will surely need that, as well as God's protection, before this day is out."

Well ahead Talon could see the scouts, moving cautiously and fully alert, seeking any sign of the Sultan's army itself. They rode for many hours; noon came and went, with the army stopping only to rest the horses near a stream to allow them to drink while the men refreshed themselves as best they could with whatever meager rations they had seized before they left Gaza or Ascalon.

The Templars shared what they had amongst each other, so Talon received a little bread that threatened to break his teeth and some nasty looking cheese. Despite the lump in the pit of his stomach at the impending battle he was hungry, and he needed all the energy he had left for the battle to come. During one pause he took his helmet off and pushed back the chain mail hood to allow his head to cool.

Men around him were doing the same; the heat, although not harsh, was oppressive when a man was covered with chain and steel. He wiped the sweat off his forehead and contemplated the army around him. It would be a near thing if they could just meet up with the enemy this day, let alone fight him, thought Talon to himself moodily. While he was thus occupied with his bleak thoughts he received a big thump on the back and whirled to see a grinning Thierry standing there, Vorhert beside him.

"We could barely believe it when we saw the knights from Gaza, Talon. We thought it more likely that we would see your head on a spear in the morning. Thank God and his mercy you survived," said Thierry happily.

Talon was embraced by both men, and after they had talked a while, they heard the call to remount. Thereafter the three of them stayed together, a mutual respect and liking having formed between them. The army of eighty Templars, and one thousand seven hundred mounted men and infantry, pressed on through the early afternoon. The dust and heat worked their discomfort upon the men, but there was an eagerness to avenge the humiliations of the past few days and to put a stop to the marauding Egyptians. Towards early afternoon they could see a column of smoke billowing into the sky.

The men all around growled their anger at the sight of it.

"That is Ramla! God curse them, they have fired Ramla!" called Lord Odo angrily to his men.

Talon estimated that they were about four miles from Ramla, but it seemed clear that the enemy had already taken the city and had sacked it.

The men in the army grew more tense as they marched. The enemy would soon be in sight, and every man now knew roughly the odds against them. Talon hoped that the small disciplined army the king led would be able to hold against a much larger force, but he could not discount the Mamelukes, who were the personal bodyguard of the Sultan and his best troops. If they numbered several thousand, the Franks were in for a very bad time.

Reynald began to move the army in an easterly direction and Talon realized that the commander wanted to gain the advantage of elevation. They were now only about thirty miles from Jerusalem, and Talon could make out small groups of mounted men coming from that direction to join the King's army. There were even some Templars who had answered the call put out by Baldwin for more men. These men were well received into the ranks of the Templar lines. Talon looked for any of his friends, but they were not present. He missed having Max by his side.

It was while they were moving over one of the low rises that led up to the heights overlooking the coastal plains that they received their first glimpse of the Egyptian army. Even Talon, who had already viewed the army, was awed by what he saw.

The slow-moving behemoth had spread itself over a wide area of the coastal plain, generating a huge dust cloud that hung over it. Looking down the gentle slopes towards the Egyptians, Talon could see vast numbers of men walking or trotting alongside camels that carried great baskets on either side of their backs in which sat archers. Most of the men on the camels wore little armor, just cotton robes and light chain vests, but they were well defended nevertheless: foot soldiers and servants in their thousands walked alongside the camels.

From the distance Talon could see the immense baggage train, mainly camels carrying huge burdens, much of it looted from the villages and Ramla. It was roughly in the center of the hoard and undoubtedly slowed the movement of the army as a whole. He could not even see the rear of the army and surmised it was only just leaving Ramla. The mass of men and beasts resembled in some grotesque manner a hoard of locusts moving across the land.

It seemed to Talon that the Egyptians would have to cross the Wadi Al Sarar if they wanted to achieve the main road and march on Jerusalem. It was a wide, ancient river bed that had steep banks of sand and rock. There were small islands in the form of water-chiseled sandbanks interspersed with dried up channels where water flowed when it rained in the mountains. Already the forward half of the army had entered the lower levels of the Wadi, descending in ragged formations that sometimes dislodged the banks, which gave way in great clouds of dust and sand, tumbling men and horses down along with it.

Those in the forefront were scrambling up the further banks, in some cases on hands and knees as the sides were steep. There did not seem to be any order to the army whatsoever. Talon squinted, concentrating on the van of the army; there he could make out a dense mass of men on horses and the glitter of sunlight on many spears. The Sultan was most probably there with his Mamelukes, the crack cavalry regiments that formed the strike force of his army.

He strained his eyes to see beyond the dust of the front ranks of the enormous number of men. He knew the Egyptian way of moving an army. It would place the baggage trains in the middle, line after swaying line of camels with huge panniers of fodder or loot and baggage; around them the infantry and camel archers as protection. Further out would be the cavalry, Egyptian and Turkish and Mameluke cavalry, who rode light, fleet horses, out on the wings of the army, both protecting it and providing it with the horns that could sweep around an enemy and surround him. They were armed with lances, and the late afternoon sun glinted on their polished razor sharp points as though a wall of diamonds was moving on either side of the main body.

One thing was clear to him despite the dust, and that was that the army was widely spread and did not seem to expect any danger. He also observed that the vast majority of the people, other than the cavalry, were only lightly armed and might not withstand a concerted charge of the kind he had been part of. He discussed this with his friends, who were heartened by the news, although each of them knew the odds were still hugely against them. There were nervous mutterings from the less experienced men, who thought the whole idea of stopping such a mass of men was sheer suicide. The more senior cast worried glances at one another; the morale of the men was going to be of great importance.

The Templars and the king's army were now placed on the higher ground between the Egyptians and Jerusalem, just where Reynald wanted them. It was strange, but despite the fact that by now many Egyptians must have seen the King's army there was little reaction. It seemed as though they dismissed the small army of Christians hovering in the heights above them as insignificant and not worthy of concern. To keep his mind from the coming conflict, Talon questioned his companions.

"What is this place?"

"I think this high ground where we are is known as Montgisard," said Thierry. He pointed to the hills behind them and said, "Ramla is over to the west, down on the plain. They have indeed sacked it, and perhaps also Lydda, God curse them!"

They were interrupted by a rider who came with a message from the king, asking that Lord Odo attend him and his lords further along the lines.

Odo separated himself from his knights and rode at a canter to learn what was going on. The King seemed to have recovered enough to stand up, and his lords went into a huddle around him. They were too far for anyone to hear anything, but as usual his lords each seemed to have a lot to say, most of it forceful with much gesticulating.

Finally Odo came riding back and his men noticed a look of satisfaction on his bearded face. "We are to be the van, right in the front!" he exulted. "God's troops will cut a path to the very center of their army."

There was a roar from his men as his words were passed back. Fearful they might be, but when Odo said this they were encouraged and put their fear behind them. The Grand Master gave his commands and indicated who should be his successor if he should fall. His eyes searched for Sir Parsifal and he beckoned him over to ensure that the battle standard would be near him as the rallying point during the confusion that usually followed a charge. He enjoined them to remember what it was the knights did best in battle. They were to hold the line no matter what.

The King's cavalry would come right behind them to add weight to the wedge the Templars would force through the ranks of the Egyptians. Then the infantry would fan out on either side and complete the wide triangle of the wedge, mopping up as they went.

The Templars immediately moved into position. Men rode alongside and shrove each other. Talon, Thierry and Vorhert stayed together and made their confessions in low voices, taking the absolution, then they kissed one another on each cheek.

"We must stay together after the charge, or we will perish alone," Talon warned his companions, "They will not fight three of us easily, but one they will swarm over and kill. And they will try to hamstring our horses, so we must keep moving at all costs."

His companions knew enough of Talon by now to respect what he had to say, so they nodded their heads in assent. He knew more than they did about the enemy.

Talon noticed a small mound that rose up out of the plain behind the Egyptian army on the south side of the Wadi.

"What is that hill, Thierry?" he asked, pointing with his lance.

"That is the Tell al-Safiya," said Thierry. "Why do you ask?"

"Because I think that is where Salah Ed Din will place his forces so that he has his back covered when the battle starts," replied Talon.

"Look! The King is coming. By the Lord God, he is mounted! How did he find the strength?" exclaimed Vorhert in awed tones.

"I could have sworn I heard that he was on his deathbed back in Ascalon," said Thierry. "God must be holding him up, there is no other explanation. What is he about to do?"

Indeed, the front ranks of the Templars and the King's Army were about to witness a most extraordinary sight. The young king dismounted and, holding onto the cantle of his saddle to keep himself upright, called out loudly for all the men to hear.

"Bishop of Bethlehem! Come to the front of the army and raise the relic of the True Cross on high for all men to see and gain courage for the battle to come!"

The Bishop, a diminutive man who bestrode a donkey, came trotting up to the King. He dismounted, then raised an ornate box containing the splinter of the Cross of Jesus on high. The young, wasted king immediately prostrated himself on his face, his arms wide in the form of a cross in front of the Bishop. After a pause he rose to his knees and addressed the open sky.

"Dear Lord," he cried, tears now coursing down his cheeks, "forgive us our sins and give us the courage to perform your work in your name and for your glory! Help us, your true soldiers, to win this day and to save Jerusalem from the destroyers of the Church of the Holy Sepulcher."

The Bishop raised his right arm and made the blessing.

"In the name of the Father, the Son and the Holy Ghost, Amen!"

*****

The siege of Ramlah had lasted but a few hours before the town fell to the overwhelming numbers of Egyptian soldiers who swarmed over the walls, opened the gates and began to sack the cit. Fires broke out as the soldiers overran the town. It took longer for the sultan's officers to drive the men who were intent upon looting the town back onto the road than it had to sack the city.

"The way to Al Kuds is open and we cannot waste more time here!" The sultan had to shout over the din to his his generals and then he ordered the march to begin.

Twenty-six thousand men climbed onto their camels and horses and resumed their march. The light cavalry by custom took up their positions on the wings of the vast array of men and animals, while the baggage and transport animals were kept in the middle. Deep inside the Egyptian army, Salah Ed Din and his senior officers observed the small force of Christians hovering along he low foothills to the east of his gigantic force. The sultan of Egypt had to hold a cloth over his lower face to ward off the cloud of dust raised by the mass of men and animals as they moved slowly eastward. The only obstacle in the way of the army was the deep wadi that crossed their path, but that was dry. There was little concern that the enemy would dare to attack such a mighty force.

"If that is the best the boy king of the Frans can muster then the road is open to us," remarked one of his generals. Salah Ed Din could not disagree. The puny force the Christians had fielded was a fraction of the size of his army and would be swept aside if it dared to stand in his way. He confidently ordered the army to head for Jerusalem. "We will be there in less than two days," he stated.

All the same he sent out messengers for units of the cavalry to close in, and he ordered the Mamelukes to come to the center and cover his front.

As the moon rises on a cloudy sky
I cry out my curse.
My feet are standing in a puddle of blood,
blood shed from the innocents
slain by my own hand.
Blood feeding the thirsty ground,
with pain and death.

—Lucirina Telor Vivan

Chapter 11

The Battle of Montgisard 1177 AD

King Balwin IV climbed painfully to his feet, shaking off a helping hand from the bishop. He faced his army, then shouted to his men.

"Today we do God's work and will have no fear. Do not be faint of heart, for God is on our side. We shall prevail. God go with each and every one of you!"

There was a roar as every man who had witnessed the young king's devotions shouted his support, and as the word rippled through the ranks of the entire army the air shook with the roars of men, few without tears in their eyes, who now found their courage and wanted only to do battle for their king.

Suddenly the fear and uncertainty were gone. All around the king, who was now helped back on his horse, the men looked to their arms and strapping, grimly certain that while they were surely about to die in the face of the enormous odds, they would be

God's servants and would be blessed this day, the 25th of November in the year of our Lord 1177.

Talon's mouth was dry and he had a lump in the pit of his stomach, but he managed to say to his two companions through parched lips the words that Max had used when they were last in battle: "Stay close. Stay close."

Both nodded without words. There was nothing more to say.

Talon could see that to their front the Egyptians were finally taking the threat seriously and the light cavalry were galloping in from the wings to try and get to the center where a large formation of Mameluke troops had gathered.

Just as Talon had predicted, the Sultan had decided to center his army in front of the Tell al-Safiya, thus giving himself a hill behind his army upon which to place his archers. The mass of troops hastened to put their backs to the low hill.

Talon could see in the distance that couriers were galloping in all directions in what appeared to be an attempt to summon reinforcements and to get the baggage train out of the path of danger. It was time to hit them as hard as they could and give them no further time to prepare.

There was a deep rumble behind him. Glancing back he saw that the horizon was black with storm clouds. He saw huge jagged flashes of lightning in the distance and the rumble of thunder followed close after. The air around him was charged and the dense heat caused him to sweat copiously under his thick tunic. He wished he could wipe his face within the stifling confines of the helmet. The storm would soon be upon them, he thought, as he turned his attention to his front. The stink of sweating men and horses assailed his nostrils.

Lord Odo now took the front and center of the Templars and raised his arm. The Templar lines moved forward as one. Each horse was held firmly in hand, although many wanted to run, sensing the energy and tension of the army all about. The saying went that when the knights were in this closed order each man was closer to his neighbor than he could have possibly been with his wife if he had one. They were knee to knee and shoulder to shoulder, their shields overlapping their left-hand neighbor and protecting his right shoulder.

Talon prayed that the King's men would be right behind them and that the enemy would not swallow this pitiful force of Templars when its charge was done. He was convinced that they were going to their end, but despite his fear he felt an exultation that he could not explain, nor did he care any longer.

Then he heard another roar behind him, and glancing back he felt the hair prickle on his neck. The grievously ill king, his hands bound in white bandages and his disfigured face half covered with a scarf, was mounted on a large fresh horse just behind the Templars, and his army was crowding in behind him. He just had time to notice that Lord Reynald was riding alongside the King and next to Joscelin.

Then Talon forced his attention to the front. Odo had raised his arm, and by dropping it the command to walk forward was given. Every eye of the Templars was now fixed on their leader. Shields were shifted tighter into place and their long wooden lances came down as men settled them in. They advanced at the walk for about fifty yards, then the arm went up and down again. This meant they should trot. As one the horsemen switched gait and picked up speed. The line held as straight as any Talon had ever seen before. Another fifty yards and the arm went up and down for the final time, and the double lines of Templars put spurs to horse.

There was a flash of lightning that lit up the sky from behind as the Templar line commenced to gallop, and the following thunder seemed to shake the very earth and sky. Talon directed his eyes forward to the enemy.

He could see that there was real consternation on the faces of the soldiers directly in the path of the charging Templars. Now the Franks were only a few yards from the van of the Egyptian army. The camel drivers were frantically trying to get their beasts out of the way, but they ran into one another and simply bunched up, making it impossible to flee. The infantry broke and ran in all directions, shrieking their fear as the terrifying sight of the charging knights and the thunder of the hooves of their huge horses became for many the last thing on earth they ever saw or heard.

Most of the fleeing men were unable to climb the banks of the Wadi, so they ran instead down and away from the oncoming danger. Those who could not get out of the way simply disappeared under the flailing iron hooves of the chargers, their shrieks of agony cut off abruptly and barely noticed as the juggernaut swept over them.

Lord Odo had picked the center of the enemy force as his target. Suddenly there were no auxiliary Egyptian troops in their path and the way was clear for the Templars to strike to the very center of the Egyptian army. In front of him Talon saw the Mamelukes milling around in massed ranks, while on the hill behind them were the archers he most feared. These men almost always shot for the horse and not the heavily armed man.

There came a shout from Lord Odo, "Deus Lo Volt! Deus Lo Volt!" It came high and clear to the Templars over the thunder of hundreds of iron shod hooves. With a roar the Templars took up the battle cry: "Deus Lo Volt!"

Talon shouted the cry along with his companions and continued to shout as they galloped across the remaining yards of sand and scrub to crash into the massed ranks before them. Later he wondered at the ease with which the Templars cut through the men and horses arrayed in front of them. As they came together with a sickening crunch of man and horse in collision he did not have time to think beyond staying mounted, staying with his companions as they struck the ranks of the Mamelukes, and staying alive.

He felt the shock as his lance pierced straight through the light shield of a large man directly in front of him. The man and his horse vanished as quickly as they had appeared. Talon allowed the lance to carry the man down off his horse, then dragged his lance out of the body as he swept past to swing its gory point over his head in a light spray of blood and lock it into the crook of his arm again. Men all around him were doing the same amid the thunder of hooves, the demonic yells of the knights and the screams of their victims. A mace flew through the air and clanged against his shield with a thud that shook his arm, but it fell away having done no harm. Another man appeared before him and again he felt the lance penetrate and heard the shriek of agony as the man died. His lance was so slippery with blood that when he tugged at it his hand slipped off the shaft, so he drew his sword and drove his horse hard forward to the front.

Then it was a frantic mêlée of screaming men, hacking swords, axes and maces. Talon could hear his companions yelling next to him and was aware that he was doing the same as the impetus of the Templar charge drove ever deeper into the ranks of the Mameluke cavalry ahead of them. He stabbed and hacked at any one who came within reach of his sword, as did Thierry and Vorhert and all the men along the line. Their Destriers stamped over the bodies of man and beast as they drove onward. The huge horses used their iron shod forefeet to strike at men and horses, crushing bodies and breaking limbs as they surged forward, driven almost mad by the spurs of their riders and the smells of the battlefield.

Talon hacked down on the shield of an Egyptian rider to his right and split it in two. The man shrieked as his arm was cut off and then disappeared under foot. Talon's horse lunged forward over the bodies—and suddenly there were far fewer of the enemy ahead of them than before.

The Templar charge had carried them to the base of the Tell. Now they were subjected to a flurry of arrows, but the effect was minimal, for the long shields afforded them protection and the intervening chaos and thick press of men made it hard for the archers to aim at horses. Apart from a few wounds the Templars had suffered little; now they rode straight up into the archer lines and the slaughter began again. Within seconds the lightly armed archers were running for their lives and had abandoned the hill. The Templars came to a halt in a shower of sand and dust, fighting to bring their huge horses under control, The animals, maddened with blood lust and fear, fought their bits and bucked but came under control.

Talon instinctively looked to the center where Lord Odo should be and saw that he was signaling for the line to turn and face the left flank; the battle standard fluttered in his wake. Once again the Templars formed up, and on a shouted command charged into the milling ranks of the light cavalry who were trying to organize themselves around a group of turbaned men and a large baggage train.

Again Talon was knee to knee with his two companions on either side; again they bellowed their defiance with the battle cry "Deus Lo Volt!" Once more the solid line of Templars crashed into the lighter horsemen of the Egyptian army, who were completely overwhelmed. Talon used his sword like a piston. Leaning out over his horse's shoulder he stabbed forward at anyone who came within reach, while on either side of him Thierry and Vorhert of the huge arms hacked and bellowed at the shrieking Egyptians, who now seemed to want only to get away from them.

Wide, wild eyes and gaping, shrieking mouths in grimacing faces came and went. The crash of steel on steel, the sickening crunch of breaking bodies and the shrieks of wounded and dying men all around numbed his mind. The great Destriers the Franks rode were trained to battle and were ridden as battle weapons themselves. They would rear and strike out with their front iron shod hooves at the smaller horses of the enemy cavalry and do such damage that the rider was often also incapacitated. Talon's horse had the smell the blood in his nostrils. He was almost frantic and hard to control; he whinnied with rage and fear, as did other horses all around, adding their noise to the general din of battle. It took a lot of work for him to use the animal effectively.

Blood sprayed high from dreadful wounds they inflicted on the enemy, drenching the battle-maddened Franks. Their victims were decapitated, disemboweled, or had limbs hacked off, and still the slaughter continued. A new sound, a rising, concerted shriek of dying men and horses, could now be heard ringing in the ears of every man on the field of battle.

*****

The Sultan of Egypt was dismounted and his men hopelessly disoriented, shocked and now terrified. The ferocious charge of the Templars had stunned all of them to the point where men lost their nerve completely and simply galloped away from the ghastly killing machine that was coming at them yet again. He did not even have archers at his disposal. They had fled over the top of the Tell after the first charge by those Christian knights

Salah Ed Din found himself in short order with only a few retainers in amongst his former baggage train, which was now strewn all about. His horse had been killed and he himself had barely escaped with his life when he tumbled out of the saddle of his dying horse to fall between two other dead animals. The Templars had thundered through the train after sweeping aside his light cavalry as though they barely existed. He realized that his cavalry could no longer be counted on to save the battle, and the vast numbers of infantry were being slaughtered like sheep all along the wadi. His generals were gone, either dead or wounded or fled, leaving him to fend for himself on this field of slaughter. One of his men was shouting at him, the voice barely penetrating the numbness of his mind. He could not understand how this destruction had happened so quickly and so completely, but the servant's shouts finally reached him.

"You must leave, Sire. You must leave and now!"

"I need a horse!" Salah Ed Din shook his head to try and clear him mind.

"They have killed the horses, but there is this camel, Lord. God protect you, but you must flee as they cannot be stopped."

The servant hastily assisted him onto the camel and then ran over to his own animal and mounted. They thrashed their camels into motion and raced off through the milling groups of men. Some were fighting the Christian footmen in savage little battles, but others had dropped their arms were streaming in large numbers to the south and relative safety. The sultan abandoned the field in a desperate attempt to save his own life; no knowing how the battle might go without him, but he was sure of one thing, should he survive this battle. He would never again allow himself to underestimate the Templar knights, and never again would he grant them mercy should they surrender. They were far too dangerous.

*****

"They are broken, they flee!" came the shout from somewhere, and Talon drew new heart from the cry. The shout was taken up by the king's men, but Talon knew it must be far too soon. He shouted to Vorhert and Thierry to stay close and snapped his head around, searching for danger. They found themselves in the middle of a baggage train full of loot and other riches; camels were running, bellowing, in all directions, trailing their loads as they galloped off.

These were rich pickings for the men of the king's army if they won, he thought briefly. This must have been the Sultan's train, he realized, and looked for him. But there was no sign of Salah Ed Din. Talon knew he would recognize him if he were still here. He saw a group of men on horses grouped around an individual who seemed of high rank attempting to make an escape.

"Those men, Thierry, we should attack them now!" he shouted as he snatched up a lance that was sticking in the ground, only noticing in passing that it was in fact protruding from a corpse.

Both Thierry and Vorhert rode with Talon as they spurred their horses into a gallop straight at the group of men. Brave men tried to stop them but it was an unequal contest. The three

Templars bored deep into the group, opening a wedge for other Templars to exploit. Talon drove his new spear straight through the light shield of a rider, though his chest and out the other side, then drew his sword and hacked at another man in front of him. Blood from a shrieking victim of Thierry's sprayed high into the air, drenching him as he went by.

He felt the jar of steel on steel as the man parried the blow, but then Talon flicked his sword round and under, plunging it into the side of the man. The man's turban fell off and his mouth gaped in a silent scream of agony before he tumbled off his horse. Talon was carried forward straight at a dark man in rich clothing just behind. He had his mouth wide open, displaying good teeth in a shout of defiance; he raised his shield high before slicing at Talon with his curved sword.

Talon dropped his left arm low across his pommel, received the blow on his shield, and then stabbed straight at the man's chest. His sword glanced off the breast plate, but it shook the man enough for Talon to batter him in the face with his shield. The man swayed back in the saddle, giving Talon the opportunity to hack at his exposed shoulder as he rode by.

Talon whirled his horse on its haunches in a spray of sand to see how his companions were faring. This particular fight was over. While the other knights charged off to find more targets, the three Templars paused and looked down on the havoc they had wrought.

The group of men they had attacked had been the bodyguard of the man Talon had wounded. Now they were dead or had fled, while the man he had struck was lying on the sand in a spreading pool of blood, but still he appeared to be alive. Talon told his companions to hold his horse and lance while he investigated.

Dismounting but holding his sword at the ready, he approached the wounded man. He was dying, but could still recognize that one of the hated Frans was now standing over him.

"Leave me alone, Infidel, can't you see I am dying?" the man whispered, his eyes half closed with the pain. For all the battle clamor raging around them there seemed to be an oasis of quiet surrounding the two men.

"Even an enemy can give comfort to a dying man," said Talon in Arabic.

The wounded man's eyes snapped open. "Who are you, that you speak my language?" he demanded, peering up at him.

"I am Talon de Gilles, Templar. What is your name, so that I can send word to your family?"

The man blinked. "Ah... " he gasped and writhed with pain. "My name is Abdul-Basit ibn Kaliq, and I am related to the Sultan, Salah Ed Din. Will you truly send word for me?"

"I shall say the prayers necessary for you to make the crossing and respect your body. I will see to it that you will be buried as a Moslem should and no one will despoil your body when you are departed, Abdul-Basit ibn Kaliq."

"I thank you, Talon de Gilles, may Allah, who is all-seeing, be kind to you. There is gold in my saddle bags that will help with this.... Do you have some water? I am terribly thirsty," the dying man croaked.

Although he was desperately thirsty himself, Talon returned to his horse, took the small skin of water and went back to where Abdul lay. He put the water spout to the man's lips, but the man had gone. His open eyes were lifeless and dull in death. A fly had already landed on his bearded face.

Talon stood up slowly, then went and took his cloak from the roll on his horse and laid it over the dead man's body. He could only hope that the pillaging that followed every battle would leave untouched a body under the cloak of a Templar.

He then went over to the horse that the man had ridden. It was standing forlorn with head down; it seemed reluctant to leave its master lying on the ground. After quieting it with gentle words Talon lifted the heavy saddle bags off the animal and placed them on his own. He took off the ornate saddle and bridle and placed them near the fallen warrior. Then he slapped the animal with the flat of his sword and drove it off. The horse whickered as though to say farewell to its master, then galloped off southwards, to where Talon hoped it would find its home. He suspected, however, that the Bedouin in the Sinai would be the beneficiaries.

Talon remounted, and he and his companions joined a larger party of Templars who were looking for isolated clusters of the enemy who had not fled nor yet surrendered. Each time a group of the enemy tried to face them they were simply run down and slaughtered. Talon's arm was weary as he repeatedly hacked down at shield, sword, head or limb that presented itself as a target to him. His sword arm was covered with blood up to his shoulder.

Soon there were no more massed cavalry for the Templars to strike at, so they broke up into groups to attack whatever other targets presented themselves. Talon's instincts told him that they must continue to fight as hard as they could, for they would surely lose if the enemy managed to rally even a few thousand.

His shield arm was numb with the hammering his shield had taken. He was deeply tired but knew there was more to come, so he braced himself and shrugged off the fatigue. Following his advice the three men stayed together, even when they would join a larger group of Templars from time to time.

Many of the King's infantry, those who were not busy looting, encouraged by the solid presence of the knights, stayed with them and worked to attack groups of the enemy in a concerted manner that overcame any resistance. Often, however, the infantry would be distracted by the opportunity to loot the dead or wounded, so the Templars would leave them scrabbling over some rich pickings, brandishing their finds to one another and yelling with glee like grotesque blood-covered trolls.

Their luck held until they were confronted by a larger body of men whom Talon thought might be Mamelukes. These men would not flee the field as easily as so many of their comrades. The two groups charged each other furiously, and soon another mêlée developed where each man had to fight for his life. There were Egyptian footmen involved too, and the Templars needed to work together to beat them off. The enemy would try and isolate one knight and then swarm over him, footmen and riders hacking at him from all sides with axes, swords and spiked clubs, trying to bring him off his mount.

This occurred twice before Talon realized that he and his companions needed to watch not only each other but the other knights as well. Now as they roamed the battlefield they would catch the enemy at his own game, and as the Egyptians, footmen and riders swarmed a knight the three of them would descend upon the enemy and hack them off the beleaguered knight.

The fighting was savage, with no quarter given by either side. The Mamelukes were fighting with the desperation of men who could not surrender, but the by now weary Templars wanted to finish it quickly. More than once Talon saw a dismounted knight and a Mameluke standing facing one another, staggering on the blood-slippery ground, both so tired that they just swung weakly at one another, neither one defending himself from the blows of the other. On one occasion the Templar knight finally paused and wearily pointed with his arm as though to say, “Leave this place!”

The Egyptian took the hint and began to walk away, only to be spotted by another knight, not one of the Templars, who ran him down, running him through the back with his lance. The body was flung away as though it were a rag doll, and the knight went on to look for other victims. Talon turned away, sickened.

The exhaustion was telling on the Templars; they were not as quick as they had been to avoid a blow. Talon took a spear point in the thigh that, although superficial, was painful and bled a lot; and he saw Vorhert take a nasty slash on the right shoulder that rent his chain mail and cut his flesh. He too bled profusely and cursed, but then stood in his stirrups and, with a roar, brought his sword down with both hands, cleaving in two the head of the man who had caused the wound.

Then Thierry gave a great cry of pain and Talon saw the broken shaft of a spear embedded in his back, the point protruding through his chest. Thierry slumped over the saddle in agony. Both Talon and Vorhert backed their horses alongside, and reaching down Talon took the reins from the wounded man, dragging the horse out of the fray going on all around them. He ran down a spearman who tried to stab upwards at him from the ground and heard bones break and the man's shriek as his body was trampled by Talon's Destrier.

In a relatively quiet place on the sands of the wadi, where there were more dead men than living, they dismounted and eased Thierry off his horse. Talon saw immediately that his comrade was dying. There was blood dribbling out of his mouth. Thierry tried to speak but coughed out a gout of blood and convulsed, his heels drumming on the sand as he died.

Talon shook his friend's body, unable to accept that he had gone. He knelt on the blood-slick ground and bowed his head, too weary to do more than hold his friend in his arms and murmur the absolution for a comrade.

"We must stay mounted, Talon, or we will be cut down as well," Vorhert croaked through parched lips.

Talon nodded, barely hearing him, and laid Thierry back on the ground. Then he hauled the spear out of the body and threw it away. He dashed the tears from his eyes with his gloved hand, not even knowing that he left a wide smear of blood over his face. He could not remember when he had lost his helmet. He felt a keen sense of loss, but Vorhert was right, they had to try and survive. The terrible battle was not yet over.

But even as he mounted he heard cheering and saw in the distance the King's banner being raised on high. Staring around with bloodshot eyes and numbed senses, Talon saw that there were no enemy banners on the battlefield, but in the distance he saw the standard of the Templars. Far to the south he could see dust from the defeated army as the survivors fled the field, pursued by the king's men.

Later, he knew, the Bedouin down in the desert of Sinai would harass the remaining survivors, killing and looting, feeding off their defeat like carrion crows. The Bedouin had little liking for the Egyptians despite the fact that they were of the same faith. Salah

Ed Din had harried their tribes because they had tried to live alongside the Christians and remain independent.

The men they had so recently been fighting were gone. They had heard the sound of their fate and now all they wanted to do was to escape the vengeance of the Christians.

He wondered if Salah Ed Din had survived the battle. The carnage was immense; as far as the eye could see there were dead and dying men, horses and camels. The Egyptian army was destroyed, and the plundering had begun. The King's men were catching the surviving camels and tearing open their loads. Only small pockets of resistance from men who had been trapped and unable to escape were left, and either Templars or the King's knights were summarily dealing with them. There was no quarter in most instances, as the blood-maddened troops vented their rage upon luckless men screaming for mercy.

Wearily Talon looked across at Vorhert; his gaze was met by the haunted, hollow look of a man who has gone to hell and is still there. Vorhert was covered with gore, some of it his own or that of his horse, but most from his victims. His tunic was in rags, his coat of mail was rent in several places and he was bleeding from his arm wound. Talon rode alongside and tore a rag off his own torn and filthy tunic and bound the wound as best he could. Then he made a rough bandage for himself, wincing at the pain of the wound.

They surveyed the battlefield together; wordlessly trying to understand what had happened. Neither could believe that they could possibly have won against such odds. Talon was desperately tired and thirsty. Slowly he took the water skin that he had tied to his saddle pommel and lifted it with shaking hands to his parched lips. He only then realized that it was shredded by blows from enemy swords: empty and useless. He tossed it aside tiredly and looked around to see if there was any water nearby.

Vorhert dismounted slowly, like an old man with rheumatism, walked over to the body of an Egyptian who was lying under his dead horse and removed a skin of water from that man's saddle.

He then walked back to Talon and offered it up to him. Talon took it wordlessly and drank the warm water, caring little where it might have come from, then gave it back to Vorhert, who drank the rest.

Talon dismounted and stood with his Destrier, which was trembling with fatigue. Its large head was down; it badly needed water. He found another sack, again from a dead man, and squirted the water into its dry mouth. The animal slobbered over the little water it was given until it was finished. Talon patted its wet shoulder, then he and the horse stood together and surveyed the carnage.

All around them and as far as he could see there were mounds of the dead. Horses and men were heaped together, many with weapons still protruding from them or with huge gaping wounds. Disemboweled bodies of men and animals were sprawled together loosely in death, many atop one another; their eyes staring blindly up at the sky and their bloody teeth bared in a last grimace of rage and agony, as though their souls had been torn from them as they died.

He felt sick with exhaustion and utterly drained. Vorhert had found an unbroken spear and re-mounted. Now he sat slumped in his saddle leaning on the spear, his head down with his battered and dented shield hanging off the pommel of his saddle. His horse, equally exhausted, stood with its legs apart, head down and trembling. Talon remounted; his movements were those of an old man wracked with pain. He instinctively examined the distance to see from where the next danger might materialize.

Talon noticed that the sun was setting, casting a wide red stain over the western sky as though the very heavens were streaked with blood, while the sky above them was jet black with the onset of night and full of rain clouds. There was flash of lightning close by that cut a jagged path through the dark, followed by an ominous rumble of thunder overhead; the storm was upon them. A large rain drop splashed onto his face. A gust of hot wind blew by, stirring the rags hanging off the dead and lifting dust from the ground they stood on.

Lord Odo found Talon and Vorhert near the tell. He rode up with some of the other Templars he had managed to round up.

"Is that you, Sir Talon?" he asked, peering at the two motionless men in the dusk.

"Lord Odo!" croaked Talon. "Did we win?"

"God saw fit to grant us a great victory, Sir Talon. You will be remembered for your work this day in bringing the Templars to this battle."

*****

Slowly the surviving Templars came together. They had suffered awful casualties. No one was sure how many had died, but less than half the original number of men who had followed Lord Odo in that first charge were left in the saddle. All had wounds and all were dark with blood from head to foot.

Within an hour the heavens opened, thunder crashed and the lightning bolts struck, hissing into the dry sand where the living cowered and the dead lay sprawled. Then the rain poured down. Talon welcomed the slashing torrents of water. It seemed to him as though the heavens were cleansing the men who lived and the bodies of those who had died. He could not but ask himself if God played a part in this. The thunder and lightning were a fitting end to this slaughter, he thought.

Talon and Vorhert had one last task to perform that night. Stumbling though the rain they found Thierry and then the body of Abdul-Basit and brought them back with them, loaded onto the back of a horse that was easily caught in the rain.

Lord Odo brought the remainder of his knights together and they searched for some kind of shelter, but there was none to be had. Within minutes of the commencement of the tempest they were all soaked to the skin.

Despite the pouring rain the king's footmen and cavalry were plundering everything in sight and chasing the survivors back beyond Ascalon. What discipline there might have been among their ranks was completely gone.

The Templars took what was immediately available that would go in their saddle bags. One imperative was to recover as many loose horses as possible, to provide mounts for Templar knights who had none of their own. Then at Odo's insistence they climbed out of the Wadi Al-Sarar, leading their sodden, weary horses, and made camp on the banks. Talon noticed that the Wadi was already beginning to flood and was glad that Odo had had the presence of mind to take care of his men.

Few could do more than to fall asleep on the rain soaked ground, huddled under their cloaks while the storm lashed at them like a living thing.

Vorhert went straight to sleep and snored loudly, but Talon could not sleep despite his huge weariness. He huddled under a borrowed cloak; the adrenaline from the battle was gone and left him utterly drained, weak with fatigue. Nonetheless his mind relived the battle almost blow by blow and would not allow him any peace until near dawn, when he began to weep, sitting quite still. The tears poured down his bearded, filthy face mingling with the rain; soon after he fell over on his side in an exhausted slumber. His horse stood over him, its head down, as though protecting him from the elements while he slept.

The next day dawned cold and wet with a mist that came out of the ground that chilled the weary men and horses to the bone. It continued to rain in a persistent drizzle all day; the clouds were level with the top of the foothills of Montgisard.

The Templars took stock of their pitiable condition while standing around in the mud and the rain, clutching their sodden cloaks to themselves with the water pouring off their hats and helmets. The Order had lost fully half their number dead. All of the remainder were wounded, some seriously, and these were now on pallets waiting to be taken back to Jerusalem. Most of them were so exhausted they could not share in the incredulous jubilation of the king's army all around.

Gazing down with bloodshot eyes at the turbulent muddy waters now flowing by in the Wadi Al-Sarar, Talon saw the detritus of the battle, the bodies of men, horses and even camels being washed slowly down stream. It seemed to him as though God wanted to cleanse the battle from living memory.

Messengers arrived from the camp of the king telling them that he was now once again incapacitated and on a pallet himself. His strength had given out late the night before, but not before he had recognized his victory and promised God that he would erect a monastery dedicated to St Catherine of Alexandria and to the glory of God for the incredible accomplishment achieved by his tiny army and the Templars. Of the King's army more than seventeen hundred had died, fully half of the force that took to the field. But the losses to the enemy beggared belief.

Lord Odo told his men that Lord Reynald and his officers had estimated that of the twenty-six thousand who had been with the Egyptian army, fully twenty thousand had died on the field, in the Wadi al-Sarar or around the Tell al-Safiya.

"Did the Sultan fall in the battle, my Lord?" asked Talon

"The rumor goes that he escaped on a racing camel!" Odo laughed.

There were dry chuckles at that as the men imagined the great sultan clutching at the reins of a camel and fleeing for his life. Talon and his companions could hardly believe the news, but the messengers insisted they had the truth of it, and then asked for Odo to attend the King.

He came back several hours later and told the men that the King had heaped praise on the Templar knights, stating that this battle had made them immortal in the eyes of Christendom. He was jubilant, saying that the name Templar was now one to be held in highest respect everywhere in the Christian world.

It was time to depart. Under lowering skies that continued to pour rain upon them, the men who were to go back to Jerusalem bade farewell to their brothers in arms, the Templars from Gaza. As he embraced his newfound comrades one by one, Talon noticed with anguish that Sir Parsifal had fallen in the field. His body would be taken by his knights back to be buried in the chapel at Gaza.

Thierry's body would be returned to Jerusalem; Lord Odo, Talon and Vorhert would take him with them.

So we are more than conquerors,
The victory is begun;
For His work has been completed,
The battle He has won.

—Michael Stace

Chapter 12

Victory

The army of Baldwin IV was welcomed by huge crowds who screamed their relief and joy from the walls of the city of Jerusalem. When the van of the army entered the gates, throngs of people crowded the streets, cheering and throwing palm fronds and what flowers they could find at the young king and his men as they rode or marched into the city.

Although there were drums beating and trumpets blaring, they didn't look much like a victorious army; fully half of the men who had set out were missing, dead, or wounded to the point of incapacitation, and the men who could ride or march arrived at the city gates looking more like the rag-tag remnants of a defeated army than one that had won against impossible odds. Even the young king was strapped onto his horse, accompanied by nervous and attentive companions, Lords and men at arms nearby to ensure that he did not fall.

Although the tattered banners of the King's army flew proudly from the standards held high, from the young king down their tunics were rent and torn, hanging off them in rags. The persistent rain of the last two days had washed off most of the blood of their enemies, and their own, but the stains were still there and encrusted on their chain mail, weapons, and harness; and so very many of them wore make shift bandages, red with the wearer's blood. They were soaked by the persistent drizzle, and despite the jubilation they all bore that hollow-eyed look of men who have descended into hell and come back, forever changed.

The singular difference that distinguished this army from that of a defeated one was the enormous number of camels and donkeys carrying the booty taken from the retreating Sultan's army. For despite the rains and the flooding of the great Wadi Al-Sarar, the king's men, and indeed many Templars, had been able to capture and bring home huge amounts of wealth in the form of rich cloths, gold, silver and livestock. There were prisoners too, but pitiably few; the King's men had killed off many potential ransoms in their crazed hunt for victims. The remainder of the defeated Sultan's men had not had the courage to face the ferocious Frankish army; they knew where home lay and had departed with alacrity.

Those who had survived the blood lust of the victorious army but were too slow to depart were roped together in lines and staggered along behind their captors, eventually to be separated into those who could be ransomed and those who would become slaves.

The remaining Templars, with the proud Lord Odo in the place of honor at their head, followed the King in the van of the parade that entered the city at David's Gate. The roar of the crowd from the battlements and along the streets, coupled with the clash of the ringing bells from every church in the city, numbed Talon's senses, but their shouts were in praise of the knights.

Word of the Templars' now famous charge had preceded them and they were the heroes of the moment. They were showered with flowers and cheered as the procession headed down the Street of St David to the large square known as the Syrian Exchange, where they turned left to ride up the now relatively clean street of

Vegetables that blended with St Stephens towards the Church of the Holy Sepulcher. Again they turned left onto the Via Dolores, and there ahead of them was the small square that opened to the church of the Holy Sepulcher.

Here waiting for them was a crowd of dignitaries standing in front of the scaffolding that still surrounded the small church. The Bishop of Jerusalem was there, wearing his vestments of state, surrounded by lesser dignitaries of the church and the city, while all around a crowd of Christian residents of the city continued to cheer without ceasing.

The young king was helped off his horse by Lord Reynald, who had the place of honor as the commander of the army, and then with two attentive men prepared to support him should he need it, he paced deliberately towards the assembled nobility of the church. Suddenly he stopped and called back to Odo.

"My lord Odo, will you not join me? Bring the standard of the Knight's Templar with you, my Lord, as I would have it blessed and consecrated."

Lord Odo dismounted and carried the standard of the knights forward to kneel before Bishop William, who disliked Lord Odo intensely, but who kissed the standard and blessed it. As Odo was heard to remark later on, the Bishop would rather have kissed the arse of a donkey than to have had to bless the Knights Templar!

King Baldwin then entered the church with the bishop and his leaders and said prayers of thanks to God for their deliverance, after which they said the prayers for the dead.

The Bishop led the prayer with the Requiem and the congregation repeated his words in a loud murmur after him while he stood facing the altar:

Requiem æternam dona eis, Domine, et lux perpetua luceat eis. Te decet hymnus Deus, in Sion, et tibi reddetur votum in Ierusalem. Exaudi orationem meam; ad te omnis caro veniet. Requiem æternam dona eis, Domine, et lux perpetua luceat eis.

"Eternal rest grant unto them, O Lord, and let perpetual light shine upon them. A hymn becomes you, O God, in Zion, and to you shall a vow be repaid in Jerusalem. Hear my prayer; to you shall all flesh come. Eternal rest grant unto them, O Lord, and let perpetual light shine upon them."

The songs of praise soared high into the vaulted roof of the church and carried out to the men kneeling on the flagstones of the square., The Requiem was followed by the Offertory and the Sanctus. As the voice of the Bishop rang out and the songs of the monks filtered out to the exhausted men, some of them wept while others gazed into space with that distant, unseeing look of men who have reached the edge of their sanity.

Later Talon and Vorhert made their way back to the Temple Knights' barracks on the southeastern corner of the city, hard up against the palace of the king. As they walked slowly along the narrow, offal-strewn streets towards their destination, Talon could see clearly the chapel of St James the Lesser built on the remains of the Temple of Solomon. He resolved to pray there, to give thanks for his delivery and that of his companions, and to pray for the ones who had fallen. There was much for the tired knights to do before the day was done and they could finally retire to their Spartan sleeping quarters.

The burial of their comrades came first, and when the prayers were over they then had to take care of their horses and equipment, making all ready for the next day. Talon also arranged with some men to have the body of Abdul-Basit taken to a small mosque near the temple and buried with the rites proper to his religion. He paid the men handsomely and was assured that the work would be done well. The man who was going to perform the work looked into Talon's haunted eyes and meant what he said.

As he was too tired to go to his billet in the town, Talon went to the barrack room with Vorhert. He only had the strength to remove his boots before he fell back onto a truckle bed and fell into a deep, exhausted slumber and slept there the rest of the day and all that night.

While he and his comrades dreamed, cried out in their nightmares and twitched in their sleep, the city continued to celebrate its deliverance. Most of the inhabitants spent the night drinking themselves into a stupor on cheap ale and mead, while their fellow celebrants danced and sang around impromptu bonfires lit in the small squares around the city.

*****

Talon woke early the following morning. After dressing in a tunic that the Quartermaster provided, he walked out onto the battlements and stared towards the east. He needed time to think.

The battle was still vivid in his mind and would, he knew, haunt him for a long time to come. He stared out to the east, forcing the awful memories to quiet, watching with eyes that did not see the camels and donkeys as they walked the road under the walls towards the valley of Kidron. He thought back to the only other great battle he had taken part in, making comparisons, even though he knew that was pointless. The battle of Myriokephalon had been a complete disaster and he and Max had been lucky to even survive. Both battles had been nightmares of screaming madness, and somehow had to be sent as far from his mind as possible. Victory or defeat: neither provided him with any pleasure.

He berated himself; was he not a warrior? A Templar in all but name? Why then did he not feel like celebrating a victory that by any standards was extraordinary? He knew the reason well enough. He knew too much about the people they had fought. They were not faceless, soulless enemies, but men such as the ones he had befriended in his time in Egypt. Yet could he have done otherwise? He doubted it, as fate had placed him on the one side and he was unable to refuse, for too many reasons.

From where he stood he could look over the Tanner's postern and watch the coming and going of the travelers at the gate. Some townspeople were still celebrating in the streets behind him, but he paid them no attention.

His mind was focusing on what he had heard at the castle of Darbsak. Rav'an was alive; and he was still here in Jerusalem, weeks after he had heard the news. His memories drifted to the time they had been together and he wondered for the hundredth time how she could have lived, if indeed it had been the truth he had heard that day.

For the hundredth time he tried to figure out how he could travel that vast distance to see her and ask for forgiveness for having failed her. But he was a member of the Templar Order now, although an auxiliary, and could not possibly desert his brethren.

Sir Guy found him there on the walls, coming up quietly to touch Talon on the shoulder and saying, "Your name is on everyone's lips, Talon. The King remembered you in his prayers and Lord Odo is saying that you are on the ladder for a high rank."

Talon turned and smiled at his mentor and friend. He had known Sir Guy was near for some time before the knight touched him, or it might have gone badly for the knight. Talon's reactions were lightning quick, especially when surprised. But Sir Guy had known that too. They embraced hard, both aware that life and its uncertainties could have taken either of them in the last week.

"I had thought you were still up in Tripoli with the Count, Sir," Talon said.

"I arrived back four days ago and was commissioned immediately to help defend the city, as there was fear of an attack by Salah Ed Din."

"The Bishop gave us our due at last at the church of the Holy Sepulcher yesterday," said Talon.

"I wonder sometimes that he had the permission of the Greeks and the Copts to use the church at all!" said Sir Guy with a wry grin. "The Franks have been in control of the church since the Bishop complained to the king that he could not even hold a service without interference from the Greeks or others. There is no harmony within that church! None can agree as to who should be in charge of what. We Christians have no room to sneer at the Muslims and their confusing sects, when our own differing churches cannot even agree on how to maintain the most sacred church in the holy land," Sir Guy remarked dourly.

Talon smiled and shook his head with a shared exasperation.

"I am not concerned about those petty quarrels, Sir. The battle lives still with me, and I wish that it did not, as we were butchers even if it was in God's name."

"You will doubtless be haunted for the rest of your life, my boy, but you should not forget what they would have done to the people of this city had they won, Talon," Sir Guy said. "What you and the Knights did at Montgisard was more than heroic, it was the stuff of legend, and news of it will fly to Europe faster than the wind can drive the speediest ships. The Templars are now assured of a place in the palaces of every King in Europe from Germany to England."

"I am in need of your advice, Sir Guy," Talon broke in abruptly.

The older knight contemplated his younger companion in silence for a moment and then said quietly, "It is to do with the 'Assassins, Talon?"

"It is to do with them, but not of them. I have something I swore I would do when I left Acre the first time those many years ago, before ever I was made a knight, and I have yet to honor that oath."

"Your oath is to the brotherhood of the Temple now, Talon. All other oaths were made null and void when you took the oath to obey the Rules."

"Have I not followed the Rules with care and faith? Have I not fought in battle for the Order and shed my blood?" grated Talon. He turned away and gripped the wall with white knuckles.

"You have indeed, Talon," said Sir Guy with a sigh, "but the brotherhood is not one that you can leave on a whim."

"Sir Guy," said Talon with force, "I am not asking to leave the Temple. I am asking for time to find out what has happened to someone who was... is important to my peace of mind."

"A woman!" said Sir Guy, his tone sharp.

"A Princess! To whom I made an oath of allegiance at one time," responded Talon equally sharply.

"I remember now! You were pining for her after you were captured in Montfort! This is still with you, Talon?" said Sir Guy incredulously.

"It gnaws at me!" Talon responded with a catch in his voice. "I am never at peace, I have never been at peace since I was taken away from her, but now it is a hundred times worse, for I am told she is alive, but I cannot see for myself if it is true!"

Sir Guy watched Talon, reading the anguish and the pain, and pulled on his beard fiercely.

"How can I explain your absence if you leave? You will be named a deserter and excommunicated. I could never wish that on you, Talon. I not only owe you my life but I know you for a singular soldier of this Order. Do you not understand that with your knowledge of the people here and the praise you have garnered for your bravery you could one day be the Grand Master yourself?"

Talon gave a short laugh. "Lord Odo will live for another fifty years, and there are many behind him who covet the title more than I do. Why, I am looking at a man who is already a Seneschal and should be the next Marshall, if not the Grand Master! You have earned that title many times over, Sir Guy!"

Sir Guy gave Talon a rueful smile.

"You always did underrate yourself, young man. Were you not a knight of the Temple I would wager that you would have carved out a whole state for yourself in this part of the world by now!"

"We both know joining the Order was the only way I could manage to come back here without having a rope around my neck!" said Talon tersely. He was alluding to the accusation of witchcraft that had been leveled against him before he had fled Languedoc.

"Ah... on that note I can reassure you that the Order protects its own. I have been made aware of the situation in Acre by Max. The Bishop will be reminded that the Templar order is responsible to the Pope and to him alone. Have no fear, Talon, in that regard."

It was no secret that the Order took in many who were of questionable background. Its need for good fighting men was so great that they were prepared to bend many rules in order to get men out here to this inhospitable country. Once in the Order none could leave except the dead. Some knights even referred irreverently to the Order as the "God's Legion of the Damned. Why is it that we can never have that which we most want in life?" Talon said to Sir Guy

"Those very few on this earth manage to Talon but most of us only catch a glimpse of it from time to time. Talon, you are distraught from the fatigue of battle. It is not uncommon; there are those to whom slaughter means nothing. You are not one of these and that makes you the better man for it, and I pray for God's compassion upon you. However, I cannot just give you my permission for this insane thing you ask of me. I must think on it, and then I shall tell you my decision. In the mean time, please do not do anything that will jeopardize your life in the Temple, nor your soul. Do you promise me?"

Talon hung his head in defeat, but then he lifted his head and looked Sir Guy in the eye.

"I promise to you, Sir Guy, I shall not leave Jerusalem without your permission. But this is my destiny and I shall follow it one day."

Sir Guy nodded, then placed his hand on his shoulder and in a conciliatory tone said, "We are bidden to the palace tonight, I in my role of intelligence and you in your new capacity of hero. You are not allowed to refuse."

"I would prefer not to go, Sir, but if it is your will then I shall go with good grace," responded Talon woodenly.

Sir Guy sighed but kept his hand on Talon's shoulder.

"Hear me, Talon," he said gently. "You could ask the King. Perhaps he will grant this wish. He is the only man aside of the Grand Master who can, and he is in your debt this day. I am not sure that Odo would, but if you persuaded the King then he might relent and give you dispensation. Odo is also well aware of what your contribution to the victory."

He looked Talon in the eyes for a long moment, smiled his crooked smile, then turned and left Talon staring after him.

Talon limped down to the barracks to collect his baggage and head off to the small house where he was billeted. He had the unusual privilege of being one of only a few knights who could live in the town without the company of three others. That too was part of the Rules, but it had been waived by Sir Guy, as he wanted to have Talon able to slip away in the guise of a local Arab from time to time to assess the condition of the city from the other inhabitants' perspective.

Before he went he searched out Vorhert and asked him how he was. Vorhert shook his close cropped head and winced as he disturbed his wounded arm, which he now had in a crude sling.

"I shall have to go and see Bones today or I shall have trouble with this," he indicated his still bandaged arm,

Talon made up his mind.

"If you go to Bones, you certainly will have nothing but trouble with that arm. You are coming with me, and no arguments. Go and get your saddle bags and meet me at the gate shortly."

Within ten minutes they had left the barracks behind. Talon was limping; Vorhert, looking somewhat perplexed, was carrying, despite his wound, all he possessed in the world in his own saddle bags, plus the saddle bags they had picked up in the battle.

At the house which belonged to Talon, located near St Peter's church not far from Zion's gate, they ran into Dar'an, who excitedly asked Talon about the battle.

"Later, Dar'an. Go and put some water to boil for me at once, then go and buy some baklava, and ask the hakim, to come and see me as soon as he can. Ask him to bring his medicines for cuts and wounds," Talon told the excited boy, tossing a couple of small coins to him. Dar'an dashed off to comply with his orders.

Dar'an was now fully attached to Talon. His father had died the week before the army left for the war, and Talon had taken the distraught boy in as his house servant.

Half an hour later Dar'an came back, with the hakim, or doctor, in tow carrying a small wooden box. The doctor was slightly bent with age but his keen intelligence shone bright in his eyes.

"As-Salāmu `Alaikum, Tal'on," he said with a smile. "I hear the Frans had a great victory against Salah Ed Din?" he spoke in Arabic.

Talon nodded and responded, "Wa `Alaikum As-Salām, honored Doctor. The Peace of God be upon you. Can you provide some of your skills on our behalf? Our own leech would kill us with his ways."

The doctor, whose name was Hindrîn Ed Kareman, smiled and said, "I hear that very few of the Egyptians made it out of the field of battle, that the Templars won the day, my Lord."

"It was an act of God, my friend. I truly believe that we could not have won if God had not been on our side that day; we were so few!" said Talon, who really believed that of the battle.

Talon introduced Vorhert, who was sitting on a bench looking pale. Talon had taken the boiling water, removed the blood-encrusted bandages from his friend's arm, then meticulously washed the wound while Vorhert growled, clenched his teeth, grimaced with the pain and swore loudly, but he had had endured it. Talon had then told him to do the same for his wounded leg while he gritted own his teeth in turn.

Hindrîn placed the box on the table and opened it, displaying many small bottles and jars of various types of medicines. After inspecting the cleaned wounds approvingly he took out a needle and some fine thread.

"You have cleaned them well, but the wounds will not close properly on their own, so I shall sew them with silk to ensure that the scar is thin," he said.

Talon grinned nervously at Vorhert.

"Did you hear what he said, my friend? He is going to sew you back together like a torn sheet, with silk no less!"

Vorhert bared his teeth in a frightened grin.

"Do you trust him, Talon? He is a Saracen, isn't he?"

"I would trust the doctor with my life, Vorhert! You have a lot to learn about the people in this part of the world. You have a choice: either him or the Bones in the temple, who will probably want to cut off your arm!"

Talon smiled at Hindrîn as he said this, and the old man smiled back. He also knew the damage the leech could do to men who had only superficial wounds.

"Here, bite down on this leather while he is busy, Vorhert," said Talon, handing him a leather strap.

His friend clenched his teeth on the strap while the doctor completed his work, after which he selected a jar of some particularly smelly light brown ointment; taking a wooden spoon he pasted some over each man's wounds. Then he told them he would bind up the wounds tight so that they sealed shut and were protected from the evils of the air around. He used clean cotton pads and strips of clean rags that he had also brought with him.

Later a much relieved Talon asked Dar'an to find a bottle of wine and to bring out the baklava. These were little cakes made with extremely thin layers of pastry. The boy had brought several different forms of the mouth-watering delicacies; some were made into a type of bird's nest pastry, others were shaped into cylinders, called borma. All were filled with a mixture of pine nuts, hazelnuts and even Talon's favorite, pistachios, blended with honey. They were baked, and then coated with sugar syrup; they were very sweet and had a distinct flavor of orange blossom water.

Vorhert, who was more used to corned salted beef, stone hard bread and the occasional vinegary wine, suspiciously tried one, then exclaimed. His face took on a look of bemused pleasure.

"How do they make this? It is made for the angels, Talon!" He licked his fingers and eyed the rest of the cakes greedily.

"Then let's pretend that we are angels for today, my friend. Eat! They are made for all men, not just the angels."

Vorhert needed no further persuasion.

Later, when all that was left of the food were a few crumbs, they sat around the table and answered the many questions that Dar'an and the hakim asked about the battle. It appeared odd to Talon that the two, who were Muslim and hence should by rights be appalled by the events, did not seem to view it that way. On being questioned about this they remarked that the army had been Egyptian, while they were Kurds. It was different. Talon refrained from mentioning that the defeated Sultan was himself a Kurd.

After they had downed another cup of wine each, Talon asked Vorhert to bring the saddle bags to him. He then untied the flaps and, reaching in, he withdrew a small bag that chinked. Loosening its draw string he let the contents fall onto the wooden table. It was gold and the coins rang as they fell and rolled about on the rough wood of the table. There was an audible gasp from the others in the room.

"This is what Abdul-Baset ibn Kalik left to me when he died during the battle. Vorhert, you were there, and you as my witness know that I have had him buried as a person of the faith should be."

He turned to Hindrîn Ed Kareman, "Honored Doctor, I need to send a message to the Sultan, if he lives, to tell him of the death of Abdul-Basit, who is a distant cousin, to inform him and his family that he was buried near to the small mosque by the temple. This is a right good place to be interned for one such as he."

Hindrîn looked at Talon. "Are you asking me to send a messenger, my Lord?" he asked uncertainly.

"Half the gold on the table is yours if you send a reliable man on a good camel, and the other half is for you when the messenger comes back with an answer, as there will be."

The old man tugged on his beard. "That is more than is necessary for the journey, Lord Talon."

"This is for you, my friend. Pay the messenger what you will, but pay him well. This rest is for you to have and should allow you to make your way home to Mosul which you told me was your family home. Can you do this for me? I gave my word to a dying man."

The old man's shoulders shook and he bowed his head for a few long moments. When he looked up he made no attempt to hide the tears that had sprung to his eyes. He reached forward and seized Talon by the hand and bowed his head over it, and before Talon could withdraw his hand he kissed it, his tears wetting Talon's palm.

He cleared his throat noisily. "You are a kind and generous man, my Lord. As Allah is my witness it shall be done as you wish. In shah'Allah, the Sultan shall know who has done this for his relative."

Talon gave the saddle bag to Dar'an and winked. "Hide it well in this house, my lad, somewhere only one such as you might find it!" They all laughed.

After the hakim had left, with Dar'an escorting the frail old man through the still noisy streets, Talon and Vorhert settled in.

"You are a man of your word, Talon," said Vorhert reflectively. "I wonder if I would have done the same."

Talon clapped him on the good shoulder.

"Whatever you once were, Vorhert, you are now a soldier of God. You would have done the same had you known what to do. Despite the carnage that we were witness to and were part of, we have to have honor, honor for ourselves and honor for our enemies when they are vanquished, or we are no better than savages."

When a man is busy in earnest,
He is blind to the sight of his pain.
Like a warrior in battle, his arms cut and bruised,
His soul does not see what he is doing.

—Rumi

Chapter 13

'Assassins

Talon arrived at the entrance to the palace late. The sun had already settled just above the western hills, a great red ball of fire, its rays staining the remnants of the storm clouds. The slanting light threw the west walls and towers into sharp relief. The torches in their sconces on either side of the main entrance threw flickering shadows all about the walls as the evening breeze stirred the flames.

The guards, alert and professional, were very respectful to the limping Templar auxiliary and turned him over to the captain of the guard who, having noticed the limp, personally escorted him to the main chamber doors, taking care not to stride out too quickly.

The doors were opened by more guards, and Talon found himself in a large but stuffy chamber full of people. Everyone seemed to be talking at once. The wine had been flowing, and the tables looked as though a tribe of starving vagrants had been though. There was food strewn about all over the heavy tables, and some on the floor. Talon could hardly see the king on his throne on the far side of the chamber, it was so crowded. However, people quieted and gave way when they saw that a Templar had arrived in their midst.

Talon was not dressed well. His surcoat was not new—the quartermaster had had none to spare—and his chain mail was rent in places. There had been no time to have the armorer repair it, and he only possessed the one set of armor at present. His wealth was all in Acre. He was conscious of his lack of stylish attire, but there were others of the Order present too, most of them in similar condition, the rents and tears proudly bearing witness to the ferocious battle they had recently fought. They stood on the other side of the room gathered about Odo and the young king.

In the silence that followed his arrival, the captain cleared a way and finally stopped in front of the gathering around the throne. Talon followed more slowly, limping. As he made his way, whispering spread like ripples made in water by a cast stone, and he heard his name mentioned often as he limped by groups of celebrants. Talon fell awkwardly to one knee before the king, aware that the whole room was watching and that it had gone absolutely quiet. The leper King stood up from his throne and walked the few steps towards Talon. He held out his bandaged hand and said in a clear voice that carried in the stillness of the room, "Sir Talon. Welcome to my house. Rise please, and stand before me."

Talon took the proffered bandaged hand carefully and lifted himself to his feet. He was taller than the King, even though the King stood one step higher.

They looked into one another's eyes. The ravages of the disease were already apparent on the young king's face; his nose and cheeks were dead white. Talon felt no revulsion, as he had learned long ago in Isfahan that leprosy was not contagious from mere contact. Then Baldwin spoke.

"Were you a lord or a simple knight I could reward you with gold, land, and other baubles of this earth. But you are a knight of the Order and have no need of these things.

"What can I give to a soldier of God," he asked in a lowered voice, "to reward him for his bravery, and his outstanding service to me?"

Talon gazed into the white face; he thought quickly, then said in a voice that only the king would hear.

"My Liege, I want no reward but that you speak to my Order and ask for me to have time to visit the lands beyond the great deserts to the east of this kingdom. I would visit them to discover for myself if a person who once gave their trust to me and to whom I owe an oath of friendship is still living. Once I have made discovery of this person, I shall return to this land and this Order."

The young king stood back a pace as though to study Talon's face more clearly and seek sincerity. What he saw in Talon's eyes was a tortured man who besought his help.

Talon in turn had time in those long moments to study the young king. Despite the ravages of the disease, in some places the skin of his face was still young and supple, and one eye was clear and intelligent. It stared back at him appraisingly.

"This is an unusual request, Sir Talon. How long would you be gone?'

"A year, my Lord, not less," was his brief reply.

"I am loath to lose one of my best warriors to some quest. But you talk of honor. I shall not pry, because I sense this goes far deeper. I give you permission, Sir Talon." He turned to Lord Odo and said for all near by to hear.

"My Lord Odo, I ask the Order to release this knight from the constraint of the Rules for a period of at least one year so he may travel to the lands far to the east of this kingdom."

He turned back to Talon. "I expect you to record your experiences, Sir Talon, and make full report when you come home."

Talon bowed deeply. In front of all the assembled people he took the young king's hand, and although the king tried to pull his hand away, he held on firmly and placed his other hand over the bandaged limb.

"I shall pray to God that he might deliver you from your illness, my Liege, and restore you to full health again. We have need of a King such as you. May God bless and protect you."

Baldwin looked back into his eyes and said quietly, "Come back to me, Sir Talon. I have need of men like you." Then he turned and walked carefully out of the room, followed by his closest retainers.

Talon did not have much time to dwell upon his good fortune. A red-faced Lord Odo was pushing through the throng and demanding what this was all about. At this point Sir Guy came deftly to the rescue. He moved swiftly to Talon's side, placed his hand on Talon's shoulder, and said to Odo, "My Lord Odo. Talon is going to spy on the countries east of this kingdom. We have a need of intelligence that we can trust as to what the Arab is thinking in Baghdad and beyond. We know so little."

"Why did he not ask of me what he asked of the King?" demanded Odo truculently.

"Because you are a hard-headed Templar, my Lord," laughed Lord Raymond of Tripoli, who had remained when the other nobles had followed the king, to observe with interest the Templars' reaction to Talon's request. "You do not understand the need for information of the enemy, as do I, Sir Guy and Sir Talon here."

Odo faced Lord Raymond with a frown on his florid features.

"My Lord Raymond! I am so pleased that you could find time to come to Jerusalem."

He turned back to Talon. "Perhaps I do not; but, Sir Talon, you should have asked me first," he stated in an aggrieved voice. "But I know Sir Guy. He has his reasons, I suppose."

He turned away to talk with Lord Reynald and his other friends. Lord Raymond flashed a sardonic smile at both knights and said, "I suspect there is another reason for the need to go east, Sir Talon. But I shall not ask, for if you survive you will bring back good information to us."

He sighed. "I can see that Lord Reynald and his cronies will be too difficult to get past soon for access to His Majesty. The success of the battlefield has placed them in unassailable positions as they take the credit for what your knights accomplished. Sir Guy, please allow me to take Sir Talon away for a moment. I have to return to my family, who are demanding my attention."

Sir Guy smiled and bowed. "Of course, my lord. Talon, I shall see you before you leave." He turned away.

The Count placed a firm hand on Talon's elbow and moved him around the crowd towards a couple of ladies. They were admiring a sleek hunting hound that stood in their midst, seemingly enjoying all the attention. As they approached, the ladies noticed the count and curtsied to him respectfully, then cast interested eyes at Talon.

"My ladies, I wish to present Sir Talon de Gilles, a distant relative of mine and one who has distinguished himself in the battle of Montgisard. He was the one who brought the Templars to the battle, without whom it is doubtful that there would have been any victory," the Count said. Talon thought he detected some irony in the Count's dry voice.

Talon bowed respectfully.

The eldest lady smiled affectionately at the Count; it was clear that she was his wife.

"My Lord, we have missed you, but you are forgiven your absence, as you bring with you one of the heroes of the battle. We would not otherwise have been able to talk to a Templar, let alone Sir Talon."

Talon was aware that the count knew perfectly well that a Templar was not supposed to gaze upon the faces of women, so he tried not to stare. Even so, he could not but notice the beauty of one who appeared to be the Count's daughter. She was not so constrained, and gazed at him with bright, interested eyes.

Lord Raymond introduced the women as his wife and daughter. Talon bowed to each but refrained from taking a hand. None was proffered, as they too knew the etiquette for a Knight Templar. However, they made it clear that they wanted to hear from him how the battle had gone and his adventures beforehand.

"But for the bravery of the Knights Templar we would none of us be here today!" said the Count's wife.

"I think that we could not have won the battle without the leadership of the king with God firmly on his side, my Lady," said Talon.

"Sir Talon here is to be released from his vows in order to visit the lands east of this kingdom," interjected the Count.

"Indeed, I am released for the travel, my Lord. But only for a limited time."

As he spoke, another couple walked up to them and greeted the Count and his wife familiarly. After the kisses of greeting on both cheeks by men and women, the count indicated Talon and introduced him.

My Lady Sibylla, I wish to present Sir Talon de Gilles, Knight Templar, one of the heroes of the great battle. Sir Talon, my Lady is the sister of the King, and Sir Guy de Lusignan is her escort... for the time being." His eyes glinted.

Sir Guy de Lusignan obviously disliked this description; but Talon noticed that Sibylla tightened her grip on his arm, and he subsided with a glower.

Lady Sibylla gazed at Talon with wide eyes.

"I heard about your exploits, Sir Talon! By now most of Jerusalem must have as well. You must stay in the city and visit the palace more often, so that we may get to know you better."

"My Lady, I regret that I shall not be staying long. I am to travel east to discover more of the Saracen and to learn of his intent."

"Is that not reckless and dangerous?" asked the count's daughter. "What if you are discovered? Would they not harm you then?"

"It is indeed dangerous, but Sir Talon here speaks the language of the Arab fluently, and he knows their ways better than any of us," said the count. "What would be impossible for any other man of us here, Talon might live to accomplish."

"Will you be gone very long?" inquired Sir Guy de Lusignan in his deep voice that was almost a growl.

"It is a very long way to the land of Persia, and I have to travel over land, as the seas between here and there are quite unsafe, so it could take almost a year, Sir," responded Talon.

The Count kept Talon with him for almost an hour, during which time he answered many questions from the ladies and de Lusignan. But then he excused himself, saying he was tired, and went off to search for Sir Guy.

Before he left, however, the count took him aside and said quietly, "Sir Talon, I do not see you as a fully committed Templar following blindly in all they do, which I have found on occasion to be impetuous and foolish. I am not popular here, but then I have noticed that few of us who understand the "Saracen" are. We are too close to the enemy for comfort, it would seem, and although the King appreciates our occasional useful information, he relies upon hotheads like Reynald and his ilk instead for policy and direction. He should pay more attention to men like Sir Guy here.

"If and when you come back, I have a proposition for you to consider that will be of advantage to us both. Please do not forget to find me when you return, Sir Talon."

He turned abruptly and walked away, as Talon clumsily bowed to his retreating back.

*****

Later that night, Sir Guy and Talon were walking along the Street of Mal Cuisine; ahead was the count of Tripoli with his family and some of the Count's guards, who had come with the Count of Tripoli to the King's reception. The two knights had bid the count good night, but were going more or less the same way; they would take another street further down, whereas the count and his family would go to a small villa near Herod's Gate.

The street was dark and deserted; very quiet apart from the clip-clop of the horses' hooves ahead and the low murmur of conversation betweent he count and his wife. This was odd, even at the late hour, for Jerusalem never seemed to sleep. Talon put a hand on his mentor's arm and said, "Sir Guy, I do not like this. There is danger here."

Sir Guy stood still. He glanced down the darkened street, then asked very quietly, "How do you know, Talon?"

"My instinct tells me that there is danger and we should close ranks with the Count, Sir."

Sir Guy said nothing, instead he quickened his pace, as did Talon, closing the gap between them and the count's entourage.

The Count and his wife and daughter were all mounted, the ladies riding side-saddle, with the count's men at arms before them and behind them. There were a few other men in attendance, some holding torches high to light the way. The men at arms heard the approach of the two knights and called out to the Count a warning.

He reined in his horse and peered back at the two men hastening on foot towards them. He recognized them and called out.

"Sir Guy and Sir Talon! Why the haste? Have you forgotten something?"

"No, my Lord, but Sir Talon here senses that there is danger and—"

Before he could complete his sentence, nine dark figures appeared in the street to the rear of the party.

Talon shouted to the count to protect the women, and he and Sir Guy turned to deal with the four men running silently towards them from out of the dark. They drew their swords hissing out of scabbards and were instantly engaged. Behind him Talon could hear the men at arms yelling and the ring of steel as swords clashed.

He allowed the first man to come in close before he feinted with the tip high for the eyes. The man raised his knife arm to parry, but Talon twisted the point down and stabbed in a lunge with his sword at the man's chest; he felt it bite into the man and grate on his backbone. The long dagger fell to the ground as the men choked and tumbled sideways.

Retrieving his sword Talon took it in both hands and slashed sideways at the second man and nearly cut him in two. There was a shriek nearby as Sir Guy ducked a blow and rammed his sword into the belly of his attacker. His sword got stuck in his victim's spine, so he had to stamp on the screaming man to pull it out. As he did, the fourth dark figure leapt onto him, his dagger raised high. Racing over, Talon brought his sword down on the back of the man, who tumbled to the ground, writhing and shrieking. Sir Guy finished him off with a downward stab of his sword.

The two men glanced at one another, then turned quickly to see how the count was faring. Three of his men were down, but so were three of the attackers. The count could not do very much on his horse in the confined space with the more agile attackers flitting in and out of the shaddows, and two of the dark figures were closing with him. The two women were still on their horses but had been shoved against a mud wall, and their terrified horses were more than they could deal with.

"Watch the rear, Sir Guy! I shall help him."

Not waiting for a reply Talon skipped the couple of paces to place himself between the count and the attackers and stood on guard, his sword raised, facing them.

"You come closer at your peril," he said.

One of the men started.

"By Allah! Who is this Frans who speaks our tongue so well?"

"I know you, Fida'i; leave now and you will live," said Talon.

The man's companion stared in the faint light at Talon. "What have you to do with this Frans whom we have orders to kill?"

"I tell you," said Talon softly, "that he is under my protection, and if you are here to kill him then you must go through me!"

The men were clearly disconcerted. They hesitated. Then one said, "We are fida'i. We have to kill him, and if that means to kill you too, then it is Allah's will."

The discussion cut short. With a shout the count drove his horse directly at the two men, intent upon running them down and stabbing them as they fell.

They both dodged the horse easily and were about to leap up and stab him as he went by when Talon lunged forward and drove his sword though the side of the one nearest him. His victim gasped and fell back, his mouth open in a soundless scream of agony.

Without pausing Talon dived around the rear end of the horse and lashed out at the leg of the other man, who was already clinging to the count, trying to thrust his dagger into the count's side.

Talon's sword almost cut his leg off. With a cry the man fell off the count, his mission uncompleted, and tumbled in a welter of blood to the stony street. Talon followed him down to disarm him, but one of the retainers ran up and stabbed down at the prone figure, driving a spear into the man's chest. There was a convulsion, and the man was dead.

"By God, why did you do that, you fool!" shouted Talon, "Now we will never know why they attacked the count!"

The man staggered back in the face of Talon's fury, babbling, "I thought we had to kill them all, Sir!"

Talon turned away in disgust; just as he did so he saw in the dark shadows down the street a figure slide out of sight. So there had been another, perhaps more. He wished that he had brought his bow; he could have taken a shot at the man.

Sir Guy picked up one of the torches lying on the muddy street that was till sputteringly alight and came up to them, glancing over his shoulder from time to time to make sure that there were no others of the enemy. He held the torch over the two bodies, while Talon kneeling made sure there were no signs of life left in either.

The count dismounted and came over to the two men, shouting at his surviving retainers to face up and down the street and be on guard. The three of them stood in the circle of light cast by the flickering torch and contemplated the bloody bodies at their feet.

Sir Guy was the first to realize that the women folk needed attention. He strode over to the women and said, "My Lady, it is over. The 'Assassins are slain and you are safe now. Do you wish to dismount?'

The count's wife had the presence of mind to retort, "If we should dismount with no one to hold the horses, we would be stranded here, Sir." She was tearful and very frightened, as was her daughter, but they both made a valiant attempt to regain their composure in front of the men.

The count heard this and called out, "You are right, my dear Lady. Stay mounted and we shall leave very soon. Come over here where I can see you better, and the men shall hold your horses."

The two retainers who were left jumped to assist the two women and brought the horses closer. The count looked hard at Talon. "I owe you and Sir Guy my life. But why do you think they attacked us? Were they vagabonds? Were they seeking money?"

"No, Sire," answered Sir Guy. "I heard Talon talking to them. They were 'Assassins, were they not, Talon?"

"Yes, and I think that you know that, my Lord." said Talon quietly, so that the women could not hear.

"You are correct. They murdered my father in this manner, but in broad daylight. They would have killed us all had you not been here," murmured the count.

"By God's good grace we were, but I know this, if Talon had not sensed something wrong, things could have gone very badly for you, my Lord," said Sir Guy. He clapped Talon on the shoulder.

"This is the work of Rashid Ed Din. He knows that Tripoli would be very vulnerable if the head of the county were killed. Not like with you Templars, eh? Kill the Master and another comes to take his place without any fuss."

"It occurred to me that this might be the case, Sir," said Talon thoughtfully.

"If you ever want other employment than with the Knights, Sir Talon, I have work for you. Remember what I said earlier," the count said, and it was clear he meant it.

The two knights escorted the small party to their lodgings at the rented villa and then walked back to the Temple. Both were on the alert alert, as now they were only two and it was quite late. They would make a good target for any fida'i who wanted revenge.

As they walked down the quiet streets Talon mentioned that he had seen another figure leaving the scene of the attack.

"That means that they know how it ended and might even know who I am; we did talk, and he could have heard."

"If the other did hear, then you are now also in danger, Talon. Why do you think that they attacked the count?"

"It is as he said. He is not like the Templars, Sir Guy. Were they to kill our Master we would simply replace him. That would gain them nothing. However, he is the ruler of Tripoli and as such is more like a sultan; his death would demonstrate that his neighbors the 'Assassins were more powerful, and then his descendants would have to pay them a tithe for their protection instead. Rashid El Din is getting greedy." Talon paused. "I am sure there is some other reason though. The Count was evasive tonight."

"You might not have heard, Talon, but his people intercepted a large consignment of gold that was being brought south to the city. We think that the people carrying it were 'Assassins who were bringing the yearly tithe to the Templars."

"Rashid would be incensed if that were true!" said Talon.

"I think it might well be true, Talon. In which case the Count will have stolen from us, his allies the Templars! That is a very bad thing, as we help to protect him."

That night Talon barely slept. The attack of the 'Assassins and then the thought that he was about to embark upon the long journey back to Persia were more than enough to keep him wide awake. He got up from his bed and paced the downstairs room restlessly.

He was finally sitting still in the darkened main room, the embers of the fire barely lit, listening to the small sounds of the night and the snores of Vorhert, when he heard the scrape of something on the door, and then a thump as though something had struck the door a blow.

He reached for his sword and slipped alongside the door and waited, but nothing happened. In the darkness he listened hard for another sound, his senses wide awake, but there was nothing else to alarm him.

Very cautiously he unlatched the door and opened it, alert for the slightest indication that someone might be outside waiting for the opportunity to ram it open and surprise him. What he saw instead made his blood run cold: a dagger plunged into the door holding a scrap of parchment.

He peered outside at the dark street but it seemed empty. Quickly he tore the thin blade free and snatched the paper, then shut the door in one swift motion.

He went over to the fire and blew on a small brand to light a candle with the flame. He then peered at the scrawl on the piece of paper.

It was written in Farsi and it read:

> *Talon the Templar, we know who you are. You stopped the attack on the Count but we can wait. Now you will also die.*

The next day Talon showed the note to Sir Guy.

"It is just as we thought, Sir. They now know who I am, and being a Templar will not protect me any more. Rashid Al Din has been thwarted more than once by me and will not permit me to live to do so again."

Sir Guy was shocked. He gave the piece of paper back to Talon.

"They are very sure that it is you because they wrote this in the Persian language, Talon. Few others in this city know Farsi. What will you do?"

"I was planning to travel the well worn road via Damascus, but now it must be by another way. They will be watching my every move now, so if I do leave by that way they will catch me. I must make it look like I am leaving for Ascalon to the south instead. They might not follow me there, thinking that I must return sooner or later."

Book II

Journey to Persia

I speak of Desert without repose
Carved by relentless winds
Torn up from its bowels
Blinded by sands
Unsheltered solitary
Yellow as death
Wrinkled like parchment
Face turned to the sun.

—Chedid 1995

Chapter 14

A Journey Begins

Talon rode his recently purchased horse, an Arab stallion, up the last rise of the mountain ridge and reined in. He shielded his eyes with his right hand and adjusted his vision to see through the shimmering heat into the distance ahead. What he saw was more of the bare, sun-scorched countryside he had been riding over for the last two days since he left Jerusalem behind to find his way to this remote place, which the guide had told him was the starting point for the journey to come.

Two other horsemen urged their horses up alongside, then halted. The man Abd'allah, the guide who had accompanied Talon from Jerusalem, pointed.

"There is Al-Batrā', the home of my people," he said quietly. "We are on Umm el Biyara. Over there," he pointed to the far eastern hills, "is the Christian fort. We call it Wu'eira. We do not want to be seen by them."

The man had a sword or knife scar that ran from his right eyebrow across his cheek bone to taper out on his cheek. It had healed badly, puckering into a savagely twisted scar that distorted the right side of his face, giving him a sinister look. Talon found him taciturn but polite, so he dismissed the ugliness. They all wore similar clothing: a disha dasha under a voluminous cotton tunic of off-white with a darker abaya, or over-robe, that had seen better days. Each head was covered by a segal, a large loose cloth of mixed woven cotton, with a head band of black goat's hair holding it in place.

Their pantaloons were tucked into calf-length boots. Under Talon's abaya he wore his sword, hung from a stout leather belt that was well made and very ornate with silver decorations. This was the only concession he made to wealth, which is what he wanted. A man in these regions was not respected for wearing too much of his wealth on his person. There were those who would take it off him if they could. However, he was expected to demonstrate that he wasn't poor either. Talon's young companion, Dar'an, was dressed in similar garb, but less ostentatious. The two of them held their restless horses in check while they and their guide surveyed the surrounding country for danger, looking down upon the ancient ruins, their destination.

"I do not see any living thing over there," remarked Talon.

"That is because they have seen us and are waiting to see who we are."

Talon had been told that this was one of the furthest outposts of Outré Jourdan, and he could believe it. From their vantage point they could see the valley of Al-Batrā' and its ruins, but the canyons were so deep and closed in that they could only see part of what Talon assumed to be a large area of abandoned dwellings.

However, what he could see in the distance was spectacular. There were huge columns of rock pillars carved directly into the sides of the cliffs, which were colored a dark ochre. All along the cliff he could see black oblong openings denoting chambers that had been carved deep into the cliffs.

The work was beyond anything he had ever seen before, and he wondered who had created this. On being questioned his guide only shrugged.

"This work was done a thousand years ago when my father's people ruled the land as far as a man could ride for a month in all directions, long before the Arab invasions... and the Christians." He spat.

"Now we cannot even live here in peace, because the Frans in that fort won't let us."

Their guide, who was a Bedul, one of the Nabataea tribe who had lived here since time immemorial, had warned them both not to stray far from him at this dangerous phase of their journey, as questions were often asked after the arrow had flown or the spear had struck.

Talon looked over at Jebal Haroun, the highest peak in the area to the north, and saw a monastery clinging to its slopes. Less than two miles away, just outside just outside the ruins of Al-Batrā', was the fort that had been erected to protect the monks. He could see smoke from cooking fires rising from behind the stout walls, but he had no intention of going there, as he did not want his presence known to the garrison.

Two days ago they had ridden out of the city of Jerusalem like thieves in the night. He had bid Sir Guy farewell at the small gate that was nearest to the Temple, then they had warily made their way down the slope to the main road that led south towards the Dead Sea. He had wondered whether he would ever see Sir Guy or his friends again.

Last night they had ridden past Karak des Chevaliers castle, stealing by like fugitives. The moon had lit the way along the white stone road, throwing its cold light on the massive walls that towered, silent and brooding, over them as they walked their horses, ready to flee should the alarm be raised.

This castle was the largest and best manned fortification in the kingdom of Jerusalem. Its purpose was to guard the southeastern approaches, dominating the caravan routes used by the Arabs who traveled between Egypt and Damascus. However no alarm had been raised by the sentries, who must have been on the ramparts and surely had noticed the travelers; the castle maintained its menacing, inscrutable front in the silence of the night.

It was dangerous to approach the ruins of Al-Batrā', but Talon needed a guide who could take him across the desert along the ancient trade route that led to the south, bypassing the cities of Baghdad and even Basra. The people he wanted to contact were known as the Nabataeans. They were the finest navigators of the desert, and perhaps the most trustworthy. Talon knew they were the people who went into the deep deserts west of the kingdom of Oman, then moved far down to the south, to the city of Ubar near to Yemen. From here they brought back the perfumes known as al-luban or 'the milk'. Talon knew it as Olibanum, the Oil of Lebanon. Its fragrance was much prized by both the Christians and the Moslems. He hoped that they would take him to the region near the Gulf of Aquaba where he could take a boat and strike out on his own, as he the knew the way to Isfahan from there.

Abd'allah nudged his stallion forward and they descended the sandy slope of the boulder-strewn mountain towards the palm trees that marked the ancient city of Al-Batrā', following the baked ridges of the Umm el Bayara along a steep thin path to the Wadi Thugra, a rocky stream bed with a wide base and low, sloping banks. There was no water left in this particular wadi, although there was the persistent sound of crickets in the crevices of the banks. But as they walked their horses slowly to the place where the Wadi Thugra joined with another stream-bed that the guide called Wadi Kharrubet, there were a few signs of water.

There were some gnarled and stunted trees that barely made it to head height; in a few places there were reeds, and they could hear the trickle of water over stones. It was hot down in the wadi and Talon felt sweat running down his back and neck. Abd'allah was tense and watchful; Talon and Dar'an adopted the same attitude of alert wariness. Apart from the click of the horses hooves on the stony path and the light jingle of bits and bridles, there was now no sound at all in the canyons.

Suddenly there was a small sound, like that of a stone being thrown. Abd'allah stopped his horse immediately and called out something in a language that Talon did not understand. Both he and Dar'an stopped their horses and waited. There was another long silence; then a voice responded and a young boy of about twelve came out of the recesses of the canyon and beckoned them forward.

They did so, fully on guard. Abd'allah told Talon in a whisper, "They know me, but are suspicious of you. Do not put your hand near your sword."

The boy spoke and Abd'allah replied, and then led the way forward.

The three of them rounded a corner and entered a small courtyard. Some goats corralled in one corner of the rock-sided courtyard peered at them as they rode up. Talon observed dark recesses cut directly into the rocky hills all around, as though human moles had been at work for centuries.

There were people in the courtyard facing them, so he could not continue his observations. He concentrated on the men. There were six in all, dressed in the dark flowing robes of the Bedouin, although these people were not strictly speaking of the Bedouin, being better known as Bedul; still their ways seemed to Talon to be close enough.

Abd'allah stepped off his horse and, letting the reins trail, walked forward and knelt in front of the lead man, an old man with sun darkened skin, much gray in his head and a long gray beard, who raised his hand in a form of benediction. Talon heard him say some thing to the guide, and then they embraced. Then Abd'allah exchanged words and embraces with the other men gathered around, followed by a short laugh.The men seemed to know Abd'allah well, for their discussion became friendly and animated. They spoke for a few minutes, Abd'allah turning and gesturing at Talon from time to time. Eventually the leader of the men lifted his hand and indicated to Talon that he should come closer. Talon dismounted and handed the reins to Dar'an and walked the few paces; he bowed low and spoke the time honored words, "As-Salāmu `Alaikum."

The man inclined his head and responded, "Wa `Alaikum As-Salām. Welcome to my humble house."

"I honor myself by approaching your house. I am Suleiman al Abbas, this is Dar'an, my servant. Peace be upon you and your house."

"My man Abd'allah tells me that you wish to travel far to the south," the old man said in rough Arabic.

"I wish to travel to Persia, and perhaps even further," responded Talon in the same language.

The old man nodded but asked, "Why then do you not travel the northern routes from Damascus to Baghdad along the merchant roads with the great caravans?"

Talon had expected this question to arise, so his response was careful.

"A man who wants to avoid the robbers who infest that path, along with the hungry and ill paid soldiers who also use that road, would want to use another. I also wish to go further south than Baghdad."

"And where would that be?"

"The kingdom of Oman, where I have an uncle I have not seen for ten years," Talon lied. "I have heard that there is none better than the Nabataean people to navigate the vast wadi and sand seas that are to the east and south of here."

The old man nodded, and the men around seemed to relax a little as though they approved of the flattery, but then a crafty look came into the old man's eyes.

"Look around you. Do you see a people who look like men of the deep desert?"

Talon looked at his former guide.

"I see a man with a very expensive Jambiya in his sash that could only have come from the Yemen. I see other men who might not be traveling anywhere today, nor do I see the ships of the desert either, but if Allah is watching he would see that you do not keep the animals of the tribe here, nor the main tribe. Your people are all around, but most are in the wadi near to the desert today."

The old man looked his approval.

"I would pay in gold for the protection of a caravan going south of Baghdad," Talon added.

He took out a small bag of the gold he carried and held it in his hand for them all to see.

The old man looked hard at the small sack of gold in Talon's hand and seemed to come to a decision.

"You may stay for the night, Kharagi. I am undecided about whether we will take you with us when we leave for the seas of sand." He turned and led the way deeper into the courtyard, where some children had come out to play, followed by women in dark chadors, their faces almost completely covered in the presence of this stranger.

The Hajj clapped his hands imperiously. A woman came out bearing a small pot with a long spout and two small cups; these she gave to the old man.

He poured a thin stream of hot liquid into one of the cups and offered it to Talon.

Talon knew the symbolism of this gesture and felt somewhat safer; with the gesture the hospitality of the tribe came a mantle of safety... for the time being. He accepted the tiny cup and sipped the bitter chai.

"I am honored, Oh Hajj," he said. "May the Blessings of Allah be upon you and your family!"

It was clear that the people here were about to prepare for the evening meal. Talon and Da'ran were shown where to put their horses, and then made their way back to the central courtyard where there was now much activity.

Talon understood that the hospitality of the tribe was a sacred thing; but he could not expect it to last, and he might even find himself ejected in the morning by a hostile people, after which he would be in grave danger. Tonight, however, he and Da'ran could sleep safely, as the rules of the tribe would protect them. The sun shone red on the western hills as the people began to prepare for prayers. The old man led the ablutions and Talon was offered water from a goatskin to do the same.

He remembered how he had been taught; he washed his face, rinsed his mouth and throat and then blew water from his nose. Then he washed his arms up to the elbows, making sure that the water dripped from his fingers to the elbows and not the other way. As his prayer mat was buried in among the baggage, he used his cloak spread on the stony ground.

He stretched his arms towards heaven and repeated the mantra.

"I bear witness that there is no Allah but Allah, and that Mohammed is his messenger."

Then he bowed deeply along with all the other men and listened as the old man recited the Opening.

"Praise be to Allah, Lord of the worlds.
The Bountiful, the Compassionate,
King of the day of Reckoning.
Thee alone do we worship, to Thee alone do we look for help.
Guide us in the Right Path,
The path of those Thou hast favored,
Not of those who incur Thine anger or go astray."

Talon and all the men nearby prostrated themselves with their foreheads in the dust as a reminder that they were nothing but dust to Him.

Talon sat up, kneeling on his cloak, and thought about what had just transpired. He was now completely outside the Christian world he belonged to. The familiarity of the world he was about to enter was coming back full force, emphasized by the prayers they had just performed. If he was to live, he would have to observe the prayers properly at all times.

*****

After prayers, the old man went and sat on a rug near the entrance of one of the caves with his men, and called for Abd'allah and Talon to come. Talon put his hand on Dar'an's shoulder and led him over. They again exchanged greetings, and Talon was shown to a place on the right of the old man; Dar'an, who was treated as a servant by all, had to sit on the opposite side of the circle in the back where he would not have access to the best of the food.

With a flourish of his hand the Hajj offered Talon the food laid out on copper platters placed on a rich looking carpet in the middle of the circle. There was rice and flat bread, and the smell of roasting kid wafted to them with the light evening breeze. Talon carefully took some rice in the fingers of his right hand, formed a ball with it, placed it on a flat piece of bread and then lifted the whole with his right hand and took a bite. He expressed his appreciation politely and elaborately in his best Arabic.

He realized that he was being watched very carefully, but then the old man seemed to relax; sitting forward he too began to eat. The men took this as a signal to relax as well, and the meal began. It was a simple meal of rice, which Talon knew was prized, succulent, fresh killed kid roasted on a fire just behind them, and the ever present flat bread that came with all meals in the desert. There were also boiled lentils and yogurt that made his mouth water.

Talon remembered with nostalgia the sharp taste and loved it. The yogurt had been made that day; it came from a skin he had seen suspended between an A-frame of sticks and shaken for hours to separate the milk. The whey would be used to drink; the rest went towards the yogurt and the dry white cheese that accompanied the meal.

The Hajj was curious. "You do not look like an Omani, Suleiman al Abbas."

"I was taken as a boy from Armenia to Persia, Al Hajj. My uncle is an Armenian Christian who trades in Oman," said Talon both respectfully and carefully. He knew he was being tested and a mistake could mean death."I was trained as a Mameluke in Egypt and converted to the faith, then sent back to fight for Sultan Nur Ed Din. Later I was given my freedom by my master for saving his life, and with his help became a merchant myself. My travels brought me here to Palestine for intelligence of the Franks, may God curse them, and now I wish to go home to Isfahan, as I am tired." He told half truths; Dar'an had been sworn to secrecy and willingly complied. His loyalty to Talon was absolute.

The old man pulled on his beard thoughtfully for a few minutes, then, using the two front fingers and thumb of his right hand, took another ball of food. He did not question Talon's story, instead he indicated that Talon should continue to eat, and they settled into a conversation that covered a wide range of topics.

At one point in the discussion Talon asked him if he had made the Hajj. The old man said, "I have indeed done the Hajj, Suleiman al Abbas; it is mandated that all men should try to do this once in their lifetime. When will you, a merchant, do this thing for God? Or are you only interested in making your fortune?"

Talon smiled back at the grinning old man, whose teeth were sparse in his mouth.

"Indeed Sire, I intend to make that journey once I am in Oman, In shah'Allah. It is but a short journey by ship to the Red Sea, where I can make the journey from the port. Is it hard to make the pilgrimage, Oh Hajj?" he asked respectfully.

"It is hard," said the old man, "But it is Allah's will and so written. We all should all attempt to do it, hard though it might be."

Talon was becoming used again to the flowery language of the people of the desert that contrasted with the sharp language of the Franks. He settled in to absorb the moment.

The conversation shifted to the events that were going on in the Kingdom of Jerusalem and the surrounding countries of Syria and Egypt. Talon was curious about the Hajj's reaction to the defeat of the Egyptians, which was still on everyone's lips.

"We, the Bedul, know about the great defeat of Salah Ed Din, but we are indifferent. Allah willed that he be struck down this time. He has offended God somehow and needed to be taught humility," said the Hajj, with seeming satisfaction. "We neither like him nor hate him. To us he is just another Sultan with great designs upon the world, and the Nabataeans win nothing to their advantage."

Talon was very careful not to let his knowledge of the battle be known. They talked late into the night and only went to bed when the light from the nearby fires died down and the stars were clear in the sky above the canyons. There was an almost full moon, so Talon asked permission to explore the great carvings in the walls of the canyons.

"You may look at them but you may not enter them, as they are sacred to our people," said the Hajj gruffly.

Talon knew that to show too much interest would be considered an intrusion, so he said, "Old man, I will respect your command. I am simply awed by the size and designs. I have never seen such a place before."

"Go carefully then, and Allah protect. The Franks will not be abroad at this time of night. Since they think they chased most of us out of here they have not troubled us, even in daytime."

Talon bid him good night, then with Dar'an in tow he went down the streets of sand that wound between the canyon walls on either side. The moonlight threw the huge columns and ornately carved entrances into sharp relief, with dark shadows in the recesses. Within a few paces of the encampment the night closed in around them and the silence was profound. The only noise was the scuffing of their boots on the sand and the occasional subdued hoot of an owl calling to its mate.

As they walked they stared in awe at the fantastic constructions of ancient temples and tomb entrances. Some were so high that Talon had to tilt his head back all the way just to see the top of the buildings.

They walked through a very narrow canyon at one point and came out in a wide open space with the remains of columns standing stark in the night as though a petrified forest had once stood there. Now they stood on a stone road, and Talon could guess that perhaps the Romans had been here; in one location he noticed a sunken series of stone seats which reminded him of the huge stone works he had encountered in Byzantium: it could only have been a small amphitheater. Behind the columns, etched into the walls of the cliff, were even more huge columns, facades, and entrances that went deep into the rock.

It was very late and the moon was waning. They heard the yip of a desert fox in the distance and once again the hoot of an owl. These sounds only seemed to emphasize the ghostliness of the strange city. Talon was tired and Dar'an was stumbling with fatigue, so they walked back towards the encampment.

The guide Abd'allah was there to ensure that they did not cause alarm, and showed them to a place out on the small maidan where they could sleep the rest of the night away. Talon rolled into his blanket, after first taking his knife out and placing it near at hand. He was not unduly concerned that they would be attacked, as the rules of the desert were clearly defined and they were under the protection of the Hajj, but old habits remain. He went to sleep easily and dreamed of giants who carved stone entrances into high cliffs.

A hand touched his shoulder and he was instantly awake. His knife flashed and nearly cut the arm of the man who had wakened him, then slashed towards the man's throat. There was a startled exclamation, and Talon heard the whispered voice of Abd'allah.

"Oustad, it is time to go!" he gasped.

"Where to?" Talon demanded.

"We go to the desert," was the brief reply as the man stepped back hurriedly, his hand going to his own jambiya.

But Talon forestalled him. "Peace, brother, I was surprised, that is all. It is good that we go to the desert, Allah be praised."

Abd'allah took his hand off his knife and grinned his ugly smile, but he looked shaken. "You were indeed once a soldier or Mameluke. You are not easy to surprise, by God!"

Talon's heart leapt. It looked as though his journey would finally begin. The moon was a distant ellipse on the western horizon when ten men and several women, Talon and Dar'an finally left Al-Batrā'. They rode out along the wadi known as the Siq, the men on horses, the Hajj with his body guard, while the tribal women stayed in the rear keeping up on donkeys. Abd'allah stayed close to the Hajj.

Talon got a good look at the Crusader castle as they went past it in the pale light of the dawn. The guards on the walls could be seen as dark shadows, but they paid scant attention to the small group of riders as they went past, following the wadi. The garrison was probably still asleep or at prayers, Talon decided. The castle was a mean place, square and small, abutting against the forbidding, sun tortured rocks of the cliffs behind it. He didn't think there were many Templar knights in the castle; not even they would want to be in a place like that for any length of time other than perhaps as a penance. The group moved at a deliberate pace that suited the donkeys, leaving the incredible site of Al-Batrā' behind as the sun rose golden in the east.

They travelled for several hours, climbing slowly onto a large desolate plateau then taking a route directly to the east. It became very hot quickly as the sun baked the rocky ground they were traversing. Talon covered his face and told Dar'an in a quiet tone to do the same to protect himself from the sun and dust and wind. They had water skins, but the water at Al-Batrā' was brackish and unpleasant to drink. It was, however, all they had. He hoped that there would be better water at some oasis ahead of them.

The sun was high in the sky by the time they started to descend towards a patch of green that Talon could just make out in the distance. He assumed that this was where the main body of the tribe lived. In this he was proved right, as he could see that although the whole region was a tortured series of winding wadis, this seemed to be the only place where there might be water on the surface.

When they came within a few hundred yards of the oasis some men on camels rode out from among the palms. They were armed with spears and rode cautiously until they could see who approached, and then they kicked their camels into a clumsy canter and started to shout.

They rode up waving their spears and yelling greetings to the men, and in particular to the old man. He greeted them as though he were royalty, and then the whole party moved at a fast pace towards the swaying palms. There they were greeted by a large number of people, men and women in their tribal dress who ululued them into the main encampment. There was joyful shouting and singing as the men waved their weapons in the air and the women chanted the curious li li li sound that shrilled the air all around and made the hair on the back of Talon's neck rise.

As they rode into the camp people regarded him curiously and talked of him as the party went by, but there was no sign of a threat so he didn't feel uneasy. Now Talon could make out the numerous camels further into the oasis and the herds of goats that fed off the sparse grass available around the palm trees. Furthermore, it was clear to him that a caravan was preparing to leave.

Big bundles of possessions were laid out among the black open tents and in the large open space that constituted a maidan for the tribe while it stayed at this oasis. Although the old man had said that they were no Bedouin, or nomadic tribes of the desert, it was clear that these Nabataeans were exactly that and had been for some time.

There was a feast that evening and Talon was invited as a guest by the sheik. By now the old man was beginning to treat Talon as a welcome guest, and the people of the tribe accordingly did the same.

He could observe the womenfolk here. These were blue-lipped women with tattoos on their cheeks. They wore azure robes and did not shield their faces in his presence. They worked the goatskin shakers and baked the bread called nan in the glowing ashes of the open fires dotted all around. In fact there were so many fires they created a haze that clung to the ground in streamers in the cool of the evening.

Some young women were walking towards Talon carrying large water jars on their heads. They walked with a graceful carriage and seemed to exaggerate their swaying; they glanced at him from under their brows when they went past, and Talon smiled greeting. The women smiled back and continued on their way, chattering to one another, and he knew it was about him.

He turned away, as it would not have been polite to stare, and found a man scowling at him from a tent nearby. Talon looked hard at the man, who abruptly turned away and went towards the large tent of the sheik.

After prayers Talon made his way towards the center of the caravan, where he found the sheik surrounded by men. He was seated on cushions, and they were drinking chai from small cups prepared by the colorfully dressed women, who were behind him at the entrance of one of the black tents. It was a large tent that could if necessary accommodate twenty men comfortably for a meal.

He greeted Talon with a wave of his hand and bade him sit with him. "Suleiman, these are my sons," he said expansively. "They will stay here, while I leave for the Oman with only one son. This one!" He pointed at a young man who stared back at Talon coolly as though evaluating him. Talon realized that this was the same man who had glared at him earlier when he had smiled at the womenfolk.

"Absalom, where are your manners!" the Hajj almost shouted at the man, who glowered but said, "As-Salāmu `Alaikum!"

Talon nodded back and said, "Wa `Alaikum As-Salām."

He didn't think much of the young man at this first encounter. There was a brooding look about him, but he dismissed him as being of little consequence.

"Suleiman, you will ride a camel for this journey. You will take your horse, but it is camels we shall be using for the sand."

"I regret that I do not own a camel, my Lord,' said Talon respectfully.

"Allah always provides; we have camels and you can ride one of mine. She is sulky and temperamental, but she is very good on the deep sands." He pointed to the massed ranks of camels across the wide space of the wadi. There were at least a hundred of them; most were the darker working camels, while others of a lighter hue were clearly better bred.

"Absalom, show our guest the darling I have in mind for him. It is Lehlah, go now and get her!'

Absalom was not happy at having to go, and left with bad grace. While he was gone the Hajj explained that the caravan would take about thirty camels with them and some horses.

"Will our horses be able to keep up with the camels, Hajj?"

"Easily until we get to the deep sands of the south; then we will go slowly, so they will be able to keep up, Insha' Allah."

Talon was encouraged to eat. The fare was much the same as the former evening and he realized that it would not change much during the journey, other than to become ever more sparse. There was kid meat, as the arrival of the sheik demanded some ceremony, but the rest f the food was the ubiquitous nan and rice, with green leaves wrapped around small roasted buttons of ground meat and dried fruit.

Eventually Absalom came back with another man leading a female camel by a halter. Her pelt was almost white. She was in very good condition as far as Talon could judge and seemed docile enough.

"Ah, here is your camel for the journey, Suleiman. You must look after her and she will look after you."

"Can I buy another for my companion, Hajj? asked Talon.

"Your gold has already paid for that. Absalom shall see to it that he is mounted too."

The tribe celebrated the arrival of the sheik till late that night. Talon went to his resting place with the sound of singing and the light tapping of drums in his ears.

*****

A solitary traveller arrived at the gate of the secret Ismaili stronghold in Damascus late that night with information for the General Esphandiari. After prostrating himself before the seated General, he repeated the message he had been given by the leader of the 'Assassins hiding in Jerusalem.

The General listened carefully as the messenger described the fight in the streets and the failed attempt to kill Count Raymond of Tripoli that had been ordered by Rashid Ed Din. He derived some satisfaction from the failure, as there was no love lost between him and Sinan. All too often the leader of the 'Assassins in this region had gone against the commands of the Grand Master in Alamut. What interested the General also was that the knight Templar known as Sir Talon had once again been involved in thwarting the Teacher, as Sinan was also known. This added up to a series of efforts that had come to nothing because of Talon.

In retaliation the furious Teacher had placed a watch for Talon in Jerusalem, Acre, and just in case Damascus, but he appeared to have disappeared into the Sinai, evidently on a spying mission for one Sir Guy de Veres for whom he worked. The General knew of Sir Guy and liked what he heard of him. The man seemed to genuinely understand the people of the region and had earned the respect of many.

Now the men at the disposal of the Teacher were waiting for Talon to return to Jerusalem, where he would meet his fate. The general was not sure that he wanted this to happen, but until Talon reappeared there was little he could do for him. He decided to send a message to Alamut and describe the situation to the Agha Khan.

As where the level sands extend
The Wilderness and desert o'er,
And leagues are counted by the score:
Nor can the ocean, in its space,
A warmer hint of freedom trace,
Nor, in extent, can it outvie
The Desert's wide reality

—Thomas W. Wood

Chapter 15

Wadi Buweib al Ghrazwan

Talon estimated that they had travelled in a southwesterly direction for most of the journey so far. The caravan was halted at an oasis that straddled the wadi Buweib al Ghrazwan just west of the caravanserai of Sakakah. In all that time they had encountered no one at all along the way; now there were some signs of civilization, but nothing to indicate that men lived permanently in this sun-bleached land. The camels had drunk their fill at the wells from which sprung sweet water that had once made for a significant wadi. Their loads were lying nearby while the crouched animals chewed on fodder that had been thrown in front of them. They seemed contented with their surroundings and the chance to rest in the shade of the dense cluster of palm trees that dotted the oasis.

During the time they had crossed the desert Talon had found the men of the tribe reserved but not unfriendly. He felt that he had learned a great deal about survival and navigation while in their company, and had discovered the Nabataeans were very much at home in the desert.

He smiled wryly to himself as he watched the camels being tended by the younger members of the caravan. He could now saddle a camel blindfolded or in the darkest night, pull it to its feet by the cartilage of its nose and make it kneel by pulling on its lower lip, heedless of its complaints. He had discovered that one could actually go to sleep on a camel's back as it lumbered along, and he himself could assume several positions on its back: cross legged, or side saddle, or crouched on the front, or simply draped over the saddle on the middle of its hump, he had tried them all at one time or another. He could hobble a camel with a flick of his wrist with its own head rope and dodge its teeth without even thinking, delivering a hefty slap on its nose as he did so.

He sat in the shade of one of the palms and observed the activity of the tribe as others prepared the sparse evening meal. The older men sat in the shade of the trees and talked while they rested. It was a rare pleasure, despite the ever present flies, to be able to relax in the shade of one of the palms and enjoy the pure water of the wells. Most of the time the caravan halted in the empty wasteland they were crossing and the men slept as best they could during the day; tents were only used if they were halted for more than one night, the men and animals only stirring when the fiery ball of the sun had sunk beneath the western horizon.

They had been on the journey for three weeks now, heading east by southeast at a steady pace of roughly twenty miles a day, sometimes more. He had had to contain his impatience at the slow pace, but the camels that carried the loads could not be hurried. His own camel could have far outstripped the others, but he knew he would never find the wells ahead and therefore could not survive the journey without the help of the tribe.

The Sheik Hajj Walid strode over to him; one of the black and tan Saluki hounds of the tribe was following a pace behind, padding along with its head down but its eyes alert. It acknowledged Talon with a brief wag of its tail. He knew that this was as familiar as any of the Salukis would ever get but it was significant all the same. He smiled at the thought and a memory it invoked, then stood respectfully as the Hajj drew near.

"As-Salāmu `Alaikum. God's peace be upon you, Hajj," said Talon, touching his heart with his right hand, meaning "and on you be peace."

The Sheik nodded his head and returned the greeting. "Wa `Alaikum As-Salām, Suleiman." He stood in front of Talon with his feet apart.

"I plan to go hunting with the hawk tomorrow morning, as we are going to stay here for a while and rest the camels before we go through the desert along the Nefud. Would you like to come with me, Suleiman?"

"Indeed, I would be honored, oh Hajj!"

"Good, then we go at sunrise before the sun is too high in the sky. My falcon likes the morning light, and the Salukis like it any time. We shall find small gazelle in these sun blasted hills, In shah'Allah, and feast tomorrow night on fresh meat."

Talon was relieved and happy. He was tired of the camel, it made a fuss about getting started in the morning. Tried to bite him when he fed it and even when he was riding it. When a male camel came near Talon could have sworn the wretched creature flirted with them. However it did no good to ride the horses every day as they would rapidly tire in this land of sand and rock. Although bred to the desert the Nabataeans conserved the strength of their horses as much as possible, only using them for hunting, and then only when they were well clear of the drifting sands.

He and Dar'an rose very early the next morning and hastened to prepare for the hunt. The boy had responded eagerly to Talon's suggestion that he come too, so they hurriedly tacked up the two Arab horses they had brought with them to Al-Batrā' and were mounted and ready to leave once the Hajj had assembled a small hunting party. Talon brought his bow and provided Dar'an with a long slender spear that might be used to finish off a small antelope should they run one down.

They left the encampment and headed south towards the low hills that were the beginning of the Nefud, a bleak area of sun-blasted hills and gullies that might have small game hidden in the folds of the rocky wastes. Talon had asked if there was a likelihood of meeting up with a lion, but the Hajj had smiled and said, "I do not think so. There is not enough game for them here; further north in the mountains, north-east of Jerusalem you will find them, and of course down in Oman."

He knew about Talon's encounter with a lion, having come across Talon washing at one of the wells they had stopped at and observed the scars on his chest. He had asked how Talon had received them. Talon had told him and the Hajj had been impressed. "Allah threw his mantel of protection over you that day!" he had remarked.

There were only five in the party. The Sheik had brought his son Absalom with them; the young man of twenty-two was as eager as the two Saluki hounds that came with the party. The other man was Abd'allah, acting as Hajj Walid's bodyguard. He rarely smiled, and his eyes never seemed to rest for long on anything. Talon thought he might bear watching, but so far there had never been any trouble. Had he not guided them to the tribe in Petra after all?

They reached the foothills by mid morning, and Abd'allah set about preparing the falcon. He then transferred the large bird to the wrist of the Hajj, who looked very regal with his high-stepping Arab stallion and the falcon gripping his gauntlet-protected wrist. The little bells on the falcon's hood tinkled as the bird turned its head this way and that, trying to divine its surroundings.

The salukis ranged well ahead, seeking prey. The party rode to the top of a small mound that overlooked a long low valley with some scrub dotted about. There was the possibility of some moisture in the region which boded well for small game, so the Hajj stopped his horse and took the hood off the bird on his left wrist, then released it into the air with a shout. The bird left his arm with a low cry and began to circle, gaining height rapidly.

Soon it was so high that it was only a small silhouette in the clear cloudless sky. It uttered a cry that carried to the watching men below and then ranged further forward over the valley.

Then Abd'allah pointed eagerly. Moving low and fast along the valley, having emerged from a small canyon, flew a large bird. It looked a somewhat like a crane to Talon, who had to peer through the shimmering heat emitted by the sun-heated rocks of the slopes. But the falcon had seen it and was dropping like a stone.

The Hajj gave a shout and kicked his stallion into motion. The horse needed no persuasion; indeed he leapt forward and galloped wildly down the slope, the Hajj waving his right arm, his robes flowing back in the wind of the run. The others followed as rapidly as they could. None paid any regard to the rocks or possibility of their horses tripping on the rock-strewn slope. The Arab horses were fabulously sure footed and needed no guidance. The Salukis flew after the Hajj, who was now almost fifty yards ahead of the party.

Meanwhile the falcon had struck its victim on the first attempt at a kill. There was an impact and white feathers flew, and for a moment Talon saw both birds locked together falling the ten or so yards toward the ground; but the falcon pulled up and away at the last moment, while the white bird struck the ground, where it fluttered as though a wing were broken. The falcon swept up and around, then descended to land again on the larger bird, which eventually went still, after which the falcon strutted away a couple of paces to wait the arrival of the party. The Hajj pulled his horse up in a cloud of dust and leapt off the animal before it had fully stopped.

As Talon rode up he heard the man murmuring endearments to the bird as he approached it, his wrist held out for it to jump on. As soon as it did he quickly tied the jesses and then slipped the hood over the bird's head, all the while crooning his praise to the creature for its endeavor.

He turned to Talon and exclaimed, "Did you see, Suleiman? Did you see my darling perform? She killed the first time, and so cleanly! What a wonderful bird! Allah be praised, but He has given me a bird to bet on one day. Ah, but God is great! I can win camels with this one!"

Talon agreed. "It was magnificent, El Hajj. You have a fine bird there. A clean kill and then it waits without trying to tear the flesh. Allah has indeed provided you with a good bird and us all with a meal!"

At this moment Talon saw a movement on the other side of the Hajj. In one swift motion he had drawn his bow from beneath his left thigh, snatched an arrow from his quiver and drawn the bow tight. In one moment more he loosed the arrow, which flew past the startled horseman and sped into the rocks behind him. There was a muffled thump as the arrow struck its target, and the gazelle which had broken cover to leap away tumbled to the ground. There was a startled silence as the Hajj stared at Talon in utter surprise, and Abd'allah gave a low curse, his hand instinctively seeking his sword.

The Hajj snapped his head around to stare at the dead animal only twenty yards from him, lying in the dust with an arrow protruding from its ribs and the equally surprised Salukis sniffing around it.

"By Allah, but that was well done, Suleiman!" the Hajj said at last with awe in his voice. "I almost thought... " he left his thought unfinished, but he was looking at Talon with new respect.

"I could not let the chance pass, although I am sure the salukis would have tracked it. Forgive me Hajj, I did not mean to alarm you," Talon said his tone contrite.

The Sheik frowned at him and then bellowed with laughter "You are a true bowman!" he exclaimed.

Everyone was suddenly laughing and joking; the hunt was going well for the Hajj, and this was important. Absalom looked relieved and had a wide grin on his face. He praised the bird and his father's perception at having bought the creature and trained it. Talon noted that there was a subtle lack of sincerity in his voice, and wondered at the relationship between father and son.

He guessed the small animal must be one of the desert gazelle that could survive in the deep sandy and rocky regions almost entirely without water, gleaning all they needed from the sparse plant life that existed in the crevices. It was little larger than a large goat kid but it would make a very nice change from the diet of lentils and cheese and dried meat they had lived off for three weeks. There would be a modest feast tonight.

The dead crane, probably one of the migrating cranes that had been driven off course by a sand storm, was picked up by Abd'allah and handed to Dar'an to carry on his horse. The boy treated it as an honor and carefully arranged the bird so that it would not swing or bruise as he rode. Abd'allah lifted the dead gazelle onto his mount, after having retrieved the arrow and handed it back to Talon; then they continued to move on along the shallow valley.

The low, sun-blasted hills on either side became steeper, and the valley bottom had more stunted trees than before. The heat was beginning to make the men and horses sweat copiously but the Hajj pressed on. He turned to Talon in the saddle and said, "I want to show you what these hounds can do, Suleiman. You have never seen a hound like the Saluki hunting the small gazelle that live in these hills."

Talon nodded politely. He knew all about the hunting skills of a Saluki, having ridden with Rav'an out of Alamut those many years ago when they were both in fear for her life. It seemed so long ago now.... He pulled himself back to the present and listened while the Hajj expounded upon the merits of the hounds, who were now bounding ahead of the party, their heads up, searching for any sign of movement.

Suddenly the lead one with the darker coloring bounced up almost on its hind legs, its nose pointing straight ahead; then with a small yap it bounded off as fast as its long slender legs could carry it. The other immediately bounded off too, racing to catch up.

Absalom shouted a high pitched yell and dug his spurs into his horse. The animal objected to the sudden treatment and bucked once, but then went into a flat out gallop with Absalom leaning over its neck shouting encouragement.

The remainder of the party put spurs to horse and galloped after him. They careered past stunted bushes and low trees, heedless of thin branches that whipped them in their faces. The whole party came out onto a long flat area of ground where they could see for some distance. Ahead of them were the two Salukis racing to cut off a small light brown animal that bounded just ahead of them along the sandy ground. As its hind legs pushed it off it created little puffs of dust that marked its passage along the ground before settling seconds after it was past.

The hunters were shouting and yelling as they pushed their horses harder still to try and catch up with the racing trio a hundred yards ahead of them.

The little animal skittered to the left and then the right, but each time it tried to evade pursuit one of the Salukis was there to drive it back onto a straight course. The end was inevitable, as there was no cover and the two hounds were overtaking it steadily.

The leader of the Salukis, Talon thought it might be the female, raced alongside the gazelle, and as they ran snapped its teeth hard onto the flank of the luckless creature. The gazelle stumbled and then it was all over. The lead Saluki darted at its victim and locked its teeth onto the neck. The two animals tumbled over and over for a few yards in a small cloud of dust. Talon could not see much after that. The second Saluki raced into the dust cloud, stirring it up even more, and then as they rode up he saw the animal lying dead at the feet of the two Salukis, which were standing over it and looking back at the approaching party expectantly.

Again it had been a clean kill and the Hajj was delighted. He descended from his horse, throwing the reins to Abd'allah, and walked slowly up to the two hounds, calling out their praises. He knelt on one knee in front of them and called them by name. Both hounds, heads down, sidled up to him to receive his praise and his gentling hands that ran over their heads and caressed their ears and necks. There were tears in his eyes when he turned to the party and exclaimed, “Allah has given us a day to remember. My children have made me proud today. Suleiman, do you now see why we are who we are and why we the Nabatean live in the desert?”

“I see. Oh great Hajj. Allah be praised, for it is a good life to live,” said Talon sincerely.

The Hajj decided that they should turn for the caravan, as the sun had almost reached the noon point and there would b no more game to find in the heat. It was also time for the midday prayers, which were performed somewhat perfunctorily by the group, as they all wanted to get back to the shade of the oasis.

They took up the gazelle and headed back the way they had come.

It was a cheerful party that rode into the oasis a few hours later. They deposited their booty in the care of one of the retainers and retired for the rest of the afternoon under the shade. There was little fear of attack, but the Hajj was a cautious man and placed sentries about the oasis to warn of any visitors. Talon covered himself in his voluminous cotton clothes and slept with the others while the sun burned its way across the afternoon sky.

He woke when the sun was low in the western horizon to the sound of activity and the smell of cooking meat on the fires being prepared for the upcoming feast. It would be a meager feast, as all would take part, but nonetheless twenty five men and boys would enjoy a morsel of meat that was fresh that evening and all were looking forward to it. Compared to the almost furtive behavior of the tribe when normally in camp, this evening there was joking and laughter.

Talon walked across the sand to the well head and drew some water, which he sparingly used to wash his face and hands before making his way to share the evening prayers with the others.

Prayers over, Talon found the Hajj sitting comfortably cross-legged on a small woven Ghilim at the base of the trunk of a large palm. He was alone and beckoned Talon over.

“Come and sit with me, Suleiman. I would know more of you.”

Talon eased himself down carefully on the left side of the Hajj, not so close as to crowd him but not too far away. "What do you wish to know of me, Oh Hajj?"

A few of the Sheik's men came towards them, looking as though they wanted to share Hajj Walid's company, but he waved them all away except for Abd'allah, who squatted near another tree keeping watch.

"You say you are from Persia and were a Mameluke, yet you look like a Christian. Where did you learn to ride, and that bow of yours is unusual. I have never seen its like before, nor one so well used."

"The bow came from Egypt; a man who is very skillful made it for me. He learned his trade far to the north of Persia among the Turks who use these."

"Ah, the Turks! May God damn them! The Seljuk have ruled the world for too long and given us nothing in return except trouble for my people."

"I thought the Christians caused more trouble for your people," said Talon with a mischievous smile.

The Hajj waved his hand dismissively. "They do today, but they do not belong here and will one day be gone, and then we will have to deal with another people like the Turks. It is hard to stay independent and free."

"You have the desert, Oh Hajj. The Seljuk and whosoever comes after them will not want to follow you out here. They prefer the fleshpots of Damascus, Aleppo and Baghdad, and the great plains of the two rivers, the wide plains of around Konya are better for them than this."

He looked up at the sky through the palm frond above and saw the blazing stars in the sky. The night was well upon them but it did not seem dark with this panoply of light above them. He could clearly see the features of the man seated next to him.

"This is true, but once we too ruled a kingdom larger than that of the Christian king... long ago we Nabataeans, the true Bedouin, ruled from Al-Batrā' to the sea, north to the Syrian kingdom and farther south across the Negev that separates us from the Egyptians, may locusts devour their crops. It was the Greeks who drove us away from the sea, and gradually we lost more lands and people until we are few in number now."

"I have heard that there are great numbers of the Bedouin directly east of the kingdom of Jerusalem, Oh Hajj. Are they not of your tribe too?"

The Hajj seemed in a pensive mood and wanted to talk more of himself and his people. He seemed to have forgotten his original reserve.

"You are right, Suleiman, but they are not of our people. They dwell on the edge of the desert and are a mix of the Arab and small people of no consequence; they are of many tribes. We do not like them; some are also our enemies."

"Why do you feud with others when there is such a need to unite and drive the Christians or the Turks into the sea?" Talon asked, probing.

At that moment Absalom brought them some flat pieces of nan with succulent meat tucked in the middle of it. He placed the food politely in front of them, then bowed and left them in silence.

"Have you fed the hounds, my son?" The Hajj demanded.

The young man nodded and left them to their food, but Talon was struck yet again by the demeanor of Absalom—respectful but also wary, and it seemed even a little calculating. However the Sheik bade Talon to eat and said, "We, the Nabataeans, the other tribes, and even the Arabs who are from the deep deserts of the south, were once united but are now cursed."

"I do not understand, Oh Hajj," said Talon cautiously.

The Sheik spat out a small bone he had been chewing on and indicated with his knuckle the group of men gathered around the fire.

"My son, one of my sons, Absalom, is with me to learn the trade and to understand the desert and its ways. Although he has traveled this route three times he has much yet to learn. But he is impatient; he wants my place and schemes to take it off me one day.

"My sons all scheme against one another to win my favor, as that is all they can aspire to. Only one will take my place. Absalom thinks that because he is with me now he is the favored son. That is not so. I cannot trust any of them. I cannot even trust my brother, who is back in Al-Batrā'. He too would like to take my place, and should he do so, woe betide my sons.

"We as a family cannot trust the other families of this same tribe. Indeed we are cursed, for the hatred and distrust are our legacy from hundreds of years ago. Each tribe distrusts the other and schemes to destroy it, or at least to get the better of it in some way or another. We unite for a short while and then turn on one another like jackals. There has been no one to show us a cause that will unite us since the time of Mohammed himself!"

It was a long speech from the Sheik and Talon wondered why he was being given this lesson in the tribal conflicts.

"You need to know, Suleiman, that it is only because I have taken a liking to you that you still live. If anything should happen to me you would be stripped of your protection because my son covets your possessions; you carry gold, and he is jealous of the woman you smiled at when we were at my camp."

Before Talon could interject indignantly he held up his hand.

"I am sure there was no dishonor to her or to her family, but you are a *Kharagi*, an outsider, and as such just by doing so you have earned hatred. Be warned, Suleiman, sleep with one eye open."

"I thank you for your good advice, Hajj, but I do not understand why I have earned the hatred of your son!" said Talon with some force.

"You are a friend of mine. You ask nothing of me except to come with me through the desert, which, my friend, I still find a little puzzling, but it is clear that you are a man of means and a man who has been a warrior, and that I like. I do not see many of your kind in this life. You interest me." He chuckled and pulled at his beard.

They were interrupted by a call from the edge of the oasis. Suddenly the men by the fire were standing up and looking around tense and alert. The call was repeated.

"We have company!" said Sheik Walid quietly. "Go! Prepare yourself for battle. It is too late for honest men to be abroad."

He is riding forth with ugly men,
To rob and ravish and to slay;
For deeds like those,
You may well suppose,
Are quite in the Tartar way.

—John Godfrey

Chapter 16

Robbers

Talon stood and ran to his saddle and other possessions where Dar'an stood waiting nervously, as he too had heard the alarm.

"Quickly, arm yourself with a spear and stay near to me," whispered Talon. He had no sooner said this than there was a frantic scream from one of the sentries out on the periphery, "We are attacked! Robbers!" his yell became a gurgle as he died.

Dark shadows flitted through the palms, their bare feet making hardly a sound on the sandy ground, but they did not remain silent for long. Uttering shouts and screams calculated to terrify the men of the caravan, they charged the poorly prepared Nabataeans from all directions.

Talon had his bow up and loosed off an arrow straight into the middle of the group of dark figures racing towards them. There was a choked off scream and a man fell writhing, the arrow embedded in his stomach. But the others still came on, screaming battle cries as they rushed forward.

"Quickly, Dar'an, we must find the Sheik and defend him. Where is he?"

"Over there Tal... Suleiman!" Dar'an squeaked, his voice breaking with excitement and fright as he pointed.

"Follow me!" commanded Talon and he began to run.

Together they ran towards where the fighting was at its thickest. Talon stopped thirty feet away and shot an arrow into the back of a man wielding an axe, tossed his bow to Dar'an then drew his sword and waded into the mass of struggling men, shouting to Dar'an to hold his bow ready and to stay close.

After that is was a melee of shouting and screaming men hacking and snarling at one another. It was difficult to see precisely who they were fighting, but the attackers were better armed and more organized than the men of the caravan. Talon could see that some carried small metal shields and even wore helmets.

He managed to cut his way to the Sheik, who had his back to a large palm and was fighting off three men in black robes who were goading him and trying to draw him out. The Hajj had been wounded; he clutched at his side it was all he could do to fend off the men in front of him.

Two of his companions were down, but one of them, Abd'allah, was fighting savagely by the side of the Sheik. He too was wounded, but it was only a light cut that traversed his arm.

Talon disposed of two of the attackers in quick succession and then rammed the heel of his left hand into the third man's jaw before spitting him on his sword.

During the brief respite this gained them, the Sheik lay back against the tree gasping, the dark patch on his clothes growing. Talon quickly stooped down and unceremoniously pulled open his robes. There was much blood coming from a wound in his lower chest. Tearing off a long strip of cotton from the outer robe of one of the dead men, Talon stuffed it into the wound and told Dar'an to hold it there. The frightened boy did so without demur. Abd'allah stood on guard, panting, but he said to Talon, "You are our friend, Suleiman. May Allah praise you for coming to our aid."

Talon grunted acknowledgement but he was concerned for the Sheik.

The Sheik reached out and touched Talon on the arm. "You are a mighty fighter and you have saved my life. I will not forget, Suleiman."

Talon said nothing; he did not like what he could see of the wound and realized that the Sheik might well be dying. He bound it tight with another strip off a dead man . When he had finished, the Hajj laid back with a long sigh as though very tired.

Talon heard men running towards them. He seized his bow from the ground where Dar'an had laid it beside the Sheik and loosed off an arrow at a three men who were running screaming at them and brandishing an assortment of weapons. One man was knocked over backwards by the force of the arrow. On seeing the effect the other two hesitated. Talon managed to send another arrow whispering through the air to thump into the chest of another and then, tossing the bow to Dar'an, he and Abd'allah charged straight at the last man. He turned and ran off into the night.

There were more shouts, and suddenly there were no more of the enemy to be seen. Talon hastened back to the Sheik and found him surrounded by the remnants of his men. There was much shouting and arguing by all the excited survivors. The Sheik was propped against the bole of the palm, while his son Absalom was kneeling next to him weeping and crying out to God at the sight of the spreading bloodstain on his father's lower chest. Others were peering down at the Hajj, simply trying to see and generally getting in the way.

Talon did not join in. He was looking for any of the attackers who might still be living. He cautiously moved towards the outer perimeter of the encampment. There was one on the edge of the oasis who was trying to crawl away. He was wounded in the side and his leg had lost a lot of blood.

Talon strode over to the man, and holding him still with a knife at his throat he searched the man thoroughly for weapons. Finding none other than the man's rusty sword nearby, he dragged the now wailing and weeping man back to where the Sheik and his men were gathered, still shouting and discussing the recent attack.

There was silence as they saw what he had brought with him, and then men started shouting abuse and threats at the wounded man, who cowered in a bundle at the feet of the men where Talon had thrown him.

Absalom took his attention off his father long enough to tell someone to get the fire going. He wanted to see what kind of offal had landed in their midst. One man was so incensed that he tried to attack the wounded man with his knife, and it took a hard slap from Abd'allah and the restraining arms of his companions to keep him off.

He screamed, "My brother died tonight and blood will be paid for in blood! I shall have vengeance before Allah! Do not protect him from me." He wept while he wrestled with his companions.

Abd'allah with icy calm, told him, "Be patient, Omar, all in God's good time. This man is wounded and will not live long, but we want to know who these people are before we send this offal to his death."

Absalom kicked the wounded man hard in the side, eliciting a scream of agony. The man writhed with the pain and clutched his wounded side.

"Who are you? Why did you attack a peaceful caravan? Do you not know the rules of hospitality? We would have welcomed you to share the water and eat our meat. Speak, you goat's dung!" he administered another kick.

Talon wondered if the man had passed out, as the response was only a whimper. But then he whispered, "I am resigned to my fate. Send me to the other side as I shall tell you nothing." He spat and then sagged onto his back.

Absalom became incensed and kicked him again and again. He then decided to be more refined about it. He glanced at the now blazing fire and snarled, "Heat the irons in the fire! We will be avenged upon this man for my father's wounds and the death they have brought to us."

While they waited for the irons to heat up he had the man stripped down to his dirty loin cloth and tied to the trunk of a palm tree not far from the one where the Sheik lay semi-conscious.

Talon decided that he need not watch what was going to happen next, but he was also worried that while the tribe was indulging in the torture of the hapless victim the attackers might be regrouping. Taking Dar'an by the elbow he strode to the outer limits of the oasis and stood silently next to the wide trunk of a palm, searching the dunes and low hills beyond for any kind of activity.

From behind them there came a hideous shriek as the vengeful men proceeded to extract every morsel of information they could from their luckless prisoner. Dar'an flinched and looked up at Talon's impassive face.

"These people attacked us without provocation, Dar'an. They broke all the rules of the desert and the hospitality of the oasis. Where there is water men must put aside their differences. There is justice in this, although it is not good to witness," he told the boy.

There was another shriek and some distant laughter. The men were getting into their stride.

With only the stars to light the darkness Talon and the boy silently walked the perimeter of the oasis, watching the shadows and the hills for any sign of the people who had attacked them, but the bare stony hills were impassive and gave away nothing. The high dunes to the east and north did not betray any movement on their smooth slopes that glistened in the starlight.

But then a slight movement to the west, down the rocky furrows of the wadi, caught Dar'an's eye. He stopped and put his hand to touch Talon's robe indicating that he too should stop. Talon halted instantly and they crouched next to a tree and listened, their entire attention on the wadi in front of them. The distracting screams of the tortured man could still be heard, but they were now muted and weaker. He was being sent slowly to meet his maker as painfully as Absalom and his men knew how.

Talon heard the click of a stone and went down on one knee. He held his hand back for the bow and then sidled into the darker shadow of a bush, pulling Dar'an into the darkness behind him. He notched an arrow and waited.

A shadow slipped out of the rocks sixty yards ahead and started moving very cautiously towards him, others following stealthily behind him. Talon realized that they were about to attack again.

He aimed carefully, then let loose the arrow. It whispered through some leaves and struck the man square in the middle of his torso. The force of the strike drove the man to his knees; he looked down at himself and began to scream. The other shadows hurriedly sought cover but not before Talon had dropped another with an arrow in the back. The first man continued to scream and then fell forward and writhed on the ground. Talon dragged Dar'an up by the arm and they ran crouched low back to the deeper cover of the palms.

There was total silence in the darkness surrounding the caravan. Then men from the tribe began to run swiftly and silently towards Talon and Dar'an. He recognized two of them as they came up before they even saw him, and he whispered to them to stay down and not to make so much noise. The two surprised men obeyed, then whispered back to the others that they had found Suleiman.

Talon waited, watching the front. Eventually Absalom crept forward and was shown where Talon and Dar'an were lying. He came up quietly and whispered, "What happened?"

"They were coming back but I killed two of them with arrows, and now they are down the wadi waiting for another opportunity... or they might have gone."

"You are a great warrior, Suleiman. I thank you for saving my father."

"He is badly wounded and needs to be tended or he will surely die," said Talon, thinking that the wound was such that he doubted if the Sheik would live to the next day. It would not do to let Absalom know this just yet, he decided.

"I do not know how to treat a wound of this kind," said Absalom in an agonized whisper.

"I shall go and see if I can help him. I have learned lessons from battles that might be useful," said Talon. "Keep an eye open here with your men. Stay here for some time, as they might be foolish enough to try again, but I do not think they will return tonight. It has been an expensive one for them."

"They lost eight men, and we lost six and four wounded, including my father," said Absalom venomously. "Allah curse them for this. May a plague of locusts swarm over their genitals and their women die of the pox!"

"I will go and see your father," said Talon.

He eased himself back from the low ridge overlooking the wadi upon which he had been lying and waved Dar'an along with him.

As they walked back to the caravan Talon said very quietly to Dar'an, "Go and make all our equipment ready. Find our horses and saddle them. We leave tonight. Do not be seen."

The surprised boy simply stared, but grasping Talon's bow he ran off silently to carry out his instructions.

Talon found the Sheik lying almost where he had left him, but this time he was on a makeshift bed of rugs and blankets. Abd'allah and one of his men were kneeling near by, watching over him. Glancing over at the next tree Talon could see the almost dismembered body of the former prisoner. Absalom and his men had mutilated him beyond recognition; their rage had made them savages.

The Sheik Walid seemed old and frail under the covers. His face was pallid, his skin parchment-like in the starlight. He was very weak, but when Talon came and knelt over him he still raised a hand in feeble acknowledgement.

"I have come to dress your wound, Oh Hajj, if you will allow me," said Talon respectfully.

The Sheik made no argument and allowed Talon to open his robe and examine the wound by the light of a firebrand that Abd'allah hastened off to bring to him.

In the sputtering light Talon could see that although the worst of the bleeding had slowed, the rag bundle he had placed on it was sopping with the Hajji's blood. The wound was deep and still seeped blood in dark rivulets down his torso. Talon feared it might indicate a vital organ had been struck. Nonetheless he placed another thick wad on the wound and with Abd'allah's help tied another bandage around the Hajj's body tightly to hold it in place and to close the wound as best he could.

The Hajj asked for water, which the other attendant ran off to find, and when the Hajj noticed they were almost alone he lifted his hand and indicated that he wanted Talon to draw closer. Talon knelt and the Hajj whispered something. It was too faint for Talon to hear so he put his ear closer to the Hajji's mouth. The old man whispered.

"I am dying. I can feel my limbs becoming cold. You tried to save me and perhaps did save the caravan. For that I shall beg Allah to bring blessings down upon you. But remember what I told you today, Suleiman. Trust no one but Abd'allah. You should head north by northeast. Make for Baghdad if you can. It will be very hard, but you have learned well the navigation we taught you. Farewell, my friend."

Talon said nothing. Instead he took the cold hand of the Hajj in his and squeezed it in a gesture of acknowledgment.

The attendant had come back with the water and now stooped over them, offering it to the Hajj, who sipped a little and then lay back exhausted. Talon covered the Hajj's torso with a blanket and stood up. He nodded to the two men and walked as casually as he could towards where he thought Dar'an would be with the horses and their baggage. Fortunately they were far enough away to be invisible in the dark to the two men attending the Sheik. Almost all the other men were with Absalom waiting for another attack.

Little enough though their possessions were, the gold was vital for his journey and he needed to make sure it was with them when they left, as leave they must. He had already suspected that, and now Sheik Walid had confirmed the need for haste.

He found Dar'an almost finished. The two Arabs horses were fully loaded with the saddle bags and their weapons. Dar'an had even had the presence of mind to make sure that the items they needed most were loaded, while he had discarded the excess that could have been carried by a camel. Neither had he had neglected to ensure that they had full skins of water. Talon blessed the boy silently.

He would have rather taken a camel across the desert, but he knew with certainty that they would be followed, and the only way to put distance between them and their hunters was to use horses. He hoped fervently that they would get across the sandy wastes ahead of them without losing an animal.

He slipped silently over to the horse lines where the remainder of the horses were tethered. There were only four there. He took them all by their ropes and walked them quietly to where Dar'an was standing, then handed off two to the boy. They mounted up and began to walk the horses in a northerly direction. He hoped that they were far enough away from the western edge of the oasis, where Absalom and his men were watching, to avoid detection. He realized that they would not get far before the alarm was raised, but hoped that their lead would be sufficient to keep them well ahead of any pursuit.

He was wrong. A man stepped out of the shadows and challenged them almost immediately. He was one of the men whose loyalty belonged to Absalom, and he sounded very suspicious. He came from Talon's left side holding up his spear and pointing it directly at Talon, who had his own horse's reins in his left hand while in the other he held the ropes of the two horses he was leading. There was nothing else to do but take evasive action. Talon gave his horse a sharp dig with his spur on the left side making it dance off to the right with an indignant snort, and then with a shout Talon called Dar'an to follow him.

The man with the spear also shouted and tried to lunge at Talon but missed, and then he had to dodge out of the way as the two following horses came by.

He shouted, "Absalom! The Ferengi escapes! He is getting away! Help!" The man flung his spear after the retreating horses, but it fell harmlessly to the ground behind them. Within seconds they were on the outskirts of the wadi and galloping wildly out onto the starlit desert.

Talon held onto the ropes as hard as he could, but his horse was plunging wildly forward and the following horses were dragging him backwards. Talon could no longer hold the two horses, but they were now scared and running anyway and would take time to recapture, so he let them go, then drew his sword and slapped the nearest with it hard with the flat of the blade. The animal promptly galloped further off into the desert with its companion following hard on its heels.

Talon looked back and saw Dar'an in the same predicament, so he circled round and seized one of the ropes from the boy and led the way off to the north.

Behind them he dimly heard the sounds of alarm. The shouts and threats receded as they galloped deeper into the rocky terrain till they were finally alone and the only sound was that of the horses' hooves. When they came to a high sandy knoll Talon halted long enough at its base to hand back the rope to Dar'an and tell him to keep following the North Star.

"I shall wait and see who comes after us and meet you about five miles further on. Wait under cover for me," he told the boy, who did not argue but lead his horses on in the northerly direction indicated by Talon.

Talon then drove his horse in bounds to the top of the knoll and looked back the way they had come. As he had suspected, Absalom had sent men after him. No doubt he believed that he could still take what he wanted from Talon, and that it would be easier to kill him and the boy in the open rather that abuse the hospitality of the desert while they were still within the protection of the oasis as the rules of the Bedouin dictated. Talon decided that the Sheik must have died.

There were four of them and they rode camels. They carried long spears and he suspected they might have bows too. He estimated that they would take about fifteen minutes to reach him; he needed to make the best of the element of surprise. The first dim shards of light were showing in the east, which would help him, as he needed light to shoot by.

He plunged his horse down the knoll in a flurry of sand and waited on the north side for the first sign of his pursuers. It was not long, as they were pushing the camels hard. The sound of their urgings and the slap of their sticks on the rumps of the animals sounded loud in the quiet desert air.

One of them called to the others, his voice carrying clearly to where Talon sat his horse.

"Hurry, we must catch the *Ferengi*! Absalom promised us sport with them and we share their wealth. The Sheik cannot protect them any more."

He waited until the four men trotted by on their swaying chargers, and then, when they were clearly silhouetted against the pale gray of the dawn, he shot the last rider. The twang of the bow string almost coincided with the thunk of the arrow as it embedded itself in the man's back. He gave a gasp, tried to reach back and touch the arrow, and then fell off his camel. The others were concentrating so hard on the trail they followed that for a few seconds it did not dawn on them that anything was amiss. That is when Talon shot the second man out of his saddle. He died with a scream on his lips, and that got the attention of the other two.

Talon rode his horse out of the shadows of the knoll and shouted to them to stop or he would kill them too. They drew their camels to a halt and turned to face him. Both realized that he had the advantage of the light and that they were facing death if they tried to do anything. His reputation with the bow was now well known to all of them.

One of them, it was Omar, tried to talk him into going back with a wheedling tone. "Suleiman, the Hajj told us to find you and ask you to come back with us. Why do you think you should leave us now, Suleiman? Have we not treated you with honor and courtesy? Why do you abandon us like this?"

Talon remembered the fate of the prisoner and the oath that Omar had sworn before he killed the man.

"I know the Sheik is dead, or you would not be pursuing me. I do not trust you or Absalom. But I do not wish to hurt anyone else, Omar. Go back to Absalom and tell him that if he sends others after me they shall meet the same fate as your two companions."

For a long moment the two men stared at him, and then the other said venomously, "God's curse be on you, *Ferengi*. I wish the Sheik had not taken you in. Absalom was right; you have brought death to our house. We should have killed you long ago. Go, and may Allah strike you with the madness of the sun before you get to new water."

Talon did not answer. He rode in a wide circle around the two men, who had made their camels crouch while they retrieved the bodies of their dead companions. He rode up to the two camels that were standing aimlessly in the sand abut two hundred yards away from the others and took their ropes. He talked to them and gentled them as he took them away with him. The camels, although they didn't like the horse smell, didn't resist him and followed in a docile walk as he led them off, followed by the curses of the two encumbered men.

An hour later he rode towards the shadows of an overhang and Dar'an came out to meet him, still holding one of the other horses. The boy exclaimed with delight at the sight of the camels, because he too knew the dangers of relying upon horses alone.

Talon grinned at Dar'an. "We will need the camels more than extra horses, Dar'an. We will take the horses with us until we have some distance and then let them go. It is the camels we want for the journey ahead."

He led the way into the silence of the sand and rock of the northward part of their journey. He wanted to put as much distance between him and the oasis before it became too hot to go on. They would travel at night once they had rested up.

He estimated that with the Sheik either dead or dying slowly and the loss of so many men, coupled with the added deterrent that Talon had demonstrated, Absalom might want to consider very carefully what his options were. Pursuit might not be the best one at this point.

The silence of the desert settled in around them and they rode on into the north, keeping the now rising sun to their right. Talon listened to the hissing of the shifting sands of the great dunes they were riding into and felt a little tug of apprehension. Their horses, although bred for this country, were not as capable as camels of negotiating or even enduring the waste lands they would have to cross. He hoped that the camels were up to the task ahead.

He shifted their direction slightly towards the east and began to watch their tracks in the sand as the last stars disappeared and they took the new direction. The great ball of the sun lifted above the eastern horizon rapidly and it was not long before both Talon and Dar'an felt its heat. They covered their heads and faces with their long cotton head cloths, leaving only their eyes exposed. Talon felt the sun suck the very moisture out of his mouth within minutes. He watched a scorpion hurriedly burying itself in the sand as they rode by. It knew what was to come.

Talon paused on the top of a large dune to take his bearings. He saw in the distance a cliff of rock that stuck out of the side of a gigantic sand dune and decided that that was their destination for the day. He prayed that the tribe would not follow them into this furnace.

The sun was burning the sky white when they made their camp. The small cluster of rocks at the base of the overhang provided only just enough shade into which they could crawl. The camels were made to squat then tied down, and the horses were given some of the precious water from the skins that had been tied to their saddles and hobbled. Then Talon and Dar'an covered their heads with their cotton head cloths and tried to sleep.

For your sake, I hurry over land and water:
For your sake, I cross the desert and split the mountain in two,
And turn my face from all things,
Until the time I reach the place
Where I am alone with You.

—Al Hallaj, *Poetry by Al Hallaj*

Chapter 17

The Desert

Talon woke suddenly and lay still, listening hard. His instincts told him that something was wrong. He carefully raised his head and looked about him. Dar'an was still asleep. The cool of the evening had allowed him to slip into a deeper slumber. At first Talon thought it might simply have been the fact that it was now evening and time to move on that had awakened him, but when he looked at the horses and the camels he realized that it was more than that. Their attention was focused on something just outside his line of sight.

In one swift motion he reached for his bow and notched an arrow while rising to his feet. Then he slipped over to the corner of the overhang and peered out. He heard the faintest of sounds and then nothing. The silence of the desert was broken only by the sound of a camel's stomach rumbling and the grate of teeth as it chewed some cud. None the less the attention of all the animals was concentrated back along the way they had come the night before. Their ears were hooked forward and they stared as one at something back along the trail.

Talon stood still and waited. He contemplated waking Dar'an but realized that he would lose precious time should an enemy show just as he was doing so. There was another sound, this time the light thump of a camel's feet as it came walking slowly towards the encampment.

Soon Talon could make out the animal and its rider walking cautiously towards him along the sandy defile. There was only one in sight but Talon was taking no chances. As the man came by him, his eyes on the camels ahead of him and not noticing Talon hidden in the shadows, he called out in a low voice, "My bow is drawn and aimed. Now make your camel stop and sit."

There was a surprised exclamation and then the figure on the camel said, "Suleiman, it is I, Abd'allah, do not shoot your arrows. I come in peace!"

"Do as I tell you!" said Talon sharply.

Abd'allah hastened to comply. He forced the camel protesting to its knees, and then waited, sitting rigid on the saddle.

"Are there others?" Talon demanded sharply.

"No, I swear by Allah's grace it is only I."

Talon noticed that Dar'an had woken up and was standing just behind him with his spear ready.

"Why have you come?" Talon asked, peering into the darkening south, searching for others who might be lurking behind and waiting the opportunity to attack while he was occupied with Abd'allah.

"The Sheik, may Allah be kind to his soul, has taken the difficult path to the other side and must now make his peace with God. Before he went he told me to stay with you, saying that you are a great warrior and I should serve you as I had served him."

Talon released the tension on the bow and with a nod to Dar'an he indicated that the boy was to go and take the camel.

"And do you want to serve me, Abd'allah? Do you agree with the Sheik? I would know what is in your heart despite his command."

"I have seen you fight, my Lord, and I know that you are a warrior. I am a warrior as well, with nothing but contempt for the son. I would serve you if you will have me."

"If this is true then you are welcome, Abd'allah. I mourn the Hajj, as he was a great man. But if you are lying then before God I swear, you will regret it very slowly till you are sent to the other side."

Abd'allah dismounted and walked cautiously towards Talon, who was still watching him carefully for any signs of treachery. He kept his hand on his knife, the bow still in his left hand down by his side.

To his surprise Abd'allah went to his knees and prostrated himself to Talon.

"If you will have me as your poor servant, my Lord, then as Allah is my witness I am yours to do with as you will. If I betray you then treat me as a dog and kill me, but believe me when I say I am here to serve you, oh noble warrior."

"I cannot help but notice that you have the Sheik's Jambiya in your possession, Abd'allah. Did you then steal it as he lay there in his own blood?" Talon did not hide his contempt.

Abd'allah got to his feet slowly, his face darkening with anger. "The Sheik, may God see him safely to Paradise, gave me this Jambiya as a mark of his trust and honor, my Lord. As God is my witness this is the truth. He did not want to give it to his son, who would have used it to make himself the Sheik of the tribe." He spoke this slowly and then said, "I shall put my life in your hands my lord. If you do not trust me nor believe me then send one of your arrows to my heart now."

Talon stared for a long moment into the man's eyes and then nodded soberly. "I believe you, Abd'allah, for your are a man and a warrior. Forgive me for my suspicion; we have been betrayed once and I am wary of this happening again."

Abd'allah seemed to relax a little. "My lord, there is nothing to forgive now I am your servant." He went down again on his knees in front of Talon.

Talon was uncomfortable. "Stand as a man should, Abd'allah. I am no Sheik, and I would you were my companion in arms. I have seen how you fight. Now tell me what has happened and why you no longer wish to stay with the Tribe."

Abd'allah stood and dragged his hand across his brow as though to wipe something away from his mind then said, "Because I belonged to the Sheik, body and soul, I could not be safe with Absalom, who knows my loyalty was only to his father. If he had trusted me I would have served him, as he is the son of the Sheik and could become the leader himself with good guidance. But I overheard their treachery against you that went against the orders of the Sheik himself, and then his words after his father died. There was no respect for his father and it angered me. My time was going to be short, as Absalom never liked me. As God is my witness he is not fit to follow in his father's footsteps."

Talon glanced up at the night sky. The stars were beginning to shine and the constellations were starting to become clear. A light wind moaned among the rocks and the sand hissed on the peaks of the dunes.

"We must leave at once. You can tell me the rest while we travel," he said. "Do you know if you were followed?"

"I left while the tribe was asleep, even the guards. If the robbers come back they will have but to walk in. Absalom is no leader, my Lord."

Their breakfast was meager: some dried nan and a handful of damp cooked rice. There was nothing else. They all took a small sip of water although the impulse to take more was strong. They mounted up on the camels and, lead the horses, set off northwards keeping the North Star just on their left.

The wind had picked up and now drove stinging grains of sand into their faces. They covered themselves with their shemaghs, the long head cloths that covered their faces leaving only their eyes uncovered to peer out through slits. The camels seemed unaffected but Talon could tell that the horses suffered.

Other than the whispering wind the desert was quiet, all that could be heard was the hissing of the sand on the tops of the huge dunes, the quiet thud of the camels' pads and the rumble of their bellies. Talon wondered how long they and the horses could go without fodder.

He rode closer to Abd'allah and they talked some more. Abd'allah it turned out was not of the tribe. He had come to the Sheik through a business transaction that had included him as an orphan. There were many these days, for the wars had shattered families the length and breadth of the Palestinian land. The Sheik had taken him into his tent as a boy slave. Over time he had proved himself worthy of the Sheik's trust, cemented when he had saved the Sheik's life in a brawl between tribes. The Sheik had made him an honorary son, but Abd'allah pointed out that had not been the kindest thing he could have done.

"The sons of the Sheik went out of their way to make life miserable for me when I was but a boy, as I was the newcomer, but I survived, and moreover proved that I was a capable warrior when I grew into a man," he said, fingering his ugly scar they learned to leave me alone.

"The Sheik's death meant that my allegiance to the tribe was severed. They are mostly good people, the Nabataeans, my Lord. Do not, I pray you, judge them by Absalom's actions. But I knew my life was in jeopardy, so I collected food and skins of water and placed them ready to take when I left."

He volunteered that he knew the navigation methods of the Nabataeans and would be able to take them to Baghdad via the wadis with water and the obscure wells along the way. He pointed out they might not survive without this knowledge. By way of demonstration he drew out of his robes a knotted string and the board that Talon had seen the other men use to locate their position relative to the stars.

"What is that called?" asked Talon.

"It is known by several names, but the most common is kamal," said Abd'allah. He showed it to Talon as they rode. It consisted of a small rectangular board with a hole in it through which a long leather string had been passed. There were knots at regular intervals along the string.

He held the board towards the horizon and put one end of the string between his teeth, then stretched the string between the board and his teeth. He moved the board along the string towards a star that he had formerly pointed out. There was a knot placed at this point and He called the distance he measured a number of 'Isba' and said that this gave him the exact altitude of the star.

"With this we can always know our position with respect to the North Star and keep our sense of direction."

He also showed both Dar'an and Talon how to use their fingers to assist with the same navigation, but said that the kamal was more accurate.

The swaying of the camels and the silence was hypnotic. Several times Talon felt sleep creeping up on him. Dar'an almost fell off once, so Talon told him to ride nearer and tied him to the saddle so that he could not fall off.

Talon was still not completely sure of Abd'allah, so he forced himself to stay alert. He also kept an eye on the direction they were taking and constantly looked back to check for pursuit as they climbed one monstrous dune after another. The camels with their large padded feet made relatively easy work of the soft sand both up and down, but the horses floundered after them, making heavy work of the soft-sided sand dunes. On more than one occasion Talon considered just letting them go, but he was reluctant to do so.

The wind abated somewhat late that night, only playing across the crests of the dunes, and the silence in the depressions became if anything more oppressive. The small party plodded on. The view ahead was one of dark waves of the huge sand hills like a petrified ocean. The land was featureless other than the wind distorted shapes of the sand mountains that sometimes had a small cloud of fine dust and sand spraying off their tops.

The thirst came to torment them and they each sucked a small round pebble, not daring to take more water until they stopped. The light wind tugged at their robes, penetrating the thin fabric. It became very cold, as though the night were sucking the heat out of the sand. Talon shivered and wished for a sheepskin to wear under his outer cotton robes. He pulled his shemagh tighter around his neck in a vain attempt to keep warm.

Abd'allah rode closer to Talon, who watched him out of the corner of his eye while his hand strayed to his dagger.

But the Bedu wanted only to talk. "My Lord, two days ride from here there should be a well. It is not well marked, so we have to make sure we reach it in daylight and do not ride past it, as could happen easily in the darkness."

"Will you not recognize it in the dark? The stars are so bright it is almost daylight; even now the view is clear."

"A man who is not paying attention can ride past a well that is only a few hundred yards away without noticing. The next water is at a wadi three days ride beyond, my Lord. We will die if we miss this one. I am not confident that I can recognize it in the dark, as it is several years since I came this way with the Sheik. We were on our way to Kabala al-Muqaddasah."

"Is that not the shrine of Husayn ibn Ali?" asked Talon.

"It is indeed, my Lord. We are on the only path from the southern desert to go directly there."

They stopped at roughly midnight to rest the camels, to take a miserly sip of water through parched lips, and to provide the same to the animals. While Dar'an was tending to the camels, Talon noticed that one of the horses was not doing well and pointed this out to Abd'allah. It was the mare and she was panting, although it was cold, and seemed in some distress.

Talon looked over the other horse, but it appeared to be doing better. The camels stoically sat and groaned quietly to themselves. Their stomachs rumbled. They were hungry but could manage until they reached water. The forage would have to wait; as long as they could provide water to the animals they might survive, thought Talon, but he was uneasy.

Abd'allah walked up to the mare and felt her over with gentle hands. He turned to Talon.

"She will not make it to the well. I am loath to do this, but we should kill her and dry some of her flesh to take with us. That way we save on water and we live ourselves."

Talon was reluctant to agree but realized that Abd'allah made sense, and he recognized approvingly that the man did not want to harm the mare needlessly.

"Do you wish to do this now?" he asked. His throat was dry, and he coughed.

"We need to ride till dawn, Lord, then we should kill her and the meat can dry in the sun while we sleep."

They mounted up and continued in the direction indicated by Abd'allah. Talon kept an eye on the sick mare, which became progressively more exhausted as they continued. Some of the sand dunes were so steep that it took all her strength to flounder up the slope, and then they went down the other side in a flurry of sand as the horses bounded down, the mare almost tumbling she was so exhausted. The camels maintained a constant swaying motion that ate up the miles, seemingly without effort, but Talon could tell that they too were beginning to feel the strain.

Finally the mare could go on no longer. They had come out of the dunes briefly to walk in single file along a hard flat area strewn with rocks when she stumbled and went down with a low whinny.

They all stopped and stared at her as she went first to her knees and then rolled over to lie on her side. She bared her teeth with the effort of raising her head and whinnied again, but weakly, eliciting a nervous response from her companion, who tugged at his lead to try and go over to her.

Talon released the rope and the stallion trotted back to the mare. He stood over her and nudged her with his nose. Again she tried to lift her head and whickered softly. Talon made his camel sit and dismounted. Abd'allah and Dar'an did the same. The boy ran back to the mare and tried to lift her head up, then sat with her head in his lap. Talon walked up and placed his hand on the boy's shoulder.

"Dar'an, we have to leave her, she cannot go on."

The boy nodded and turned a tear-streaked face up to Talon. "Do we have to kill her, Lord?" he asked. These were the first words the boy had spoken for many hours, and they struck Talon hard. The boy was a Kurd; they loved horses as though they were part of their family.

"It would be a kindness, Dar'an. You do not have to watch. Go with the camels till you come to the sand and wait there. Abd'allah and I will take care of it."

The boy nodded and gently placed the mare's head back onto the ground. She grunted and shivered.

Dar'an rode off into the shadows of the towering dunes ahead of them, taking the other horse with him, while Talon and Abd'allah took out their knives and approached the mare.

Talon talked gently to her while he placed his razor sharp knife on her jugular and then drove the blade deep. The mare jerked and struggled violently, forcing him to get out of the way while she tried to get up, but fell back with flailing hooves to lie trembling and groaning, spurting dark blood into the air from the severed artery. The rank, metallic smell filled the air as her blood puddled around her head. Talon again knelt near her and held her head until the eyes glazed over and the trembling stopped. She seemed to sigh as she died.

The two men immediately began to cut strips of flesh from her rump. They laid them out on a cloth, cutting enough to ensure that they would have plenty of dried meat for a week, then wrapped the bloody bundle with leather thongs.

They left the dark still form of the mare lying alone in the starlight, loading the bundle of meat onto Abd'allah's camel, which objected strenuously to the smell of blood. He shouted and beat it with his stick until it was subdued enough to allow them to tie the bundle. Then they mounted up and rode after Dar'an. Nothing was said as they came up to the boy, they simply continued in silence into the next ocean of sand dunes, constantly heading north by north east.

Dawn came quickly. The darkness to the east cleared and they could now see details of their inhospitable, bleak surroundings. The only color that emerged from the darkness was that of the sand, a wild array of streaked yellow and orange with bands of red and black from the shadows still to be dissipated by the sun. Despite the company with him Talon felt very alone in this vast place.

This day dawned with a reddish halo around the sun that displayed a dark brown line on the southern horizon. Abd'allah seemed uneasy and turned his head to point with his quirt.

"The weather is going to change and a wind will come soon," he called across to Talon and Dar'an. "It could be the Khamsin!"

"Will there be a storm Abd'allah?" asked Dar'an nervously.

"There might be, but we need to find shelter soon or we will cook in this sun," said Talon.

They crested yet another massive dune and paused on the top to survey their surroundings.

As far as the eye could see there was an ocean of dunes like huge petrified waves that seemed to lap against the occasional red streaked rocky cliff that jutted up into the sky, sometimes several hundred feet. In some cases the dunes actually looked as though they were cresting, as the wind had undercut them leaving a cornice of sand that looked like a wave top about to foam down.

Abd'allah lifted his hand and pointed. Far away in the already shimmering horizon Talon glimpsed what might have been another rocky formation emerging from the sand. But the distance was great and he was not sure.

Dar'an, who had the sharpest eyes of all three, exclaimed, "I see something like a tree! Is that the oasis, Abd'allah?" he turned an excited face to the man on his left.

"I think it is, but it is very far off and we will not make it there today," said Abd'allah gruffly. He seemed to be taking a liking to the boy.

"Where can we stop? There is nowhere here." The boy was becoming frightened by the tension emanating from the men.

"We must go into one of the valleys and get as close to a cliff as we can to shelter from the wind. We cannot ride through what is to come," said Abd'allah to Talon. His lean dark features were tense, his dark eyes fearful.

Suddenly they heard a high-pitched wailing sound from the south followed by a low booming. The camels groaned as though they knew what was coming. The men turned their heads as one to stare in that direction. The sky to the south was darkening. Instead of the deep indigo blue of the normal day, a brown cloud was rising out of the horizon.

They heard again the booming sound and saw the sand being driven off the tops of the distant dunes by an oncoming wind.

"The sand demons are singing!" cried Abd'allah. He struck his camel hard on the rump, driving it forward with frantic slaps of the reins, striking it hard over and over. The beast bellowed and began its shambling run.

"Hurry! We must reach shelter! The devils are playing their evil music and we shall die if we stay here!"

His panic was infectious. The other two followed him down the slope of the sand dune in a flurry of dust and sand.

The booming and the high-pitched notes became louder and more frequent. To Talon as he rode after the fleeing Abd'allah it was as though monstrous stringed musical instruments were playing to accompany the deep resonant booming from the desert behind them.

Almost as though responding to its cue the first wind gusts struck the party. The sound they had heard at a distance was now all around them, accompanied by stinging sand driven off the tops of the surrounding dunes.

They hurried as fast as the camels could take them towards the rocky island that stood out from the dunes in the hope that they could find shelter in the lee of its form.

The wind seized at their clothes, tearing and whipping them, threatening to pummel the men off their perches on the backs of the camels. The animals themselves needed no persuasion to flee to shelter, meager though it might be.

Within a half hour, with the howling wind pursuing them all the way, the riders came up against the rocky wall of the cliff. It faced west by north and only provided minimal shelter, but this was all there was.

Abd'allah shouted over the wind. "Get the camels down against the cliff and we will get between them and the rock! Hurry! The storm is upon us!" His last words were torn away by the wind, but the others knew what he had meant and hastened to comply. In the process however, the stallion slipped out of Dar'an's hands and pulled away.

It was clearly terrified and scuttled backwards as the boy tried to catch him, running after and crying out for him to come back. Talon ran out and seized Dar'an by the shoulders and shouted, trying to be heard above the keening wind.

"Leave him! We have to look to ourselves, Dar'an. Come quickly."

They ran back the few yards to where the camels were now squatting and dived behind them. The stallion was swallowed up by the swirling dust.

Glancing up Talon could see the sky had changed completely to dark brown and black. The air was full of fine talcum-like dust mixed with stinging sand particles that swirled in from all directions; it became denser by the second. They were being engulfed by a storm that had started in the Red sea and come deep inland. It was already finding its way into their eyes and noses, burning and blinding.

Talon huddled closer to the other two and did as they had: he covered his face completely with his shemagh, wrapping it several times around his face to keep it in place. Then they felt the real fury of the storm as it swept over them. The singing they had previously heard was drowned out by the howling and shrieking of the wind. It plucked savagely at them with talons of sand as they cowered behind the crouching camels. To Talon it sounded as though the demons of hell were reaching in to tear them away and carry them off. He crouched lower and prayed for it to stop.

Talon felt his camel shift and it gave a nervous rumble in its stomach, but it stayed put and did not try to get up. He could see nothing but could feel Dar'an with his hand. The boy was on his knees like Talon, but he was bent over with his head almost on the ground and he was wailing. Talon felt the boy beginning to panic and try to get up but he pushed him down hard, shouting at him, but the wind tore his words away. To go out in this was sure death. The boy subsided but Talon's hand was exposed for a few seconds. He pulled it into the folds of his clothing sharply when the whipping particles scoured his flesh. He could also feel the sand accumulating all round him and felt a sense of panic at the thought that it might completely cover them up and bury them. He found it difficult to breathe, as the air was so dense with the flying dust it threatened to choke him whenever he tried to open his mouth to gasp for more air.

The storm seemed to last for hours before it finally eased off and then fled northwards, the howling of the wind sounding like a thousand wailing spirits as it departed.

Talon felt the great weight on his back and shoulders and stood up with an effort; sand cascaded in rivers off his body. He slowly unwound his face cloth and stared out with bloodshot eyes at a land that had changed shape. Above them the sun was a distant red orb in a still dark sky that was slowly lightening as the storm moved away, while all around them were piles of sand that had accumulated against the walls of the rock and themselves. The camels were half buried and there was no sign of the stallion.

Something stirred behind the other camel and Abd'allah lifted his cloth-covered head from the sand that had almost buried him.

He looked more like some strange desert creature coming out of its hole than a man. He unwound his face cloth, peered up at the sky and then glanced over to Talon. His face was caked in a whitish brown dust that was streaked where the tears from his eyes had dribbled. His eyes were bloodshot and his hair almost on end. Talon laughed and stooped to lift Dar'an out of the hole he was now crouching in. The boy came out slowly and fearfully.

"Are they gone, Suleiman? Are the devils gone?" he quavered.

"Allah be praised, we have been spared. The storm, for that is what it was, is gone to the north. There is nothing more to fear from it, Dar'an."

Talon stepped carefully around his camel and checked it for injury. The animal, apart from seeming annoyed at the storm and the discomfort that came with it, was quite unharmed. Abd'allah did the same with his camel and so did Dar'an.

Dar'an was mortified at having lost the stallion. The horse had carried some of their possessions. The climbed the rocks behind them and stared out at the shifted dunes, some still smoking dust from their tops, to look for the horse, but there was no sign of him.

"I am very sorry I lost him, Tal— Suleiman. I could not hold him. He was too frightened of the wind."

Talon placed a kindly hand on his shoulder, "In his state of fear I do not think I could have held him myself, Dar'an," he lied to relieve the boy of his guilt.

"We shall make camp here and leave at dusk for the wells that Abd'allah has shown us," Talon said.

They took some careful draughts of the by now filthy greenish water and gave the camels just enough to keep some in reserve, then laid out the meat on the rocks behind them to dry. It was a crude method, as they did not have any salt, and for sure some would spoil; but the rest might keep long enough to be edible over a couple more days.

They went to sleep up against the wall of rock. Talon hoped that a scorpion would not come out during the day and bite one of them. The sting would cripple a grown man.

Talon woke just as the sun was sinking below the horizon, a giant red ball in the west, and noticed that one of the camels was very agitated. It was hobbled and standing on its feet but it was looking down at the ground near it and literally barking at it, rearing back and snorting then prancing back again. Talon leapt to his feet and stared at the enormous insect on the ground in front of the camel.

Abd'allah had risen from his sleeping position and he seized a stone, jumped forward and threw the stone at the insect.

"It is a camel spider and the camel knows it! We must kill it!" he cried, buy the thrown stone missed. The spider seemed to realize that there was danger about and proceeded to start running out onto the sand.

Talon ran after it with his sword drawn and slashed down at its torso, slicing the creature in half. He stared fascinated at the wriggling legs of the huge spider as it died in front of him. It was almost twice the size of one of his hands. He felt a revulsion for the creature and for what it could do to a camel or a man, and no remorse for having killed it.

Abd'allah strode over with Dar'an behind him.

"I have seen the face of a man who had half of his cheek eaten by one of these while he slept. I am glad you killed it. The camels know it for what it is and fear it," he said.

"What happened to the man, Abd'allah?" asked Dar'an.

Abd'allah turned to him, "Why Dar'an, he went mad! Would you not?" he said calmly.

Dar'an shuddered. "I want to leave this place," he stated.

They needed little persuasion. They retrieved some of the meat that they thought might have cooked, leaving the rest to the vultures, as Abd'allah said, although Talon found it hard to believe that any large bird could survive in this emptiness. But Abd'allah pointed to the remains of the spider and said, "There are many creatures that live here in the sand; they are shy and one does not see them often, but they are there."

After the stars came out Abd'allah, with Talon at his side, checked their position with his kamal while Talon used his fingers, and they agreed that they needed to head a few more points to the east. They pushed the camels hard as they reckoned that they should make it by dawn if they were lucky. The water being almost gone and what there was left being foul and greenish, it was not a comfortable time. The animals were now weak from lack of food, but they plodded on.

Talon was tired; the storm and the uncomfortable rest during the thunderous heat of the day had taxed him, so he dozed on the camel as its swaying motion continued up a dune and down the other side or along a rocky defile that led in the right direction. The others did the same.

The night descended and within an hour sucked all the heat out of the sand. The desert cold wrapped itself about them so that they shivered and breathed the sharp clean air through dried up nostrils that hurt because there was no mucous to wet them. Their lips, already dry, began to crack.

Abd'allah led the way with Dar'an in the middle and Talon taking up the rear. They spoke very little, each man huddled within his own thoughts. They stopped twice during the night to rest the camels and to give the last of the water to them before they remounted and headed north by north-east, always keeping the North Star just to their left by a few points.

Dawn came in gray streaks that dissipated into light blue, and then the white ball of the sun rose above the horizon, seeming to race into the sky; and the cold that had chilled them all night changed to a heat that almost as rapidly seemed about to to boil their heads. Within a few hours the sun's remorseless heat seared the dunes and reflected off the glowing sand to burn the eye with a glare that remained seared onto the retina some time after the watcher had turned his head away.

Abd'allah led the way up yet another huge dune to stop at the top and stare ahead. He raised his arm in a tired gesture and pointed, and Talon stared through the shimmering heat to where he indicated. There, some distance still to the north, there seemed to be something, but he could barely make it out. It seemed like a mirage of some kind, as the distant palms set against a rocky formation seemed to dance in the waves of heat coming out of the desert ahead of them.

"How far away are the trees?" he asked. He had to repeat the words for they came out as a whisper, his lips were so parched and his throat so dry.

"It is more than five miles away, but In shah'Allah we shall make it there today. We have no choice but to keep going," Abd'allah croaked.

"Will the camels be able to make it?" asked Dar'an. He too sounded as though his throat was full of dust.

"Look at them! They can smell the water and they can see just as well as we can," Abd'allah said.

Indeed, when Talon glanced down at his camel it seemed as though the creature had regained some of its interest in life. Up to this time the animal had been slowly flagging, and he had wondered when he might have to get off and walk on his own.

They set off at a slightly faster walk than before. The riders gave the camels their heads to make the pace they wanted to.

But it was still a long distance to cover in the burning heat of the day, and Abd'allah reined his camel in when it seemed too inclined to go faster. "Even a camel will miscalculate and over tax itself," he grunted to the others.

Talon learned during those last few miles how thoroughly the heat of the sun and the desert could suck the moisture out of a man. He was glad for the cotton robes that billowed about him and prevented the heat from burning him and drying him out completely. But it did not prevent his lips from cracking painfully and his throat from feeling as though he had poured hot metal into it. The only exposed part of him, his eyes, burned, and he had to blink frequently to keep them from drying up completely. There seemed to be no relief and each breath that he sucked in scorched his lungs.

He could tell that Dar'an was in much the same condition because the boy was hunched over in the saddle and coughed once or twice a dry hacking cough that Talon did not like to hear.

The wind picked up a little and once again they heard the strange music of the dunes around them. Dar'an looked back at Talon fearfully but Talon reassured him with a raised hand. He could not understand what it was that made the eerie music and the booming sounds, but they did them no harm so he concentrated on their path ahead.

Slowly, painfully slowly, the palms of the oasis became larger and ceased their irritating dance just above the shimmering heat of the desert to become real palms in the distance. The camels quickened their pace. They even groaned their yearning to be at the water that they could now smell clearly.

Then the distance was less, just a few thousand yards, and men and camels could not be restrained any more. Abd'allah gave a shout that came out more as a loud croak and applied his quirt to his camel. It lumbered eagerly forward and the other two followed, groaning and bellowing. It was almost a race to the oasis. The great ungainly animals, weak with hunger and thirst, still managed a shambling gallop.

They came in a rush to the trees, and the men threw themselves off the camels. Talon looked around for a pool of some kind but there was no water. Incredulous and fearful, he stared about him, but Abd'allah knew what to do. He went immediately to a damp patch of sand near some reeds and began to dig, first with his knife and then with his hands. Soon he had scooped a shallow depression out of the sand, and into this seeped water.

He pushed aside the eager head of one of the camels and lifted a little water in his cupped hands and sipped. He seemed to be tasting the water like a connoisseur. Finally he nodded and began to scoop more sand out of the way, making the depression even deeper and wider.

"Keep the animals away for a little longer, my Lord," he commanded. Talon, relief flooding over him, let Dar'an hold his camel and joined him to scoop the damp sand away to make a pool about a yard wide. The seeping water was brackish at first, but it began to clear after a couple of minutes. Dar'an shoved the camels' heads back whenever they tried to reach the water.

"I needed to test the water for salt before the camels got to it," explained Abd'allah looking over at him. "Salt water would kill them, but this water is sweet; it is safe to drink."

They then let the excited, grunting and groaning camels drink frugally of the water while they sipped from cupped hands right next to the animal's sucking muzzles.

They had to stop from time to time and let the water seep back into the depression, and then they all stooped as one to drink again.

For Talon the simple pleasure of taking a sip of cool water was exquisite. After the first gulps he allowed the water to stay in his mouth for a few seconds before swallowing slowly, enjoying each moment, allowing his pores to soak up the precious fluid. He could feel his skin and the inside of his mouth and throat become normal again. His cracked lips were still painful, but he welcomed the pain. Abd'allah admonished them not to drink too much at first, but the temptation to gulp the water down in feverish haste was almost overwhelming.

It was hard for Talon to restrain himself from putting his face in the water and gulping down huge mouthfuls. The camels sucked the basin dry many times before Abd'allah forced them back and hobbled them near some reeds that grew along a depression that must have been followed by the underground water. Although there was none to be seen above ground other than their own man-made well, there were reeds aplenty for the camels; they seemed to find them edible and began to graze contentedly.

Abd'allah took charge and began to look for palm fronds and other wood debris, which he gingerly gathered for a fire, wary of scorpions, and indeed he did once disturb a scorpion that scuttled off into the rocks to the east of the oasis.

They managed by the use of a flint and stone to start a stream of sparks into some fibers that Talon had gathered, and with much gentling and light blowing they managed to get a fire started.

Abd'allah wanted to cook the meat thoroughly before they ate another morsel because, as he pointed out, it would make life miserable for them if it made them sick. They charred some of the meat and tested it, each taking a small mouthful. It was delicious and suddenly Talon realized how ravenous he was.

After the meal of horse meat and some stale nan that they still had with them, the men sat back and relaxed for the first time. Dar'an looked exhausted and murmured that he needed to sleep. He covered his face and head and rolled over without another word and fell into a deep slumber.

The two men sat in companionable silence for a while. Talon regarded Abd'allah with new eyes. Not for the first time he remarked to himself how resilient, self-dependent and courageous were these people. Abd'allah was a true Bedu and had just demonstrated his determination and his ability to survive in the harshest of environments. Talon reflected to himself that the desert stripped away all the superficiality that came with men from the more populous places, leaving the individual bare, and showing no mercy should they fail to understand its harsh conditions.

Talon finally broke the silence. "I am thankful that you came after us, Abd'allah. I am sorry for the death of the Sheik, because he was also your father. May Allah be kind to him in the hereafter and give his soul repose. You have guided us and shared our hardship and are therefore welcome company. You do know that I go beyond Baghdad, do you not?"

"I do, Suleiman. I will go with you to Baghdad and there I might stay, as they say it is a wondrous city with many thousands of people, all living in palaces. I want to see the city and to walk its streets of gold. How can so many people live in one place and not run out of food?" he asked innocently.

Talon smiled. "You might indeed like to see the city, my friend, as indeed I would again, but you might also be disappointed. The people of cities are not as the Bedouin, they do not have the clean desert nor the clear skies for their roof. Neither are they as close to God as perhaps we are here in the desert. There are things that you will surely not like there."

"How is that possible, Suleiman? Does not the Caliph, the representative of Mohammed himself and therefore of God, reside in the city? If this great man of God, the companion of the Prophet, lives there then it must be a city of God's creation and therefore wondrous." He sounded a little indignant that Talon might question this simple fact.

Talon raised his hands in the gesture of peace. "My friend, it is as you say and more, much more. I want to visit the great libraries when I get to the city, as they are the greatest in the world. I did not have the opportunity the last time I came through, so I intend to tarry for a while. You will be awed by the beauty of the palaces. But do not be surprised that not all people live in palaces, as does the Caliph."

"It does not matter, Suleiman. We will no doubt stay in a palace. The Sheik, may Allah make his journey to heaven light, said that you are a rich man, and as I am now your servant it should be so that we live well too."

Talon laughed. "I am tired, Abd'allah, do we need to take turns to stand guard?"

"I do not think we will have visitors here. We might at the next well though. I think we can sleep safely here, Suleiman," said Abd'allah.

They slept, and Talon dreamed. He dreamt of a garden with cool water fountains surrounded by green shrubs that created a bower of flowers, and that Rav'an was there with him smiling into his eyes. He felt a great sense of well being. She leaned forward to kiss him and he was sure he caught her fragrant scent of jasmine; then he saw how the fabric of her blouse stretched over her breasts and longed to stroke them, but as he reached for her she was gone and he was alone again. He woke feeling lost, the loneliness that had haunted him for so long, that he had continually tried to put aside, came back full force, leaving him empty and hollow.

The others still slept, so he got up and explored the oasis. It was so small that he could well believe Abd'allah when he said that it was easy to miss in the dark. There were but eight trees in all and a dark patch of sand that indicated where there was water. A full sized caravan would not do well here, he thought.

They stayed for two days at the well. Although the men were perpetually hungry, the rest of the meat lasting only the two days, the camels seemed content. They were well watered and reasonably well fed when they left the oasis to continue north.

The land changed imperceptibly as they moved northward. The huge sand dunes gave way to low hills of sun- and sand-burned rock formations that looked as though they had once been vast mud drifts that dwarfed the men and camels, now frozen into their distorted shapes by time and the sun. The path they followed became more firm, and at times they moved across great areas of bare rock that were hot even into the late hours of the night during which they traveled.

According to Abd'allah the next water was in a well-known wadi and therefore frequented by men. The Bedu of the region south of the town of Karbala came to water their animals before proceeding on into the hinterland or north towards the rich flat lands of the Mesopotamian region.

The rock formations became more pronounced, serried with streaks of color layered from pure white to dark red all the way up their weather-riven sides, and a path slowly materialized out of the dry sand the camels trod. Talon recognized the signs and became more alert. They were coming out of an empty quarter to a region where men traveled.

The days passed and once again the water became a source of concern, but Abd'allah reasoned that they had made good progress and were drawing near to the well that he had visited many years ago with the Sheik.

Sure enough, just when Talon was again feeling parched and nervous about the chances of reaching water before the camels went down, they came to a stony rise and Abd'allah pointed confidently to the northeast. Talon peered into the shimmering heat, but could not make out what Abd'allah was pointing to.

Dar'an, who had been shading his eyes from the glare of the morning sun said, "Are we going to that cliff, Abd'allah?"

"We are going to that cliff, Dar'an. There is a large well situated at its base where the water comes up from the ground, In sha'Allah. There is a cistern there that our people and the local Bedu know about, but few others."

Once again Talon was glad that Abd'allah had come to them. He doubted that either he or Dar'an could have survived without him. They came upon the unlikely location of the well at about noon, having traveled all night and the entire morning. Once again the camels were exhausted and the men in not much better condition. But the camels knew there was water and headed unerringly towards the point that Abd'allah had indicated.

They came to the base of the cliffs, but all Talon could see was a small ring of stones situated nearby. Abd'allah made his protesting camel sit and then dismounted and walked over to the stone ring. He peered over the low wall and then beckoned the other two over.

"Long ago the Nabataeans built this place for others and themselves to use. Our people have been in the desert for hundreds of years and therefore know all the places where water comes to the surface. Here we have a well that is not known to many," he said softly.

Talon peered down at the dark opening in the ground. A cool breath of air seemed to come out of it and his nose told him that water was surely down there, but how to get it out?

"How do we get to the water, Abd'allah?" he asked though parched lips.

"We will make a bucket out of one of the skins and lower it in. It will take time but we can pull water out. I hope that no one has been here recently, as the water might be down."

They hastily fashioned a crude rope from their own clothes and straps and then cut one of the large goat skin water containers into an equally crude bucket and threw it down. There was the satisfying sound of a splash as it hit water and Abd'allah drew it back up, careful not to stress the cord too much.

They dutifully watered the camels first. That took time and patience, as the animals were greedy for more and bellowed their frustration at the slowness of their masters. Finally the men could drink, and then they were able to fill the skins and rest for a few hours.

"We are within a day of the edge of the desert, but men can still die for lack of water if they do not know where to find it. However, we will now find water frequently between here and Baghdad, In shah'Allah," said Abd'allah quietly.

"I hope you are right," said Talon fervently. "Allah be praised for our deliverance and your help. We could not have made it without your skill, but I am a little tired of being thirsty all the time."

Abd'allah smiled his distorted smile, but it was a warm one and betokened pleasure at the complement. After resting for the hottest part of the day in the cover provided by the cliffs, they mounted up, and again Abd'allah led the way along the track that served for a road in these parts heading again north by northeast.

Before they left the wells they prayed, and because they could now use water they performed the ablutions carefully in the prescribed manner. Before, when they had been without water they had had observed Tayammum (dry ablution) by touching clean dry soil, then wiping their faces and hands with sand and asking forgiveness from God for being unable to use the vital remains of their water.

They were walking slowly along the dimly lit path in the darkness when Talon was witness to the extraordinary sight of the moonrise.

For some time now the moon had been growing more each evening, but now it was full. Talon knew it would come up over the distant hills several points to the north from true east. He could see a dim light that grew in that quarter; very slowly it became more intense, during which time they continued in silence, the soft thump of the camel pads being the only noise.

The three men stopped their mounts and stared fixedly as one, as though in the grip of some religious happening. It was with an instinctive sigh of awe that they all witnessed the first glowing silver curve of the moon rise above the top of the dark range of hills to the east. The ball of glowing silver light seemed to move swiftly after that. It rose out of the darkness like a cold, bright sun that bathed the desert with light. It was enormous, its size somehow much greater than Talon could remember when it was overhead the night before. The desert was illuminated from horizon to horizon as the huge silver orb climbed high into the night sky bathing everything around them in an eerie silver light.

Talon gazed at the full bright moon and wondered at the world he was traveling in. He had found time for reflection while traversing the desert. Men had walked this way for centuries and left almost no mark on the land. He recalled the other lands that he had visited, and despite all the hardship of the last week he still felt that he preferred this place to the lands full of men with their quarrels and jealousies which had no relevance here.

His thoughts drifted back to Jerusalem and the petty intrigues that seemed to be endemic within the court. He hoped the King was still living, as he had liked and respected the brave young man. He reflected upon his decision to take the southern route and avoid the risk of running into the 'Assassins and the chances of being denounced as a Frank.

Although they had nearly paid the ultimate price for coming this way he was somehow content within himself for having done so. The desert gave one a sense of proportion. Here life was utterly insignificant; survival trumped all other needs and pared man's emotions to the most basic senses, yet still he could gaze up at the moon with a sense of mystical awe and feel close to some unfathomable being. As though to punctuate the advent of the moon they heard for the first time the distant call of a jackal. Its yapping song was crystal clear in the otherwise silent desert all around them.

They journeyed for another two days, stopping at clearly marked wells and encountering no other men on the way, although there was more and more evidence of man's presence.

They met Bedu when they stopped briefly at the wells of Ar Ruthiyah. The men of the tribe called themselves the Bani Asad and they were goat herders. They followed the traditional rules of respect for the water and offering of chai, but it was clear that these people were very poor, and although they left the three travelers alone there was a wariness. There were about ten of them, so Talon and Abd'allah took turns that night for the first time at guard.

Talon had meticulously followed the routine of prayers during their journey and was careful to do the same while in this area, performing ablution (wudu), purity of the whole body, clothes and ground used for prayer, and facing the Qiblah (the direction of the Ka'ba at Mecca) as closely as Abd'allah could calculate it. They also resumed their prayers five times a day.

What worried him was that these men might be of the Sunni following and object to them, even to the point of denouncing them, which could mean death should someone make a case out of it. They therefore prayed alone and away from the tribe.

"*Fitna* sleeps for the time being: God's curse upon him who wakens it." Abd'allah murmured as they settled down for the night. Talon knew what he meant. The Sunni-Shia divide, often described as *Fitna,* was like a smoldering volcano, an ever present danger, but for the time being it was still.

Early the next morning, however, one of the men walked over to them and told them that they would be safe on the journey to Karbala al-Muqaddasah, as they were good Shi'ites and would be welcome. Talon was shaken. They had been observed; it was just as well that they had not been praying in the Sunni manner, he thought to himself.

They bade the people gathered around the wells farewell. Calls of "Go with God and may Allah protect you" ringing in their ears, they left the tribe during the night with the moon to guide them along the well worn track that headed ever northeast.

After another week they passed a huge body of water that seemed to comprise two large lakes on their left, and another half day later they arrived at the small but significant town of Karbala al-Muqaddasah.

While Talon was aware that this was the burial place of Husayn ibn Ali and a very holy place, he had never been here before. He was curious as to what it might look like. Abd'allah, on the other hand, had come this way as a pilgrim some years ago.

Their way took them onto a busy road with traffic composed of camels, donkeys and people making their way towards the town overlooking another body of water.

He knew from his Arabic studies under the good doctor Farj'an that the name derived from the words for Torment and Tribulation, and associated that with the fact that Husayn ibn Ali, the grandson of the Prophet, had been slain here and beheaded while leading a revolution against the Caliph Mu'awaya and his army from Baghdad.

Soon they could see the great shrine dedicated to Husayn in the distance. On enquiry they were told it was called the Masjed Al-Husayn.

The road they traveled was filling up with people taking goods to the town bazaar. Trains of camels laden with ripe dates and other produce lumbered along in strings, one man or even a boy leading five or six at a time. The women and young children perched between the loads that draped the sides of the heavily laden animals.

There were herds of goats and long tailed sheep being driven alongside the road, the monotonous music of the copper bells hanging off the necks of some of the goats giving a musical tone to the air. The incessant bleating of the sheep coupled with the smells and dust of many people and animals using an unpaved road was in sharp contrast to the quiet Talon had become used to in the desert.

He noticed many pilgrims walking along the road who were coming to worship at Husayn's tomb. Some were quite old and were being helped along by children or other members of their families. Talon learned later from Abd'allah that many elderly pilgrims traveled there to await death, as they believed the tomb to be one of the gates to paradise.

Talon remembered the day of Ashura, the mourning of the martyrdom of Husayn ibn Ali and his followers. He wondered how it must be here when the maddened and grieving Shi'ite mourners, many bloody and covered in ashes, reached this town. He was glad that Ashura was not taking place while he came through.

There were no great walls about the town; this was a holy place and required none. The Masjed itself dominated the surrounding township that had grown up around it, but there was a lot of construction going on around the tomb.

Talon and his companions did not pause for long to admire the workmanship that was being lavished upon the shrine by skilled craftsmen, but they learned that a great fire had destroyed much of the town and damaged the shrine itself. It looked as though a great deal of money from pilgrims and rich donors was going to rebuild the shrine and the town to an even more magnificent monument to Husayn.

The minarets, a relatively new idea since the introduction of baked brick, would tower over the surrounding countryside, a clear landmark for pilgrims. The great dome was being renovated with even more intricate fret worked stone that was being carved into elaborate prayers, and many colored tiles that would overlay the brick foundation and add a glow to the otherwise drab construction.

Talon would have liked to linger but he needed to press on and get to Baghdad, where he could perhaps join a caravan going south to the Arabian Gulf or even find a boat.

Talon heard Farsi spoken for the first time since coming to the East, and his ears listened eagerly to the words spoken by the pilgrims, trying to place the speakers. But he could not pause and talk; they needed replacement camels, and then he wanted to continue on to Baghdad.

Obtaining new camels was easy; gold talks. The left their tired old camels behind with a skinny and pockmarked camel dealer, who stank of camel himself, and who would doubtless sell them on to some luckless pilgrim for a huge profit.

It was hard not to notice that there was money to be made at the expense of the pilgrims who had come from far and wide to worship at the shrine. Merchants were doing a roaring trade selling crudely carved wooden or clay mementos and souvenirs from stalls near to the great building, while food vendors cried their wares to tired pilgrims promising fair prices and good fare while delivering neither.

They left the holy city behind that day and pressed on to join a caravanserai that Abd'allah had learned about from the camel dealer.

Four days later they crested a low range of hills and saw before them the slow curve of the river Tigris in the great flat plains, and on a hook of the river the famous round walled city of Baghdad.

O Queen of Beauty, who hast conquered kings,
O woman wonderful, in pity be
Most merciful to one who softly sings
Thy matchless glory; yea, to one who brings
His broken songs, sung but in praise of thee.

—Charles H. Towne

Chapter 18

Baghdad

The first thing that struck Talon as they gazed at the distant city of Baghdad was the height and symmetry of its round walls. The river Tigris made a huge bend at this point in its travels across the green verdant plains, and in that bend, protected on almost three sides, was the 'Round city' as it was known far and wide. The side facing the west where the waters of the river did not flow was probably the most imposing, as the walls for some reason had the appearance of being taller.

As they approached the great walls of this fabled city, Talon was reminded of the time long ago when he had ridden up to the walls of another city, Isfahan. Despite his need to move on he was tired and wanted to pause in his journey and explore the wonders of the center of the Islamic universe. There were comparisons to be made with the great city of Constantinople.

Unlike the white stone of Constantinople, the walls of Bagdad were made of sun baked mud brick and therefore bore a reddish hue. They were tall and imposing to the newly arrived traveler as he approached.

But there was much else he saw that disturbed him. As they rode with the caravan towards the city through the countryside, he noticed much that had changed. When he had come though six years ago, the outlying farms and estates had been on good condition ; and although dusty, as it had been a hot summer, there had been much green, and the canals had been in good repair. The fields had been well tended and the variety of crops had been wide.

Now, although it was very green and the palms looked tall and healthy and the fields seemed to be well watered, it was almost as though there was too much water. It lay in large pools in muddy fields where the crops were sticking out of the mud, looking sickly. Dyke walls were crumbling and the walls that surrounded estates, indeed many houses themselves, were badly damaged and had a look of neglect about them.

On being questioned the others of the caravan told Talon and his companions that the floods this year had been the worst anyone could remember. If they thought the countryside looked bad, they should see the city. It had been a disaster!

As they passed alongside the many canals that made up a complex network of waterways, Talon noted that the banks, once well repaired, were crumbling and in some places broken so that this or that field was completely under water. The whine of mosquitoes reminded him that this meant more of these stinging creatures and the increased risk of the shaking sickness.

The caravan they had accompanied, which was carrying dates and some cotton bales, was going to settle outside the city walls; so Talon and his companions Abd'allah and Dar'an took their leave of the Rais, who accepted payment cheerfully and told them where to go once in the city to find the Souk. There they would be able to find someone who would in turn know where they might find accommodation.

As they rode their camels through the awesome entrance, Talon looked about him at the massive gates, which were made of wood that was the depth of a man's forearm with great studs of iron holding iron bands in place. There was a gruesome line of skulls and newly severed heads decorating the ledge above the gates, a warning to criminals that swift, cruel justice was meted out at the hands of the Caliph's police.

The gates were open, so they followed another small caravan as it came through and paid the small entry tax. Talon noticed with some surprise that the guards at the gates were Turkish. He assumed that they must be Seljuk and wondered about that, as he had thought the power of the Seljuks might have waned somewhat over the last ten years. He soon noted that Seljuk mercenaries were to be seen everywhere. However, that did not concern him at the time. To the guards they were merely another group of ragged Bedu who had come to trade in the city, so they were dismissed without even having their meager baggage searched.

The most pressing thing on Talon's mind just at that time was to find secure lodgings, a safe place where he could relax and rest. After which he wanted to have a bath so badly that his skin itched just thinking about it.

Passing through the gates was quite an experience for both Dar'an and Abd'allah, neither of whom had ever been to a city this large before. Even Talon found the walls were imposing. He guessed that they were more than one hundred feet thick at the base, and their height somewhere at about one hundred feet high. The gates themselves were immense, but because of the thickness of the walls it was like entering a tunnel. There were massive towers placed along the outer wall at regular intervals, while at the gate there were several clustered in a group on either side, giving the effect of a castle.

They were no sooner through the first awe-inspiring barrier than they were confronted by the second or inner wall that was almost as imposing. As had happened at the first gate, they had to go through a cursory inspection by the guards, whom there were many. They were then allowed to go about their business, and made their way along the huge plane tree-lined avenue that ran directly from the gates towards a distant palace that gleamed in the sunlight; its many towers and domes and minarets denoting great power and wealth. But it was not the palace that they needed; it was the Souk.

Following the directions given they soon rode their camels into the narrow and crowded streets of the busy mercantile district. The street would open up into markets for all manner of foods, mainly produce brought in from the surrounding countryside. Eventually they came out of one narrow, noisy street onto a large crowded maidan full of people and animals, and there in front of them was the entrance to the Souk.

Talon knew that the souk, or bazaar as he was used to calling it, was nearly as old as the city itself. He knew that Al Mansur, the second Caliph of the Abbasid dynasty, had founded the city in four hundred years ago and the Souk, because of its value as a place of trade, had been built at almost the same time.

He gazed at its ancient frontage, tall and wide, with a high domed but rundown front that looked more like the entrance to a palace. Glazed tiles and intricate frescoes were still visible on the columns and walls on either side of the entrance, although they were sadly in need of restoration, while hanging down from the tall arched roof were many large brass lanterns that looked like closed off bells. The workmanship was beautifully done, thought Talon; and he guessed that when lit the light from the oil lamps inside would reflect off the roof like a thousand stars. he knew they would be lit at dusk, as the Souk continued to teem with life until late into the night.

A smaller curved archway was cut deeper into the wall behind the main entrance and provided the main route into the dark, covered streets of the Souk itself. All along the outside walls of the Souk were tea houses and small merchant shops set into arched recesses, while above were windows, their shutters of wood also intricately fretted to allow those within to see out but not to be seen. In many instances the upper apartments jutted out by many feet over the street below.

People and dust were everywhere, as the maidan was neither paved nor watered to keep the dust under control. The noise was deafening for men who had known only the silence of the desert for so long, but many of the smells emanating from the food shops were mouthwatering. The aroma of roasted lamb and chicken mingled with those of spices and the dusty stink of animals, bleating sheep and goats that were being driven by, churning up more dust into the noonday air.

They dismounted and for a small coin negotiated with a scrawny herder who provided Abd'allah with a place to rest the animals. His even scrawnier slave took the animals and led them off to be watered. Abd'allah elected to stay with the animals while Talon went for food.

"I am uncomfortable with all these people about whom I do not know or trust, Suleiman. I shall guard the camels. Send the boy over with some food for me."

Talon had to agree; the temptation for anyone to rob them might be high, and then they would be adrift in the city with no transport. He and Dar'an walked the remainder of the way towards the entrance to the Souk.

They were immediately surrounded by the mass of people going about their morning business. Laborers and slaves, and many of these black people from the Nubian lands carrying huge loads, shouted hoarsely for a path through the crowd while others from far distant countries walked their thin camels towards the back entrances of the Souk to unload their wares.

Men in rich over-robes and huge turbans, seated on small donkeys, pushed past men dressed in simple cotton shifts and a round prayer cap on their heads. Others who looked more like the Seljuk kind in pantaloons and fine horsehide boots pushed their arrogant way through the press of bodies on horseback, their guards or attendants opening a path with lance hafts. Rough looking men with thin wisps of mustaches from the lands to the far east, still wearing sheep skin jerkins and leggings despite the heat and carrying bows on their backs, rode sat on small hairy ponies and watched the bustle with black, impassive, slanted eyes.

Every language of the Arabian world was being spoken here in this the largest Souk in the known world, to which came merchants from every nation in the Gulf of Arabia, including Persia, bringing with them the best of wares from the ends of the earth. Some had only recently arrived, leading donkeys laden with carpets from Tabriz, Hamadan and Isfahan or from Bokhara as part of huge caravans of camels; they greeted one another in Farsi, Dari and Urdu, whereupon Talon's ears pricked up. He was not so far from his destination now, he told himself, even if it had been a sharp left turn along the way.

Others from the lands of India bringing spices ambled along the road on their camels, while rich people went by on palanquins carried by perspiring slaves, the fine scent of oils and spice mingling with odors of sweat and that of old clothes hanging in the air.

Women were also there, but heavily veiled in most cases, although there were some who merely covered their heads with a light damask cloth. In the midst of noise and dust were groups of men standing like little islands of people gesticulating and talking loudly to one another, adding to the noise of the crowd. Theses were traders of large consignments of goods that lay in warehouses in other parts of the city. Talon knew they were Jews or Armenian merchants who traded with the great empire of Byzantium to the northwest.

Street vendors at rickety stalls displayed their wares, shouting at passersby to sample what they had, mainly water or chai, or in some cases sweetmeats, but their wares were more often than not covered by the flies that were everywhere, settling on any exposed surface of the skin, buzzing about the eyes and mouth persistently. Talon realized that this was why many men carried a fly whisk of horsetail or some such device; the flies were a nuisance.

He was thankful for his shemagh, as he could pull it over most of his face to protect it from the buzzing insects. Talon was very hungry, and Dar'an agreed that the first thing they needed to do was to get a real meal.

They did not have to go into the Souk for that; there were many places along the wall where they could enter a recessed shop to sit cross legged on a carpeted raised platform in the cool interior and be served, first tea and then rice and kebab. They chose one and ordered enough food to feed three hungry men. Dar'an was beginning to show signs of the poor diet they had existed on for weeks on end; so Talon, who felt he needed the same treatment, set about choosing from the bewildering number of dishes presented to them. The roasted chicken kebab with a tart lemon sauce and well cooked rice were only part of the meal. Talon wanted some green food to supplement their diet and ordered berenjena, a long, smooth, purple-skinned plant that was cut into strips in front of them and roasted, yoghurt called mast and cucumbers along with cabbage soup. The boy could barely wait for the food to arrive before he dived in and began to stuff it into his mouth.

"Dara'an you eat like a camel. Look at all the food you have spilled," Talon accused the embarrassed boy with a smile.

"I am sorry Talon. I am so hungry," the boy protested with a grin through a mouthful of food. There were morsels of rice and other food scattered all over his lap.

"Well, see if you cannot improve your manners. We are going to a place where they will not like you to act as though we are Bedu," Talon told him, not unkindly.

Later they drank chai that had been sweetened with ghant, the hard lumps of cane sugar that were placed alongside the small cups.

While Dar'an slipped across the maidan to take food to the hungry Abd'allah, Talon leaned back on the rough woven material of the cushions, sipping aromatic tea from a tiny cup. He took stock of the crowded maidan, enjoying the feeling of a full belly. The aroma of pipes drifted his way and his nostrils flared at the familiar scent of the smoke. This maidan alone made Jerusalem look like a rough village by comparison, he told himself. Baghdad was worth visiting for a while.

When Dar'an came back they would seek accommodation. Meanwhile he soaked up the noises, sights and smells of his surroundings. When he did return, Dar'an was agog, his senses overwhelmed with the sounds and smells and sights.

Upon being asked about accommodation, one of the servants, having completed a swift appraisal of Talon's form of dress, pointed to the entrance of the Souk and told them that just inside, maybe a hundred feet in, there was a merchant who sold silk and manuscripts who might be able to help them.

They made their way into the Souk and joined the moving stream of people. Immediately the sunlight was replaced by the gloom of enclosed, high roofed streets. There were openings in the domed roofs that allowed bright shafts of light to illuminate a wall here or a pillar there but did little to light the rough paving of the street. The pillars and walls were worn and dirty from much settled dust and human passage. Set into recesses in the walls were lamplit shops that sold a wide variety of goods from all over the vast Seljuk empire.

There were silks from distant China, paper from far Samarkand, camphor and bright cloth from Indian merchants who had come with the monsoon winds via Oman. Frankincense from Salahlah in the south of Oman near to Yemen, spice of many kinds and colors from distant countries the other side of India, also brought in ships by the Omani merchant lords. Tea in blocks or loose in sacks, and the tantalizing smell of khaffee beans invited the passerby to stop and drink of its bitter, stimulating liquid.

The stench of damp and rot mingled with the rich but dusty smell of many goods, spices, exotic foods and dyes. Talon heard the squeak of rats in the dark corners and wondered about the possibility of disease in this cramped environment.

The noise of conversation was much more subdued here in the souk, at least in this area; but Talon knew that deeper into the huge labyrinth would be the metal craftsmen, working in bronze, tin and iron. Apprentices along these streets would be beating brass sheeting into the many shapes of lanterns and oil lamps, or, in another area, shaping weapons and working the steel. The beating of the hammers would be deafening. In yet another street there would be men working wood into furniture or ornate designs; and in yet another, clay potters would be plying their craft.

Here, however, there was more wealth as carpets, silks and expensive cloth were on display; these had come from all over the empire. Baghdad itself was famous for them and Talon stopped to admire some. The moment he did, of course, they were accosted by the eager merchant, who offered tea and sherbet with sweet honey cakes and invited them to sit and bargain. Shaking his head and bowing politely, Talon led the way on towards their objective, another shop that sold silk, but there were also many parchment rolls in this alcove and even some books.

Talon approached the shop carefully, as there was a large black man wearing a small turban and dressed in long cotton robes standing outside. He was armed with a sword that, although sheathed in its scabbard, he had swung in front of him, and he was standing with both hands on the pommel. He looked businesslike. Talon, with a glance at the guard, stood waiting for someone to come and see him.

It was a little unusual for the merchant not to come immediately, but then Talon noticed that the only man in the place, who seemed quite elderly, was talking to a woman in at the back of the alcove. They were looking at a book that had been opened and were discussing the contents. The man looked up, noticed Talon and Dar'an, said something to the lady, and then came towards them.

Talon bowed politely and said, "Salaam Aliekum, Master."

The old man made a perfunctory bow and returned the words, "Aliekum Salaam, Sir. Welcome to my humble shop; I am honored by your presence. May I be of assistance to you?"

"The honor is all mine, Sir. Your name was given to me as one who might be able to guide us."

"Please be seated." The old man waved to a comfortable place on the pile of carpets and clapped his hands for chai. A servant hastened out from the dark recesses with a brass tea pot with a long elegant spout and poured steaming tea in a long stream into tiny glass cups. Although he had already had enough to drink Talon accepted the cup, and when the merchant had taken his, Talon sipped it, making appreciative noises.

"What may I do to assist you, honored Sir?" The old man asked politely.

"I seek good accommodation. I can pay well for good rooms and a place for my animals. I have journeyed from far Al-Batrā', that is why I look travel stained, but I am a man of means and will not cheat you," Talon said. "I also hold papers for money that I can obtain from the Jews here in the city."

This last was to reassure the merchant as to his credentials. The old man looked thoughtfully at Talon as though assessing him. Then he said, "I know where there is a widow who has a property not far from here that she might be able to rent to you. You will understand that even a little extra income will be welcome to one such as she."

He turned to the veiled woman, who had remained in the back of the shop motionless in the shadows while the conversation took place. The merchant called over to her.

"My Lady, do you still have rooms available at your property? There is a man here who wishes to rent them."

The woman moved closer to them and Talon could make out her features. In the dim light she seemed to be in her mid-twenties and she was quite attractive, with regular features and none of the blemishes that were often the curse of those who had had the childhood diseases. He could not tell much more about her because of the veil, and he did not want to be rude and stare. His nostrils caught the delicate scent of roses. He remembered his manners and bowed from the waist to her politely.

"My Lady, I will pay well for good accommodation. Please do not fear that we are thieves who have come to rob and steal. But we have traveled a long way and are tired and in need of accommodation. I am a merchant in my own right, but I am traveling to Persia where I used to live."

"My Lady Melilla, do you wish to rent to this gentleman?" the old merchant asked.

The lady nodded her head and spoke softly, "I have rooms over the stables of my former husband's property which are available if you wish to see them, Sire."

Talon bowed again and said, "Whenever you are ready to show them to us, we shall follow you, my Lady."

The woman looked at Talon. "The floods caused much damage to our street, Sir, but I can offer you the three rooms within my compound."

The old man then said, "I did not hear your name, Sir?"

"My name is Suleiman bin Mahmud Omar, Master. That of my companion who is guarding our animals is Abd'allah, and the boy here is named Dar'an."

The old man seemed interested in the comment Talon had made before. "You say you are a merchant from Persia? What do you bring with you to sell?"

Talon replied carefully. "I have come from Egypt and Damascus, where I concluded earlier business, and am on my way home with my companions. My wish is to stay here in Baghdad for a short while, to visit the House of Books and to study the way paper is made, and to learn of medicine if I am able to. There is money to be made in the western countries from such knowledge."

The old man nodded his head. "The House of Wisdom I can take you to when you have found your accommodation. Please visit me here when you have the time and we can talk more of books then."

He seemed satisfied with Talon's explanation and turned to his visitor. Just as he did so the call for noon prayers came to them from a distance.

Talon said, “I shall go to the maidan and pray with my companions, after which we can follow you to your house, my lady?”

“I shall send a servant to you to show you the way to my house,” said the lady Melilla. Through her chador her eyes seemed to be appraising Talon.

Talon bowed politely, bidding them both goodbye, “Ma'a Salaama, God protect you and may his blessings be upon you,” and backed out of the shop respectfully.

As they came out of the darkness of the souk Talon noticed that now there were very few people about. It was noon and the city was at prayers or settling into the midday rest period. Gone were the crowds and noise, replaced by a sleepy quiet that was only broken by the occasional bray of a donkey or the grumping of a camel near by. The shutters were down on most of the street side shops, their owners gone to the mosque to pray or to stay with their families until the heat of the day had subsided and the city could wake up again.

Abd’allah was deep in conversation with the animal caretaker; the slave asleep was on the ground near by, and theirs were the last animals. The maidan was almost completely deserted.

Talon and his two companions decided to pray where they were; they could hear the call from the mezzanine but they wanted to stay and wait for the servant of the lady sent to show them the way. Eventually a man in a clean white tunic that came down to his bare feet came out of the entrance to the Souk, looked around, then walked over to them. He salaamed to Talon and introduced himself as their guide.

Talon hastily explained to Abd’allah what they were going to do, whereupon they bullied the protesting camels to their feet and set out after the servant. They were led along the narrow streets with the top floors of the houses almost touching, so that in some cases the heads of the camels were nearly brushing the base of the floors above.

But then they came to some slightly wider roads with walled properties on either side. These were not estates; they were houses set back from the street within courtyards. Their guide led them up to the gates of one of these and banged on a stout wooden door within an archway for attention. There followed an exchange and the door was opened by an old man who seemed to be the gate keeper.

Talon and his companions were beckoned forward and led into a spacious courtyard with a moderately large house set well back towards the rear of the compound. There were walls all around and Talon thought he spied a tree and perhaps a garden behind the house. Along the walls were set stables, and to the right at the top of a set of steps there were rooms that the servant pointed to, saying that they could stay there. There was no sign of the lady of the house.

The apartment proved to be well aired and reasonably clean, although sparsely furnished. He didn't mind that. A good sleeping mat, a clean carpet on the floor and the means to cook were all they really needed. There was plenty of water in several jars. After the dryness and lack of water of the desert, the three men were overwhelmed by the plentitude of water. Talon found that he was actually appalled at the way water was wasted in this city.

He asked about a bath house or Ham'am for men. He was desperate for a bath and wanted one immediately. On being directed, the three of them set out for the first baths they had enjoyed since leaving Jerusalem.

Luxuriating in a hot pool with half a dozen other naked men, the three of them talked of what they would do during their stay in the city. Talon was going to visit the maktabah, the House of Books, and informed the other two that they were free to do as they pleased for each day as long as they met for the evening prayers and the evening meal. He encouraged Dar'an to come with him but did not press it; he knew the boy would be bored to death in the library.

Talon decided that he had time to visit the hospital as well as explore the libraries. He had been fascinated by the advanced medical treatments he had witnessed in Isfahan and in Byzantium as practiced by some of the Greek and Arab physicians. Compared to these men, the leeches of the European countries were primitive and ignorant to a frightening degree. If he had learned nothing else from the good doctor Farj'an he had learned the value of treating wounds with care. He intended to learn more.

The following days were a joy for Talon. He could walk the streets in relative safety, and to his pleasure Abd'allah and Dar'an did accompany him on many of his explorations.

Abd'allah explained that he had watched Talon once they came to the city and it was clear that he needed a bodyguard, as he walked about with his eyes on heaven and his mind in some other world. It would be a simple matter for any thief to come and relieve him of all his worldly goods and Talon would probably not even notice. Talon laughed and agreed up to a point, because he was indeed enraptured with the city, but also somewhat sad.

The destruction of the flood had been extensive. There was a lot of repair work being done, including in the area where they lived. Few places were left intact or without the need of repair. There were mosques that had simply fallen into the water, leaving bizarre half domes open to the skies, as though some giant with a sword had cut vertically down and taken half away. Because of the manner in which houses were built, of sun dried mud, few being baked hard, the houses and walls had melted into the flood waters. He compared the city to that of Constantinople and found it wanting in that regard.

He visited the old merchant in the Souk again to open the discussion about a visit to the libraries, and stayed for long hours at the man's shop, drinking little cups of hot tea as he listened to the old man describe the current situation in the city. He also read his books and bought one or two for himself.

"How did you fare during the floods, Diya al Din?" he asked the first day, after finding out the man's name.

The old man stroked his beard slowly and Talon realized that he was talking to a Hajj.

"The floods were the worst in living memory and they brought with them pestilence and disease. Following on the floods came the frogs; they were everywhere! A man could not walk without stepping on them. Then they died in the sun and the flies came! Much, much worse than they are today, Suleiman. The city lost many people in the floods from drowning alone, but later disease, the sickness and wasting diseases, came and took many more, and the flies came again."

To change the subject, as it seemed to be a sensitive one, Talon asked when they might go to the libraries, and also he wanted to meet with a Jewish merchant. "Could you provide me with a letter of introduction, Hajj?" he asked politely. " I need to obtain money with some scripts that I have."

The old man seemed delighted to help and agreed to write a note that would provide access to a Jewish merchant who could provide cash, and then one to admit him to the inner sanctum of the library.

"I too am a student of science and poetry," he told Talon. "My shop belonged to my father and to his father and now to me, but I have lost my only son to the Marsh fevers; so now I am here to make a living, although I would prefer to stay at the library every day. I shall be glad to take you there, Suleiman." He paused as though thinking and then said carefully.

"This is a beautiful city, Suleiman, but it is also a city of intrigue and much danger. A young, good looking man like yourself must be careful. Say little, and listen."

Talon looked at him, seeking to find out if there was more than the message in the old man's words, but Diya had turned away and was doing something with his books.

"I shall be circumspect, Hajj," he said.

Later Talon made his way into the entrance of the great library and upon showing his letter was allowed to wander through the great halls. It resembled a palace full of bearded men in huge turbans attended by slaves. He smiled to himself as he imagined that there was a competition to see who could have the largest turban of them all and still walk upright.

There were also many young students who were either reading in the numerous alcoves or actually attending lectures in small groups in a corner one of the larger rooms. The whole atmosphere was not unlike the libraries his young friend Theodora had taken him to in Constantinople; however, unlike Constantinople where he had seen many girls and young women in the libraries, here there were only men. He nonetheless found it very stimulating to listen to this speaker, an older man with a huge turban, who talked about the mathematics, or that one explain a detail of astronomy, and yet another discourse on medicine.

The library was set among some large gardens that had fountains in several corners; the paths took a person under the shade of lines of plane trees, palm and willows, and citrus fruit trees in profusion with a background music made from birds of many kinds. He found that simply walking in the gardens was a rare pleasure; in some way it calmed him and he found he could reflect on his life and think more deliberately of what he hoped to find in Persia and what would follow.

*****

Max Bauersdorf, Sergeant of the Templars, returned to the house that Talon owned in Acre, he was in a thoughtful mood. The wind was blustery and swirling dust and debris were being thrown about and congregating in corners. He shifted his cloak about his shoulders and looked up at the gray heavens. It was going to rain again and he wanted to be near a good fire with some wine and to think.

Months ago he had received a letter from Talon informing him that he was leaving Jerusalem for Persia and did not know when he would be back. To his consternation Talon informed him that he had news of the princess.

Sir Guy had come back to Acre and had summoned Max to his chambers.

After answering Max's questions about the battle, Sir Guy had given Max a wan smile and said, "Talon's name will find its way into legend, for he brought the Templars to the battle but... soon after he left for Persia by way of the deserts."

"Then no one will find him, Sir Guy, because he does not wish to be found."

"That would be a good thing, as he has run afoul of the Old Man of the Mountain again," Sir Guy had said. "I agree he will not be found unless he wishes it. He gave this to me to hand over to you until he does come back, Max; assuming God wills it."

After Max had read the letter from Talon he had looked up at Sir Guy with an expression of great concern. "Will we ever see him again, Sir Guy? How did they... you allow him to leave?" He had sounded almost as though he were accusing the knight, who had given a rueful smile.

"Allow, no.... I almost begged him not to go. However King Baldwin gave him special dispensation to leave, for what he had done you see, on condition that he came back. The Grand Master Odo was very upset but could not gainsay the King, who has developed a special fondness for Talon." Sir Guy had given a bitter laugh. "I pray to God we have not lost him, as I shall miss him."

"But if anyone can survive and come back to tell the tale it must be Talon. He is a formidable warrior and knows full well the dangers he will encounter," Max had attempted to reassure Sir Guy.

In his letter Talon had turned the enterprise over to Max to hold and to manage while he was gone. In the event of him not communicating for a period longer than a year, Max was to assume he was dead and to make certain arrangements with the captains, Henry, Nigel and Guy, for them to be granted their ships. Max was to have control of the monies and a percentage was to go to the Templars.

Today on one of Max's infrequent visits to the Jewish quarter to see a man called Jacob, he had been informed that a script had recently been placed on some money which Talon had left in the merchant's care. The letter from Talon had stated that in this manner, should Max receive notice of a transaction, then Talon was in good health.

He was admitted to the courtyard by Simon, the door keeper, just as it began to rain. Max strode up the stairs to the second floor where the large dining room was situated and there he found the three captains taking their ease and waiting for orders from him.

They greeted Max enthusiastically and Henry pushed the wine flagon along the table towards him. They knew that because of the ongoing enquiry from the house of the Bishop Max would have to be careful as to what he said, so they were all three diffident about asking him too much.

"Have you heard anything, Max?" Nigel spoke for the others.

"I think it is safe to say that the Falcon still flies," Max responded with a grin.

There was a general sigh of relief and they all raised their mugs in silence.

"We must go to the island of Cyprus and carry out his instructions once the spring is here," Max told them.

The last man of this forlorn group
did naught except for gain,
giving only to those who gave,
was how he played the game.

—Kashif Khan

Chapter 19

Unmasked

Talon was delighted when Diya al Din found time to come with him one day. He left Abd'allah and Dar'an to their own devices and walked the narrow streets with the old man. Despite the well policed city there were still cutpurses and thieves who would not hesitate to rob an old man if they thought they could get away with it, so Talon made himself the bodyguard for the day. The old man was worn by time and illness so they went slowly; this gave Talon the opportunity, while talking, to observe the sights of the city. He noted that the Caliph's palace dominated the center.

A walled city within a city, it boasted many mosques and monuments dedicated to former Caliphs, the guardians of the faith. The pointed domes and minarets were prolific. There was one discordant note to the beauty of their surroundings; Talon saw that there were several dozen heads on spikes off the side of the main gates, and was shocked to note that some of them seemed to have light colored beards and shaven heads.

"Those are the heads of the Franks, the Templars who our warriors killed in battle, God curse them," said Diya when Talon asked him about them. "Only their heads adorn the walls of the palace, as they are the most formidable enemies of God and are cursed."

Talon realized that he was talking about men he might have known at some time and looked away. He mentioned the number of Turkish soldiers in the city.

"It is a feature of the city, and indeed of Mesopotamia; the generals who protect the Caliph have become very powerful," replied the old man. "Indeed, they are so powerful one might wonder who is in charge of whom."

Talon did not say anything but a chill went down his spine. But for the grace of God his head could well be decorating that wall too. He noted that they seemed not to be very old, the decay being not very advanced. He wondered what battle these poor men had died in while he had been traveling.

Without seeming to be disturbed by the sight Diya mentioned that there were other libraries inside the palace, but few had access to them other than the great philosophers and imams who taught, or the medical doctors who were prominent.

Talon, mindful of his mentor Farj'an, asked him, "Who are the most prominent doctors of our time, Hajj?"

"There are several today who are famous and in much demand by this or that Sultan, but the man we all revere is now dead. He was a Persian like you, Suleiman, and taught at Isfahan one hundred years ago. Come, I shall show you a portrait of him. He was one of the greatest men of Persia, perhaps of the world. His name was Abū Alī al-Husayn ibn Abd'Allāh ibn Sīnā."

Having spoken this grand name with some reverence he led the way slowly up the steps towards an area that Talon had not formerly visited in the library. The Hajj took him to a relatively small room, one that was full of books that lined the walls in shelf after shelf. There were the usual bearded men in long flowing robes seated on cushions looking over books in most of the alcoves, but there was a space available for them to sit and pore over a large papyrus that Diya obtained with the help of an assistant who knew him.

Opening the rolled paper reverently, Diya showed Talon a portrait of a man and pointed to it saying, "Ibn Sina, the greatest doctor of our fathers' times, but also I think of our own. We are seeing a change with regard to knowledge, Suleiman."

"How is that, Hajj?" Talon asked, puzzled.

The old man looked around carefully before he spoke again.

"In the past men could discuss the Book, the Koran and its revelations, and draw conclusions of their own. They could study the sciences without restraint, and medicine was open to all who wished to gain knowledge.

"But today there are men who claim to be servants of God; these call themselves men of God but, unlike the Imams, few are well educated. Unfortunately they also claim that they and only they can interpret the book and deliver God's words to the rest of us.

"Worse, these same men do not want others to question our existence on this earth and the world we see and hear about us. So now the sciences are beginning to languish ...."

He stopped and would not continue. Talon did not press him, as there were others in the room with them and some might have heard the old man's words. It was clearly a subject that was dangerous to discuss in the broad light of day.

Talon concentrated on the drawing in front of them and saw a picture of a man with a short beard wearing the usual loose turban, pushed back somewhat to the back of his head. He noted with interest the view of the forehead and profile that was presented to the observer; the eyes were looking down almost as though the doctor had been reading when the artist made the portrait. His regular, lightly bearded features were not remarkable although not unhandsome: a strong nose and firm lips with a jaw that denoted determination without being pugnacious. Somehow the artist who had drawn the face of this remarkable man had captured what was singular. It was the intelligence of the man that struck Talon most of all.

Diya left Talon to read the books in that small room. He read for most of the day and only looked up when the sun had begun to sink into the west. He hurriedly went to look for the old man and found him in another part of the library reading a parchment on Astronomy written by Omar Khayam.

They made their way back to the home of Diya through streets that were beginning to come to life again as the sun set. Talon could not remember a time recently when he had felt so content and at peace with the world. He resolved to attend some of the classes that were held at the library in the hope that he could learn more of the medicine.

Over the next several weeks Talon formed a fondness for the old man. He spent long hours at the shop discussing books and their contents and the politics of the day, which Diya was more than willing to talk about.

In all this time, Talon had never glimpsed the lady of the house; but one day, when he was walking back from a visit to the library, she had just descended from a palanquin and was walking towards her entrance, the huge black slave just one step behind her. She must have heard his arrival at the gate because as she came to the entrance of her house she turned and glanced back, then paused at the door. Her veil had slipped a little, showing more of her face. Her dark eyes found his and lingered briefly on his face and then she disappeared within.

Abd'allah, who was standing very close to Talon, spoke in his ear. "Women like you, Suleiman. You must tell me how you do it one day."

Talon grinned, embarrassed. "Abd'allah, my friend, you are imagining things!"

Abd'allah grinned his evil smile at Talon and wagged his finger.

"My father the Sheik, may Allah be kind to him, used to say, 'Women are trouble in whatever form and a man must beware of them.' All the same, I have not felt the softness of a woman in my arms for a long time. Do you think there is a place in this city for my need?"

Talon laughed outright. "My friend, this is Baghdad; I am sure that somewhere there is what you need, but do not ask me... try the servant over there later and see if he can direct you." But he was intrigued by the woman and the look she had given him. Talon had watched her as she walked and decided that he liked what he saw.

Still chuckling, he started to walk up the stairs to their accommodation, looking for Dar'an. Abd'allah remarked as they went up, "I am disappointed in this city, my Lord. You were right; it is not paved in gold, and truly it stinks at the hottest times of day. How can it be thus, when it is the city of the Caliph and therefore God's own?"

"Abd'allah, you must understand that when men come together in large numbers for trade or simply to live then there is much dung and the smell of dirt. Remember Jerusalem, where we met? That too is a city that men believe is dedicated to God. It is a fraction the size of this city and even it stinks on a hot day!"

"I am beginning to miss the desert, my Lord."

"What about the need for a soft, warm body, my friend?"

Abd'allah brightened. "Ah! Yes, before we go back to the desert I must enjoy that gift that God has placed within man's reach! My Lord, do you think the lady of this house would know where we can go?"

Talon laughed again and clapped his hand onto Abd'allah's shoulder as they entered their apartment.

"Abd'allah, my friend, if you dare to speak to the lady at all your punishment will be at the hands of that huge slave of hers and your head will doubtless decorate the walls of this fair city! We will have to find out another way. No, go and ask one of the lesser servants."

*****

On one occasion the old man asked Talon to take him to the hospital known as the Bimaristan, where he wanted a physician to examine him.

"I have been having pains in my right side for some time now and they make me breathless and weak. Will you help me to go there where I can be looked at and you can continue your research?"

Talon jumped at the chance and took Abd'allah with them to ensure the old man was looked after along the way.

The Bimaristan was located on the west side of the city, which was some way from the area of the Souk and the house of Diya, but the walk was enjoyable. They even managed to take a boat part of the way along one of the numerous canals that crisscrossed the city.

When they arrived at the Adoudian Bimaristan they were met by an orderly who asked them who they wanted to see. Diya mentioned the name of one of the more prominent physicians and the orderly disappeared.

Diya said, "I am only here for an examination, so I don't have to do more than register. If I came as an actual patient I would have had my clothes taken away and a clean shift given to me and then I would be assigned a bed."

"What of your possessions? Do they take those too?" asked Talon, surprised.

"They would take my money and other possessions and keep them in safety for me until I was ready to leave."

"How is it that they can be trusted with another man's possessions?" asked Talon incredulously.

"There are strict rules that apply to the running of a Bimaristan, Suleiman. If any of the rules are broken, if a patient complains, or something is stolen, then there is an enquiry and the perpetrator of the wrong is severely punished."

While waiting for the old man to be seen they were not allowed to wander about but could look around the ground floor, where there were many patients lying or sitting on low platforms. There was a card by each bed on which, Diya informed Talon, the doctor who was responsible for that patient wrote his daily observations. This had been instigated by a famous physician named Al Maqriz.

At one time a group of young men following an older man with a gray beard and a loose turban who moved slowly down a line of beds, picking up the cards and discussing the patient with the young men.

"Those are students who are following a teacher of medicine and he is asking them to think about what is wrong with the patient," remarked Diya with a glance at Talon who was watching them with wide-eyed interest.

"Are they then to become physicians themselves?" Talon asked him.

"If they can pass the exams, yes. Not many do," the old man said with a rueful smile. "I tried to become a physician once but I could not pass the exams, so I became a book seller and a silk merchant instead. But tell me, Suleiman, you who have been to Damascus and Egypt, do they not have the Bimaristans there also?"

Talon thought about this carefully before answering. "In Isfahan, I learned of the Bimaristans from my uncle," he said the word easily as that is how he remembered his mentor, "and now here I see it is practiced in the same manner. I was younger then and did not notice so much. In those countries, and in Syria, there are good physicians who have doubtless trained here in Baghdad; but only in Egypt did I see the Bimaristans. They are not as advanced as here, although I believe it had a place for curing eye diseases, but I am not certain. Furthermore, I can tell you, Hajj, that other than the Byzantines theLatin Christians have nothing to compare with this whatsoever."

"You make a distinction between the Byzantine Christians and the... Latin Christians? How is this?"

"The Byzantine people have interacted with the Persians and the Arab peoples for centuries Hajj. They do understand these things, but the Frans are barbarians in this respect," Talon answered.

"How then do the Christians deal with wounds or disease if they do not have the benefit of a Bimaristan?" asked the old man.

"They pray to God for deliverance from their pain, or men called leeches practice upon them and usually kill them with their inept ways," responded Talon with a short, humorless laugh.

"Here if a physician is blamed for the death of a patient and it is proven to the satisfaction of the head administrator of the Bimaristan that there is sufficient evidence of neglect, then he must pay blood money to the patient's family," said Diya.

"Then the leeches in the Christian world would never have any money, because they do not cure," responded Talon.

"It seems you have a lot of experience of the Christians, Suleiman," remarked the old man with a shrewd look up at him.

Talon felt a trickle of alarm. "I have been a trader in these places. They are hard to miss in Palestine, Hajj. The kingdoms flow into one another, if you see what I mean."

Talon was deeply impressed by the cleanliness of the Bimaristan and the orderliness of the place. The more he saw the more he compared it to the ghastly conditions of a place for wounded and sick in the Christian world. He had been appalled when he first visited one such place in Jerusalem soon after the great battle of Montgisard. The screaming of wounded men dying of infections, raving from the fevers induced by their suppurating wounds, and the shrieks of the men having limbs amputated had horrified and sickened him. Having formed his first impressions of a hospital in Isfahan he could not comprehend the hellish conditions he witnessed at that time. He realized that this hospital was even more organized and better equipped than the ones he remembered in Isfahan.

Diya even pointed out a pharmacy called the Al Sharab khana. Talon recognized a mix of Persian and Arabic in the name and again was struck at how much influence the Persians appeared to have had upon the Arabic empire.

The orderly came back for Diya and politely asked him to go with him. Talon and Abd'allah were to stay and avail themselves of the comforts of the garden where they could wait. Later they took Diya home, and he told them that the physician had recommended that he come back and stay for a week, to be put on a careful diet and given medicine for his liver that was a little too large.

*****

Several days later Dar'an came breathlessly up to their apartments and informed Talon that the lady had sent a servant to speak with him. When he descended the stairs to the courtyard a serving man told Talon that he was expected after prayers at the front door of the house. The lady of the house wanted to speak with him.

Later that day Talon bathed carefully, as he wanted to give a good impression, and then dressed in his cleanest robes, as he now possessed more than he stood up in. He completed his prayers with the other two and then went to the entrance of the house. The door opened as he approached and a male servant greeted him politely and led him through the anteroom and then through a large inner room to the back of the house, then down some steps into a garden. He noticed the black slave standing just inside the garden at the head of the stairs. He nodded as he went by, but the slave barely acknowledged his presence, staring straight ahead.

It was dusk, and the garden gave off the scent of fruit trees and flowers; his nostrils caught the scent of jasmine and his pulse quickened.

There were clay pots of shrubs and an orange tree to the side; along a short path he heard the tinkle of water and recognized the sound of a fountain. As he approached the fountain he saw beyond it a carpet laid with food and drink,with lanterns illuminating the setting.

Talon stopped at the fountain and looked about him. It was a small but well tended garden with flowers and shrubs in corners.

An ancient wisteria vine climbed the back wall and had been tended so that its branches gave a cover to a small area near the carpet. The profusion of shrubs and fruit trees provided dark shadows and corners that his eyes searched from long practice for lurking foes, but his senses told him there was no one tonight except for the lady.

Mellilah, still veiled, walked slowly out of the shadows and stood in front of him.

"My lady," said Talon and bowed low. "Salaam Aliekum, my Lady."

To which she replied quietly with the familiar, "Aliecom Salaam, Sir." He realized that the only reason he could be alone with this woman at this time was because she was a widow, and therefore master of her own environment. In any other circumstances he be breaking the law. Even so he was acutely conscious of the fact that the Nubian slave was near the doorway watching his every move.

He continued. "Kef Haalik?" (How are you, my Lady?)

" Il-Hamdulillaah," (Praise be to God!) she replied.

"Will you take refreshment Sir?" she asked, indicating the carpet and the food. He nodded and followed her to sit cross legged on the soft pile of the expensive carpet. She clapped her hands and a servant brought tea.

Mellilah joined him, sitting down across from him after he had sipped the tea and mentioned its fragrance.

It took some little time for Talon to feel comfortable with this attractive woman seated opposite him. She no longer wore her dark chador but instead wore diaphanous veils; while they maintained the decorum of the time, they rather enhanced the mystery and allure of the woman they concealed. He already knew from the old man Diya that she was well educated, but hitherto they had not had the opportunity to talk, so he listened to her with interest as she spoke and invited his discussion.

An attendant wearing flowing robes and wide band around his middle holding a well made dagger came forward and presented him with a plate of grated soap and a basin of bronze holding water with jasmine leaves floating within. Talon washed his hands ceremoniously and then dried them on a towel the servant held out to him. Mellilah performed the same ceremony.

Several other attendants then came forward and laid down hot food in front of them: mutton from the fat tailed sheep of the mountains boiled in camel milk, a platter of wild Guinea fowl, and delicate kebab lamb pieces on thin wood skewers with green peppers and rice accompanying them. Stewed meats wrapped in grape leaves with roasted aubergine strips and almonds in little dishes were near by. Mellilah told him that the delicious fritters were a delicacy from Egyptian called shebach; there were also two kinds of olives, artichoke hearts fried in batter, and kebaeba: beef, pine nuts and crushed wheat. Her husband had loved them while in Egypt and taught their cooks how to make it.

Talon sampled all the foods, enjoying the tastes and flavors immensely. They did not talk very much, usually only when Mellilah indicated a special tidbit or called for the next course. After the early courses were done they were then presented with salads and pieces of watermelons of several types that were very sweet but refreshed and cleansed the mouth.

This was followed by sherbet and honeyed cakes, and finally Mellilah called for khaffee, which was dark and bitter. She asked him if he wanted to smoke a pipe but he declined.

Talon leaned back on the cushions replete, enjoying the moment.

Mellilah had let her veil fall away and now he could see in the lamplight how well proportioned and attractive her features really were. When she smiled her teeth were white and even, and her dark eyes would flash with amusement.

She murmured quietly to the servant who had been in attendance and he signaled the others to clear the food away, leaving the sherbet and the other small sweetmeats, and they were left alone.

They talked for over an hour about the city and the library and even some books that they had both read. Talon found to his pleasure that she was well versed in the poets and even knew some of the Persian literary names such as Omar Khayam, Baba Tahir and Rumi. He regaled her with his impressions of the cities of Hamadan and Isfahan, being careful not to mention his involvement with the 'Assassins. She in turn was a font of information regarding the politics of the city of Baghdad and its factions. She warned him to stay clear of the Seljuks and the other mercenaries and mentioned the names of several high ranking people whom her husband had known before his untimely death.

Talon wanted to know how she had become a widow. She told him, "My husband was the son of Diya the merchant, whom you know well by now. He died of the fever, but before that he was also a merchant like yourself. He was wealthy and visited Egypt and even Palestine. Diya has told me much of you and your interest in the medicines, my Lord."

"My name is Suleiman, my Lady, and I would have you call me by that name," answered Talon.

The moon was high in the sky when Talon realized that he was forgetting his manners and made to leave. She inclined her head and lifted her hand to stay him.

"Suleiman, I would know a little more of you. You are here to see the library and the Bimaristan, but you look more like a warrior than a merchant or student of medicine. My people tell me that you practice almost every day on the flat roof of your apartment with your slave."

Talon decided to chose his words carefully. "My lady, ..."

"You may call me Mellilah while we are alone, Suleiman," she said quietly.

His pulse quickened. "Mellilah, I used to be a Mameluke," he lied. "I fought the Franks for Nur Ed Din before I became a merchant. But I have found that even a merchant must stay well prepared in this time if he is to survive the dangerous journeys he must make to sell his goods."

She nodded at that, but it was clear to Talon that her mind was on other things. He waited.

Mellilah seemed to be hovering on the edge of a decision of some kind and he did not want to disturb her while she thought about it. Then she said, "I would like to meet you again, Suleiman. Will you take pity on a lonely widow and tell me of your adventures another time?"

Although there was a moon it was merely a sliver of light and it was now dark in the garden. The lamps had almost all gone out.

"I would enjoy that very much," he said and stood up. She rose to her feet in one lithe movement and waited until he had come round the carpet and was close. Her hand reached out and touched him on his chest. It was an intimate gesture. He reached out and took her hand gently and kissed it. Her fingers were slim and cool and pressed his hand as he did so. She gave a little sigh but then said, "Go in peace, Suleiman. May your dreams be of peace."

"My dreams will be of beauty, Mellilah. God protect you and may your dreams be peaceful."

Talon left the garden with her scent in his nostrils and his heart beating. He wondered if he would bump into the huge slave on the way out but there was no one to be seen. He went to bed, his mind in turmoil.

*****

He woke the next day to find Abd'allah back and looking smug, so he assumed that he had been all the night with a woman. The only person looking somewhat put out was Dar'an, who seemed to be harboring some envy of the other two for their nocturnal escapades.

Talon wanted to start preparations for leaving the city. He felt that there was much to seduce him into staying longer than he intended, even more after last night. He was, after all, only half way along with his journey and eager to move on despite its temptations.

He talked about it with Abd'allah. "Will you be staying here in Baghdad, Abd'allah?" he asked while they ate a frugal breakfast of nan and fruit.

"I might stay here, Suleiman, there is a good reason... you will understand. But I will help you to prepare to leave and obtain better camels for your journey."

"Then I shall pay you for your services and this should enable you to live reasonably well once we have gone," Talon said.

On his next visit to the Hajj the old man, whose health was now on the mend, informed him that there was to be a talk on the subject of astronomy by a notable figure at the reading house that morning. Talon eagerly agreed to go and accompanied the old man to the talk. There were a large number of young men who attended the meeting.

Talon and the Hajj, despite pushing carefully but firmly through the crowd, could not get within twenty paces of the speaker; so they were hard put to hear everything that was said.

They walked away discussing the dissertation, their heads bent, not paying any attention to the crowd, when a man stopped in front of the Hajj and exclaimed, "Hajj Diya El Din! I have not seen you here for many months! I thought you might either be out of the town or too sick to come to our humble school. My Allah's kindness shine upon you!"

The Hajj looked up and smiled, "Ah, Hakim, my dear young friend. I have missed you too. Allah be praised, you are back in Baghdad and look in good health."

"Old father, you look well too," said the young man, smiling and bowing politely.

"God be praised, he has protected me for the most part and I am well," said Hajj. "I would like to introduce a young man who is a traveler like you. Suleiman is but recently come from the region of Palestine where he has had experience of the Franks."

The young man turned and smiled at Talon, showing good teeth and a ready smile.

"Welcome to our fair city, Suleiman, what is left of it since the flooding!" he gave a rueful smile. "You are an acquaintance of Hajj Diya so that is enough for me to believe that you are a good man. I would be very interested in hearing of your experiences with the Franks. May God damn them!" This last was said reflexively. Talon didn't even blink, he had heard it said in this manner many times before.

Some other young men dressed in expensive clothes were waiting impatiently for Hakim. One called over to them. "Come along, Hakim! We have to prepare for the party this evening; the prince will be early as always, and it is getting late!"

Hakim glanced back at the men, waved his hand and then quickly said, "Hajj, I have not seen you for over six months; bring Suleiman with you to my house, we have a party in my garden tonight. Many men from this college, including some of the learned teachers, will be there, and we can talk some more. Will you come?" he asked eagerly.

Hajj looked up at Talon, who nodded. "We will come, an hour after prayers. Go with God."

Hakim touched his heart with his fingers and said, "May Allah protect you, venerable Father." Then with a smile at Talon he half ran to catch up with his friends.

Hajj turned to Talon. "Well, we have a garden party to go to now, which should be of interest to you, young Suleiman. You will have the opportunity to meet educated people more your age, and I am sure that in return they will be keen to hear of the wars in Palestine."

They made their way back to the Hajj's home, and after some tea Talon hurried back to his apartment to change and prepare for the evening.

He found Abd'allah there and asked him to come with him, as it would be late and he wanted to make sure the Hajj was well protected while on their way home. Abd'allah readily agreed, saying, "Now at last I will see how the rich live."

Talon had laughed and bade him prepare himself for an evening of learned discussion and good food.

They escorted the old man to the large house where the garden party was taking place, arriving a good hour after prayers when the dusk was settling on the city and the dust haze was glowing in the last rays of the sun. As they approached the house they heard the light sound of music being played on a qitara and lute. Someone was singing in a high, clear voice while the murmur of many voices carried over the lantern lit walls.

They were met by an expensively dressed slave, who demanded superciliously who they wanted to see. Talon could tell by the man's accent that he was from Persia and very nearly rebuked him in Farsi but held his tongue.

The Hajj's tone was level when he said, "It is Hakim ibin Sharaf who has invited me, Hajj Diya Ed Din, and my companions are my escort. Be kind enough to give him my greetings and inform him that I am here." The old man could sound very haughty when he wanted to, thought Talon with a smile to himself.

The slave deigned to look down his nose at the Hajj, but he was a trace more polite. "If you will be pleased to wait here I shall inform Hakim ibn Sharaf that you are here, Hajj."

Within minutes they were ushered into the gardens via a large arched gateway, and found that it was an extensive space populated with many fruit trees and several fountains, about which people seemed to congregate naturally. The garden was brightly lit by numerous lanterns and oil lamps that cast long shadows which were thrown up against the walls as people wandered from group to group.

Hakim spied them from afar and strode over quickly to greet the old man and renew his acquaintance with Talon. "Hajj, I am so happy that you come, and also that you have honored my house, Suleiman; my friends and I would be honored to hear more of the events in Palestine from one who has been there recently."

"I would not say recent, as I have been on my journey for several months before I came to Baghdad."

Hakim shrugged." I have never been there, let alone to Damascus, so you still have much to tell me, of that I am sure."

He drew them towards a small group of men who were standing by one of the larger fountains. There ensued the usual flowery greetings as the young men proudly pronounced their family names and heritage. Talon had to explain more than once that his ancestors came from Persi,a which tended to explain his fairer complexion and the color of his eyes. They seemed to accept this without question, so he relaxed a little and looked about him.

The young men were respectful towards the old man, but for the most part they wanted to know of the situation in Palestine. There were many questions and not a little bragging as to what they would do if they ever encountered a Frank. As they were all of an age to be able to contribute to the fighting Talon was curious as to why these firebrands were not already fighting the great battles for the Muslim world.

The talk drifted to geography and the recent dissertation as well as to medicine, so Talon was able to enjoy the rapid movement of the conversation going on around him. Abd'allah was unable to follow the conversation, so he chose to stand nearby and assume the stance of a bodyguard. His scarred face and the glower he put on it deterred anyone from coming up to him and engaging him in conversation.

The evening had progressed to the point where some people were getting a little drunk. Wine flowed, regardless of the ever more strict edicts emanating from the palace, but for the most part there was none of the rank drunkenness that occurred in the Christian world.

Talon was apprehensive, so he did not drink anything but water and fruit juice that slaves presented to the men from time to time along with the delicious honey cakes. He was being careful because he had noticed something that alarmed him. One of the men who had arrived during the evening had looked hard at Talon and had continued to watch him during the conversations that followed with a peculiar intensity.

He was somewhat older than the others and spoke very deliberately about Damascus, having it seemed just come from there. He was dark featured with the usual mustache and short beard, but there was something familiar about him that Talon simply could not place.

Then he remembered and a cold sweat trickled down his back. The man who had stared at him was none other than Aarif Mejid, the man he had ransomed after taking his ship in a storm off the port of Abydos. There was no mistaking the face now. He tried to stay in the shadows after that and find out more about the man, but he had disappeared. Talon was about to go and collect Abd'allah and leave the party when when there was a commotion at the gates with much shouting.

Everyone turned towards the sounds emanating from the street and listened uneasily. Suddenly there were soldiers running into the gardens and it was clear that they were looking for someone. With them was the young man that Talon had noticed before and his eyes were flicking everywhere as he searched the gardens for his objective.

Talon was certain they had come for him. He seized Abd'allah's sleeve and said in a very low tone, "They come for me, my friend. Save yourself."

Abd'allah barked a short laugh. "I stay with you, my Lord. If indeed you are right then you will need my sword this night."

They slipped into the shadows seeking a way out, but their way was blocked by a high wall; they might have been able to climb it but a shout from behind prevented them from trying. Not wanting an arrow in the back nor a spear, Talon spun around and found their way blocked by six soldiers, one of whom shouted, "Stop where you are! Identify yourself!"

In the small silence that ensued, while they were standing facing one another in among the fruit trees, Talon heard Hakim shouting in anger at the officer, demanding an explanation for the intrusion. But the rough voice of an officer who sounded more like a Seljuk Turk cut him off and told him that if he continued he would find himself in prison for aiding a spy.

Another voice rose above all the others, that of Aarif. "That is he! That is the Frank! I would know him anywhere. Seize him before he gets away!"

Talon looked over the heads of the soldiers and saw that it was indeed Aarif Mejid who had just denounced him, pointing straight at him, excitedly shouting, "Take him! Take him!"

With a dread sense of disaster and a lump in his stomach Talon unsheathed his sword and stepped forward in an attempt to intimidate the men in front and obtain some space. Indeed they did fall back, but then the same officer who seemed to be in charge shouted at them, "Attack, you dogs, and take him prisoner. I want him alive! Attack, or I shall have you flogged to death yourselves, you jackals!"

The men hesitated and then started forward. The one who was closest to Talon raised his sword and with a shout charged him. Talon deflected the man's clumsy downward slash and feinted high with his blade. As the man lifted his shield to protect himself Talon plunged his sword into the exposed chest. The man grunted in agony and fell forward to choke up blood as he died. The others were shocked at the speed of the killing and paused, but again the officer screamed at them, even striking one of them with the flat of his sword.

Gathering up their courage they came on in a rush, forcing Talon to give ground. But he found that he had a man on his left side acting as his shield. It was Abdullah, and he was shouting abuse at the men ranged in front of them. "Come, you dog turds! I will send you all to hell with my nice sharp knife!" he yelled, brandishing his sword in their faces.

But the troopers had spears as well as swords, and now there were many others coming to support the six men. Before long the two had their backs to the wall of the garden and were surrounded by lunging, slashing soldiers who were all yelling at the same time and getting in one another's way as they tried to attack all at once. Both Talon and Abd'allah scored with kills again, but it was a foregone conclusion that they would not last very long. To Talon's dismay Abdullah cried out and lurched back against him gasping, "They have killed me, my Lord. Save yourself, for I am gone!" He said no more as the troopers bore down upon them, and Abd'allah received several more thrusts to the body, but he was dead already. Talon had made the mistake of bending over his companion to try and protect him, not sure if indeed he was alive or dead. That was the last thing he knew, as he received a blow to the top of his head and then knew nothing but blackness.

Treacherous time has put me in prison
where I've chirped away like a bird in a snare
How pure my aspiration
is, and was, and will be there.

—Todorus Abulafia

Chapter 20

Prison

Talon lifted his head and stared blearily about him, then he groaned out loud as a wave of pain almost overwhelmed him. The wounds and bruising he had suffered from the beating administered to him by the soldiers and after that by the guards were agonizing. His face was swollen and the left side of his jaw was numb. He shook his head to try and clear the fuzziness, but that made matters worse; he felt as though his head was about to fall off with the pain the motion generated.

He felt about him in the darkness and found he was lying on some stinking damp reeds in a small stone cell. He lifted himself up onto his hands and knees and tried to stand, but something pulled at his left leg hindering him from doing so; it clinked. He looked behind him and discovered that he was chained to the wall. Carefully he moved so that he could sit up and lean against the wall and then stared about him, peering into the darkness around him.

The small cell, not more than ten feet in any direction, stank of excrement and urine along with other rotting smells that made him gag. He wiped his mouth with the sleeve of his torn outer garment and looked up at the low ceiling.

He ached all over so began to explore himself to see if there was anything broken, but apart from a badly beaten face and chest he discovered little else to alarm him. No breaks and no deep wounds. An open wound in this place would soon fester and kill him, he realized. He nearly jumped out of his skin when a voice close by said, “Ah so our friend is awake, Allah be praised!”

Talon peered into the gloom and saw a dark shape squatting against the corner furthest away from him. The figure waved its arm and there was a clink of chains.

“Who are you? Where am I?” demanded Talon though parched and split lips.

“Ah, he speaks too! I shall answer the last question first, as that is the easy one,” replied the shadow, “You are in the Citadel on the east side of the river, a guest of the Vizier; this is his palace and his prison. You have been here for almost a day. I thought you might be dead. There is a little water in the jug over there.” He pointed.

Talon saw the jug and gingerly reached for it and smelt its contents. There was nothing reassuring about the rancid smell coming from the jug but he was desperately thirsty so he trickled a little into his throat. It tasted abominable but he held it down with a gulp.

“I am sore indeed to the point where I might as well be dead,” Talon rasped.

The figure chuckled. “They will find ways to punish you and still keep you alive, my friend. Have fear of that, for then you will wish you could die. The men who work for the Vizier are experts at finding out what they need to know from people like you.”

“People like me?”

“Are you not the famous spy, The Hawk? A Templar Knight from the kingdom of Jerusalem?”

“Where would someone like you hear this kind of nonsense about me?”

"The guards were talking when they brought you here and chained you to the wall."

Talon grunted and leaned tiredly back against the wall. It was damp but he didn't care. He felt exhausted and very hungry.

"Do they feed us here?" he asked to change the subject.

"When they remember to," came the reply.

"So who are you and why are you here in this cell with me?" demanded Talon.

"I am Allam of Oman and I am accused, as you are, of being a spy. Masha Allah. God wills it."

"Are you as spy?"

"After a fashion." He paused. "But not as you might be thinking. I am not here to spy on you. I came to Baghdad to sell racing camels and the beautiful scented resin Lubban from the bushes of Salahlah in the south of my country. I came also to see the lay of the land for my Lord the Prince."

"Does he know you are incarcerated here in this prison?"

"He might well know by now that I have disappeared, as my men would have sent a messenger, but neither he nor they will know where I am nor what will happen to me."

"What will happen to you?" Talon croaked.

"The same that will happen to you, my friend! When they have finished with us we will be beheaded in the city maidan before the Caliph's palace, in front of the noisy crowd who will be baying like jackals for our blood."

Talon said nothing but he felt a cold shiver pass though him. So this was where he was to die. No chance now of getting to Persia from this fortress. He had seen the citadel from the city side of the river, a forbidding place with high walls and a huge gate that dominated its surroundings. Its great red walls loomed over the east side of the river just north of the large bend in the Tigris.

His eyes were becoming accustomed to the darkness so that he could now see the man squatting across from him more clearly. He noticed the straggly beard, the long matted hair and the deep staring eyes of a man who has no hope. The man's cloths were mere rags that might once have been expensive; it was hard to tell in this light. He turned his head to stare at the door. It was made of wood with iron bands holding it together. There was a thin shaft of light shining through a slit of a window high up the wall on his left above where Allam squatted, but it did little to illuminate the cell.

He pondered escape but felt so tired and sick that it merely flickered though his mind while he continued to take stock of his surroundings. There were rats; he could hear them in the gloom squeaking querulously among themselves, feeding on something in the far corner. His new companion left him alone, as he too seemed to be tired.

He must have dozed. Talon woke to the sound of footsteps outside; light flickered through the gap under the door indicating that someone carried a torch. The feet shuffled to a stop and then the bolts were thrown on the other side and the door was opened into the cell.

Two men peered into the shadows thrown by the torch and then one stepped into the cell and took two steps to stand over Talon who crouched against the wall squinting up at him.

"He's awake. You!" he kicked Talon in the legs, "Get up, you are coming with us."

The man who addressed him was dark; under the dirty rag that he had wound around his head he had a thin, pock-marked face and a scraggly, unkempt mustache. He had the blue blind eye that Talon recognized as river blindness. He had seen a lot of this in Dezful a long time ago in Persia.

The other was a larger man with huge hands and forearms that bespoke of strength. His turban was a long rag wound loosely about a head that seamed to have no hair on it, and it seemed he lacked a neck as well. He grinned malevolently at Talon, showing black and rotten teeth. Talon noted that both men were dirty and almost as ragged as the prisoners themselves.

Talon scrambled awkwardly to his feet. It wasn't fast enough for the man with the blind eye who gave him a slap on the side of his head.

"By Allah, when I tell you to move, you move, you infidel pig!"

Talon reeled from the blow but managed to stay on his feet. The guard stood back; he held a sword pointed at Talon while the other man stooped to turn a key into the band that held his leg and released the chain. Then he too stood and moved towards the door leading the way out, while Talon was shoved hard towards the entrance by the other guard.

"Go with God, my friend," called Allam.

"May God protect you, my friend," responded Talon automatically. He received another blow to the head from the guard behind him.

"Be quiet, Infidel, your God will not protect you from what is to come."

He went carefully but stumbled a couple of times on the uneven surfaces; despite his exhaustion he wanted to take note of his surroundings just in case he had the unlikely chance to escape. The floor was very uneven, tiled with mud bricks that were broken and sunken in places. Water had seeped into the tunnel and created dark puddles that stank, reflecting the torch light. The three of them stumbled down a long dark corridor with cells on either side till they came to a flight of steps that were worn into the mud bricks. Talon noticed that they were climbing towards daylight that filtered through the cracks and slits in the wooden door at the top of the stairs.

The leader pulled the locking bands and pushed open the door. Talon was again shoved roughly from behind through the opening. He recoiled from the bright sunlight as it hurt his eyes, and it was a few seconds before he could see properly. He stumbled again as the big man gave him a rough shove forward.

He found that they were at ground level and on one side of a large courtyard. He looked back at the door they had just exited and noticed that it was set into one of the outer walls, which appeared to be very thick indeed. From the set of the sun this wall seemed to be on the western side of the fort on the side of the river.

They walked across the courtyard, which was a hive of activity, with the man behind him prodding Talon along none too gently with the point of the sword.

There were horsemen formed up at one end of the enormous maidan preparing to leave the fort, while on the other side there were stables and syce working with the animals under the shade of a grove of trees. The main citadel was set against the north wall and towered over the outer fortifications.

Talon was prodded towards the entrance of this forbidding place. His two guards were now joined by five smartly dressed and equipped soldiers in light chain mail carrying spears. Talon was handed over to these men, who formed up around him to prevent any escape, then they marched into the main entrance of the citadel. He noted with surprise that the guards and most of the men on horseback or lounging nearby were again Turkish. He had forgotten that the Seljuks were often hired by members of the nobility as mercenaries. Apparently the Vizier felt safer with these tough men than with local militia.

He was given no time to admire the tall columns of the interior, nor the cool, beautifully decorated tiles, nor the high fluted arches of the roof of the first floor. Men in white cotton robes hurried about on the Vizier's business carrying books and rolls of paper. No one paid him much attention as the group hurried towards the wide flight of steps that led to the upper reaches of the palace. For that is what Talon decided this must be. Fortress on the outside, it was a veritable palace inside where the Vizier carried out the business of the Caliph of Baghdad.

The guards hurried Talon up the steps, even seizing his elbow to make him move faster, rushing him to his destination. They came to the top of the stairs and were stopped by a tall warrior in full armor: breast plate and pointed helmet with a turban wrapped tight around its edge, carrying a shield and sword at the ready. He held up his hand and demanded who was coming to see the Vizier.

The leader of the group escorting Talon bowed low, and pointing to Talon replied that the prisoner was to be brought to the Vizier for interrogation.

The officer made a ceremony of allowing them to come abreast of him and then led the way down the wide corridor towards a polished and carved wood door where two other guards stood. Again they were challenged, and again a little ceremony was enacted before one of the guards rapped the door with his knuckles. A man from inside opened the door a crack and peered out. The guard whispered to him and then indicated Talon with his thumb. The door was held open and they were admitted to the sumptuous room beyond.

Talon almost gasped. This was a huge room, laid out with the finest of carpets on the stone flags. Gold and silver ornaments and bowls were in abundance and glittered in the waning sunlight that shone into the room from large arched windows. There were fine cloths and cushions laid around low tables at the center of the room, while in one corner there appeared to be a full library of books and piles of rolls of paper.

A man was seated on cushions at the table with two attendants, who seemed to be clerks waiting on him.

The guards, having forced Talon to his knees, prostrated themselves then waited in that position until the man lifted his hand. Then they scrambled to their feet and stood behind the still kneeling Talon.

The man got to his feet and came towards them. He was tall and thin, dressed in white cotton robes with a modest turban on his aged head. Talon did not fail to note, however, that the material of his tunic and turban was of the finest silk and that the jewels placed in the turban were worth a King's ransom. Not only that, the man's bearing indicated that he was used to command, and his shrewd gray eyes were watching him very carefully.

They gazed at each other, observing one another for a good few minutes. Talon, still on his knees, refused to look away, and the man seemed determined to win the battle of wills that was taking place.

Finally the man said, “I am told that you are a spy from the Kingdom of Jerusalem. Is this correct?”

“I am not a spy, my Lord, as Allah the all merciful is my witness. I am not even sure what a spy is.”

“What do you, an infidel, know of Allah and his kindness?”

“I was brought up to know God’s laws, Sire.”

“You speak Arabic. Where did you learn this?”

“I was taught this too while I learned the laws and the mercy of Allah. Sire, my mother was a slave captured in the siege of Allepo and my father was an officer in the army of the father of Nur Ed Din.” Talon was determined to stick to his story that he was from Anatolia and that he was the son of a slave woman who had been captured in one of the frequent sieges that took place in that region.

“You were denounced by a man who knew you. He told a very different story in which you were a ship’s captain and captured him while at sea, what do you say to that?”

“If I might meet with my accuser I could refute the lies he tells, my Lord. I have never been on a ship and have no intention of ever doing so. I fear the sea! I am a merchant who is trying to reach Shiraz in Persia.”

“What business do you have in Shiraz?”

“I have an uncle who lives there, Your Eminence.”

The Vizier looked curious.

“Why then did you flee when you were accused instead of facing your accuser when you had the chance?” He spoke in Farsi.

At first Talon did not think he had heard the man aright, and then he decided to take a chance. He realized that he was on thin ground, but he looked back into the eyes of the man in front of him and tried to bluff it out. He spoke back in Farsi.

"I did not know for what I might be accused, and I thought I was simply being attacked by men who had made a mistake. They were not interested in my answers at that time, Gorban."

The Visier blinked, he had clearly thought his trap would be sufficient but Talon had understood and responded. Still speaking in Farsi the Vizier asked another question.

"Where did you learn to speak Farsi?"

"My uncle taught me, Gorban. This was while we were trading in Isfahan. It is the most beautiful city in the world, apart from Baghdad, of course." Talon played the wheedling merchant.

The man gave a flick of annoyance with his hand.

"Do you know who I am?" he asked.

Talon shook his head, "I know only that you seem to be a wise and just person, my Lord, and I throw myself upon your mercy."

"I am the Vizier to Al Nazir the Caliph of Baghdad, and I have the power to execute you or to release you. Your life is absolutely within my power. So far you have not yet convinced me that you are not what you are accused of. All the same, I do not think that any of those filthy Franks could learn to speak my language, let alone the Arabic, so I am doubtful that you are who you have been accused of being. However, I would learn more about who you really are. You look like a Frank, but again there are many Mamelukes, slaves who look like you, who have converted to the true faith, who serve the Sultans as mercenaries.

"I am giving you the chance to save your life and soul by telling me what business it is that brought you to Baghdad. Are you one of these Mamelukes? If so, what business are you upon that you disguise yourself as a merchant in Baghdad?"

Talon took a deep breath and then looked directly back at the Vizier, trying not to show any fear. "My Lord, I came to Baghdad only to travel much further on, to Persia where I have private business. Again I say I am neither a Mameluke nor a Frankish spy."

"Yet your accuser insists that you are a Frank. He has seen you in the company of other men from that heretic band of infidels,

God damn them. He says that you captured him and placed him in a Templar prison while his family found the ransom."

Talon knew then that he must be very careful. He stared back at the man in front of him as boldly as he could and repeated his words. "My Lord, if I were a spy for the Kingdom of Jerusalem, God damn them for infidels, why would I be here in Baghdad, far from the areas that are in conflict? It is precisely because of the wars that I am here in this city looking for a means to go to Persia as a merchant! I am a man of peace who flees conflict, my Lord."

The Vizier looked down at him for a moment longer, as though deciding in his mind what to do.

"You sound convincing, but I shall bring your accuser to confront you and then we shall see. If you are lying, you will be tortured and executed." He indicated with a nod of his head that the interview was over.

The guards again prostrated themselves in front of him and then rose, dragged Talon to his feet and marched him out of the room. As they crossed the Maidan again Talon paid particular attention to the walls and any entrances. He noted where the horses were stabled and where there were steps that led to the battlements, anything that might be of use if he could escape.

They returned the way they had come and he was handed off to the two men who had brought him up from the dungeons. Again he was roughly handled as they took him down to the cell where he and Allam were staying.

Once again they chained him to the wall and left without saying anything more.

As the door slammed on him his new companion called over to him. "Well, my friend, how did it go? You don't look as though they tortured you today. I did not hear screams."

Talon turned his head and looked at Allam. "Allah was kind to me today, but I fear that he will not be so for long. I have been denounced by one who claims to have known me in the Middle Sea as a Frank."

"You certainly look like one," was the reply.

"We cannot all look like our Arab masters," said Talon tartly.

The other chuckled. "No, and Islam is mainly blind to the color of a man's skin or hair, but tell me why would someone denounce you if there was no cause?"

Talon found this was getting difficult and changed the subject. "I am to be interrogated once the Vizier has found the man who denounced me."

"Ah, that could be weeks. Time is of a different nature here in the dungeons of the Vizier. They will find the man, of that I have no doubt, but they might just as easily put him in prison till they decide when he is to denounce you. In shah'Allah he will be treated like us."

Talon was curious. "What do you mean? Why would they throw him in prison?"

"To put the fear into him, and then it is you against him. They like their little games here in Baghdad. The Caliph, Al Nazir, May God bless him and be kind to him, is new and no one is sure of his ways or wishes. The Vizier, on the other hand, is originally from Persia and has served for a long time in the administration. He will be preoccupied with other, more demanding issues than a mere spy. Be prepared for a long wait, my friend."

"I do not want to stay here forever! How long have you been here?" exclaimed Talon.

"I have been here for I think four weeks, but am no longer sure. One day blends into another. I doubt it will be forever, my friend, but it might seem like that before long."

"What of escape?" The words were out before he had decided that he could trust the man in the cell with him. But it was too late now.

"Ah escape! I have often thought of that, but we are both chained to the wall and it is not easy to take a wall with you when you want to run away." He chuckled at his own wit.

Talon thought for a moment. "If you had a weapon could you defend yourself?"

The other's reply was scornful. "You are talking to a warrior lord who was raised on a horse and given a sword at the age of four years, Ferengi!"

Talon was relieved to hear that there was still spirit left in the man. Now he knew Arran could fight but gave no sign that he was impressed. He sat back and considered what might be done. Late that night the guards, always a pair of them, came to the cell and left some food and foul tasting water within reach of both of them.

They ate the food without relish, and because there was nothing else to do in the darkness they talked. Talon, always careful about his heritage, invented a story about his life in Armenia where the first great battles for the Holy Land had begun. His companion, on the other hand, was not reticent at all about his background.

"I am from the kingdom of Oman, and I am a merchant, but a much respected one, almost a prince in my own right. I did indeed spy for the sultan from time to time," he informed Talon. "I come from Salahlah, a port on the south of Oman, where I deal in racing camels and the Lubban that can be found in some quantity out in the desert. Do you know of this, Ferengi?"

"My name is Suleiman bin Mahmud Omar, and that does not make me a Ferengi! And yes, I know of the scented sap; it is much prized on the coast of the inner sea, including by the Franks," he stated firmly. His companion only shrugged in the darkness.

"My reason for coming to Baghdad is that the Caliphate has changed and my Lord and master wanted to know what effect it might have on his kingdom," Allam said. "I was sent to listen to the word on the street and in the chai houses, where men sit on threadbare carpets, make deals and drink the sweetened black liquid that comes from the red berries and the same place as the black slaves."

"Unfortunately I was overheard by one of the police spies who work for the Vizier, and they decided that I asked too many questions. Not only that, my accent gave me away," he explained.

Talon had noticed that the accent of the Arabic from the Gulf was different in many subtle ways from that spoken in Mesopotamia.

While his companion had been talking Talon had been seeking anything that might serve as a weapon. Little presented itself other than the chain he wore and perhaps the wooden bowl he had scraped his meal out of with his right hand.

That night he slept badly; he could feel the parasites crawling over his body as he lay in the filthy rushes. His companion slept fitfully and more than once woke up cursing and slapping at some biting insect that had disturbed him.

After midnight, when a rat started gnawing at his boot, Talon gave up trying to sleep and sat hunched against the damp wall thinking of ways that he might get out of this hellhole.

Dawn brought little relief. The daylight filtered in through the high window and lit the cell with a gray hazy light that didn't penetrate the furthest corners. The eternal call to prayers sounded faint in the distance. "Allaaaah Ak..bar!" Then followed the prayers shouted through cupped hands from the distant minarets of the city Mosques across the river, another world away now, and perhaps forever.

The filthy lay in darkness with me,
Their legs in shackles, just like mine;
Time has twisted my paths---unjustly.
My jailers are cruel. I've done no harm.

—Todros Abulafia

Chapter 21

Interrogation

During the night he tried to figure out how he would escape. He was now convinced now that his companion was not a spy sent to share his cell and wheedle information out of him, but one who would dearly like to escape too, as there was not telling when the interrogations would start. Allam had told him blood-chilling stories of how this would go.

"They will start gently by beating you and then burning your skin and pulling a few nails from your fingers. They might even beat the soles of your feet, just to warm you up," he had said with relish. "But as time goes by they will go to the more tried and tested ways of extracting a confession, and then, my friend, you will not be able to walk out of here even if all the doors were opened to you."

Allam finally woke up, and they spoke in a desultory manner, trying to wile away the interminable hours. It rained outside during the day and Talon noticed that the wall behind him was damp. That made it very uncomfortable to lean against, but in the dim light he noticed that when he dragged his hand over the bricks they crumbled.

He dug at the bricks near the staple that anchored him to the wall with his nail and then with one of the links of the chain. The brick gave a few crumbs. Hope rising, he seized the wooden bowl and used it to scrape more of the brick away. Little by little he managed to scrape a dent in the brick around the metal that was buried in the wall.

It was a full four days before they came back for him. By that time Talon felt that he was on personal terms with all the rats and had become well accustomed to the stench of the cell. They were never let out to answer the call of nature, having to suffer the misery of being near to their own body waste all the time.

He heard footsteps coming towards their cell and stopped scraping. He leaned back against the wall he had been recently excavating and stretched his legs out as far as they would go.

The door banged open and the guards stamped in and once again they unchained his ankle. This time Talon was taking careful note as to how they did it. He feigned weakness so that they would not think him dangerous and become unnecessarily alarmed. Then they were shuffling down the corridor past other cells. There were some inmates present; he could hear groans and in one case crying as the prisoners contemplated their various fates or nursed their most recent injuries.

He was taken to the far end where a door opened into a larger room. As they entered his blood curdled. It was clearly a torture chamber. Many instruments of interrogation were stacked against the walls, and in the center were a rack and table for the victims to be laid out on before the interrogations began.

A small group of men were waiting for them, and nothing about them gave him any confidence that he was going to be asked simple questions. The two men at the front of the group of four indicated that he was to be brought in, whereupon he was shoved roughly towards them and then forced to his knees.

"Kneel, you Ferengi dog. You are in the presence of an officer of our most glorious Vizier!" scolded one of his escorts.

The officer came up to him and said, "You are accused by this man of being a Frank spy and a Templar. Do you deny this?"

Talon squinted past the officer to the man behind him and felt a chill as he recognized Aaron Mejid. He knew then that he was doomed to die here, if not today then some time in the near future, for Aaron seemed to carry weight here in Baghdad and certainly bore a grudge against Talon.

"Who is this man who accuses me?" he demanded as boldly as he could, but the fear in his stomach made his voice crack and his mouth was dry.

"I do, oh *Suleiman bin Mahmud Omar*." He said the name mockingly. "I know you were not who you say you are but are Sir Talon the Templar knight who captured my ship outside the port of Abydos and then ransomed me, nearly beggaring my family in the process. Are you spying for the Templars or for someone else?"

The man laughed. "By Allah's will I have caught up with you! Oh mighty Falcon! Did you know that you are known as that because of your skill at killing? You kill they say like the Batinis, those filthy 'Assassins of Rashid El Din's." He paused and then sneered."Look at you now, not so mighty or well dressed, I see!" He held his nose and pretended to be appalled by the smell emanating from the prisoner. "I could hardly believe my eyes when I saw you in the garden as bold as you like!" He turned to the officer and said triumphantly, "This is the man, my Lord. He should be tortured to extract as much information as we can from him and then executed as a common criminal."

The officer nodded but added, "It is still your word, Aaron Mejid, against a man who claims he is a common merchant, not one of those soldiers of the Franks. If he is what he says he is then he will not lie under the interrogator's irons."

"He is Talon, otherwise known as the 'Falcon' I tell you! He is a master at deception and disguise and is a dangerous spy. I know him!" retorted Aaron vehemently.

The officer turned back to Talon. "You will be interrogated here today and many other days until we learn the truth. If you are who you say you are then Allah will intervene and you will be spared too much pain. On the other hand," he said sternly, "if you are indeed a spy of the Templars then you will die at the hands of the executioner after you have almost died under our interrogators' hands here in this room. Start the interrogations."

He indicated Talon to the two men behind him. As they came forward Talon fell forward and started to wail. He cried pitifully as they seized him.

"My Lord, I beg of you for all that is merciful that I am innocent of these crimes. I do not know this man! I am a simple merchant!" He screamed as they pulled off his outer rags and then his upper clothing, then threw him onto the table. They pulled his boots off and threw them into a corner then they spread-eagled him face down on the table. He felt genuine fear but he wanted to give the impression that he was absolutely terrified. Allam had told him that they seemed to enjoy breaking hard men and in order to survive what was coming he should pretend that they were hurting him far more than they actually were. He screamed again and again as they tightened the ropes that held him and wept while he waited for the men to start on him.

One of the men laughed as he watched the writhing and weeping Talon on the table. "If this man is a soldier I will be surprised. Look how he squeals like a sheep about to be killed!"

He was a big ugly brute who had broken teeth and eyes that seemed crossed. He hefted a coiled whip that he unwound onto the floor before he flicked the end onto Talon's back. No sooner did he feel the light touch of the whip than Talon fell to screaming and weeping even more copiously than before, begging them to hear him and calling on Allah as his witness that he was truly a merchant passing through the city. He bewailed his fate at having ever come close to the city.

But he jerked with real pain when the whip did descent hard onto his bare back. He was given seven lashes by the interrogator and each time asked to confess to being the Templar he was accused of being. Each time he wailed and wept and cried that he was nothing of the sort and begged them to stop.

The officer stayed long enough to shrug disgustedly and then took the smirking but puzzled Aaron away with him, remarking as he went, “If this crying excuse of a man is a soldier of the caliber you have described then I do not understand why we have not taken Palestine away from them long before. I think he might be telling the truth.”

Aaron blanched at that, as he knew the consequences of false accusation would mean that he would be on the rack instead of the current occupant. As their voices receded down the corridor Talon could hear Aaron vehemently trying to convince the officer that he knew that Talon was a spy.

The two men left behind went to work on Talon with rods and whips. Then they used hot irons on his bare feet, eliciting more wails for mercy as he play-acted the frightened merchant man with no stomach for pain. All the same the pain was real, and he rapidly became exhausted from lack of water and the constant renewal of the punishment on another part of his anatomy. Eventually, when he was close to passing out, they became bored and went off, leaving him lying face down on the table semi-conscious.

He heard them leave and gathered himself to lift his head painfully and look around at his surroundings. There was a fire going in a metal crucible in one corner with more irons being heated, while pulleys and ropes festooned the beams overhead. Alongside one wall were coils of rope and several heavy whips. He looked down and there in front of him was a small tray of instruments that could only have been for extracting teeth or nails. The tools were crusted with dried blood and there was even something that looked like a blackened tooth lying among them. He shuddered as he gazed at the diabolical instruments, but then his eye lighted upon one of them. It was a sharp iron nail about five inches long and a quarter of an inch thick at the shaft, with a point that might have been used to bore into a victim. It too was dark with someone's blood.

He watched the tray and a plan grew in his head. He lay forward and rested as best he could while he waited for his tormentors to come back. They returned but did not continue the torture. It was late afternoon and they had missed their afternoon naps so they wanted to take him back to his cell. While one of them went back to the door to shout for the jailers the other started to release Talon, who feigned semi-consciousness.

As the man completed untying the last of the ropes and started to pull Talon to his feet, he suddenly went completely limp and slipped through the man's hands to fall awkwardly to the floor. In doing so he managed to fall almost across the tray of torture instruments and take it to the floor with a crash. The brass tray rolled off into the corner and the instruments went everywhere across the dusty flagged floor, while Talon lay where he had fallen, moaning to himself.

The guard with a curse jerked Talon to his knees with an arm around his neck and threw him backwards away from the mess on the floor. Talon stayed on his knees, pretending to be exhausted and now wailing copiously. The exasperated guards literally picked him up and half dragged him out of the room down the corridor to his cell, where they tossed him none too gently against the wall and proceeded to chain him up. Throwing his rags at him as they parted, the man with the blind eye scoffed, "If you are a soldier my mother is a general. What a cry baby!"

Talon lay wearily against the wall trying to recover. His companion eventually spoke up, his voice loud in the confined space of the cell.

"I am sure that Allah must have at least heard your pleas! You could be heard all over the castle. What did they do to you that made you scream like they were castrating you, Suleiman?"

"I followed your instructions to the letter, Allam, and despite the fact that they seem to be the ugliest and nastiest people I have ever encountered I think I fooled them enough as they didn't do too much damage. My feet hurt abominably, though. I am afraid to walk on them."

Allam laughed softly. "Maybe not this time, my friend. But this can go on for a long time. The are working on you and forgetting me for the moment, which gives me time to recover until they remember me, and then it will be my turn again."

"Poor comfort for both of us," murmured Talon. He opened his fist and looked down at the thick pointed nail that lay there. Turning he faced the wall and began to pick at the brick around the thick iron staple embedded in the wall. To his immense relief the nail dug more than just a few grains of the brick out at one time. He knew hope then and began to scratch determinedly at the surface; soon he had created a small pile of dust at the base of the wall and there was a sizable crater around one side of the staple.

Allam was curious. "What is it about the wall that is so fascinating, my friend?" he asked politely.

"I managed to steal a piece of iron. Do you want to escape or do you want to stay here until they come and chop off your head?" asked Talon bluntly.

"I prefer the first choice, my friend," came the reply.

"This is going to take time, but we must both do it so that when the time is right we are both free to overcome the guards one night when they come in with the food. When they come for me you will dig for your life, and when they come for you I shall dig for my life. It might take us days but it is all we have."

"I agree with you, Suleiman," said Allam somberly. "Let's hope we both last and that Allah is kind to us and blinds these filthy pigs to our activity."

"Keep the dust and put it back as mud when we hear them coming so that they don't suspect anything," said Talon. "We must work night and day with one resting and the other working."

Allam whispered, "You are a resourceful man, Suleiman... for a poor merchant." Then he chuckled. "But what do I care of that? We are companions in distress and need one another, is that not so?"

Talon nodded in the darkness. "That is so, my friend. Now you dig because I am tired and need some rest."

He tossed the new tool over to Allam, who picked it out of the air and examined it carefully. "This is indeed a good tool. Sleep for a few hours and then you can continue."

Talon first used some of what little spit he had in his mouth to make a mud ball out of the dust at the base of the wall and plaster it back in place around the shaft of the staple.

Then his tiredness took over and he fell asleep on his side, oblivious of the pain all over his body and the fleas and other biting insects that came to crawl over him in the night. His companion concentrated on his work.

Late that night the jailers arrived with more slops and brackish water that they left within reach of the sleeping Talon and his companion, who leaned back against his wall looking wearily up at them as they stood over him.

One of them chuckled nastily. "This 'woman' is squawking without even getting to the real stuff. He probably is a miserable merchant, but we can have our amusement for a while longer."

Later that night there was much noise outside. Both men sat up and listened as there was a lot of shouting and some screams, the crack of a whip and more shouting, and then the crash of doors being opened and shut.

"What do you make of that, Suleiman?" asked Allam.

"It sounds like more people have discovered the cheaper lodgings of the Citadel," said Talon with a weak attempt at humor.

Allam cackled and then spat. "You have spirit, Suleiman, I'll give you that. There were a lot of people in that batch, I can tell."

Silence settled in and apart from the rats who kept the two men company the deep quiet of an underground space crept upon them.

Talon leaned back against his wall and wondered for the hundredth time what he was doing here. The loss of Abd'allah had shaken him. The man was, had been a good companion and as far as he could judge a very trustworthy man. He had fought side by side with Talon and died for it. He hoped Abd'allah's soul was headed for Paradise. The man deserved it.

Talon was woken by Allam later that night, and while his companion went to sleep he got to work on the wall. He noticed that the brick was wet through and then did some thinking. They might easily be below the water line of the Tigris, all things considered. Well, that was becoming his advantage; the brick was rotten and the deeper he dug the easier it seemed to become. However the staple was deep into the wall; so he settled down to steadily digging the rotten brick away. His hands already had blisters on them from holding the small spike and ramming it constantly into the wall. But he ignored the pain and doggedly continued the work.

It was dawn by the time he had managed to dig deep enough to sense that he was at the end of one side of the staple. His excitement grew as he realized that all he had to do was to make the hole deep enough and he could slip the chain around it, then he would be free. He continued to work furiously, and then with a push and a gasp he drew the chain out from the staple and held it in his hand dangling loose.

Allam woke up just in time to see Talon standing up despite the pain in his feet, holding the chain in his hands, a look of triumph on his face.

"By Allah's mercy, you have done it!" Allam whispered with awe in his voice.

Talon strode over to him and seized him by the shoulders.

"Yes, I have, and now we have to get you loose too. Allah be praised, we will be free this very night if we have his protection."

They knew from the dim light above them that they still had several hours before the jailers came to either feed them or to take one of them off for 'interrogation' so they took turns at working the brick. It was dryer than the other side where Talon had been but, it still gave way to the persistent picking of the small spike they were using.

All too soon, however, they heard noises from off down the corridor as the jailers banged doors and dumped slops inside cells and shouted abuse. They hurriedly spit on the dust in the little piles about them and pushed it back into the holes, then carefully leaned back against their respective walls, waiting.

It seemed that it was time for one of the other prisoners to go to his execution. The luckless prisoner could be heard wailing and crying as the unsympathetic jailers dragged his limp body along the corridor and up the stairs to the outside. There was a fearful silence from the entire prison area as people strained their ears for more sounds from outside. But the execution was most likely on the other side of the river, so they would not have heard even the roar of the crowd as they watched a procession of prisoners going to their fate that day.

"We had better wait until we know what is in store for us today, my friend." said Talon to Allam, who had turned impatiently to go to work again on his shackles.

"You are right, Suleiman," sighed his companion. "I am so eager to leave this place that I can barely wait now."

Eventually the jailers came to their door. This time the one with the white blind eye strode over to Allam and dragged him to his knees.

"Stay there while we unleash you, offal eater," he growled.

After they had released him they pushed him out of the door between them and slammed the door shut as they went out. Just before they left Allam gave Talon a wink. Talon grimaced at him and lifted his hand in salute. They both knew where the jailers were taking him, and sure enough within about half an hour the screams began.

Talon winced. They seemed genuine and he prayed for Allam to have courage and to survive the torture. He went to work on the staple that held Allam's chain urgently, hoping that no one would come for him.

After what seemed hours of intermittent screaming and crying he heard the men coming back. They opened the door and dumped

Allam back in his corner, making sure that he was secured before they left. Talon sat where he was, as he knew they would be back in a short while to deliver some slops to them.

Allam groaned and lifted his head. Talon was shocked at the sight of his face. Allam tried to sit up but could not, he slumped against the wall but managed a wry grin at Talon.

"It looks bad but I don't think they broke anything," he croaked, then he passed out on his face in the rushes.

Talon was about to go to him, but the jailers came back and, as he had anticipated, dumped a jug of water on the rushes just within his reach, as well as some flat nan and a bowl of some indeterminate soup. It smelled bad but he could just distinguish the smell of cooked lentils.

The jailor with the bad eye sneered at Talon. "You are for the rough stuff tomorrow, Ferengi. Eat up; you won't be able to eat anything by the time we have finished with you tomorrow."

When they had left Talon carefully released himself; seizing the jug he slid over to his companion and turned him onto his back. He lifted Allam's head and dripped some water into his bloody mouth. Allam choked and shook his head and tried to sit up. He spat out a tooth and then wiped his mouth with his filthy sleeve. Talon helped him sit up and propped him against the wall.

"You look bad, my friend. What did they do to you?"

"The usual things, but they were in a hurry for some reason and I screamed like a woman so that they thought I was in a lot more pain that they were actually making me suffer," said Allam wearily. "You still look bad from the beatings yesterday, so don't worry too much about me." He grinned though cut lips. Talon was relieved to see the spirit of the man still unbroken but he said carefully, "Will you have the strength to leave with me? We have to leave this place soon or they will wear us down so much we won't be able to depart even if we could."

"You are right, Suleiman. They will kill us if we stay, so we must get to work. Where is the spike?"

"I have it. You eat some bread and soup while I get to work,and later you can relieve me."

They took turns digging and eating and even sleeping when they could till late in the afternoon, when Allam let out a low cry.

Talon was instantly by his side.

"By the good will of Allah to whom all praise is due! I am almost there!" said Allam shakily. They worked frantically to get the last of the brick chips out and then it was Allam's turn to stand and hold his chain in both hands. He did a little jig of joy, and then reaching down he hauled Talon to his feet and embraced him, dancing clumsily around on the filthy rushes. Then he stopped and held Talon for a long moment in a tight embrace.

"You are my savior, my friend. Allah be praised, but I shall never forget this."

"We are not out of the prison yet, Allam, so don't count your goats just yet!" Talon rasped."Now listen to what I have to say."

Then he outlined his plan. After he had drilled Allam in the role he was to play they talked about what they would do once they escaped. They spoke for a long time about their options, arguing forcefully but amicably. Allam wanted to go straight to his encampment outside the city and then flee south to the sea, but Talon pointed out that the Vizier's men would know exactly where to look to arrest him again. Allam reluctantly agreed with him, but then pressed Talon for a better alternative.

Talon explained that he had come into the city by a much more discrete route and could still go to his rented property and get weapons and even some money that could be used to bribe the guards or others on their way. He hoped that no one had found out where he was staying, because that would also mean that the Kurdish boy, Dar'an, would be discovered and most probably robbed and killed. Abd'allah had been killed at his side, however, so no one should be able to trace his presence in the city back to the boy other than the old man, who would certainly deny any knowledge of where the merchant was staying.

They agreed that both of them wanted to go south, it was just a question of how they were to mange it. The distance was daunting and they knew they would be hunted all the way if the Vizier got wind of their direction. At the end of the conversation Allam said, "It is a plan of sorts. It will work, In shah'Allah, or we will die tomorrow instead."

They heard the distant call to prayers from the minarets across the river. It was time for the evening prayers. Allam got to his feet wearily. "We should pray, my friend, as this is Allah's grace and I have to thank him."

Talon climbed to his feet and they went through the ritual of prayer together.

That blade which lurked, 'neath passions rude,
Whose fane was war, whose feast was blood,
Now idly hung unnoticed there,
Its wearer's promised rest to share;

—Thomas W. Wood

Chapter 22

Escape

The waiting was hard. The two of them made as good a meal of the foul soup and the stale bread as they could because, as Talon pointed out, it might be their last meal for a while and they needed their strength for the coming night.

As evening approached they talked in a desultory manner reviewing the plan they were to put into action. It was clear to Talon that Allam was very tense; Talon also suspected that his companion was still hurting from the interrogation. His own body was very sore and his face and feet were badly bruised from the beatings he had received. Finally they heard the jailers making their final rounds for the night, and they could see the flickering light of the torch through the crack under the door.

"Be ready!" whispered Talon. The dark figure of his companion shifted but said nothing.

The bolts were slammed back and the door was kicked open with a sandaled foot. The jailor whom Talon now called Blind Eye entered first, sword held forward in his right hand, followed closely by his partner carrying a jug of water and some more dried nan.

Blind Eye also carried the torch, so both of them had their hands full; but they were obviously confident that they could not be attacked because the prisoners were chained to the wall.

Talon was squatting against his wall, head down, but watching the men in the guttering light of the torch. His moment came as the large man stooped to place the food and jug on the ground. Talon leapt up and swung the chain hard in an arc that landed on the back of the man's neck with a thrashing sound. The sheer savagery of the blow stunned the man and he fell forward onto his knees.

Talon didn't even look at him, instead he spun towards Blind Eye who was standing gaping as though unable to believe what he had just witnessed. Before the man could react Talon ducked behind him and whirled his chain around his neck then jerked it as hard as he could. Blind Eye let out only a choked cry that was barely audible and stepped backwards, dropping the sword and the torch as he clutched at the chain around his throat with both hands.

Talon jerked hard again and hauled the struggling man over backwards off his feet so that he fell in an untidy heap to the floor. Making sure that the man was incapacitated for the moment Talon glanced up quickly to see what Allam was doing. His companion had jumped on the other jailer and he too had thrown his chain around that man's neck and was now pulling backwards with all his strength.

But his intended victim was very strong and had recovered enough to stand up and try to turn on his attacker, reaching behind him to grab his hands as the other jerked the chain savagely back and forth. The two were performing a strange shuffling dance punctuated by wheezing grunts of pain from the jailer and the loud panting of the other. Talon could see that the situation could only end one way, as the larger man fought with all his strength against the chain around his neck. It was clear that sooner or later he would be able to close with his attacker and there was little doubt in Talon's mind as to the outcome then.

Talon looked down at the jailer with the blind eye who was coughing and choking at his feet and about to yell for help. He released the chain and snatched up the rusty sword. Without giving it any thought he rammed the point deep into the side of his victim, who gave a choking moan and then writhed silently in his death rattle. Talon knew he had only seconds left. He tugged the sword loose, turned and dived across the cell to where the other two were struggling in a manic embrace. The jailor had succeeded in twisting his body round so that he faced Allam and had then rammed him backwards into the wall.

Allam was now fighting for his life, trying to fend off the deadly grip the other was about to lock around his own throat with his massive hands. The chain was now hanging loose, but so intent on the struggle was the guard that he had not yet called out an alarm. Talon picked his place and rammed the sword with both hands deep into the back of the thickset man. The sword went right through his heart and protruded through his rib cage at the front. The tip of the blade came to a stop an inch from Allam's own chest.

The man froze for a split second and then arched his back, clutching desperately at the sword point where it protruded from his chest. His mouth opened to scream his agony but Allam had the presence of mind to slap both his hands across the gaping mouth just in time so that the only sound was a muffled gurgle. The large man fell to his knees, with both hands still clutching his chest. His eyes rolled up into his head, then he toppled forward to bang his forehead against the wall with a dull thump; then he fell sideways onto the floor. Allam skipped off to the side watching wide-eyed as the man died at his feet.

The whole thing had lasted only a few long seconds, but they were both panting with the exertion. Talon leaned on the sword and gasped.

"Be still and listen." They both froze in place and listened. After a few moments Talon whispered, "I don't think anyone heard us."

Allam staggered over to the door and shut it. The torch had fallen to the sodden rushes and was about to go out. Talon leaned down and picked it up, restoring it to its former brightness. He lifted the torch high and surveyed the cell. Their two jailers were very dead and blood was beginning to collect in a puddle near each.

"We have to get their clothes off quickly!" panted Talon.

Allam nodded wordlessly; he too was panting hard. They began to strip the blind jailor of his outer clothing. Allam wrinkled his nose at the unwashed body and filthy garments but continued till he had them in his arms. He shook them to try and rid them of some of the blood. Talon went over to the other jailor and did the same. They donned the clothes and then they sat down and took stock of their situation. They both listened again for long minutes to see if there was any kind of alarm. There was no sound other than the rasping sound of their labored breathing in the confines of the cell.

"We need to leave as soon as possible so that no one starts looking for these two," said Talon.

Allam nodded, and then said, "By Allah, I have never seen a man kill as quickly as you did tonight, Suleiman. You are a man to be reckoned with." He squinted thoughtfully at Talon in the flickering light of the torch.

Talon grunted. "We have no time to be discussing things, Allam. Yes, I was a Mameluke. We have to get moving!"

When they were dressed and had donned the loose turbans of their victims they prepared to leave. Allam struggled into the sandals of one of their victims and then pronounced himself ready.

Cautiously Talon opened the door and peered out. All was darkness beyond the light of the torch. He led the way out and they then shut and bolted the door behind them. They were now committed to the escape; there was no return.

Trying to sound like they belonged in the place they strode confidently along the corridor to the far torture chamber where Allam remembered seeing some weapons placed against a wall. He wanted at least a knife on his person if they were to end their days in a fight, he told Talon.

There they picked up a couple of knives and another rusty old sword. Talon was delighted to see his boots lying where they had been thrown and promptly exchanged them for the sandals he wore. Now they had to make their way up the stairs to the level of the Maidan and somehow get out of the fortress before anyone noticed that they were not the jailers.

Talon decided to put the torch out before they came to the entrance so that they would be in darkness as they walked out. They discovered that, although there was not much activity at that time of night, there was enough near the gates for them to be concerned, so they paused in the dark recess near the wall and looked around.

"How in the name of the Prophet do we get out of here?" whispered Allam in Talon's ear.

Talon shook his head. "I do not think we can go out of the gates; there is light there and people know the two men we left below."

He glanced upwards. "I think we have to go over the wall, but there are sentries up there too."

He had an idea. "Come back into the passage. I am going for some rope," he whispered. He hurried back to the torture chamber and located a pile of rope in the darkness that he thought might do. With the coil over his shoulder he made his way back to his companion.

"This rope will allow us to drop to the outside, but we might have to swim the river to get to the other side; can you do it?" He didn't say that they might have to kill another man to get away. They would just have to deal with it if it happened.

Allam nodded warily. "We have to swim the river?" he asked nervously.

Talon didn't wait to reply. He moved off, keeping to the shadows of the wall, until they came to a stairway that lead up towards the battlements. Cautiously they climbed the stairs one step at a time until they could just see the top. As Talon had feared, there was a man squatting with his back against the wall some paces off. It was hard to see if he was awake or not, as he seemed to be slumped. Sure enough, a low snore greeted them as they mounted the final stairs. Talon pointed out the sentry to Allam and put his finger to his lips. The heavens above were aglow with stars and they were now clearly outlined against this backdrop.

Should the man wake he would certainly raise the alarm. Allam moved with his dagger out as though to finish the man, but Talon seized his arm and again put his finger against his lips and pointed to the battlements. He hurried to the low wall in front of him and leaned out to search the ground below. Somewhat to his surprise he saw a short bank and then the river running black and swiftly beyond that. Now he understood why the foundations of the citadel were so wet.

He quickly tossed the rope out and down, hauled it in, and when he thought he had it approximately in two halves he looped the rope over one of the many crenels that protruded up from the parapet. He motioned Allam urgently to get onto the rope and whispered to him.

"Take both ropes and slide down them to the ground. Don't let go of either one or you will take a tumble and hurt yourself."

Allam nodded and Talon helped him over the edge of the wall and then made sure he had both ropes in his hands.

"Go!" he whispered sharply.

Allam needed no further bidding. He slid most of the way down and landed with a soft thump on the bank. Talon moved quickly and let himself down but had only just started when he heard voices near by.

A man said, "I knew he would be asleep! Hey you, Ali! You lazy donkey, wake up! It's a flogging for you."

There was the patter of two pairs of sandaled feet and a loud slap. The sleeping man woke with a cry and then there was a lot of shouting as the newcomers berated him for being asleep on duty.

Talon froze against the wall. If anyone looked over the edge they could not fail to see him. Very slowly he eased himself down the rope, praying that no one would do so and discover them both. But the noisy altercation continued above, so he let himself down steadily to the base of the wall where Allam was pressed into the shadows and there they stayed until things settled down above them.

Silence descended in their area of the wall. Very slowly Talon started to pull one end of the rope. It took some time but eventually the loose end dropped down to where they were standing. They waited again in the darkness for any sign of trouble.

"Now there is a good chance that they will not think we made it over the wall," he whispered to Allam. "Are you ready to swim?"

There was silence. Talon nudged his companion. "Are you ready to swim the river?" he whispered more urgently, shaking Allam by the arm.

His companion whispered back fiercely. "I... I have never learned to swim, Suleiman. I am a man of the desert, not the water!" he offered in weak defiance.

Talon smiled grimly in the dark. "Then now is the time to learn. Do not struggle in the water or you will drown. I shall see if I can find something to help us float. Stay here."

He made his way along the wall towards some darker shadows where he felt about. He was seeking anything that might support Allam and help them get across the large river.

To his surprise he stumbled into an obstruction that upon investigation seemed to be a short length of timber. Feeling for it he realized that it was an old rotten door lying with a lot of wooden beams and other rubbish that had been tossed over the walls of the fortress.

He hefted the timber and then placed it on the bank and went back for Allam, who was squatting against the wall disconsolately contemplating the river in front of him.

When Talon came up he whispered woefully, "Allah has decreed that I should die here, my friend. You have done all you could to save me but the river is not for me. I will stay here and fight them ferociously when they come so that you can escape. I shall die with no regrets, my friend."

Talon grunted, "You can stay here if you want to and be a martyr but I have the means to get both of us across. You will have to be very courageous, Allam, or we will be discovered. But we can make it if you listen to me carefully."

Allam whispered back, "By Allah, I shall do exactly as you ask, Suleiman. Tell me."

They made their way back to the door and Talon slid it into the water. It was rotten so it did not float well and he had some misgivings as to its capability to carry Allam; but he made his unhappy companion lie on the door, which promptly subsided in the water so that Allam was almost submerged and began to panic. Talon leaned over him and fiercely whispered to him to be still or he would leave him and go alone. Allam subsided but began to mutter prayers in one long continuous stream.

Talon took off his boots and placed them on Arran's back, then pushed the whole party into the river. Allam hung onto the sides of the door with a grip like death, his head lifted to see where they might be going while the rest of his body was almost totally submerged. The only sign that he was in a state of complete fright was the rasp of his breathing, his mouth wide open as though to gulp all the air he could. When he remembered he would start muttering his prayers again until some small wavelet would splash into his mouth and shut him up for a few minutes.

Talon had underestimated the strength of the current. His clothes dragged in the water and he had to fight to keep them on course, and also from capsizing, as that would be the end of them.

Allam would flounder about and cause a commotion that would bring the very unwelcome attention of anyone on the river bank.

He kicked out strongly, hoping to make it across almost directly, but the current drove them down stream much faster than he had expected. He was very glad that there was almost no traffic on this portion of the river, for if a boat had come by they would have been seen and the alarm raised very quickly after that. As it was, a small falukah sailed by about a quarter of a mile further down stream, but the people on board were preoccupied with some drinking and partying so they paid no attention to the river all about them. All the same, Talon pushed Allam's head down so that both of them had only their eyes above the water while they clung to the rotten door.

It seemed as though they had been in the water for hours and Talon was chilled to the bone by the time they were within reach of the other bank. He cautiously moved the door with the petrified Allam still clinging to it towards a part of the bank that was tree lined and where the shadows would shield them from curious eyes.

It was with profound relief that he felt the mud of the other bank under his feet and could push the raft into the reeds. Although he was very tired he had to shove Allam hard to get him to release the door, splash into the water then stagger to the dry bank. They lay there, too tired to talk. Talon retrieved his boots and then fell flat, he was shaking with the cold; he was chilled to the bone and he was sure that Allam must be as well, although his companion did not say a word. Allam lay in a sodden bundle on the dried mud, shaking visibly.

Finally Talon sat up and took stock of their surroundings. There was a faint glow of light in the eastern horizon. It was time to go. He stood up and staggered up the slope through the reeds until he stood on the main bank of the river. Sitting down to empty the water from his boots and replace them he looked over at the distant citadel, an ominous dark shape squatting on the other side. There seemed to be no alarms for the moment, but that could change at any time. There were few sounds in the night around them: the distant barking of a dog and the restless caw of a crow somewhere in the trees, otherwise silence. He figured that it would be some hours into the day before anyone realized that the two jailers were not around and started looking for them.

"Come on, Allam, we have to hurry," he said.

"Once again I am in your debt, my friend. May Allah be kind to you on judgment day," said Allam in a low voice.

"You may thank me later, we cannot be seen in daylight or people will remember us." He set off at a brisk walk, trying to get warm.

"Where did you say your people were camped?" he asked Allam.

"On the south of the city very close to here, Suleiman," responded his companion after looking about him.

The Caliph has gone to his lordly rest
Though wild is the billow that rolls in his breast;
And though the bright stars of the evening have set,
And shadows are dark on the tall minaret,
And the chamber is still, he slumbers not yet.

—Thomas W. Wood

Chapter 23

Refuge

Because they were so close they decided to take a look. The camp was one of many that were situated around the great city walls. They approached just as the first rays of day illuminated the eastern horizon, bathing the tops of the palms with gold. Talon knew that as soon as the people at the fort knew of their disappearance they would come looking at this encampment first; he wanted to make sure that they were well out of the area before then. There would be a pursuit, of that he was sure.

They were in for an unpleasant surprise. The men and camels that had constituted Allam's retinue were gone. He choked with disappointment and cast about desperately to see if he had made a mistake. Talon too was staring about him at the remains of the camp. It had all the signs of previous occupation: cold fires and camel dung strewn about. There were even a few rags lying in the dust but little else to indicate that a small but rich caravan had stayed here for many weeks.

The two men finally squatted down near the ashes of one of the fires to take stock.

"We have to get back into the city," said Talon.

"Are you mad?" asked Allam incredulously. "By the Prophet, you are mad!" He stared at Talon with wide eyes.

"We cannot stay here and get caught, for surely they will come here, my friend," said Talon calmly. He was beginning to wish that he had not left the rope behind. "We have nothing to support us on the outside, certainly not now since your men have left, whereas inside the city I have money and access to food, perhaps even a boat."

"How do you propose to get in?" asked Allam, his curiosity getting the better of his inclination to tell Talon once again that he was mad and that he would have nothing to do with Talon's scheme.

"In the morning there are many people who have been shut out by the curfew who have slept near the gates. We will mingle with them and go into the city when they open the gates. I hope the alarm has not gone off by then. We must hurry, as the gates open at dawn."

Without even looking at Allam he began to run towards the distant gate that they could see dimly in the gathering dawn. There was a fair crowd of people, ranging form wealthy merchants going to the first prayers at the mosques to peasants with goats and sheep. There were camels laden with produce from the farms and even some beggars.

Even as Talon and Allam hurried up to the small crowd the call for prayers came from within the city. The eerie, long, song to the faithful was taken up at other minarets so that it seemed as though the whole city was calling the words of God to the faithful, telling them to commence first prayers of the day. Some of the people at the gate started their prayers but hurried through them as some activity behind the doors began to take place; and then the massive gates began to creak open. They were pushed by five soldiers straining at the huge weight until they finally crashed open against the wall.

Talon joined the herders with Allam in tow, pretending that he was with them; the sheep and goats were a handful and the shepherds welcomed the help. Talon noted with relief that the river had washed off most of the blood and filth from their time in the dungeon. No one paid any attention to the two ragged men among several equally ragged shepherds as they herded goats and dirty, smelly sheep through the gates.

Talon glanced back briefly and then pulled Allam into the darkness of one of the narrow lanes, then led the way at a trot towards the street where he had left Dar'an and all his wealth. A few early risers were either hurrying to their destinations or to prayers. The calls of the Mullahs still filled the air of the quiet city. Dogs barked at them from the moment they came to the first house. Talon ignored the dogs other than to wave his sword at the bolder ones who came to investigate them.

No one paid them any attention, so they were able to continue on their way unhindered. It was only when they came to the more respectable houses that they began to see more people. Mostly it was the night watchmen, who were still on duty. Sometimes there were poor people who worked the streets, keeping them clean for a fee or collecting trash from the servants of the houses.

Talon realized that they were approaching the area where he had his lodgings. He stopped and looked about; the streets were quiet. Even the patrols that periodically came through had not put in an appearance. The early morning was when most people slept deepest. Still he was apprehensive. If the lodging had been discovered they were finished.

He need not have worried, however, as all was quiet as they came upon the street. Very carefully now and keeping to the shadows they came to the door which lead into the familiar courtyard. He tried the door quietly and predictably found it barred from the inside. He listened at the door to see if there was any early morning activity. But the mistress slept late, thus so did her household.

"Now what do we do!" exclaimed Allam in a worried whisper. They were both near exhaustion by now but they were still not within the sanctuary they craved.

Talon looked around hurriedly and then looked up at the wall of the courtyard that lay behind. "Can you give me a lift? Enough to allow me to get onto the wall?" he whispered.

For answer Allam went to the wall and leaned against it, cupping his hands. "Come, my friend, get over the wall or we are both lost."

Talon immediately stepped into the proffered hands and leapt up towards the top of the wall. His hands just managed to get a grip on the other side, but then he hung there too tired to haul himself up. Allam came from under and pushed against his feet, providing just enough impetus to allow him to reach over with the other hand and pull his exhausted body onto the top where he lay trying to control his breath and observe the courtyard below, leaving Allam to slump against the wall.

All was silent. Talon slid off the wall and landed clumsily on the ground within the yard. He waited for any indication of alarm, but there was nothing. He stepped carefully towards the door and lifted the bar. As the door opened Allam slid in and they closed it. They squatted together in the shadows and waited once again, listening for any unwanted sounds of people on the move.

Finally Talon got to his feet and led the way towards the steps that led up to his suite of rooms. When they go to the top he pushed on the door that led to his accommodation. It was barred on the inside but it rattled. There was a small noise in the room. Talon took a chance and tapped on the door. This time there was a scuffle from within, and the welcome voice of Dar'an demanded who was there.

"It is I, Suleiman. Open the door, Dar'an."

There was an muffled cry of excitement, the door was thrown open and Dar'an stood there gaping at the two filthy men standing in front of him. Talon felt a huge sense of relief. The boy was safe, which meant that they were also for the time being.

"My Lord, where have you been? You look terrible. Allah be praised you are alive. I heard that you had been taken prisoner. I did not expect to see you alive again... I... I did not know what to do or where to go, so I stayed here." He was babbling tearfully now.

Talon stepped forward, embraced the boy and said, "Allah is indeed great and has kept you safe here. I am fine, and this is my friend Allam ibn Mohamed Khalil who will stay with us for a time. We are safe for a while, but not for long."

Dar'an stepped out of the embrace and grimaced, wrinkling his nose. "Master Talon, I do not know where you have been but you need a bath. I shall take care of this immediately. You... you need to trim your beard too." He looked over at Allam and bowed. "If my Lord says you are his friend, then I am your servant, Sir."

Allam looked perplexed. "I thought your name was Suleiman?" he said to Talon questioningly.

"Until I knew I could trust you with my life, my friend, I could not take that chance."

Allam nodded thoughtfully and then bowed back to Dar'an respectfully and said with a laugh, "We have been having some adventures, young Dar'an. I accept your invitation but we are very tired and need to sleep before all else. Is it safe here?" he asked Talon and the boy.

Talon looked at the boy and took him by the shoulders. "Have you had any visitors since I disappeared, Dar'an?" he asked gently.

"No, my Lord, no one at all. The mistress is keeping to her rooms and I hear that she is doing a lot of crying." He looked disgusted.

"I stayed because I thought that those who arrested you might not know of this place. One of the servant women told me about your capture and the death of Abd'allah. She told me to lie low until the noise had died down and then to leave. I preferred not to wander about the streets, as I thought someone might recognize me and know I had been with you and Abd'allah, may God be kind to his soul."

Talon gripped the boy's shoulders hard. "You have done well, my young friend. I am sure that Abd'allah's soul will be granted clemency when his time for judgment comes. He was a good man and a friend of us both. May Allah forgive him his sins and see him for a faithful, honest man.

"Now, we are hungry and need to sleep; can you provide us with something to eat?"

Dar'an wiped his nose with his sleeve and nodded vigorously. "I have some cheese and goat's milk with some lentils and some barbari. It is cold; will that suffice for the moment, Sir?" he asked eagerly.

"We do not want to wake the household with noise and chatter," said Talon between mouthfuls as they hungrily devoured the food Dar'an placed in front of them. The food tasted divine after the swill of the prison. "So we must not move about too much and we must plan carefully our next steps."

Allam said with a wry grin, "I would have gone willingly to the executioner if we had had to put up with much more of the slop that those two cursed men dropped on us."

They wolfed the food down and then Talon made his way to his bedroom while Allam was shown a mat in the main living room to sleep on.

Talon could not remember putting his head to the pillow. He fell onto the bed and went straight to sleep.

Dar'an cleaned up and then went into his master's room and removed Talon's outer clothing, threw it in a corner and then curled up at the foot of the bed on a carpet with a blanket for cover. The household continued to sleep.

Talon woke in a panic, sweating, with a cry on his lips. He had dreamed that Blind Eye had come to his rooms and was demanding retribution for having been killed. He was pointing to the huge wound in his side and whining about payments, his bluish blind eye peering down at Talon accusingly.

Talon rolled out of bed and looked around groggily at the walls and furniture of the room. Then he lay back and took stock of their situation. There was no question of leaving in daylight, for the word would be out on their escape by now, he was sure of that. He pondered what they needed to do while he bathed his bruised face in a bowl of water that Dar'an had left him. The boy was in the other rooms making some breakfast.

Allam was still asleep when Talon came quietly out of his bedroom and whispered to the boy, "We have to stay here all day and then leave tonight, Dar'an.

"I want you to find a boat, a good one that three of us can sail out of here when the time comes. I need a boat that will sail in the sea, for we must get to the sea of Arabia. Do you think you can find one for me?"

Dar'an nodded. "Perhaps, Talon, but I don't know much about boats."

"If it has a tall mast and is long and narrow with a high back and is over thirty feet long then it will probably do for us, Dar'an."

"I will do as you ask, Talon. In shah'Allah I shall make the right choice," said the boy, then he asked wickedly, "What do I tell the Mistress of this house when she asks after you?"

Talon pretended to take a swipe at the boy's head. Dar'an ducked and grinned but then he whispered in a serious tone, "Do not fear. my master. She will not know you are here... at least not from me!" Talon grinned as well and took another swipe at the dodging boy's head. They ate the bread and spooned the maast with some cucumber and rice in companionable silence while they waited for Allam to come out of his exhausted sleep.

Dar'an had left by the time Talon shook his new friend by the foot to wake him up. Allam came out of his sleep spluttering and scrabbling for a weapon, his eyes wild and fearful. Then he caught sight of Talon standing over him grinning and holding his dagger out of reach.

"It is time to wake up, my friend, and to plan our escape from this not so welcoming city," said Talon in a low voice.

While Allam washed the filth off his face and beard Talon explained their situation. "It is entirely possible that we are trapped in this city if they think that we came here."

Allam nodded. "It was madness to come... we will surely be captured and executed. I can feel the point of the executioner's sword in my back just before he chops off my head even now!" He looked lugubriously at Talon who could not help but to laugh.

"Perhaps we will cheat the executioner even now. Listen, we cannot leave by the gates; they will be watching for riders and any one on a camel will be searched and interrogated as they leave. The only way out is by boat, and even then it will be hard, as we still have to get over the walls."

"I shall see you on the maidan and then on the way to meet our maker, Suleiman, or Talon, whoever you are; but I think that this time we are trapped."

"Have you no more faith in Allah's mercy?" snapped Talon. "Thus far I think that he has been on our side and not that of our enemies!"

Allam dried his face. "But it will not do to rely upon his benefice for too long. He has smiled upon us thus far, but I fear it might only to be to toy with us before turning us back like mice in a trap."

"Allam, I thought you were a fighting man! What is this nonsense? Do you not think it better if we relied upon our own wits? I do not think you are a coward, my friend."

Allam was goaded. He drew himself upright and his right hand searched for the knife that Talon still had in his hands. "No one calls Allam a coward! Not even you!" he said fiercely.

"Indeed not, my friend. I will not call you one either. But you have to have more faith in yourself and in me if we are to succeed in our next endeavor. Allah notwithstanding, we have to work this one out for ourselves. Now listen."

While a mollified Allam ate the remains of the breakfast Talon explained his plan.

They then rested some more, regaining their strength while listening with half an ear to the activity outside their accommodation as the household woke up and the daily tasks within the flood-damaged courtyard went on through the morning. There was still much work being done to repair the broken and crumbling walls and houses in the neighborhood; the enormous floods of the spring had done immense damage to the entire city.

At one point both men jumped up and snatched up their weapons, listening with bated breath as someone rattled the door and called out for Dar'an. Fortunately the servant or whoever it had been did not tarry but with an impatient oath finally left, his footsteps receding down the brick stairway.

Late in the morning the two men heard footsteps again ascending the stairs and a light tap on the door in the code that had been agreed with Dar'an. He slipped into the gloomy room as soon as the door was held open by a cautious Talon. He was obviously excited.

"The news is all over the city that two men escaped from the Citadel last night or this morning!" he burst out when Talon asked him what was going on.

"They say that a notorious spy called "The Falcon" and another spy from Oman killed their jailers and escaped into thin air!"

He turned to Talon. "Who is the Falcon, My Lord?"

"Never mind who he is, Dar'an; what else did you hear?" Talon glanced at Allam who was staring at him with wide eyes at the news.

"I am confused, my Lord, but they also said that today is a day of celebration, as the Caliph has ordered the execution of the heretics, the Ismaili prisoners who were captured not so long ago."

"Ismaili prisoners? What do you mean?" asked Talon, puzzled.

"They say that there was an attempt to murder the Vizier by the 'Assassins, the Ismaili ones from Persia. Don't you know about these people, Talon?"

"No, what do they say on the street? Allam, do you know about these people?"

"I have heard about them, Talon. They are terrifying people as they are invisible and can kill anyone they chose to. Everyone fears them, may Allah curse them for all eternity!"

Dar'an was into his stride now. "They say that the Ismaili and the Shi'ites of the city, mainly the Persians, have tried to plot the downfall of the Caliph and these people are taken from among the residents of the city to be executed as an example to anyone else plotting to kill him."

"What happened to the ones who tried to kill the Caliph is the first place?" asked Talon. But he already knew.

"The word is that they often try to kill themselves rather than be captured, Suleiman; they have no fear of death," said Allam.

Talon nodded but said nothing. This might be useful information. He sympathized with the poor people being executed. They were victims of a repressive regime that viewed the Ismaili and other Shi'ite sects as heretics and therefore suspect at any time of plotting to murder righteous Sunni folk, but he could not help that. He wanted simply to leave the city, not get tangled up in the perpetual sectarian conflicts that were growing more and more bitter over time.

He had even heard that the Shi'ites had been blamed for the massive floods of the past spring that had destroyed large areas of the mud brick city. There had been riots by the Sunni citizenry. They had burned the houses in the Shi'ite and Ismaili areas, making no distinction between them and the Jewish community that had also been devastated. Many innocent people had died, having been blamed for the damage caused by poor maintenance of the many canals in and around the city.

At that thought he paused and asked Dar'an, "There are many canals that lead into and out of the city. Do they usually guard the entrances under the walls?"

"I could go and find out, my Lord."

Talon thought that a good idea and packed the boy off again with instructions to find a canal nearest to the river side of the city. In fact the river Tigris swept around the city on the north and east sides, so there would most likely be many canals that opened into the river itself. He also instructed the boy to discreetly buy food for four days.

Briefly, Talon thought about letting the Mistress of the house know he was safe, but then he forced himself to reconsider. Her servants would surely find out and then there was the very real risk that someone within her compound might be tempted to betray them. He could not afford the chance.

The day was well advanced by the time the boy came back. By this time both men had discussed every detail of how they wanted to leave the city without raising the alarm.

Once again the boy was very excited when he came in. "My Lord, the crowds are gathering at the great Maidan near the center of the city just in front of the Caliph's palace gates. I have heard that there are many Shi'ite and they are getting angry because there are to be executions of Ismaili and Shia, and there will be many more troops on duty tonight when the executions take place."

"A disturbance could be just what we need tonight," observed Allam.

To Him that made heaven, Earth and Sea,
That since my flesh must die so soon
And want a Head to dine next noon,
Just at the stroke, when my veins start and spread,
Set on my Soul an everlasting Head.

—Sir Walter Raleigh

Chapter 24

A Boat

There would be no message; they were slipping away like thieves in the night. Swords were concealed in tied up blanket rolls whence they could be easily pulled if necessary, but the men carried the traditional knives in their sashes. Dar'an carried one and also carried Talon's bow in the thigh case that he normally used when mounted. They would leave all else, including the camels, to the mistress of the house. They were each dressed as poor desert Arabs but with an over cloak that could be used to keep out the cold or for protection from the sand in the desert.

Talon took care to ensure that Allam did not see the gold that he had hidden and now carried on his person in a small leather bag tucked into his clothing. He knew that Dar'an's loyalty was absolute so he was not concerned that the boy would betray them.

They waited until the servants of the house were busy in another area then slipped out of the room. It was not difficult for them to run along a flat wall adjacent to their own and to clamber down some scaffolding onto the deserted street without being seen by the old man who watched the gate of the compound.

They set off at a brisk pace to join the flow of traffic heading for the great maidan where the executions were to be held. Talon had no intention of staying to watch, but in order to reach their destination they had to pass through or by the maidan. He wanted some distraction to take place that would allow them to leave the city undetected. A riot would be helpful.

They quickly mingled with the many people moving towards the maidan. There were the usual camels ambling along at their own pace regardless of what their owners wanted. Not many goats nor sheep tonight, but many, many people. As they hurried along Talon tried to hear what people were saying. It was clear that there was an unusual amount of excitement, as a mass execution of heretics was not that common and certainly entertainment for all.

As they progressed along the side streets towards the main avenue that led from the inner gates to the gates of the Caliph's palace the throng grew denser. People carried torches on long sticks that lit the faces of the crowd and the surrounding houses where others, mainly women, stared down at the moving crowd.

From time to time now there was a shout from behind and horsemen rode through the crowd, driving people off the center, scattering them in all directions as they clattered by. Talon and Allam were careful to keep their heads down and shrink into the crowd whenever this happened. They were near to an intersection which would bring them onto the river side of the Maidan when there was a great shout ahead.

"They have begun the executions," whispered Allam. "We have to get across the maidan and down to the river before the crowd gets out of hand."

Talon heard him but did not reply. They were swept up in the movement of the now very excited mass of bodies, some of them none to clean, who pressed all around them. Then they were stopped on the edge of the Maidan itself by armed men with spears. Despite the gristly show being presented there was a festive atmosphere in the air.

The soldiers ringed the massive square in a tight circle preventing anyone from getting too close to the scene taking place in the middle. Their spears were held across their bodies, facing the crowd. There were horsemen within the circle of foot soldiers, seemingly poised for trouble. Talon didn't like the look of this; there was no crossing the maidan at this point. He cast about for a way round and nudged Allam.

"Go south from here; we can cross the avenue over there." He pointed over the crowd. Allam nodded and pushed his way through the crowd in that general direction, ignoring the curses and ugly looks sent his way as he drove on. Talon had Dar'an by the shoulder and pushed him ahead of him in Allam's wake.

To his right in the near center of the square he could see a huddle of kneeling people who looked like prisoners, while off to their right in the very middle of the Maidan were three burly men who were clearly the executioners. Again there was a roar from the crowd who were watching the gristly events unfold.

He heard a shriek as a luckless prisoner was dragged struggling to the place where the men waited with their long swords poised. Another and then another was dragged by the soldiers out of the huddle of prisoners and taken to where their lives would terminate.

There they were made to kneel, their arms bound behind them, facing the crowd. One of the executioners stood poised over his victim and he pricked him in the back with the point of his sword. The pain drove the prisoner's head up as he gasped with the pain. Almost casually the sword swept down and across. The victim's head leapt off his shoulders and the body toppled over twitching, blood pumping onto the sand. The head bounced a couple of paces in front and rolled onto its side. Blood still poured out of the prone body as the executioner reached over and picked up the head with his huge hand and raised it high. The crowd cheered and roared its approval. A skillful execution was to be admired; and besides, they enjoyed the entertainment. Talon felt that the luckless prisoner had been dealt with kindly under the circumstances, as it could have been much worse.

In fact the next prisoner failed to realize that he could have a clean execution as long as he stayed still. He screamed and shrieked his terror to the sky as he was forced into position for the sword. Then, although he had also been pricked by his executioner he fell forward. This movement meant that the sword failed to completely decapitate the man and he fell forward still shrieking, now in agony. The executioner had to finish the gristly work, clumsily trying to hack the prisoner's head off as he writhed on the ground. The crowd roared its disapproval, shouting abuse and lewd comments at the inept executioner, who looked very chastened. He could be made to join the prisoners if he did not improve his style. People shouted aloud that he should be made to do so at once!

Then a more gristly execution began to unfold. A prisoner, naked except for a loin cloth, was dragged out in front of the crowd and strapped to a cross-like frame. While the inert figure hung there, a man read a proclamation to the crowded Maidan.

"This is a member of the Batinis, a foul 'Assassin who failed in his attempt upon the life of his most holy person the Caliph of Baghdad. His punishment is to be flayed alive and then his skin will be stuffed with straw and shown to the world at large. Let the sentence begin!"

The small man who had made the announcement hurried off during the hush that followed his words.

But then one of the executioners approached the prone figure of the prisoner and, drawing out a knife, drew a deep cut across the man's back and then down both flanks. The prisoner came to life with a scream, a long wailing scream that was the only sound in the whole arena. Another man came up and then both tore the flesh off the prisoner's back in one long pull. The prisoner shrieked his agony to the world and writhed horribly, jerking and shaking his body as the remorseless executioners continued to flay him.

The crowd began to howl their appreciation of the horror they were witnessing.

The baying of the spectators and the dreadful spectacle distracted attention from the fact that three people were furtively making their way across the avenue and taking no notice of what was being enacted in the Maidan. Neither Talon nor the others wanted to see any more of the ghastly process being carried out in the name of the Caliph. Finally they had crossed over the avenue and taken refuge at the corner of a narrow street that opened onto the main avenue where the noise of the crowd was considerably lessened. Here they paused to take stock and decide their next move.

Talon asked Dar'an the way and he pointed.

"Down there is a canal that makes its way through both the Inner walls and the Outer walls of the city, Talon. When we get to the river we can take a boat; there are many on the banks."

Talon nodded and was about to turn to leave when he noticed something. Just up the avenue at another corner he saw several men who were obviously not part of the normal crowd. He stared at the group and noticed that they were all carrying bows and other weapons. Their faces were covered by their dark shamaghs; nevertheless, he could tell they were watching the maidan, but with a different kind of interest, intense and somehow sinister, almost as though they were waiting for something.

He cast his eyes about and across the street; he could see other men in hooded over clothing who were also armed. He gripped Allam and Dar'an by the arms and whispered urgently, "We must leave now! There is going to be trouble any minute!"

Without pausing to explain he led the way at a run down the dark street. They were almost out the other side when a small group of men with bows and spears came running towards them. Talon dragged his companions into a dark shadow, covering his face up to his eyes and hoping the men would not see them. They were lucky; the men were intent upon their own business and hurried by without even glancing in the direction of the fugitives.

Talon took the lead again and began to run for the canal bridge that was ahead. They ran off to the side and slipped into the additional darkness provided by the bank. In the water were several boats of the kind that plied the city canals taking passengers and produce from one end to the other, flat bottomed and wide across the beam. No one was about, the entertainment was elsewhere this night. The roar of the crowded maidan effectively hid any more of the bone-chilling shrieks of the luckless man being flayed.

They hurriedly clambered into one of the boats and pushed off. There were only about a couple of hundred yards to go before they had to pass through a tunnel that led through the Inner wall. They approached it carefully, waiting to be challenged, but there was no one to call them over and ask them their business so they entered the darkness of the tunnel. They pushed themselves along with a pole heading towards the dim light of the other end. The walls were very thick and the tunnel long and dank. Talon felt the roof near his head as he stood to push the pole into the mud and drive them forward. The roar of the blood-maddened crowd followed them into the tunnel but died quickly to a murmur, leaving only the soft sound of water flowing past the prow of the boat and the squeaking of bats.

They shot out into the open air, thankful that they had passed the first hurdle, but just as they did so a soldier on the bank shouted that they should pull alongside and explain where they were going. They heard again the distant sound of the crowd despite the thick walls between them. Talon's heart sank. The hunt was still on for the two fugitives. The Vizier would not let the executions deter him from this objective. He called back.

"Had enough entertainment for one night; going home."

"Where is home? I want to see your faces! Get over here or I will send a spear your way!"

"Hold you piss! We are coming over!" called Talon, sounding aggrieved.

"There seems to be only one man, Suleiman." whispered Allam.

"Be ready for others. I shall deal with him," whispered Talon.

They pulled into the side and Talon jumped out and walked up to the soldier with his hands out from his sides. "Can an honest citizen not go home to his family with his old father and son any more?" he said querulously.

"Come up here where I can see you, dog's offal! I have my orders to check all people going through the canals tonight."

Talon came close to the man, who raised the torch on high to see him better. Just as he came up Talon dropped his hand to his sash, slipped his knife out and in one swift motion took the man by the throat with his left hand and stabbed up and into his heart. The soldier dropped the torch, struggled very briefly, then sagged to the ground.

"Quickly, we must get him out of sight!" whispered Talon urgently.

The other two rushed up and helped him to drag the dead man into the deep darkness of the wall by the tunnel.

"Are you sure that this canal takes us to the river where the boats are?" Talon asked Dar'an.

"Yes, my Lord, there are many boats along a wharf that is just the other side of the walls. They will be guarded too, I am sure of that."

Just then they heard a different note to the noise of the crowd. It had changed from the baying that they had heard earlier to something else. Talon could have sworn it sounded like panic. Then he realized what might have happened. The men he had seen were most probably members of the Shi'ite or Ismaili communities who wanted revenge for the persecutions being visited upon their peoples and had attacked the crowd just when it was most vulnerable.

"We must move quickly now," he told the others. "There will be much death on the streets of Baghdad this night."

They drifted along the canal in the dark, watching both sides of the built up banks for anyone who might feel compelled to interrupt their journey. Often there were houses that all but leaned over the canal in places, and here they were careful to be very quiet lest they wake someone sleeping inside. But the vast majority of the citizens of Baghdad were within the Inner walls this night, and anyone who might have seen them was probably not interested in getting involved.

But the huge Outer walls now loomed in the dark and they could see torches near to the entrance of the tunnel that led out of the city. Talon wondered if there was some kind of grating like a portcullis that could be used to bar their way.

He steered the boat towards the darkest bank and told the others, "This is where we swim or wade. The water is not deep; a man can walk on the bottom and keep his head above water."

Neither of the other two answered him.

"Dar'an, you can hold onto me as we go along the bank. And you, Allam, can use a pole to help you; but we cannot get through with the boat. You do realize this, do you not?"

"Allah protect us, but I am so afraid of water!" whispered Allam.

"Then take this, it is a water skin. Blow it up and use it as a float," said Talon tersely, and he slipped down the bank into the water.

"Are you two coming?" he whispered urgently.

Dar'an gave a whimper and slipped down the bank and onto Talon's back, where he held on with one hand in a vice-like grip that nearly choked Talon. However, the boy still had the presence of mind to hold the precious bow out of the water with his other hand. Despite his terror he knew it was vital that it not get wet.

The three of them waded and swam the intervening distance towards the torches that were placed on one side of the entrance to the tunnel.

There were indeed men on the side nearest to the torches, but their attention was clearly not on the canal. Instead it was focused on the sounds that were emanating from within the Inner walls and the flickering light of fires that had begun to glow over the top of the walls.

Their excited chatter and pointing took up their attention completely and allowed the three fugitives to slip by; they waded into the tunnel without anyone noticing at all.

The tunnel proved difficult, as the water from the river now slapped against the walls and there was a slight undertow that Talon found hard to fight, and Allam seemed about to panic until Talon took a handful of his clothing and dragged him along.

They emerged spluttering and chilled alongside one of the piers that lined the outside of the wall. It was a hard struggle but they managed to clamber onto the platform above and lie there recovering their breath. Soaked to the skin, they were still jubilant at their escape.

"Now Allah be praised for our deliverance!" whispered Allam thankfully.

Dar'an nodded in the dark. "All thanks to God for saving us this day!"

Talon sat up and looked along the pier at the many falukhas lined up alongside. There were many to choose from, so he asked Dar'an which one he had decided upon.

The bedraggled boy stood up and pointed at a long, sleek looking boat that was tied up near by. "I watched it for a long time. The captain I think is Persian, as I heard Farsi. There were six men for the crew."

"That makes it difficult for us then," said Talon. "We are only three and would not be able to control the boat. We have to take something smaller."

They were all standing on the pier looking down at the boats when they heard a commotion at the entrance of the tunnel. There was a muffled shout and a boat was poled out of the darkness. There were four men on the boat, which was followed by another in which were five men, but they seemed to be in trouble. What is more, Talon noticed that they all spoke Farsi. They were tense and fearful and in the dim light provided by the stars above they seemed to be fleeing from something behind them.

Then he noticed that one of the men in the rear boat was lying on the floor and seemed to be wounded. Without thinking he shouted at the men in Farsi. "What in Allah's name is happening in the city?"

The men simply stared at him. Then one of them raised his bow and began to aim at the three on the pier.

"In God's name do not shoot! We are friends and can help," cried Talon.

There was an incredulous exclamation from both boats and the men began to pull alongside.

"If you want to help us you had better be quick! We have stirred up a hornets' nest in the city and they know we left this way!" was the laconic response of one of the men.

"We are going to take a ship out of here and you can help us take it," called Talon. He told Allam to keep his sword handy all the same and Dar'an to hold his bow ready with an arrow near to hand. He could not be sure of these men. They were killers who might feel that it was to their advantage to steal a boat and leave no one behind who could talk.

The dark forms of the men were now cautiously moving towards them along the pier, and Talon wondered if these shadows could be trusted when there was another commotion, this time at the gates that were placed in the wall about three hundred yards along the bank. One of them had opened and soldiers were pouring out. Then there were men on the walls above them shouting and pointing down at them. Several men from above threw lighted torches down so that they landed on the bank, spluttering fiercely but enough to illuminate the gathering on the pier. Very soon after arrows and a couple of spears thudded into the planking near by.

"We have no time to loose!" shouted Talon. "That is the boat we need. Do you come with us or do you stay?"

The leader of the dark shadows on the pier in front of them looked up and then at the troops running towards them.

"We will come with you," he said tersely.

Without any more words every one, including the two carrying the wounded man, rushed the short distance to the falucca Talon had indicated and clambered aboard. There were a couple of men on board who had been woken by the noise who now tried to resist. They were summarily thrown overboard, their yells quickly extinguished by the splash they made in the river.

A swift sword stroke cut the ropes that held the boat to the pier and men rushed to push it away from the bank with poles they found on board. Talon and Allam went to the mast to unfurl the sail. As the boat drifted away from the bank others assisted them to haul the sail up to the peak of the mast where it bellied in the light breeze coming off shore.

They were about forty yards from the bank when the first troopers came abreast of them on the wooden pier. It gave a slight advantage in height to the soldiers who hurled javelins and spears at the boat. Some of the spears struck the deck and embedded themselves but none struck a man. But then some archers sent their arrows whispering towards them and everyone on the boat dived for cover as the first struck wood. One of the strangers gave a sob and fell forward with an arrow embedded deep in his chest.

Hurriedly Talon took his bow from Dar'an and aimed at the crowd on the pier, now about sixty yards away. He loosed an arrow and had the satisfaction of hearing a cry of pain as it hit its mark. Others of the group also shot their arrows, but less effectively as the distance was now too great for the average bow. Talon, on the other hand, with his more powerful bow brought down several more men before the range became too great for even his.

Glancing up he could see many men holding torches lining the tall walls above them while despite the distance and the darkness he could see frantic activity on the pier near another boat.

It too began to drift away from the pier and a sail was hoisted rapidly. Talon's heart sank. They could not hold off the numbers that were on that boat. They would have to outrun it.

He turned his full attention to the sail and the river ahead. He made his way quickly up the steps from the main deck to the second deck where the unmanned tiller was situated and took it. He could feel a satisfying bite to the water as he leaned on the tiller bar. The boat responded eagerly, too eagerly, and the sail flapped, loosing wind. He hurriedly changed direction and the sail once again bellied and filled. The boat leapt forward.

One of the men who had come aboard with them approached him as he stood near the large tiller on the high rear deck. Talon wondered if the man intended him harm, but instead the man stood facing him and glancing back towards the pursuing boat said.

"You saved our lives with your quick thinking, for which I thank you. May Allah bless you for that, but I do not understand why. Who are you and why are you fleeing Baghdad?"

He stepped closer and then peered at Talon. "By the Prophet, I think I am beginning to understand! Your face... it looks as though you have been badly beaten. The word on the street all day has been about two men who escaped the Citadel. That was you?"

Talon nodded silent, wary. He assessed the man in front of him, almost his height and wiry, lithe and balanced on the balls of his feet. This was a fighting man; he had a couple of long scars on his strong forearms to prove it; he carried a sword easily in his right hand. His dark, thin features reminded Talon of the Ismaili he had known in the region of Alamut. But they were a long way from there. Why had these people come to Baghdad, he wondered for the hundredth time.

Talon became aware that the man in turn was scrutinizing him as though he had not made up his mind about them as yet and they might still be in danger.

Then the man abruptly laughed. "Anyone who can escape the Citadel is my friend!" he said. "You must tell me about how you did it some day, but now we have to leave those goat turds behind or we will all be back in the Citadel! Do you know how to sail this boat?"

"I do not, but I was hoping that you did," said Talon with a grin to he man standing in front of him, who grinned back.

"No, I do not either, but I think we have someone on board who does. Behzad, bring the man we found in the stern cabin."

There was a scuffle and a yelp, then three heads showed themselves over the edge of the steps. The man in the middle was fighting the other two, who hung onto him with all their force, dragging him up the steps.

They finally got to the top and flung the man down on the deck in front of Talon and his new acquaintance. The figure on the deck was dressed in only a night shift, a dirty one at that. He was middle aged and fat around the waist. He sported a gray beard but was already balding on top; his turban fell fallen off when he was dumped on the deck.

The man who had formerly addressed Talon nudged the prone figure with his toe. "Do you know how to sail this boat?"

The figure on the deck said nothing.

The man squatted next to the prone figure and addressed him again very patiently. "Do you see this fellow who is holding the tiller now? Yes? Well he is going to carve you into little pieces and drop them into the river in two minutes if you do not answer me." He then stood and administered a kick to the ribs that made the prone figure gasp.

"Yes, yes, I can sail this boat! It is mine... I am the captain."

"Ah good, the man can talk. Now listen, you piece of offal, you will sail this boat down the Tigris river to the sea and if you are successful we might even give the boat back to you."

"I... I understand. In shah'Allah I shall do this for you, your Highness!" croaked the man.

"Allah does will it! Stand up and look behind us. Do you see that boat back there? If they catch up to us then you are a dead man. Do you understand?"

In the darkness Talon could almost see the man pale under his beard, but he nodded. Talon handed the tiller over to him and watched him as he took control of his ship.

Then the man who had done all the talking said to Talon, "I think we are comrades now. My name is Hussein; what is yours?"

"My name is Suleiman; I am grateful for your help. None of us could have done this without the other, I think, so we are all in one another's debt, including that of God the Almighty."

"We might well have to thank Allah in due course, but for the time being what do you think we should do about that boat behind us?"

Talon looked over the stern rail at the falucca loaded with men that was behind them. It seemed that it might actually be gaining on them.

An idea occurred to him. He turned to the captain and asked, "Do we have fire on this boat?"

The captain looked at him as though he was mad. "Fire? There is no fire on this boat."

"Then what do you cook with when at sea?"

Talon took his dagger our and put it to the captain's arm. "I shall hurt you enough to make you tell me, but you will still be able to steer this boat. Is there fire on this boat?"

The man looked into Talon's eyes and knew he was not bluffing. He swallowed and said huskily, "I keep live coals in the metal pot for cooking below in the cabin."

"Thank you. May Allah's blessings be heaped upon your head, Hajji," said Talon softly and left to check.

"You are fortunate that it was not the coals that are to be heaped upon your head, you sad old goat!" said Hussein as Talon left.

He found the pot and brought it up on deck. His memory of the pirate ship incident still fresh in his mind, he showed the others with bows how to form little tight bundles of cotton rags mixed with cooking oil that they tied to some of their arrows. While they attended to this chore he stoked the flames of the pot and told the eager Dar'an to find some fuel if he could, to make the fire larger. He looked up at the hovering Hussein and told him what he was going to do.

"We will only get one chance at this so we have to let them come closer."

He thought that Hussein would object at first, but Hussein looked at Talon, then at the boat and only nodded, then climbed up to the stern deck and talked to the captain.

Pretending that they were disorganized, the men on the boat lowered the sail enough to let most of the wind out. The falucca slowed and started to wallow in the dark waters of the river.

It became clear to the men on the other boat that they were gaining on their victim and they began to cheer and shout abuse and threats as to what they were going to do to the luckless fugitives when they caught them.

Talon explained to the others what he wanted, pointing out that they needed a tight little bundle of oily cloth with enough loose ends to catch the flame. It had to burn long enough to ensure that the flame was not be blown out by the flight of the arrow. Once they understood they got down to work and several arrows were prepared for each man.

Then Talon and the other bowmen crouched in silence on the rear deck and the mid section of their own boat and waited. Hussein, peering over the aft of the boat, watched the other close on theirs, all the while calling out the distance.

When the other boat was forty yards away he shouted and the archers stood up and loosed with flaming arrow tips. Their arrows arched high in the air leaving sparks and flame behind. One went out but the other four landed among the men on the pursuing boat. There were yells of surprise and anger and some of pain.

Another flock of arrows flew and this time one struck the sail, then another. The fabric, dry from the desert winds and sun, caught quickly and within seconds flared into a tall pillar of flame. Then more landed on the deck of the boat among the cordage and cargo which caught fire quickly, the flames speeding out of control despite the desperate efforts of the men on board to stop them from spreading. Within minutes the boat was a blazing beacon on the river, afire from stem to stern, and men were jumping overboard. Talon called down to the waiting Allam and crew.

"Haul up the sail! We must make some distance between us!" They needed no persuading and hurriedly pulled their own sail high where the light breeze caught and drove the boat on.

The screams of rage and fear from the men of the other boat were slowly lost in the night although the bright flare of its burning could be seen long after the shouting had died away in the distance.

I never hear the word "Escape"
Without a quicker blood,
A sudden expectation –
A flying attitude!

—Emily Dickinson

Chapter 25

River Journey

"What is your name?" Talon demanded of the captain of the ship.

"It is Kadeen, Your Honor, at your service," the man replied.

"You work for us without treachery and you will live to keep your boat," Hussein said.

Once the captain realized that he was not going to be butchered, he became effusive.

"I am from Bandar Abbas and was about to sail for there when... when you arrived," he told them.

"We will be happy to go there too," Hussein told him, and Talon breathed a silent sigh of relief.

As the captain chattered his nerves back under control Talon's thoughts drifted. Despite the gnawing concern that carrier pigeons might have been sent south to the Vizier's forces, he knew that there was nowhere other than the river for them. Hussein presented a serious problem which could become a real danger when they made land in Bandar Abbas, assuming they made it there. Initially Talon and his two companions kept to themselves as much as they could because Talon did not want to draw too much attention to himself, least of all with the Ismaili. But this proved harder to do than he wished.

Hussein was very curious about him and never let an opportunity pass when he did not probe Talon about his past and why he had been imprisoned in the first place. Allam proved to be a good foil on those occasions when Hussein pushed too hard, explaining that the Vizier was a man who decided much on a whim as to who or who did not inhabit his prisons.

"Look at me!" he insisted one evening when they were seated on the high deck at the back of the boat talking. "I am from the Oman, a mere merchant who sought to bring my racing camels to Baghdad to sell for a fair price, but I was arrested as a spy with no proof whatsoever. They have confiscated my darlings without payment, Allah be my judge! God's curse upon the vizier and pestilence on all his children! How I will ever get home is in God's his hands. In shah'Allah."

"But who is the Falcon they were all talking about in the city? I could believe it is your friend here... " Hussein persisted with a keen glance at Talon.

"Mistaken identity for sure," said Allam, as he snorted with derision. "I spent a lot of time with Suleiman in that offal hole, may God's curse be upon the men who tortured us. Suleiman yelled the moment he saw the torture chamber. You should have heard him! I thought that they were torturing him to death but they had barely begun. He is no spy!" said that worthy with an apologetic glance from under his brows at Talon, who was seated with his head down trying to look pathetic on his right.

Talon pretended to shudder at the memory and looked fearful.

"I am a merchant from Shiraz who is trying to get home after a mixed success in Egypt, mostly not so good," he said with a whine in his voice.

"You don't sound quite like a Shirazi to me, Suleiman." remarked Hussein, his hooded eyes watching Talon. "Besides, you took control as soon as we were on the boat. You don't seem to be a stranger to danger." He smirked and repeated it, liking the rhyme.

"No, I am not. I was a merchant for many years in Egypt. But my uncle lives in Shiraz, and he is my last remaining relative. From time to time even a merchant has to take control of his life or go under," Talon attempted an indignant glare at Hussein as he lied. He most definitely did not want to tell the same lies he had told the Vizier. The man seated across from him would not be pleased to hear that Suleiman had been a Mameluke fighting for Nur Ed Din. Nur Ed Din had been obsessed with the destruction of the Ismaili sect before he died and had often attacked their castles in the region of mountains north of the county of Tripoli. Hussein seemed to accept this story for the moment, as he changed the subject and they began to discuss the recent events in Baghdad.

"The Caliph and his Vizier, God's curse upon them, have persecuted the Shia' and the remnants of the Ismaili for many years. It is easy to call us heretics and then throw us to the ravenous crowd who love executions. That takes their minds off their problems with the poor harvests and gives the Vizier someone to blame for the disaster of the floods."

"Are you Shia or Ismaili?" asked Talon with respectful diffidence, sounding ignorant to his own ears.

Hussein shot him a look, hesitated and then said, "I trust you, Suleiman, so the answer is we are Ismaili."

Talon nodded and shot a fearful look at Allam, who also looked awed and frightened, but genuinely so. Talon most certainly did not want to give Hussein any clues as to his knowledge of the 'Assassins so he did not pursue that line of discussion.

"You were responsible for the recent attack on the Caliph and then the riots that followed the executions?" he asked.

Hussein's features tightened. "We were sent to protect the few Ismaili left in the city and to put an end to the Leader of the heretics who call themselves the Faithful. But for ill chance we would have succeeded. The Vizier has spies all over the city so we were discovered before we could even begin. They flayed one of our people but the others are in paradise, as they fought to the death when the soldiers came."

"Did you avenge the men at the riot?" asked Allam, his curiosity getting the better of his fear.

"We did indeed. Even to killing our own man before they could finish their foul execution. I sent an arrow to his heart and then killed the men who were carrying out the obscenity."

Talon despite himself drew some satisfaction from this. No man should be executed like that, and his respect for Hussein went up a notch or two. The man was not afraid to get into the thick of things.

Later Hussein asked if he knew how to treat wounds. "You said that you had been a merchant in Egypt, Suleiman, so you should know a little of their medicines? We have one among us who is gravely hurt."

"I have some experience, but not as much as I would wish," returned Talon. "Take me to him and I will see what I can do."

Talon was taken down to the wounded man who lay on a pallet on the hold. The man had taken a spear thrust in the upper part of his thigh. He was feverish and there were beads of sweat on his brow.

Talon removed the bloody rag that was bound round the man's thigh and had a look at the gaping slotted hole in his leg. He noted that the blood did not pour out the moment they took the bandage off so assumed that no vital blood vessels had been severed. Bending over the man Talon could not smell the fetid stink of gangrene so he had some hope for his recovery.

Talon asked for boiled water and cleaned the wound carefully. The young man groaned just once but then set his jaw and made no further complaint as Talon probed deeper, looking for dirt and scraps of cloth that would fester. Then while some of the man's comrades held him Talon stitched the wound crudely, using a needle and thread borrowed from the captain for repairing his sail, wishing all the while that he had learned more when he had had the chance in Isfahan.

He left a small length of straw in the stitching as a drain and then instructed the men to take the man on deck where he would be better off in the cleaner air rather than in the smelly hold. They were to make sure he had a lot of clean water to drink and food to keep his strength up.

Having accomplished all he could Talon went below deck himself and slept deeply. He dreamed of a great battle where he and some close comrades were faced with a never ending array of grimacing, screaming enemies. He awoke with Dar'an shaking him and telling him that it was evening and that supper was served.

The journey down the river took a week. During this time they anchored on lonely shores at night or simply sailed at night, the brilliant light of the myriad stars guiding their passage.

Talon was impressed with the sleek lines of the boat and the speed it could attain with a good wind behind it. The wooden hull was well set and caulked and the high prow carved intricately with signs of the Koran. The men slept comfortably on deck every night as there was no rain. Despite the light wind that drove them along, however, the days were very hot and muggy. He was glad of his light cotton robes.

They fished as they went and enjoyed their succulent catch on the charcoal fire that was carefully nursed day and night. Allam and Talon spent time together watching the distant river banks and talking.

"Tell me about this Oman of yours, Allam. It sounds like an interesting country."

"It is, my friend. It is rich because we Omani are seafarers. Well, the ones that live on the coast are. I am more fond of the wide spaces of the desert and my beloved camels, and I wander the deep desert where the tribes purchase my beauties from me for good prices. I am a wealthy man in my own right, as is my father.

"Oman is a rich country because we have boats that are much larger than this one that are designed to deal with the great storms of the Indian seas; they are called Al Ghanjah. They can carry huge cargoes. Our people go to and from India bringing spices and cloths made there, as well as skins of rare animals and precious hard woods that go towards making our ships."

"How do they know how to reach these places that are on the other side of the world?" Talon asked, his curiosity aroused.

"This has been done for many generations, Suleiman. Our people were trading with the Indian lands when the prophets of the Jews were alive!"

"But the wind? How do they manage to go one way and then come back the other way? Does the wind change?"

"Oh yes, the monsoon winds blow from the southwest in the hot wet summer, then in the cool of winter the winds turn to blow from the North East and take our merchants back to Oman. Through God's blessing of the winds we have become wealthy. My father is a great sailor and so is my older brother; I too have travelled once to India."

Talon was impressed. Nevertheless, he wanted to learn more about the travel routes.

"Do they also sail to the south? What is there in the south?" he asked.

"Ah, now you have asked a good question. Where do you think those large black slaves come from? Have you ever seen the teeth of an elephant? The land south of the Arabian countries and the Red Sea is known as Africa and it is full of huge animals and fierce tribes, both of which will eat you!"

Dar'an, who had been listening, gasped and his eyes widened. "Allam, is this really true?" he asked, half disbelieving.

"As Allah is my witness that country is immense and full of animals like a paradise, but there are huge creatures that will surely eat one such as you in one gulp, my young friend," said Allam with a laugh.

"How do you know all this, Allam? Have you been there?" Talon asked skeptically.

"No, my friends, but you see the sultan of Oman is a wealthy man and the riches that he possesses come from Africa and an island off the coast called Zanzibar. From there his ships can trade with India for the spices. We Omani hear tales of Zanzibar all the time from the seafarers who land in Muscat and south in Salahlah. It is from there that his great ships begin their journeys carrying the teeth of the elephant and the slaves for Oman."

In the early hours of one morning Talon was on watch and the captain, who was at the tiller, called him over and pointed towards the south east.

"Do you see that line over there in the distance, my Lord?"

Talon peered at the eastern horizon and saw a long dark line that was the southern shore of the great river they had been following.

"Beyond that point there is the Arabian Sea," said the captain. "Can you not smell it? The small harbor village of Basra is situated almost at the entrance of this river and it is the last place where we can obtain water and provisions for the three or four day crossing of the sea."

"Then we will be clear of the land and any risk of pursuit, In shah'Allah," Hussein said as he came up on deck.

They all repeated the words, "In shah'Allah."

Allam, who never seemed to want to be far from Talon, also came on deck rubbing the sleep from his eyes.

"What are you talking about? Is it Basra? Are we finally there? I would like to go to Basra if possible to see if I can obtain a passage to Muscat," he said, cocking a wary eye at Hussein.

Talon looked at Hussein. "We are low on provisions and clean water. I checked yesterday; we have no reserves for a long voyage and there is almost nothing to eat other than a little dried fish."

The captain added his opinion, "If we do not take in water we will be in serious trouble. We cannot take it from the river; it is not sweet and men get sick from it. Allah willing we won't have a storm, but..." he left the rest in the air.

Hussein leaned against the rail squinting out at the growing line of the shore. They could make out the distant masts of large seagoing dhows and the spikes of a couple of the new kind of minarets. The tops of some tall palms became visible. The sun was racing into the sky, its great white orb already burning off the light dew that had settled on the deck. The heat of the day shimmered off the water and made it hard to see clearly.

It promised to be a hot day with high stretched clouds that added to the already humid air around the boat. Talon compared the heat of the river and gulf area to the hot dryness of the desert and decided that he preferred the desert heat to this suffocating muggy heat.

"We will stay out here until dusk and when they are all at prayers we will go in quietly and see what we can do about the water and provisions," Hussein said.

That evening just as the sun set they inched towards the shore. The captain, who had taken a liking to Talon, perhaps because he feared him less, pointed to the other larger ships anchored near the beach.

"Those are feluccas and dhows in the harbor; ours is called an al Baum but those are Shu'i, and I think there is an al Ghanjah from Oman; but there... that one, the very large ship is called an Xebec. It carries two masts and has several decks. That might be going to Oman; they build these kinds of boats for the monsoon run to India. It is built for the high seas of the ocean."

There were few lights showing other than a couple of lamps on the mastheads of the larger boats, very few from the town. Talon guessed that it was more of a port with a mud fort than a town of any consequence. However it was the last place along the river where a boat could put ashore and obtain sweet spring water and provisions. They were not challenged, so they dropped anchor near to the larger boats away from prying eyes on shore. The anchor fell with a splash into the muddy waters of the river, the sail came down, and their boat turned in the flow to face upriver.

They could clearly hear the call to prayers in the distance and the murmur of voices carried over the water from the other boats. All seemed peaceful to the silent watchful men on board.

Hussein gave a warning to the captain. "Do not try to warn anyone or tell who we are. Be quiet and you will live to see your family and home again."

The captain nodded, mute in the gathering dusk. He was very afraid of Hussein, knowing full well that he meant what he said. The men in the skiff were tense as they came to the wooden jetty; there was a lot of activity on the wharf and along the main street of the town. Basra's only importance was as a useful port of call for ships about to leave the relative safety of the river and head out to sea.

There did not seem to be any interest in them so they cautiously sought out vendors and, keeping an eye open for trouble, negotiated for supplies. Talon used some of his precious gold to pay the vendors; the others had nothing to offer. His gold spoke, however, and before long they had all they needed, including access to a spring to fill some barrels and skins with sweet water. Then they hastened to return to the boat.

When they reached the boat Allam asked if they could talk to the captain of the large ship in harbor. It turned out that the captain was Omani himself and was going to Muscat in Oman and agreed to take Allam with him, but he was leaving within the hour as the wind was favorable and he wanted to get out to sea, even at night, as he could navigate from the stars. Talon gave his friend some of his coins to smooth the way.

Allam was delighted and hastened to bid his friend goodbye.

"Suleiman, Talon, whatever your name is, my friend," he said in a low voice as they parted, "I owe you my life, and as Allah is my witness I shall repay you one day.

"I do not know what you are planning to do in Persia but I suspect that you are going into much danger, and these men are very dangerous companions. If you can ever come to Oman then find me there. My father is well known and he will assist me to provide help if you need it. I shall never forget you, my friend," he said wiping a tear away as his emotion began to get the better of him. In a low voice he gave Talon detailed instructions as to how to find his father's house.

"God you with you, Allam. I shall commit your instructions to memory. We will meet again, In shah'Allah," Talon said. He had come to like the cheerful young man.

They embraced hard and then Allam hurriedly embraced Dar'an and told him, "You have a Lord who is great, Dar'an; you should protect him well."

Dar'an laughed and sniffed, his eyes wet. He too had taken a liking to the bright nature of their companion. Allam was taken over to the skiff. The last Talon saw of him he was waving and calling as the huge boat went by, rocking theirs in its wake.

"Go with God! My prayers will follow you, my friends."

"God protect you!" called Dar'an as he stood next to Talon waving.

It was time to leave; they had the basics necessary to get them across the sea and if the weather stayed good the journey would be short according to the captain, who was nervously watching the shoreline for signs of trouble.

Soon they were moving away from the cluster of ships and riding into the middle of the great river again. Hussein strode over to Talon, who was standing on the steerage deck on the starboard side, and said, "I think we left just in time, Suleiman. Do you see over there?" He pointed toward the shore they had just left.

There was a crowd gathering on the river bank. He could see many torches being held high and even some horsemen waving and pointing. Even from this distance Talon could see clearly that they were not actually waving but threatening and shaking their weapons.

"They won't be able to catch up with us now," said Hussein comfortably. "This boat is a fast one and will show them its tail."

Talon laughed. He looked ahead to the now distant Omani ship's sails and felt comfortable that Allam too was safe from the Vizier.

Three hours later the wind freshened and the hull tilted as the sail became taut, the rigging began a low hum. The boat now dipped and rose in the gathering swell, gaining speed. Talon sensed that this boat was more at home on the wide sea than in the delta, it strained like a war horse to be let free. Even the captain seemed more at ease now they were finally at sea.

A light spray blew back over the bows to wet Talon's face as the vessel seemingly shook itself as it began to play in its proper element. There was a palpable sense of relief aboard as the men gazed back at the receding flat coast line.

Stars streaking clover skies
wet flakes in winter white
sulphur gauze sweeps
across cobalt east
river a mirror of crimson
brushed with leaves
roses on Isfahan's old bridge
silk and doves, turquoise
mosque, wild moss
bees swarm around
white orchid moon

—Shireen Bakhtiar

Chapter 26

Isfahan

The garden looked much the same from where he sat on his horse looking though the gates. The same avenue of shrubs and low palms with flowering shrubs dotted about the well trimmed grass spaces. In the distance he could see the fruit trees near where he and Reza had tested their skill with their bows. Somehow the place seemed smaller than he remembered it, but the trees had matured so that the house seemed to crouch comfortably within the shade of the tall poplars and palms nearby.

He glanced down the avenue towards the building and felt a strong mixture of emotions wash over him. It seemed so long ago that he had arrived here with the Doctor Farj'an, and Fariba, Rav'an and Reza. He felt his heart begin to thump louder as he rode slowly down the avenue towards the building.

He soon realized that he had been noticed; indeed one of the gardeners bowed deeply to him, but there was no recognition. He dismounted at the main entrance and handed off the reins of his horse to the syce who ran up.

"Stay here until I come back, Dar'an," he said to the boy, then he walked the short distance to the main doors which opened as he approached.

A well dressed servant in billowy pantaloons, red leather slippers and a wide red sash around his waist over which was a long silk coat that came down almost to his knees, his regalia topped with a neatly wound turban, stood at the entrance and after bowing low asked his business. Talon stood in front of him, looked him up and down then told him, "I have come to see Fariba, the lady of the house if she is here; please inform her that an old friend is come to visit."

He knew that he was being rude but he wanted to have a few seconds to observe Fariba before she recognized him. The servant looked nonplussed for a minute but then remembered his manners and bowed him into the living room to the right of the high entrance. Talon stalked past the man and stood in the center of the room. It was just as he had remembered it. The well cared for look of the room with its rich carpets on the floor and the low tables stacked with books and rolls of paper denoted an owner who was studious as well as interested in decor. There were cushions of silk against the walls and flowers in vases distributed around the room giving it a cheerful as well as restful atmosphere. The dreadful destruction he had witnessed the last time he had been there was a distant memory. Indeed, the memories flooded back and threatened to overwhelm him.

Forcing himself to control his emotions he glanced up at the wood beams of the ceiling and noticed that they were newly painted. Of course, it had been No Roos not so long ago! The time when households all over Persia conducted a spring cleaning ceremony.

He was standing with his back to the door when he heard a very light step behind him. He turned slowly and saw before him the slim figure of Fariba; how could it not be her? He had the light behind him so while he could see her clearly she could not make out his features and was eyeing him quizzically.

"My Servant told me that a friend had come to see me but..."

"Fariba, do you not remember me?" asked Talon. His voice was husky as he was almost overcome with emotion. His eyes swept over her. She was a beautiful as ever, if anything somewhat more ethereal; there were white strands in her hair, but her figure was straight, slim and as elegant as he had remembered.

She took a step forward, staring at him still with a question in her eyes; she even pulled the diaphanous veil more closely around her head. "I am sorry, Agha..." she began, but then a light dawned in her eyes. Her hand went to her heart.

"Talon? No! It... it cannot be!" she whispered then seemed to dismiss the idea and stood irresolute, looking confused. But then he stepped closer and said, "Yes, Fariba, it is I, Talon. Auntie, it is I."

Fariba's nerveless fingers released her veil, which fell away. Now he could see her beautiful features, but they were bloodless, white, and she would have fallen if he had not stepped in quickly and taken her arms to hold her gently upright even as she sagged weakly against his chest.

She gasped, "Dear God! Allah be praised for his mercy. Talon, is it really you?" Then she began to cry silently.

He took her frail frame in his arms and held her shaking form, whispering as his own tears began to flow. "Yes, my Auntie Fariba, it is Talon.... I have come... at last."

Fariba stopped weeping and pushed back against his chest looking up at him with tear-stained cheeks.

"Oh, I must look at you! How you have changed! Ah, my Talon, how you have changed, but I still see you. She traced the scar on his jaw and then placed both hands either side of his bearded face and shook his head gently. "Ah, but you have so many scars of the warrior, my Talon!"

She kissed him then on both cheeks; he felt the wetness of her tears.

"Come and sit with me, my long lost boy, and tell me how you came and what became of you when you got to Palestine. We thought you were dead; there could be no other explanation for what happened... but there were strange rumors too!" She sniffed and wiped her nose with a kerchief giving an embarrassed laugh.

He sat down on the cushions, controlling his impatience as there was one thing he was desperate to know.

With a visible effort Fariba brought herself under control then clapped her hands and gave instructions to the servant who appeared like magic. She needed tea and cakes and now! The servant, with a curious look at Talon, vanished.

Talon turned from where he sat and begged the question.

"Auntie, I shall tell you of all that has befallen me, but first in the name of God and for the sake of my tortured soul, I have come to understand that God in his mercy might have spared her but I must know from your lips, my dear Fariba! Is Rav'an alive?"

Fariba wiped her eyes with her light silk kerchief. "My dear Talon... yes... yes, she is alive."

She stopped, a concerned look on her face because Talon had bent over as though in pain and stayed there doubled up rocking himself for a few long moments, his arms crossed about his middle. She then said, "And so is your brother Reza." At this Talon jerked upright and his whole being radiated joy.

"Then they are both safe? Tell me, Auntie, they are safe?" He went on one knee before her and seized both her hands in his. She nodded but then released a hand and placed it on his arm and said gently.

"There is so much for you to tell and much for you to know, Talon. But for the moment calm yourself; she is alive and so is Reza, so we shall talk more of this at the right time. Today Allah has been kind and heard my prayers.

"Yes, my dear Talon, I prayed for you many a day when I finally heard the news. He has brought you back to me before I die, and for that I am so very thankful." She leaned over to him and kissed him again on the cheek, her slim hand on his forearm as though the touching could reassure her that he was really there. Her lovely green-gray eyes were still wide with emotion and surprise.

They began to talk, pausing briefly to drink some hot fragrant tea, and then they started again. She made him begin at the beginning from the time when he had disappeared into the ill-fated castle of the Templars.

"Reza came back for you, Talon. He had seen some of those knights...I cannot remember what they were called, but he somehow had a bad feeling, you know how perceptive he is. He told me that he saw you taken prisoner and watched them beat you, after which he saw them take you off towards a castle just like a prisoner. He was very confused because he thought that they were your people; he said they were Frans. That was the last he saw of you because he had to ride back to be with Rav'an and tell her the dreadful news."

"I was indeed taken prisoner by the Templars; they would not believe me when I told them who I was and then would not let me go, Aunt Fariba. From then on I was a prisoner until they put me on a ship for my homeland," said Talon, and he too had to wipe the tears away.

"I raged and begged them to let me go but they would not, and all the time I knew that Rav'an was carrying my child, and I knew that this was a sentence of death. My soul has been in torment ever since."

Fariba was looking at him, she had paled again. "You knew all this when they captured you? Ah, my poor boy, the torment must have been terrible."

"It has been a lifetime of torment Auntie... I finally had dispensation to come and find out for myself because I could not bear to live without knowing any longer."

Just then a high pitched voice came from outside the doorway.

"I want to see my Grandmother now, Salem, and there is nothing you can do to stop me!"

There was the sound of a scuffle and then a child ran into the room. It was a boy of about six years dressed in wide loose pantaloons but bare footed. He wore a light shirt and a loose turban on his head that was almost falling off. He ran into the room but stopped short at the sight of the two adults seated on the carpet near the center of the room.

"Grandmother, they said that you had visitors and that I could not come in!"

"Indeed, you should not have come in the way you did, Rostam, it was very rude of you. I know your manners are better than that!" admonished Fariba trying to look stern. "But now that you are here you should be very respectful and greet my visitor. This is Talon, a very dear friend of mine who has come a vast distance just to see us."

The boy, a slim but strong looking child, bowed very low and said, "Salam, Agha, Halla shuma khobe?"

"Salam, Rostam. Man khob hastam. Va toro, khob hastin?" said Talon politely and he smiled. The boy looked curiously familiar. He turned to Fariba and found that she was looking at him strangely. Then she did something very odd. She put a finger to her lips and shook her head. He decided that she wanted him to wait with his questions so he said nothing further.

Fariba called out to the servant who had been hovering by the entrance and said. "Salem, Rostam will go with you now. It is almost time for his bath anyway. Go along with you, Rostam, and be good to Alia. I shall come up and read to you later."

Rostam came over to her and gave her a kiss and then stalked off with his servant calling over his shoulder, "It was nice to meet you, Khoda Haffez, Agha Talon." Talon smiled and responded. "Khoda Haffez, Rostam, I hope to see you later."

*****

When the boy had gone there was a short silence in the room. Talon turned to Fariba to find her staring at him with an enigmatic expression on her face.

"You have a grandson?" Then, questioning the look in her eyes, he asked, "What is it, Auntie, what do you want to say?"

"Talon, how long is it since you left Rav'an?"

"An eternity, Auntie, what are you saying? It has been almost six years if I am not mistaken."

"How old do you think Rostam is, Talon?" she asked with a smile.

He gasped and stared at her. "You mean...?" He could not go on; his mouth fell open and he just stared at her.

"Yes, my precious Talon, he is your son."

He sat there gazing off into the distance, a bemused expression on his face. After a few moments like this he turned to Fariba, and despite her squeak of protest he wrapped his arms around her delicate frame and hugged her.

"Talon!" she protested, "What will the servants think?"

"Indeed, my dear, what will the servants think?" said a gruff voice.

They both looked up and there was Doctor Haddad standing in the doorway looking surprised.

"My husband! Look who is here! It is Talon! Allah has been kind and answered my prayers!" Fariba cried, jumping up and gliding over to him to plant a kiss on his bearded cheek.

"I think I heard aright; is it really you, Talon?" exclaimed the doctor staring hard at the stranger in the room.

Talon rose and walked the short distance to the doctor, who had an arm around Fariba's waist; both were smiling up at him.

"Indeed it is I, Agha, and right well pleased to see you both." He bowed low to the doctor who unceremoniously reached forward, took his arm and gripped it hard, then embraced him, patting him on the back.

"You honor our house, Talon. This is your house for as long as you wish to stay," growled the doctor, his eyes were wet. Fariba put her hand on his chest. "My dear husband, go and have a bath, for I am sure that you have had a busy day at the hospital and need to be refreshed. I shall order food and then we will talk together."

She looked up at Talon. "You know that you are our guest, Talon; you did come intending to stay?"

He smiled at her fondly. "Auntie Fariba, honored doctor, I hoped so much that you would both be here, but I needed to find out if that were so first. I shall go now and bring my baggage and my companion, a young Kurdish lad who came from Jerusalem with me."

"No! Give our servants directions to bring your servant and your baggage to this house," exclaimed Fariba.

"There are many stories within this statement and I intend to hear them all," said Haddad with a chuckle. He bent to kiss Fariba and then left them with a wave and stumped off up the stairs, calling for his servants.

Fariba turned to Talon and said, "Yes, Talon, he has been good to me and yes, I am now his wife in all things."

Talon took her hands and said, "I had so hoped that he would be good to his words and it has proved to be true. Do I now call him uncle?" he asked mischievously.

Fariba smiled. "Your uncle Farj'an would not object, I am sure, Talon. He would understand, as you loved him dearly. Haddad will pretend to be indignant but I know he will be pleased." She laughed with him then.

Talon kissed her on the cheek. "Indeed I did and still do, as I do love thee, Fariba, for he was my mentor too."

Talon and Fariba went back to the carpet and continued their animated conversation. Finally Fariba stopped and said, "It is as though we both want to collect as much information from each other as possible within the shortest time, Talon. There will be time; we shall make time, but in the meantime I hear the servants and I must see to your needs. Also I have to see to our dinner tonight; there is much to prepare for! You have come back to us!" She rose, and telling him to stay where he was she went to see to the preparation of his room and a bath.

Talon realized only then that for all the talking she had not once mentioned Rav'an.

Dinner was a convivial affair and the food a delight. Talon had not eaten like this since Baghdad, and Fariba insisted on his trying out all the old favorites that she remembered. There were tasty pieces of dried, spicy meat with goat's cheese mixed with herbs on biscuits. They sampled smoked olives in oil with garlic and herbs. Small quail eggs were provided, along with eggplant cooked crisp in sesame oil. She even had some roe from the huge fish to be found in the sea to the north.

Talon tasted again badhinjan buran, pureed eggplant with yogurt and spices. The main course, Fariba reminded him, was called bastaniya and was composed of spiced chicken and lamb with pears, peaches and almonds. This was followed by a desert of honeyed dates stuffed with almonds and scented with rosewater that he recalled was called rutab mu'assal.

Talon found that he had to eat and at the same time answer a hundred questions about the life he had led during the last six years. He told them again of his capture and the torture to his mind as he agonized over his loss of Rav'an, and then the return to his homeland. He told them of the events that had led up to his leaving and then of the years of his life in Egypt, other countries, and finally Palestine. His journey back to Isfahan held their interest, especially his capture and imprisonment in Baghdad, which fascinated them. His escapes and the hardships he glossed over, but Fariba was watching him and it was clear that she read in his story much more than his words.

Later that evening when the servants were gone to bed and the three of them were seated sipping chai Talon asked the question.

"My Auntie Fariba, tell me now where is Rav'an? Where is Reza? Are they together or is Reza still in the Alborz? I must know."

Fariba and the doctor glanced at one another and then, taking a deep breath, she spoke.

"Talon, Rav'an is a woman now, and as you know her brother the Agha Khan had plans for her."

She sighed. "Talon, I am not sure how to tell you this, but I must somehow."

Her husband touched her on the arm.

"My dear, we must have courage and say what has to be said. Talon must know the truth."

With a sinking feeling in his heart Talon listened to this exchange and waited.

Finally Fariba looked up, and there were tears in her eyes when she said, "The Agha Khan made a treaty with the sultan of Shiraz, Talon." She paused but then went on. "For years Rav'an stayed here and we pretended that she was ill and could not travel, but one day, only a few months ago, an emissary from her brother came by and met with her. He must have reported back to her brother that she was well and able to become a wife, even if she was older than the normal wife would be. The sultan had word of her beauty and wanted her.

"Very shortly after that the command came from her brother that she was to travel to Shiraz with an entourage of some extravagance, and there she was to become the wife of the Sultan."

Talon sat very still saying nothing while Fariba and the doctor watched him fighting his emotions.

"She did not go willingly, Talon. I was sure she was close to taking her own life," said Fariba, reaching out to touch him, tears streaming down her face. "But I persuaded her that she must live no matter what, and one day she would see her son again."

*****

Talon went to bed that night in a daze. He could not sleep, tossing and turning this way and that, trying to understand the situation and what he could do about it. Many choices came to mind but all of them came down to what he could do about Rav'an, now a Sultan's wife. He remembered her saying that she had dreaded this, as she was a mere pawn in the hands of her brother, and now she was locked away in the depths of some fortress in the Sultan's harem where God only knew what she was being subjected to.

In the faint light of dawn he finally came to a decision.

He spoke with Fariba and the doctor in the privacy of the living room and watched their incredulous expressions as he did so.

"You are quite mad, Talon!" the doctor exclaimed in horror. "Shiraz is one of the great fortresses in the south. The Arabs built it for a reason, and that was to keep the peace in the region. It is impregnable and has withstood many sieges from the Baluchi, Afghani and other foreigners before. What makes you think you can gain entry? Then Allah protect you, but how will you get into the harem and take Rav'an out! It is madness!"

He was almost wringing his hands with agitation.

Fariba was in as bad a state. "Think of your son too, Talon. What will become of him if you are taken? They will kill you most horribly and then Rav'an's life might be in jeopardy if they extract that information from you with torture!"

"I have been trained by the best in the world, my dear friends. Fariba, you know this! And, good friends, what would you have me do? Leave the woman I came from across half the world to find in the harem of some balding old lecher? I cannot bear the thought! And besides, my son has a home here if I do not succeed. No one need know if I fail, as then neither Rav'an nor I will come to collect him from you, and he will not have the grief to bear either."

They tried all morning to dissuade him but his mind was set. Finally, Fariba and the doctor, realizing that he could not be persuaded otherwise, decided that they must try to ensure his success by helping him. There was no time to lose so they made preparations.

The doctor would send a trusted servant to accompany Rostam and his nurse Alia south to the port of Bushehr, where they would wait for him to bring Rav'an to them. If they succeeded they would take a ship to Oman.

"I have a friend there who owes me his life and has often told me that I should come and visit him," Talon reassured them.

Neither Fariba nor the Doctor liked the plan at all but could not find an alternative that would persuade Talon to change his mind, so they reluctantly went along with it.

Alia wept when she was brought to see Talon. He embraced her against all decorum and thanked her for looking after Rav'an. There were more tears on all sides. Talon wanted to know if his old friend and caravan leader was in Isfahan. A servant was sent off to find out if Al Tayyub was in the bazaar.

In this world I need a Brave Knight,
Who would never give up any fight.
A knight who would dry away my tears,
Telling me to overcome my fears.

Anonymous

Chapter 27

A Dungeon

She woke in the dark to hear noises outside the wooden door, which although thick could not mask the screams and pleading. She tensed as she sat up on the mat and waited for the door to crash open and the men with the silk ropes to enter and her final journey to begin. But the noises subsided and finally there was silence. In the darkness of her cell she found that, although still exhausted from the harrowing days preceding her imprisonment, she could no longer sleep.

Her mind drifted to the time when she had been living in very different circumstances.

Her every wish granted and every comfort possible had been provided. When she arrived she had been welcomed to the city with fanfare and extravagant feasting as the union was officially recognized. She barely remembered the sultan other than his sweating presence nearby as the ceremony was concluded. Of course her brother had not been there. He never was.

Drums and cymbals had clashed and horns had sounded as she was escorted to the harem. All eyes upon her, admiring the rich embroidery and silks, and laden with gold bracelets and jewels, presents from her brother. He had also sent a pure white horse from the Turkoman world, and while there had been many words of praise for the gift she could well believe that the sultan would not be able to ride such an animal; he was too fat.

At the entrance to the harem, where she had been led with much ceremony, she had been greeted by the eunuch and the lady in charge of the women. Both had been unctuous and fawning, which had not helped her, longing as she was for a familiar face.

Still dazed and bewildered by the events which had led up to this moment she had barely responded to their words, allowing herself to be led to an alcove which she was told would be her private accommodation. They divested her of her outer clothing and jewelry and left her with bows and soft words as they went out, pulling the thin curtain across to allow her some privacy at last. The babble of conversation that had greeted her arrival from the number of other women clustered about the edge of the pool had subsided into silence as they watched her being led by, but now the murmur of hushed but excited voices began again as they discussed the new arrival.

It had been two days before she had been able to surface from the apathy that had overwhelmed her. She was dimly aware of her surroundings as the eunuchs and other ladies proudly showed her the large pool of water with a small fountain that made a continuous low music. The women and some children lingered here for most of the day, gossiping and bored. It was lined with glazed tiles and sunlight could enter the domed area from arched windows high up in the walls. The ache in her heart grew as she looked around her at the finery of her new home.

How she missed the garden, the sound of birds and the wind in the poplars, even the shriek of that tiresome strutting peacock. She had burst into tears and returned to her alcove. They had regarded her with surprise; wasn't this paradise? She knew better, this was a prison from which she would only leave as an old woman or dead.

By then the eunuch in charge had started to complain to the woman who called herself Abeer that it would not be long before the sultan wanted the new girl to appear before him, ready for the consummation of the marriage.

They had come and cajoled her to her feet, and then with the help of another eunuch called Basim had then led her to the bath, away from the curious eyes of the other women and girls, where they had stripped her of the light clothes she wore and the eunuch Basim had remained while she bathed. He was a black man from the African continent and still young with a dark frizz of short hair on his head and two bright black eyes that regarded her with approval and sympathy.

He clucked at the bush between her thighs and muttered about having to do something about that, but for the moment he concentrated upon bathing her and washing her hair, then he dried her and made her sit in towels while he fussed over her and brushed her long hair until it shone.

Despite her depression she felt better and even hungry. As though he sensed her need, Basim disappeared for a few minutes, saying he was going to fetch some sweet meats.

While he was gone another person had entered the baths. A very pretty girl of about sixteen, who exclaimed when she saw Rav'an seated by the water.

"Oh! You are so beautiful. They said you were but now I see it."

After a tentative start it was not long before Rav'an and the young princess, who called herself Jannat, were deep into a conversation and Rav'an had taken a liking to the girl. Evidently Jannat returned the sentiment as she opened up about herself as though someone had turned on a flow of water long held within. They were deep into Jannat's previous life in Kerman when Basim returned with a plate full of small pastries and sweets, which he enjoined her to eat.

That was one of the few moments of pleasure that Rav'an remembered, but very shortly after that her life changed.

"You are too thin, my Lady, we must plump you up, but that will take time and I must prepare you for the day after tomorrow. The sultan wants to see you then," Basim said, not unkindly.

He chased Jannat away and then tactfully indicated that he needed to do something about the light bush of hair at the junction of her thighs. He explained that it needed to be removed completely and the only way to do this was for her to lie back while he administered some smelly ointment that stung painfully.

It had been an ordeal which she ruefully realized would take place often in the future. He left her to endure the pain, telling her that he would return in due course and remove the residue.

An hour later he had come back and, telling her to remain still, had gently but surely removed every hair he could find from her pudenda. Basim had been very gentle as he performed the process, all the while telling her in poor Farsi how beautiful she was and how lucky the sultan was to have married her.

Rav'an barely listened to him; her thoughts were far away.

The process completed she had bathed again and Basim, having inspected her, had pronounced her fit to see the Sultan; but there was one other necessary thing to verify. He had asked her to lay back and then had called in the woman Abeer.

What followed had not been at all pleasant. Abeer had told Basim to leave them, then had placed her hand on Rav'an's stomach, gently caressing her there and then murmured, "You are the most beautiful woman the sultan has ever found, my dear. We will be calling you our queen very soon, of that I am sure,"she purred.

Her caresses had continued with her other hand, which had travelled up Rav'an's thigh and then slowly but firmly opened her legs. Then she had moved her fingers onto her inner thigh, close to her junction, almost as though she was inspecting Basim's work. Rav'an had nervously begun to try and sit up. Abeer pushed her back down with her other hand.

"Lie still and do not move!" the woman commanded in a sharp tone. Rav'an lay back, tense and unsettled. No woman had ever touched her in this manner before and she was almost certain Abeer was enjoying herself. The exploring hand continued to her junction then Abeer had begun to stroke her there, clearly with the intent of exciting her.

With an indignant exclamation she tried again, this time with more determination to get up. "What are you doing! Leave me alone!" she exclaimed.

Without warning Abeer had thrust two fingers into her vagina. It had not been rough but the very act had surprised Rav'an so much she jerked into a sitting position then fell back as the woman shoved her forcibly back. With horror she noticed the expression of surprise and even satisfaction on the woman's face.

"So... you are not a virgin!" she said slowly. "I wondered. I thought I saw those little signs indicating that you have carried a child and now I am right. You are not as young as the others, so I needed to verify. By God, but you are in trouble now!"

Rav'an stared up into the face of the woman who hovered over her. There was a look of cold triumph in her dark eyes. The once beautiful woman seemed to be glad of the discovery. Rav'an suddenly realized that this woman had seen her as a competitor.

There was no denying it. They stared at one another for a very long moment. Then Abeer said, with a smirk of satisfaction on her face, "You cannot go before the sultan and we cannot disguise the fact. You are here on a lie and the sultan will not be pleased. We should have known. Your people are not to be trusted in anything, not even in something as important as this! "

She had swept out of the room, leaving Rav'an to hurriedly cover herself and stand, but within minutes and some loud words outside the eunuchs had returned with Abeer and Rav'an was hustled to her alcove to await the pleasure or displeasure of the sultan. There had been an ominous silence outside of her curtain for a long time; then gradually other occupants of the harem began to discuss the incredible event in hushed whispers.

Jannat had tried to enter but the woman Abeer had harshly told her to stay clear, adding with some venom that no one wanted to have anything to do with a spoiled goods. Jannat had courage, that was sure, as she had said none too quietly, "You did not have to denounce her. There are ways; we all know about them, but no, you had to do this. You are a witch with evil in you."

This had been followed by a slap and Abeer had said, "This whore was sent as an insult by her brother. You would be well advised not to see her or you too might go to the dungeons. She will be dealt with, and you know what that means, so don't tempt me to make you join her."

Jannat had retreated in silence, and then for two days Rav'an had been left alone to contemplate her future with fear in her heart.

*****

The sultan and the vizier had been notified by the woman Abeer in person after the chief eunuch had alerted them as to the situation. After a horrible silence, during which the sultan's face had gone puce, the Vizier had waved everyone out of the room and stood before his master who was now almost gobbling with rage. The tantrum went on for minutes until the vizier, who was well used to these rages, decided it was a good time to step in.

"We have to be very careful, Your Eminence!" He had almost whispered, glancing about him with nervous eyes. His spare frame, slightly stooped, was hovering over the sultan, who looked almost as though he was going to have some kind of fit and die forthwith. He was slumped back on the throne with his feet spread out in front of him, twitching with emotion.

The sultan glared up at him with eyes sunk deep into the flesh of his rotund features and ground his teeth. Then he opened his mouth. "She must be executed!" he almost screamed.

"My Lord, you are right of course, but... remember who's sister she is?" the Vizier pleaded.

The sultan pushed himself upright on the throne. A sudden thought came to him. "I shall not return the dowry."

"Of course not, my Lord. But if we execute the woman in public, then... there could be questions and perhaps unpleasant repercussions. You know how dangerous those people are."

"You are not suggesting that I let her live?" gobbled the sultan, but his eyes showed a flicker of fear at the thought of retribution from that quarter. It was always terminal.

The vizier gave a strained smile, his thin lips tight against his teeth. "No... No. Of course not, your Eminence, but if we can keep her out of sight for long enough, memories of the woman will fade; then we can... " his slim fingers made a twisting and pulling motion as though he were wringing a bird's neck.

"I should have her anyway! Her beauty is gnawing at me! But ... but she is spoiled goods, and they *knew* it!" the sultan wailed. He sat up, his turban was askew. "How will we do this without those abominable people knowing? They have eyes and ears everywhere!"

"A weighted sack in the qanat one dark night. No one will know who it is in the sack, and there will be no signs of violence to be discovered when we bring the body back for burial. A physician will be present to make a note of this, which we can send to the Khan. There are innumerable ways a person can die from sicknesses."

"What should I do, my vizier? You know what should be done," the sultan pleaded. " I have been unforgivably insulted."

"I will give orders for her to be sent to the dungeons, my Lord... to await your pleasure."

*****

Deep in the bowels of the fortress and in a darkness that was so dense Rav'an could not even see her hand in front of her face, she let her mind wander to her memories of her child, her aunt Fariba and the gentle doctor. She wondered how they were and prayed that no harm would come to them. Her thoughts turned as they ever did when alone to Talon. Fariba had told her that one of the great healing forces of life was time. In time Talon would fade enough for her heart to heal. But she knew that her aunt was only saying this, as Fariba had loved Talon almost as much as she did. Had he not saved their lives in Isfahan before he had disappeared back into the world of the Frans?

Apart from that one tantalizing time when Reza had brought exciting news of an event in Egypt when they had both decided that it might be him, there had been nothing. But his memory had not faded and sometimes in the pre-dawn darkness she had thought his soul might be nearby and had woken to call our to him, then had wept as she did not know if he was alive or dead. She had poured out her desperate love onto her son, glimpsing in him on occasion the Talon she was now never to see again.

Now she would never see any of them again, as she had been assured by the jailers that this was her final destination. Execution would be brutal, but then perhaps her soul would know some peace. She turned and lay down on the mat in a fetal position, oblivious of the tears that wet her face, and fell into a troubled sleep.

But the shadow of God brings the seeker to find.
Knock on the door, knock enough times,
And a head will come out from behind.
So the lover of hope kept on trying and trying,
Till a meeting was granted by chance and by fear.

—Rumi

Chapter 28

Shiraz

A dark figure, its face covered to the eyes with a shemagh and a loosely wound turban on his head, eased slowly over the edge of the mud wall battlements that were part of the sultan's huge fortress, rolled over the low wall and slid into the shadows at the corner of a tower nearby.

The sentry who stood inside the archway sheltering from the cold wind on this moonless night did not seem to have heard nor seen anything; he remained motionless at his post. But he was an obstruction that had to be removed as he was standing in the way, the only route down into the courtyard.

Sliding along the wall in absolute silence the figure came up behind the sentry; he was just about to reach forward to take him down with a knife in his back when he noticed something peculiar about his intended victim.

Instead of standing upright the man was leaning limply against the wall. Talon looked harder and noticed that the man was being held against the wall by his own spear! Its shaft was set on the floor with the point deep inside the man's throat up under his jaw. There was blood dripping down the shaft of the spear and down into the vest of the guard; it had just started to drip onto the mud brick floor. The man was quite dead, but had died only minutes ago!

In the silence of the night Talon felt the hair on the back of his neck rise and a cold sweat break out on his forehead. All his senses were screaming alarms. He slid quickly and silently deeper into the shadows. Someone had come through here just before him and could still be near at hand, well within striking distance.

As still as the mud wall he had his back against, Talon's eyes swept back and forth across the deserted battlements and the dark shadows and crevices nearby. Nothing moved. He remained crouched, his ears straining for the slightest noise to warn him of an attack, sifting the night sounds for any sound that might prelude an attack, his knife held tight and close. His objective was the compound on the other side of the opposite wall,behind which towered the domed palace with its many halls, chambers and corridors. He knew it was a mad venture and that it had little chance of success. But he also knew deep down that he had not come all this way to Persia and then on down to Shiraz to abandon Rav'an, just because something might be taking place that he had not anticipated.

Forcing himself to breathe calmly and to still his fear, his eyes swept the walls and nearby shadows repeatedly, seeking the slightest sign. But all seemed very quiet with no movement or darker shadows to betray another person poised to strike.

He wondered about the person who had come through before him, without doubt a very skilled 'Assassin and one who could easily have noticed Talon coming after him and be lying in wait nearby.

Talon had his back safely to the wall behind him. From here he could look down into the wide stone -trewn path that ran between the buildings below the battlements. Then he noticed a flicker of movement about sixty paces away down by the corner of a wall and at the foot of the wide round towers. A dark figure emerged slowly from the shadows and moved swiftly along the base of the wall in the direction of a portal further along the path. It moved silently and furtively, keeping to the darker patches. He could barely see the figure in the darkness of the wall, but surely it moved.

Talon knew it had to be the 'Assassin who had just killed the sentry. Why? He could not think what the 'Assassin might be here for, but it threatened to disrupt his plans irrevocably. Talon felt a wave of frustration combined with anger; he had not come here to have his plan ruined by someone who was trying to break into the palace. He had to know who it was, but more importantly he had to stop him before the alarms were called and he had to flee, his goal of releasing Rav'an from her imprisonment abandoned. It would be next to impossible to come back another time. Guards would be more numerous, and far more alert.

As silently as his quarry, Talon swiftly descended the wooden stairs and followed the figure in the distance. His grass woven sandals made hardly a whisper on the sand. But he had barely covered fifty paces before the figure suddenly disappeared into the shadows again. Talon could not see where the man had gone, so he was forced to move forward as silently as he could and much more carefully to check on the whereabouts of his quarry. His senses were screaming at him that danger lurked ahead but he forced himself to keep moving.

He did not get very far, as suddenly the figure leapt out at him. Talon's first reaction was the stab upwards as the figure came hard at him but his blade was parried with incredible swiftness, and with equal speed a blade was flashing up towards the underside of his ribs.

Talon danced aside only just in time and the razor sharp blade of his adversary sliced through the fabric of his outer clothing. There was the hiss of expelled breath and the figure followed through as swiftly as a striking snake. Again Talon had to dodge back, his own blade just parrying the other's as it flickered in towards him. The rasp of steel on steel was loud in the quiet of the night. In the darkness it was very hard to tell from where the next strike might come. The blades rasped together again and the two men locked wrists. Talon sensed something then. His adversary was strong but was lighter than he.

He used his own strength to force the other man back, still with blades locked, as both knew that to pull away now was certain death. Talon reached forward with his other hand and clamped his fingers onto the knife wrist of the other in a vice-like grip, effectively preventing him from escaping while at the same time taking the initiative away. Again there was a hiss of breath as the other struggled briefly and then slammed his palm towards Talon's head. Talon ducked, but the palm of the thrusting arm and hand that glanced off his temple still hurt.

He shook his head and then used all his strength to lift the lighter person enough to unbalance him then spun him back into the nearby wall. The man's head thudded against the wall and he slumped a little as though stunned. Talon snatched the head covering off the head of his victim and gasped.

It was the face of one he could never have forgotten. Although the years had matured the face and there was a well trimmed beard and mustache it was Reza without any doubt, a slightly dazed Reza who was desperately trying to recover his balance.

"Reza! Reza!" Talon whispered urgently. He prayed he was right. In this darkness he could easily be wrong and then his opponent would attack again. The man shook his head but went on guard instinctively, although he stared hard at the covered figure menacing him.

"Who are you?" he whispered back just as fiercely.

"It is Talon, your brother, you idiot!"

Talon tore off his own head covering.

Reza stared hard and then gaped.

"Talon? Is it really you? What in the name of the Prophet? You have changed! And what are you doing here?"

"I think I am doing what you are!"

"Then you are seeking Rav'an?"

Reza put his knife away and stepped forward to give Talon a bear hug. The two danced silently in this manner for a few long moments. There were tears in their eyes when they finally separated and held one another at arm's length.

"You have changed, my brother; I see a warrior."

"You have changed too, my brother. Once we were boys, today we are warriors! Are we together in this?" Talon returned.

Reza nodded soberly. "Yes, Talon, much has changed, and us with it... but you are still my brother and I thank God for it and that you are here and alive. How did you know she was here?"

"Fariba. We shall talk later; for now do you know where she is?" asked Talon.

"I know that she is kept in the harem, but that is all. I was looking for a way to get deeper into the palace. We are on the right side, as this wall is one of the walls of the courtyard of the harem."

"How do we get over this wall? It is very high, even for us."

Reza grinned in the dark.

"Neither of us is as light and nimble as we once were, Talon. But we have to get over this wall. There are grooves and small footholds, and it is made of mud. We can do this, and then there is another."

They ran silently together towards the lower section of the wide mud wall, their faces once again covered. Scaling it was not as hard as Talon had dreaded, but he still thought he made too much noise. Reza simply sped up the wall like a spider and gave him his hand to pull him up behind him onto the top.

Reza whispered to Talon, "It is quiet, but we must be very careful as there are people still awake all over the place and we could disturb one at any time. I have taken care of the sentry."

Talon nodded. "I bumped into him on my way over the wall. He told me that you had come by there."

Reza snapped an alarmed look at Talon.

"How...?"

"He was quite dead though; nearly scared the life out of me!"

Reza chuckled quietly at that. "You have not changed, brother! Still joking."

"Listen to who is talking. Come on."

They moved quickly along the darkened pathways to the courtyard and then made their way towards the compound that was their objective. They eased themselves up amd over ayet another wall and down very carefully to the ground and then ducked into the deeper shadows.

As they sped silently along the path Reza whispered, "I am guessing that Rav'an is in one of the innermost rooms of the harem but I don't know where she might actually be within the building. The search must be carefully done. If we wake the many women they will undoubtedly start screaming like a bunch of frightened geese; that would lead to our capture, and you know what would happen then!"

Talon could guess. They would be tortured until they were mad and then there would be a public execution where they would be cut into small pieces while still alive. He didn't want to contemplate failure at this juncture.

They found the section of wall that surrounded the compound easy to climb, but they had to remain lying on the top, for below in the inner courtyard were two men walking together and talking just beneath them. Talon assumed they were eunuch guards there to prevent any intruders who might want to sample the goods belonging to the sultan. He leaned close to Reza.

"Do we have to kill them?" he whispered.

Reza's face could not be seen under the dark shemagh that he had rewrapped around his face but he nodded. He put his face close to Talon's.

"I do not think we have any choice, as we have to come back this way, and if they have even a tiny suspicion, getting past them on the way back will be very difficult without them raising the alarm," he murmured.

Talon drew his knife and prepared for the encounter.

While the men were walking the other way and had their backs to them Talon and Reza slid quickly and silently down the wall. Daggers held in fists they ran silently up behind their victims and slammed their blades deep into their victims' backs. The only sound was the thump of hilts as they struck. Neither of the guards knew what had happened, they died silently with the knives deep in their hearts and a hand over their mouths; their struggle for life was brief and then they were in their death throes, but one of them kicked his spear so that it rattled against the wall. Talon and Reza stopped and listened but there were no alarms.

They dragged the corpses into deeper shadows and waited, listening to the night. Nothing happened, no alarm; just silence. The distant roaring of a male camel followed by the bleat of a young goat disturbed the night but the animals stopped and again there was deep silence. The fortress appeared to sleep. In his heightened state of tension Talon felt that he could hear the dust slipping off the stones of the walls it was so quiet.

Now they needed to find their way into the building behind them. They crept along the wall until they came to an archway; there they paused. There was a snore from within so they investigated.

A very fat man was seated on a cushion, leaning against the archway of a small door. He was obviously supposed to be guarding it but had clearly felt safe enough to go to sleep, relying upon his companions outside to alert him should there be any disturbance.

Talon knelt by the man, ignoring the stink of wine on the man's breath and prodded him with his knife. The man woke with a start and stared blearily up at the dark menacing figure leaning over him. A sharp knife was being pushed against his throat. He shrunk back with a moan.

"Tell me where the harem is and I shall not kill you," whispered Talon.

The man was obviously terrified; his hand went to his heart and saliva dribbled down his chin. Talon prodded him to remind him.

"Speak or I shall finish you now!" he whispered more fiercely.

The man nodded mutely towards the door.

"It is in there; go down the long corridor and you come to the main entrance to the harem," he croaked.

Reza leaned over the man. "Get up! You will show us where that door is and if there is an alarm you die first."

They pulled the now copiously sweating man to his feet, and while Talon tied his hands behind his back Reza tore off his turban and wrapped it tightly around the man's lower face, effectively gagging him and putting a stop to his low moans of terror. He had a key on him which Reza took and used to open the door.

"It is only a matter of time before they find the men outside," whispered Talon. "We have to hurry."

Reza nodded. They pushed the whimpering man ahead of them into the dimly lit interior, making sure that the door was bolted shut behind them. Just as he had said there was a long corridor ahead, lit only by smoky oil lamps placed in recesses in the walls. The three of them shuffled down the dimly lit corridor until they came to a large, well-carved door located on their left. There was a frieze above the door which allowed anyone within to look out without being seen. Both Talon and Reza saw this immediately and ducked out of the line of sight.

Talon pulled the fat man to him and removed the gag. "Stand close to the door and tell them to open it," he ordered.

Reza knocked on the door and they waited. Eventually a small grill was slid open and a high pitched voice asked querulously, "Who is it at this late hour? Do not bang on the door or you will wake everyone!"

"It is I, Jamal. Open up."

"Very well, but do not make any noise." The grill snapped shut and they heard the sound of bolts being withdrawn inside. Reza and Talon looked at one another. There was no choice. As soon as the door opened Talon slipped through and before the eunuch within could cry out he was dying from a knife in his heart. Talon laid him down in the dark recess just within the entrance.

Their prisoner began to cry out with fear but Reza brandished his knife in his face so all that came out was a tiny bleat of terror. They all three moved past the corpse into the darkness of the room beyond. This area was very different from the austere décor of the passageway they had just left. They had entered a high roofed central chamber with its roof supported by many slim and fluted pillars of finely worked stone. Talon swept his gaze around the room and noticed that there were many dark recesses in the walls all around. These walls were sumptuously hung with tapestries and rugs, their images and the gold threaded Arabic scrolls glimmered in the poor light of the night lamps placed in a few niches.

He noticed rich carpets strewn on the floor below the marble steps the men were standing on, and low seating platforms; Talon could see in the dimness beyond that there was a pool somewhat like a large bathing area, and he could hear the sound of a small fountain playing into the pool of water. The sound of splashing was loud in the cavernous silence that greeted them. The sultan took care of his women, it seemed.

Talon nudged Reza and pointed at the alcoves leading off from this chamber, which he assumed served as a living room for the women, and he wondered how on earth they were going to find Rav'an. He was also afraid there might be children here or other women who would screamat the sight of intruders, and then they would be in trouble.

The man with them was whimpering to himself and sweating, a stink emanating from him, and his clothes were wet with perspiration. The room itself seemed well lived in, as there was an overabundance of stale perfume and other old smells coming from the interior.

Talon pulled the man close and whispered.

"As you value your life you will tell me where the lady Rav'an is sleeping," he hissed.

Before the man could answer, however, a figure rose from one of the low beds alongside the walls and began to walk towards them. Talon and Reza froze but the man began to shake, so Talon forced him to his knees and Reza glided very rapidly down towards the figure approaching them. He was so fast that the person, a woman, only had time for a stifled squeak before he was holding her fast with his knife at her throat and a hand over her mouth. He whispered urgently to her and she relaxed enough for him to release her, but the knife was still hovering in a menacing manner before her eyes.

She was an older woman who Talon could see by the dim light of the chamber had once been beautiful but was now overweight and bore herself more as a matron.

"Where is the woman called Rav'an?" Reza hissed. The woman put her hand to her mouth; she was trembling with fear but then she seemed to collect herself and replied, "She is no longer here."

Reza and Talon heard her words with shock. "Not here? Then where is she? Tell me or I shall cut you!" Reza snarled. He waved his knife threateningly at the lady again.

"She left for Isfahan."

"When?" Both Talon and Reza were aghast at the news.

She was about to answer when a figure darted out of one of the alcoves and came towards them. It was a much younger woman, almost a girl, and she ran with a light step.

As she came up she whispered in a harsh manner. "You lie! You lie, Abeer!"

Reza was moving even as she spoke to keep her in sight as well as the older woman. Talon glanced at the eunuch but he was on his knees staring at the scene in front of him with shock and fear written all over his face. Talon hauled him down the steps so that he could threaten both the eunuch and the older woman.

Reza reached out and seized the girl by the arm but she wriggled out of his grip and kicked out at him in a fury. Reza was so surprised that he loosened his hold and she was free but tripped and fell to her knees, gasping out something as she fell. As quick as a striking snake he was on her and this time he held her by her hair. "She... she is not in Isfahan!" the girl gasped and pointed at the woman she had named Abeer. "*She* knows where she is! Tell them, you witch! Rav'an is not in Isfahan!" she was no longer struggling and Reza said, "Do not move, stay where you are."

He released the girl advanced again on Abeer and said menacingly, "I asked you where the lady Rav'an was. This time do not lie to me or I shall finish you here and now." His voice, even as a whisper was so savage that she flinched and took a step back, but he followed her and then Talon was right behind her so she had nowhere to go.

She was shaking with fear now and stuttered, "I know that she is in one of the dungeons of the palace, but which one I do not know. She was taken there directly from the chambers of the Sultan."

"Again you lie!" The girl snapped in a hissing whisper. "You denounced her to the Sultan's servants when you found out that she was not a virgin. It could have been hidden from them! Men are so stupid!"

Talon and Reza glanced at one another, at the girl and then at the woman at their feet.

The girl continued as though they were not there. "They see what they want to see. But you betrayed her for your own selfish reasons and now she will face death by execution! You witch!"

Again Talon and Reza looked at one another, but this time with alarm. Talon was looking around them nervously. This bitter exchange was threatening to become louder and then the entire harem could wake up any minute, whereupon they would be finished.

He edged in closer to the woman and said very quietly. "Your life depends upon telling us the truth as to where she is. If you lie we can come and find you, no matter what is done to protect you. We are *Fid'ai* and have come from Alamut. You understand?"

She gasped, even though she must have understood who they were almost at the onset, but she nodded.

"She is in a dungeon below the main palace." With some prodding from Reza she proceeded to tell them how to get there. All the while the other girl was watching her with anger in her eyes but she said nothing until Abeer was finished. Then she pointed at the Eunuch and said, "He would know... I am sure Jamal would know."

I shall have to ask him nicely," Reza whispered to Talon.

"No, its my turn, I will be able to find out for sure, within moments."

"Talon, my brother, I am better at this than you. I have had more practice."

"And you don't think I know how to make him talk?" Talon asked with surprise in his tone.

They were interrupted by the girl who placed her hands on her hips and said in a scathing manner, "When you two have finished squabbling over this... this insect like a pair of donkeys it will be dawn and too late to do anything. Decide and then save my friend Rav'an!"

Reza and Talon gaped at her. Without another word Talon went over to the man, who was still on his knees, and dug his knife blade into the base of his throat. That was all it took; the eunuch began weeping and wringing his hands. With great care Talon took off the gag and asked him. "Can you take us to the cell where she is?"

The man nodded. "No more, I beg you! I will take you," he sobbed.

Talon and Reza exchanged looks again. They had a huge task ahead of them, and how could they leave these women behind while they went looking for Rav'an?

As though divining their thoughts the girl whispered, "You must take me with you! If *she* is allowed to live then she will make sure that I am punished and I will surely die. You must!" she pleaded, reaching for Reza's sleeve. "Take me out of this prison, I do not want to die here." She was tearful now. Reza turned and stared at her as though seeing her for the first time. She was a young woman of perhaps eighteen, possessed of very fine features and a slim form. Talon thought he saw a change come over Reza then and wondered what he was going to do next.

Reza said nothing. Instead he reached for the older woman and forced her to her knees. "Leave the chamber, my brother. Take those two with you."

Talon became aware of the sudden change of atmosphere and the woman too realized that her time had come. In one last desperate attempt to save her life opened her mouth to scream. She did not have a chance to utter a sound. Reza's knife flashed.

She seemed to relax suddenly, but then he was supporting her as she fell to the ground to lie limp on the polished tiles in a growing pool of blood. Talon was surprised but the man he was holding fast was even more shocked. He gave a groan and the stink of his voided bowels filled the air.

The girl let out a tiny moan and put her hand to her mouth, her eyes wide with shock, but did nothing more. Talon watched her approvingly as she held onto her self control and stumbled past him towards the entrance of the chamber as though she had gained permission already. Talon retied the gag on his prisoner, hauled him to his feet and dragged him after the girl.

Reza with a quick glance around the silent chamber sped after them and closed the large doors silently behind him. They were back in the corridor but this time their prisoner indicated that they should continue along towards another set of ornate doors just ten paces away.

The girl had taken off her slippers and was now as noiseless as the two of them, although their prisoner was still making far too much noise for Talon's liking. Talon was still thinking about the ruthless gesture he had just witnessed his friend commit, but told himself that they would receive far worse if captured. Not only that, the woman had betrayed Rav'an who now faced death herself. The urgency of finding her was now paramount.

Reckless love is not afraid to explode
while reason seeks profit;
As Love suffers
She remains steadfast, solid and strong.

—Rumi

Chapter 29

A Drain

Reza took off the gag and asked the eunuch how far it would be for them to go to find the dungeons.

"It is one level below, if we take the tower we will not encounter more than one or two sentries," the man gasped.

"What do we find behind this door?" Talon asked him.

"A... a sentry, just as I was," the man gargled.

Easing the door open was a slow business, but on the other side they saw a eunuch, asleep sitting on a bench sprawled among some cushions. His snores reverberated around the small antechamber. With great care they all tip-toed past the sleeping man. Their prisoner was so cowed that he made not the slightest effort to sound the alarm. He indicated a small door across the room away from the main archway to their left. There were curtains drawn across this archway, which effectively hid them from any prying eyes.

Talon was sure that there would be guards somewhere on the other side, so he put a finger to his lips and glared at the girl and their prisoner. The small door opened upon a stone stairway that led both up and down. They closed the door with great care, aware that every creak of the hinges could waken the sleeping man, and slipped down into the darkness below.

As they moved slowly down the stone stairs they could make out the dull glow of light from below. No noise at all could be heard, not even the sound of men snoring or people moving about. Talon led the way, his sword held in front of him, while Reza held onto the eunuch by the scruff of his neck, his knife close to the shaking man's throat, and the girl hovered close by as silent as a mouse.

Slowly Talon turned the last curve of the stairway and found himself at the end of a long corridor. There were several doors set in the mud brick walls all along the passage, but they did not look as though they were prison cells. There were lamps burning in recesses along the corridor that gave off a dim light. Some had gone out, leaving dark patches along the narrow corridor. He glanced back and motioned the eunuch to come and join him at the doorway.

"Where will she be?" he whispered.

The eunuch looked confused. "This is not the dungeon!" he whispered his eyes rolling with fear and clearly bewildered by what he saw.

Talon seized him by the throat. "Then where is it!" he hissed.

The shaking man pointed to another door and said, "It must be that door, another level..." Shaking his head at Reza, Talon pushed the man out into the dimly lit corridor and then they all crept towards the other end of the passage where yet another door opened onto some steps that led down into the darkness below. Talon thought he heard the sound of water but was not sure.

When they shut the door behind them they found themselves in pitch darkness and absolute silence other than the persistent sound of water flowing somewhere below. There was an unpleasant smell wafting up towards them. Reza returned through the door and took one of the lamps out of its recess, then they descended the steps in its flickering light.

Talon knew that time was running out; before long someone would discover one of the slain guards or the dead woman in the harem and all hell would break loose. He was desperate to be out of the city with Rav'an and on their way to the coast. If only they could find her!

Once again they emerged into an open space and the first thing that struck them was the smell. Dust and excrement mixed with urine and other filth. Talon wrapped the loose end of his turban around his nose, as did Reza, while the girl put her hand over her face with a whimper of disgust. The sound of running water was more pronounced that before. It came from deep underground beneath a worked metal grill set in the middle of the passage.

"Where does the water come from?" Talon demanded of the eunuch.

"It is the qanat that diverts the water from the main river Khoskh to the palace," he whispered tremulously. Talon filed the information away in his mind.

"Where does it lead?"

"It falls back into the river when it has passed under the palace. All the water for the palace is taken from this flow."

Reza jogged along the barred corridor past one of the two lighted torches illuminating the tunnel, peering inside the cells. There were sleeping forms in all of them and one or two woke up to peer back at him with wide frightened eyes. But none of them was Rav'an, of that he was certain.

Then came a surprise. One of the forms in the cell woke up and stood up. "What do you want at this time?" he asked querulously. Another stood up in the same cell. "What is going on? Do you need prisoners for something?" he jangled some keys as he got up.

Talon realized with surprise that these were the jailers who were there to guard the prisoners but who slept in an open cell.

Reza recovered very quickly. "We come from the Officer of the Guard to check on you... and guess what we find! You were asleep, you dogs!"

"We were only resting, your honor, please do not report us," the first one pleaded, clearly frightened by Reza's tone and arrogant bearing.

"We are here to take the prisoner Rav'an upstairs. Which cell is she in?"

"I will show you, your honor, at once!" the second man said, waving the keys with a jangle in the air. Reza nodded. "You! Stay inside there," he warned the other man with a wave of his sword, who subsided onto his pallet. By now the other prisoners were waking up and taking an interest. Some were even asking what was happening. Talon was glad of the darkness that hid him and the other two for the moment.

Reza let the man with the keys out of the cell and then asked in a casual manner, "What key works for this cell?

Before the man thought about it he had shown the key to Reza, who snatched it out of his hands and locked the cell door with the other guard inside. The man reacted with anger and fear. "Why have you done this? You cannot do this to me! Who are you?" he exclaimed, grabbing the bars and shaking them.

"Shut your mouth and you will live," Reza said and smacked the man on his knuckles with the flat of his sword. "Make any more noise and I will come in there and cut your throat myself."

The man retreated, sucking on his bruised fingers, a frightened look on his face.

Ignoring him, Reza motioned to Talon and his companions to join him, and then put the edge of his sword against the neck of man with the keys, who was facing him with a confused and fearful expression on his face.

"You are not from the guard! Who are you?" he quavered.

"Lead me to the cell where you have the Lady Rav'an." His voice carried to the other man clearly enough for him to hear.

The trembling man nodded mutely, then waved his hand at his partner, who subsided. Talon and his two companions had now joined Reza, to the surprise of the jailers and also to those prisoners who were now awake and becoming aware that something very strange was taking place.

"Who are you? What are you doing here? In Allah's good name let us out!" they called.

Putting her finger to her lips the young girl smiled at them and waved her hands for them to quiet down. "No noise. No noise!" she whispered. The filthy, starved creatures stopped calling and stared at this beautiful apparition who had appeared in the middle of their night.

It was time to hurry. Talon shoved the eunuch forward. "Lock him up with the jailor. We no longer need him," he said to Reza, who was quick to comply.

Talon then motioned the jailer outside the cell to hurry. There was another torch flaming on the wall nearby. Reza took this and followed the jailer, who was desperate to obey and avoid the point of Reza's dagger. They moved a few more paces along the passage to a wooden door sunk into the wall, and he opened the cell with another key. The smell of dank air came out of the pitch darkness within. There was a scratching sound of a rat scuttling away and then silence. Reza lifted the lamp high to better see within.

Talon's emotions threatened to overwhelm him but he held himself in fiercely, knowing that much depended upon their safely escaping before he could release them. He motioned Reza to wake the form lying on the rough pallet on the floor, while he turned his back and watched for any danger. The girl next to him gave a gasp of shock at the conditions of the cell.

Reza moved over to the pallet and touched the form on the shoulder. There was a muffled sound and then the person on the bed sat up and peered at him. Reza went on one knee and held his finger to his lips then whispered something. There was a stifled exclamation and the figure scrambled to get off the bed. Talon stepped back and stared, his heart pounding.

He would have recognized Rav'an anywhere, even in the half darkness of the cell, even in the condition he now found her, but because he had his back to the light she could not make out his features. She stood up and whispered back to Reza.

"It is you, Reza! I knew you would come! I prayed so hard that you would come! But who is this?" She peered up at Talon, who stood a good hand taller than she in her bare feet.

"Do you not recognize me, Rav'an?" he asked in a hoarse whisper.

There was absolute silence as she stared at him, then her hand went to her heart and she swayed. He stepped forward quickly and reached to hold her, whereupon she almost fell into his arms.

"Talon?" she asked softly, pulling back and staring up at his face.

"Yes," he whispered simply. She put both hands on either side of his face and held onto him, gently caressing him.

She shook her head. "It is a dream; it can only be a dream. You come to me in dreams and then I wake up and I am so lost that I weep. It is so cruel of fate to deal with me thus, in this place; it is all I have left," she murmured wretchedly.

"Does this feel like a dream?" he asked huskily, reaching for her and holding her tight in an embrace. He felt hot tears running down his cheeks as he held her.

"Oh no! Ah Talon, is it really you?" she asked again, her voice muffled against the cloth on his shoulder. Her hands were fists gripping the fabric of his shirt at his chest.

She turned and stared at them, her eyes wide in the poor light. "I see you, Reza, and it is you, Talon, but is that you, Jannat? What are you doing here?

Jannat was weeping and rushed to embrace her. "We, your strange friends and I, have come to take you away, my Rav'an. I have to leave with you or they will kill me for helping them. But I wanted to find you, I have missed you."

While they embraced Reza came close. "There is no time left. We must leave, my Lady, or we will all become ghosts," he whispered.

Talon awoke to the urgency of Reza's reminder.

"We must leave immediately. Do you have any other clothes for the road, my Lady?" he asked. He felt her lift her head and could see the gleam of tears on her cheeks. Her hand strayed back to his face.

"My Talon, I have no clothes other than these clothes I am wearing, and only slippers. They would give me no others."

"Then we must leave as we are. We can find clothing as we travel," he whispered back. "I have a cloak with the horses which you shall have."

Reza grabbed the jailor who had been standing off to the side watching, and before the man could make even a sound he found himself slammed against the far wall of the cell and the key turning in the lock behind him. The pounding on the door was muted and would disturb no one while they attempted to escape.

Reza whirled about, his face a mask of anger. "They did this to our princess!" he exclaimed incredulously. I shall be back in a few moments."

Before Talon could stop him he had run to the door at the end and disappeared up the stairway.

*****

Reza ran silently all the way up the steps and then along the corridor to speed up the next set of steps and stopped in front of the guard who slept.

This guard woke up to find a knife at his throat. "You will tell me where the Sultan sleeps," the dark form hissed in his ear. Reza's face was so close that the man jerked back, but the hand that held his collar remained firm.

"Tell me! Tell me now!" Reza demanded. The now sweating man lifted his hand to point upward.

"Above us in the main chambers," he croaked.

It was the last thing he ever said. Reza sped up the stairs, leaving the man in a pool of his own blood, his body still twitching, his throat cut from ear to ear.

Reza had little difficulty dealing with the sleepy guards and was finally rewarded by seeing two men leaning against the wall of an imposing wooden doorway. They died silently and he slipped like a phantom into the room.

At the far end was a large platform decorated with silks and cushions upon which a rotund man was sleeping. On either side of him were two women. The females were very young, while the man himself was lying on his back, his belly a large mound in his middle. They were all fast asleep with the coverings of the bed strewn in untidy folds all about them.

Reza's intent had been to kill the sultan, but then he decided against it. The effect would be just as devastating if he used another way to demonstrate his rage.

*****

He reappeared in the dungeons like a wraith just as Talon was about to come after him to find out what he was doing.

"Where have you been, Brother!" Talon snapped; he was not pleased.

'Reza gave him a cold grin. "I left a message."

He got no further, as Talon heard a noise above them. He pointed upward and they listened hard; what Talon had most dreaded was beginning to happen above them. Their escape route was blocked.

"What have you done?" he accused Reza.

"It was not I who disturbed them, Talon. I suspect that the eunuchs in the women's chamber discovered the dead and raised the alarm."

Talon's eyes sped around the hall and arrived at the grating, which covered the hole in the floor. It was raised just off the ground, rather like a small wellhead. An idea occurred to him. He snatched the keys from Reza and ran to the cell which held the eunuch and the jailor. At the point of his sword he drove them to the former cell that had been occupied by Rav'an and then shoved them with his foot to stagger against the surprised man already there and shut the door turning the key as he did so.

Reza was watching him with alarmed eyes. "Talon, we do not have time for this!" he exclaimed.

"No indeed, listen to what is going above. Can you not hear it? They have discovered the bodies. I have an idea, Reza. Release the prisoners and tell them that is the way out, up the stairs, and they are to rush out as fast as they can. *We* go down the qanat!"

Reza had cocked an ear to the muted sounds taking place above them. He nodded, then laughed and shook his head.

"Of course!" he said.

He rushed about, opening the cells and telling the bemused and confused prisoners that their only way out was up the stairs. He brooked no arguments and even used the flat of his sword to drive them through the doorway. Most of them needed little persuasion and scampered up the darkened stairs to what they thought might be their way to freedom. But then an ominous sound came from above. It was the sound of more shouts and pounding feet.

"Hurry, we have to disappear!" Reza called out in a harsh whisper as he closed the door on the last of the prisoners.

Talon heaved at the heavy grating; soon it was forced off enough to allow them to peer down into the darkness below. He prayed the confusion created by the prisoners would be enough distraction to allow them to vanish below.

"It is perhaps only ten feet down," Reza stated. "I shall go first and help the women as they come down. Lower them to me, Talon," he commanded, and then without hesitation he dropped out of sight. There was a muted splash, then he called up urgently. "Hurry!"

Talon heaved a frightened Jannat onto the rim and then let her down by one arm and had the satisfaction of knowing that Reza had been able to reach up and catch her. Rav'an slid onto the rim and then with a lingering look at Talon seized his hands and allowed herself to be lowered down to the arms of Reza.

By now the former jailers had become aware of the noise above and were banging on the door to their cell, creating enough noise to bring people to investigate. It was time to disappear. Talon climbed into the opening and braced himself so that he could hold onto the rim of the well and then attempted to slide the grating back into place. He only partially succeeded but it was all he could do, so he let go and dropped the distance to land in the cold running waters of the stream below with a splash.

"Come, there will not be much time," Reza said from the darkness just down stream from him. "We are mad to do this, but if it works then we have a chance," he said into the darkness that now enclosed them.

The rushing water was knee deep and threatened to pull their feet from under them, the current was so strong. Talon and Reza were forced to brace themselves against the sandy walls to prevent themselves and the women from being swept away. Jannat gasped as she floundered at one point but Reza took her by the arm and hauled her behind him as he staggered down the length of the pitch black tunnel. She was eager to go, and then Talon seized Rav'an by her hand and followed them.

At one point there had been a cave-in, which they had to crawl over, fighting the current that threatened all the time to sweep them away.

Then they came upon a problem. The water seemed to be rising and the flow slowed, but the undercurrent was still very strong. Soon it was level with their chests, and Jannat and Rav'an, who could not find the floor, were clinging to the men who supported them. Reza turned to Talon and said, "There might be a blockage, or, I pray to God, only a narrowing of the stream. I have to find out.

He passed Jannat to Talon and, taking a deep breath, sank under the water. After what seemed to be far too long he surfaced, gasping for breath. Although Talon could not see him he could sense him and called out to tell Reza where they were.

Reza responded between gasps of air, "There is a constriction below; it is narrow, but one person at a time can go down. I shall go first and try to dislodge a rock."

"Do we know to where it is going?" Rav'an asked for all of them.

There was a long silence after her question, broken only by the swirling waters and a whimper from Jannat.

Reza answered. "No, my Lady, we do not know, but there is no other way. In sha' Allah, this leads to the river as the eunuch said. If so we might survive; if not then I shall meet you all in another place. Come with me, Jannat. He took her hand in a firm grip and said, "Do not fear, my Lady. Just take a deep breath and hold it, then trust me. Dive deep, my brother and sister," he said as he departed.

Jannet struggled instinctively but Reza's grip was too firm. They vanished into the water, leaving Talon and Rav'an clinging to one another in the darkness.

"It would be a cruel fate to lose you now, my Rav'an. We must trust in God." He had to raise his voice to hear himself speak.

"I love you, Talon," she gasped, clasping herself to him with a desperation born of fear and emotion.

Abruptly the water level began to lower, but then the force of the current increased. It fell to waist level then remained there, tugging at their legs.

"Reza must have dislodged the rock he was talking about," said Talon. "Allah protect you, Rav'an. I shall see you in the river."

He kissed her on her lips hard and then let her go.

Rav'an took a deep breath and vanished into the darkness as though she had never been there.

He took a deep breath himself and then followed her to the bottom of the stream, allowing the current to drag him down. He knew a moment of sheer panic as the water seized his body and dragged him feet first into an opening that barely accommodated his shoulders. He was swept through and along what he could only think must be a smooth clay pipe, and then to his surprise after only a short distance he was ejected into space to fall with an arc of water into another body of water. He plunged deep and then struggled to the surface, gasping for breath, desperate to fill his lungs and regain some form of control. He heard a faint cry to his right and reached out to grab the flailing arm of Jannat, and then swept his eyes about their destination.

There were in a deeper part of the river sheltered by a high bank from which came the jet of water that had ejected them. Jannat was clinging to him like a monkey and spluttering as she tried to regain her breath and babble prayers of thanks for her deliverance at the same time. He all but ignored her, as he was desperately looking for Rav'an. He could see nothing in the fast flowing waters of the river, but then as he staggered to the side a strong hand reached out and Reza seized his collar.

"Where is Rav'an?" Talon asked when he had regained his footing on the bottom of the river. He had a sinking feeling in his stomach as he searched wildly for her in the dark river.

"Fear not, she is with me. She landed on me in the river and nearly broke my neck!" Reza hissed, rubbing his shoulders and neck resentfully

"Then get this monkey off me and we can find the horses," Talon hissed back, and prized Jannat's death-like grip from around his neck. Talon's relief at seeing Rav'an, who was lying on the bank next to Reza, was almost overwhelming.

"I... I cannot swim. I am sorry, I'm sorry. Allah be praised, but you saved me!" Jannat stuttered.

"Here, Reza, take her." Talon pushed the sodden girl off him. "We have woken up a hornet's nest up there and must put as much distance as we can between us and that place, once we have the horses. Where have we landed?"

Reza helped the half-naked girl onto the bank, where she rested on hands and knees next to the panting Rav'an. He inadvertently leaned back and by accident his head connected with Jannat's soggy bottom. She gave a squeak of surprise and fell forward, while Reza hastily pulled himself back up to a kneeling position.

"I... I am sorry my Lady," he stammered, embarrassed beyond words. She turned her head and regarded him in indignant silence.

The mutual embarrassment would have been comical had it not been for the urgency of their situation, but Talon sensed that Jannat had not minded so much. He almost laughed.

Rav'an now sat up. "Thank you for catching me, Reza," she said, her tone very sweet.

Reza wanted to get back to the subject of their escape as fast as he could. "Those are the walls of the palace above us. The city is to our left, so my horses are just around the corner. Where did you leave yours, brother?" he whispered as he scrambled to create some distance between himself and Jannat.

Talon thought about it for a moment while he tried to orientate himself. The city was down stream, which meant that his horses were not much further around the walls from those of Reza, tied to the branches of a tree in a copse of willows near to the river bank.

"There is a copse of trees further along the river, but let's go and get yours first, they are much closer," Talon suggested.

They set off along the bank of the river, keeping the walls to their right. There was no doubt that the alarms were being sounded; torches were being carried along the battlements as confused and nervous soldiers rushed about peering into the darkness below and trying to follow conflicting orders, and there was much shouting from within.

The soaked and bedraggled group soon came to a small copse of trees and paused while Reza stared into the darkness. Satisfied he waved them on and they came upon the two horses he had brought to take Rav'an away with him.

"Thank God no one found them," Reza whispered. "But two horses will not carry four people very far. We must find yours, Brother, or we will be overtaken far too soon."

Talon nodded in the dark.

They mounted up. Reza lifted Jannat up behind him, whereupon she wrapped her arms around his waist and clung to him.

Talon hoisted Rav'an up behind him and she did the same. She was trembling with cold and reaction but said not a word, simply holding onto him, her arms tight around his waist and her head on his shoulder as they moved off.

He led the way around the palace walls, keeping to the cover of the trees along the river bank, heading to where he had left his horses; but as they approached he knew something was wrong. They were still there, dark shadows against the light color of the sand, but his senses told him they were not alone. Reza eased his horse alongside and they both stared hard at the trees ahead and the two horses seemingly alone hitched to a branch.

"There are others with the horses, Talon."

Talon nodded in the gloom. Fortunately they had been staying among the trees as they negotiated the riverbank, so it was possible that they had not been seen. He indicated to Rav'an that they had to dismount. Reza and Jannat did the same and they stood in the shadows of the trees along the riverbank in silence, trying to see if there was any movement near the horses.

"I can see two of them; they look like they are soldiers, " Reza breathed, almost in his ear.

Talon felt a chill beyond the cold of his soaked clothes.

"We have to have the horses. They must have been a patrol and were suspicious of the horses, " he whispered.

"And waiting for the owner to return, no doubt, but now you and I must go and get them," Reza said; his tone was very calm but the intent deadly. "Can you kill from this distance?" he asked.

Talon stared at the shadows. "If they come out of the trees I can, it is only about sixty paces."

By now the noise from above them had intensified as the entire palace woke up to find itself in a state of pandemonium. They could also hear screams, which Talon attributed to the prisoners who had been unlucky enough not to escape, if indeed any had. They would get short shrift from the panic-stricken guards this night. Talon felt regret that they had done this to them, but his own needs were paramount now.

All the noise served as a distraction to two guards, who now strode out to the edge of the copse to stare up at the walls talking in low tones to one another and gesturing up at the battlements. They were not paying any attention to their immediate surrounding they were so distracted.

Reza handed Talon his bow. It was an act of faith to do so, as Talon was not familiar with the weapon. His own bow was in a sheath with the horses ahead of them. But Reza clearly remembered how deadly Talon had been.

He knocked the arrow Reza handed him and drew back the string. Just at that moment someone jumped off the battlements of the palace to fall with a thump at the bottom, followed by a scream of agony. It must have been one of the former prisoners who had made it to the walls and risked death to escape the horrors awaiting him if he remained.

One of the men turned sharply to see what it was and this presented his front to Talon. There was a sharp twang and the arrow flew off into the dark to land with a thump. The man fell over, clutching his chest. He writhed for a moment and then lay still.

The second man let out a startled grunt and began to run away. The second arrow struck him high on the back of his thigh. He gave a choked cry and stumbled off. Reza raced after him and Talon watched in silence as he caught up with the man; there was a very brief struggle and the man lay still in the dark. There was a cluster of torches gathered on the walls high above them, but no one seemed interested in what was going on near the river.

Reza urgently signaled his friends to hurry up with the other horses. He dragged the inert bodies into the undergrowth by the riverbank and then rejoined them.

The women's wide eyes and pale features told of their shock at witnessing such a sudden and efficient killing.

"Allah has protected us thus far, but now we must leave!" Reza said in a low harsh tone.

They hastened to mount up, each to a horse, and then they took a route along the riverside that would lead to a shallow crossing which Talon had forded earlier in the night. Soon the noise and shouts of the chaos in the palace were left behind and the only sound was that of the pounding hooves of the horses, which were fresh and ready to run. Talon was now leading them; heading west towards the dark mountains and the sea.

It was only when they were fully several thousand paces away that Talon was able to relax and ride closer to Rav'an. She was staring at him as though she were still seeing a ghost.

"Where did you come from, Talon?" she asked almost timidly, reaching out a hand to touch his forearm as though to reassure herself that he was real. Just then Reza came up alongside. Jannat was close by on Reza's other side; he glanced over at her.

"Will you be able to ride a long distance, my Lady?" he asked; his tone was polite.

Jannat nodded and tried a smile. She was soaked in her flimsy palace clothing and shaking with reaction, so he took out his cloak from a saddle bag and threw it over her shoulders. Talon hurriedly did the same for Rav'an, who was also trembling with cold.

"Who is he? Who are you?" Jannat asked. Now that they were temporarily out of danger she was becoming frightened. The entire night had been a terrifying experience after the sheltered life she had led.

It was Rav'an who spoke for them. "Reza is my brother and Talon is my long lost love. They came to rescue me, Jannat, and now you are with us. I am so happy at this moment."

"Where did you come from, Talon? It has been six long years since I saw you taken by the Franks," Reza asked.

"It is a long story, Reza, my Rav'an. But you know this, that I could not stay away any longer once I knew you were alive, Rav'an. I... I was so sure that you would be dead because of what you told me in Banyas castle that dreadful day I had to leave you. I was intercepted by the knights Templar while following you north the next day. They took me to their castle where I was imprisoned. I could not convince them that I needed to find you."

Reza nodded. "I saw them just after they had taken you, when you tried to escape, brother. I saw that you were their prisoner. Your own people took you prisoner! I still do not understand that, but I saw it and came to Rav'an and told her."

"My heart was broken before even that news, Talon, but when Reza told me this I fell into the deepest despair. Only the strength of Reza kept me from finding solace in death at my own hand after that."

Reza interrupted. "My brother and sisters, we must now ride like the wind, as it will be dawn very soon and then the people in the castle will learn the truth about what happened and we will be fugitives. The sultan will send men in every direction to seek us and hunt us down with all the vengeance and resources he surely has at his disposal. We must make all haste to put many miles between us and our pursuers."

Talon looked back at the massive towers of the fortress of Shiraz in the distance and shuddered to think that Rav'an had been a prisoner there. Not even as a wife of the sultan, but in that stinking prison awaiting a fate that he dared not even contemplate.

"But where will we ride to?" Rav'an enquired.

"We ride for Bushehr, my Rav'an. Our son will be there and we must take him with us!"

"You know!" she cried, shock in her voice as they set the horses to a gallop.

"Yes, my love, I know, and I have seen Fariba and the good doctor. Servants are waiting for us, including Alia!" Talon laughed joyfully as he rode beside her.

For time has deadened the cries of pain
That tortured our ears of yore;
The heat–the dust–and the chilling rain,
Forgotten forever more!

—Frances Bartlett

Chapter 30

The Chase

The second night was almost over and the first streaks of dawn had appeared in the east. They had stopped to rest the horses and to ease their own aching limbs. Talon and Reza were seated slightly apart from the women, who were resting by some small trees. Talon had woken up to see Reza's dark silhouette seated on a rise that gave him a good view down the steep valley behind them. He had joined him, seating himself close so that they could talk in a low tone without disturbing the exhausted women. He instinctively checked that the horses were calm and resting. They were tired but would last for some time to come. They sat in silence as each absorbed the fact that they were together again after so long.

Then, as though hesitating to say it, Reza began. "We have missed you, Talon. Where have you been?"

"I was taken from the world I knew and thrown into another. I have learned much, but I too have missed my brother and my Rav'an. Which... is why I came back," Talon responded.

"You know that she gave you a son?"

I do, and I have met him. My heart nearly burst when I knew but... I think I knew I had a son well before I ever met him." He put his arm over his friend's shoulder and shook him. "I am happy that I have found you again."

Reza smacked Talon on the knee and gave him a tired grin. "How is my brother after all the excitement of last night?"

"For a while I did not think we would make it. That stream was a crazy idea."

"But it worked, Talon. You think clearly, you always have. I was so scared when we came to the end of the tunnel and that drain I pissed myself."

Talon grunted a laugh. "Hmm, in the circumstances I doubt if anyone noticed. I was too scared to do even that. Allah gave us a chance, but how those girls did not just die of fright is amazing to me."

Rav'an is a strong lady. You know that, Talon, but the new girl, Jannat, a nice name, she is a surprise!" He hunched his shoulders and ducked his head. Talon grinned in the dark.

"Does Reza, the famous man of women, like her? She clung to you like a frog on that horse earlier," Talon teased

"She is better looking than a frog." Reza hit him on the arm. "Even a very good looking woman, there is no disputing it. Rav'an will have to tell us more about her," Reza said, keeping his tone noncommittal, but his dark features if anything grew a little darker. He picked at a piece of dried grass and picked at his teeth. "I am not a noble and I am sure she is from a great family, sooo, there is not much chance there."

Talon was not so sure. He had seen how Jannat looked at Reza.

"We heard rumors, Talon. There was one where a Frank with the skills of an assassin stole a ship and slew some of the men that Sinan Rashid Ed Din had sent to kill the Sultan Salah Ed Din. Did you hear anything of that?"

"Hmm, yes, it might have been me. About two and a half years ago I was in Egypt because my ship was wrecked and I became a slave but... well, one thing led to another and I escaped with a ship."

Reza grunted with amusement. "I told Rav'an that I did not think that it could have been anyone else! That rumor made people smile in Alamut. They still remember you there. Sinan is not liked very much here in Persia. I suspect that even the Master was not displeased, but we, Rav'an and I, were sure it was you. But after that... nothing. What did you do after that?"

"I was sent to Constantinople. Ah, Reza, that is a city of dreams. You would love it. Now I have three ships and am a wealthy man!"

Reza turned to look at him in the starlit night. "You have become a man of means, Talon. I am glad for you. Are you some kind of lord now? Plenty of beautiful women, I suppose."

Talon chuckled. "By Allah and his kindness. You have not changed one little bit, Reza," he laughed. "No, I am not a lord but I have more control over my destiny than before and some good friends to help. Did you go though all the whores in Isfahan?" he asked, evading the subject."

"A man has a spear for a reason, despite what those miserable mullahs tell us. So I use it. Including with the one you neglected to service, my brother. She thought you were wonderful. I cannot think why." He grinned at Talon's discomfort.

"So do we have a plan? You mentioned one but I see no one to assist us," Reza continued.

"I went to see Al Tayyub and asked for his help. Even now I think he is down in the plains giving someone misleading directions about our route."

Reza turned to him. "You are a thinker, my Brother. I had not thought of that."

"Al Tayyub and Youssef were hurt that you did not ask for their help. They were still smoking that funny stuff and giggling with their friends in the bazaar, but they were glad to see me and we talked about what could be done by way of diversions. They admire you for some obscure reason and of course they love the lady Rav'an. Youssef is somewhere in these hills waiting to help. I pray he is, or we might have a problem."

*****

It was not until early in the morning of the second day, as the sun begun its fiery climb into the sky, that they knew they were being followed. It was going to be a hot day and Talon was already feeling the heat when Reza, ever alert for trouble, strode up onto a mound and looked back along their previous route. He shaded his eyes and squinted into the sun. Then he called the other three up to join him.

"They are coming," he said simply. "We have been careful with the horses up to this moment but now we must ride hard."

"Youssef should be waiting for us a few miles further on at the passes," Talon said. He hoped he was right. "There we can make a stand, but we have to try to make the port. We must now hurry."

"Youssef is over there?" Rav'an asked, pointing behind them.

"Both he and Al Tayyib are in this with us, Rav'an. If Reza only now sees pursuit then Al Tayyub has completed his task. We gained a full day's ride when we would have had nothing."

Talon and Rav'an peered into the distance towards the north east almost into the rising sun. Talon could just make out a thin plume of dust on the plain below. They were in some foothills so they could see a great distance back along their trail; the dust plume was still many miles away and could have been anything, a dust devil or simply wind picking up the dusty desert and blowing it around. But he knew it was not so. He felt a trickle of fear in his guts; he trusted Reza's eyes and knowledge; the pursuit was on. The men who were following them were very determined. He marveled at how fast they had been to catch their trail despite the distractions placed in their way. They hurried down to their hobbled horses and mounted up.

"How far to the port of Bushehr?" Talon called to Reza, who had Jannat by his side. She seemed to want to stay near him as though she gained some strength from his presence. But when they halted she sat with Rav'an. Both women were bedraggled, their long hair in loose strands Rav'an had bound hers and Jannat's hair in thin leather straps, but they were badly in need of grooming and their flimsy clothes were in rags. Although exhausted they were seemingly indifferent to their attire and still possessed the cloaks Reza and Talon had provided them. It seemed to Talon that Jannat might almost be a younger sister to Rav'an, and it was clear that they were fond of each other.

"Today and a night of hard riding... if we are lucky!" he responded.

Talon looked over at Rav'an and they locked eyes. There was no need to say anything. Capture was not an option. He turned away, his heart heavy. If they could just make it to the port then they stood a chance of escape; but if they were caught on the road, which was for the most part across open country before the town, they didn't stand a chance. There were still nearly thirty miles to go and that was over some very harsh mountainous terrain.

Reza tried to lighten the mood. "I wonder how the prisoners fared? I hope that most of them escaped." He chuckled. "They would have needed to swim once they made it to the Khuskh river. If they managed that they could have disappeared into the bazzar which is just around the bend."

"I suspect that most will be caught again, and then Allah be merciful to them, but some might have escaped," Talon remarked.

They had made it past the caravanserai which marked the cross roads. The road which led to Bushehr traversed the low but rugged mountains they were now climbing while the other led many weeks' journey to the west and eventually the headwaters of the great river Dez.

Many miles behind them, the leader of the large group of armed men stamped around the well, impatient to get going again. Captain Kanaan had been charged with the mission of getting the princess back. He had brought a large party of armed men with him, as it was supposed that the treacherous Ismaili would have a large party themselves. He had understood from the Vizier that they had reneged on the marriage and stolen the bride back.

He had been summoned to the Sultan's chambers early in the morning the day before. Riding up to the imposing fortress from where the main garrison in the city was quartered alongside the growing bazaar, he had wondered just what the summons was all about. When he had ridden in through the gates of the palace he had found nervous soldiers in the courtyard, none of whom was willing to say anything. His keen gaze probed the yard and what he saw was not reassuring.

There were some bodies piled in a corner, already covered in flies. There was a pall of fear hanging over the palace; heads were already coming off. In fact there was a scaffold in on corner covered with blood, some already had rolled, he surmised. He wondered who the unfortunate had been this time. His own neck felt uncomfortable and he touched it involuntarily.

He had noticed in the past that when he was summoned for an award that everyone wanted to be noticed by him, but today no one would meet his eyes. This was ominous, and there was an atmosphere of terrified confusion everywhere; the word was that the Sultan was in one of his rages.

Kanaan was an old hand at soldiering, battle scarred and competent, but even he approached the palace doors with some trepidation. No one could tell who the Sultan would point his finger at next and demand their head when he was throwing one of his tantrums.

So it was with some relief the captain noted that the vizier was in attendance, evidently trying to instill some order into the chaos all about him. But even he seemed to be having a hard time calming the Sultan and the attendants, most of whom were hysterical eunuchs prostrated with either genuine or simulated grief on the floor and carpets around the throne.

When he had arrived and prostrated himself to the unheeding Sultan, the Vizier had turned on Kanaan, then almost dragged him aside into an alcove.

"I am glad that you have come, Captain Kanaan," he had said evenly, but it was clear he was very tense. "I was beginning to wonder who in this palace had not gone completely mad today! These idiotic goats seem to think screaming and wringing hands and wailing to God are not a good prescription for calm, and his eminence is not helping one little bit!" He snarled between clenched teeth, his mustaches bristling and his Adam's apple jumping up and down in his skinny throat.

Kanaan had to admire the man's composure under the circumstances. His turban was impeccably wound on his long head with every jewel in place. His robes were hung just right on his spare frame, while all around him people were tearing at their turbans and clothes and were very disheveled.

"In what manner may I be of service your Honor?" he asked, his tone carefully polite.

"You are to discover out what happened and to find the culprits!" The Vizier said above the din going on behind him.

"Sire, can you please explain what has happened? Er... it will help me to understand better and so I may find who has done... what?" Kanaan asked. His tone was very respectful but insistent.

The Vizier leaned over the captain, who could now smell the expensive perfume that man used, which did little to hide the vizier's foul breath; he resisted the temptation to take a step back.

"Do you know that they killed dozens of my eunuch guards and only God and the remaining eunuchs know how many of the poor sleeping women in the confines of the harem? The murdering sons of offal! May their souls burn in hell for eternity!"

He glared at the Captain. "Are you paying attention, Captain?"

"Of course, Sir. May I speak to the Officer of the Guard to find out more?"

The Vizier waved his hand dismissively and then gave what Kanaan took to be as near to a smirk as his stern features were capable. "Of course, but you will have to have a conversation with his head alone, as it has been parted from the rest of him."

Kanaan blinked.

"That worthy neglected to protect this palace and our persons!" The Vizier's voice rose an octave as the din behind them increased. He leaned closer to the captain.

"They, I mean those murderers and killers, left the heads of the two sentries to the bed chamber of his eminence, on the pillows right alongside him while he slept! Can you imagine that? The sheer horror of it when he awoke and the utter terror he has been subjected to! I rather doubt if he will ever be himself again after this, and if his physician does not get here soon his head will also decorate the battlements alongside all the others!"

"People have been slaughtered all over the palace, and furthermore," his voice now took on a shrill note, "ALL the prisoners were allowed to escape! They were running about in every direction around the palace for most of the night like a bunch of chickens with their heads off!" He leered, liking his pun. "But now they are most surely without their heads. Why, one even made it to the entrance of my own chambers. He was killed before he could do any harm, of course, but the attackers just... vanished into thin air! Can you believe it? Nearly thirty prisoners don't just escape from the dungeons without help!"

"Those murdering assassins, I have no doubt at all they were the phantoms of 'The Master'... they came, they killed and then they just vanished! No one saw anything." He took a deep breath as yet more wailing and screaming came from the throne area.

Kanaan glanced nervously towards the din. The sultan wore a glazed look on his bloated face and Kanaan could have sworn that he was drooling. The sultan held the town of Shiraz in brutal thrall so Kanaan doubted if any of the prisoners would be given a safe haven there.

"May I talk to the commander of the palace guard, Sir?" he asked carefully.

The Vizier had been watching the performance of the eunuchs with disgust written all over his thin features. He glanced back at the captain.

"What? No of course not! The commander of the palace guards has been punished. You will have to talk to some of the surviving people." The Vizier's tone was abrupt and almost dismissive.

"So I am to chase down the prisoners wherever they might be, Your Honor?"

The Vizier closed his eyes for a brief moment as he visibly tried to calm down. He pinched the thin bridge of his nose with slim, beringed, well manicured fingers as he did so.

"Yes... No. I don't care about the prisoners except for one, and only one. The rest we will find soon enough. You may ask questions of those who were left behind. The main thing is to find the princess Rav'an of the Ismaili and bring her back alive. Do you hear me? Alive! I do not care about anything else nor anyone else... you may dispatch the bandit scum as you please. If you are able to do so bring some back, as the Sultan, may God protect him, will want to see them executed publicly and as painfully as possible. They are a stench upon the earth and an insult to God in any case. You can bring their bodies back, as we will then skin them and stuff them with straw. On second thought, bring them back alive if you can and we will skin them alive!"

Kanaan blinked again. This was serious; the Hashashini had come back for their princess and kidnapped her while leaving carnage in their wake? Well that was their reputation, but why would they do this for a mere woman? he asked himself. Besides, the Sultan probably had dozens of beautiful women in that famed harem of his.... He was jerked back from his envious thoughts by the Vizier, who prodded him with a long thin finger in the middle of his chest; Captain Kanaan concentrated on the words.

"Take as many men as you can muster and leave as soon as you have questioned the guards who were locked in the prison when those dogs left. As soon as you are done with them they will be executed. Then you are to leave within the hour! Do not come back without her. Do you understand, Captain?" the Vizier hissed.

Kanaan nodded. "I will come back soon with the Princess, my Lord... In sha' Allah," he said deferentially. The Vizier was one to treat with great respect and the message was clear.

"Then what are you waiting for? Get going, Captain, get out of here."

"My... My Lord, does anyone have any idea which direction they might have gone?" Kanaan asked.

"How in the Prophet's good name would anyone know that, you imbecile? They came at night, killed everyone, and left at night! Use your men to find their trail and do not come back with excuses!" the Vizier shouted.

Kanaan flinched but he saluted correctly and said meekly, "Khoda Hafez Gorban." The captain hurried out, only just remembering to make hurried obeisance towards the Sultan and his wailing entourage as he left.

He had spent the next hour visiting the dungeons and talking to the ex jailers, who were quavering with fear as they knew their time was almost over. To a man they said that there were more than ten men in the group who had come to release the princess. They had had no chance to defend themselves, having been overwhelmed by the phantoms and their numbers.

"You know how those people are, your Highness! One moment there was no one and the next they were all over the place and they overpowered us. There was nothing we could do!" they wailed, wringing their hands and blubbering with fear.

He had noticed the grating seated on the round low opening in the middle of the floor and asked about it. "That leads to the qanat that runs below the palace," one of them responded.

"Where does it lead?" he'd asked.

To the river, your Highness," the man had told him.

He examined the well-like structure, listened to the rushing water far below, and noticed that the grating seemed to have been shifted. He tried to move it and with some effort could do so. He thought about that. That might explain why there had been no evidence of the escaped assassins, he reasoned. But why had the

Hashashini left such a trail of blood to get in when this entry would have been so much better? Eventually, after much questioning, Captain Kanaan, who was an intelligent man, reasoned that they had not known about it when they came in but had most probably left by this route.

He resolved to find out if there had been any sightings on or along the river. He took some men from the palace but then went to the barracks in the town itself and ordered his company of men, all thirty of them, to saddle up and prepare for a long couple of days.

The investigation of the river had yielded up some useful information, but only after a good half of a day had been wasted scouring its banks looking for the exit to the underground stream and then for anyone who might have seen something.

Not all the prisoners had been able to hide or get away as dawn approached. His men brought him a couple who had been hiding under some bushes along the riverbank, and after some persuasion with knives they had screamed that they did not know of the Hashashini following them out to the river. Neither, even after some very painful sessions with the sharp knives of his men, could recall seeing those particular people although one mentioned that they had all seen a beautiful girl and some strange men in the prison just before their release. Lying on their backs, their feet tied to a cross bar, they wailed and cried as their feet were beaten and cut, writhing and begging for mercy. Eventually he had tired of asking the same question over and over again and had had them dispatched by one of his more eager men.

In the silence that followed their killing he had pondered the situation and concluded that the Hashashini had most probably left using horses already stationed outside of the walls for their escape.

Then another unpleasant discovery was made. His men had been investigating the corpse of one of the prisoners who had jumped from the walls during the night. The poor creature had died at the base of the walls having broken both legs and his back.

But an urgent call from the group of men patrolling the river bank brought Kanaan hurrying to stand over two other bodies that had been discovered hidden in some bushes not far from the dead prisoner. These men were clearly soldiers and had been killed with arrows and knives. Kanaan wondered what they might have been doing there.

His men told him that from time to time the palace officer of the guards, a careful man, had sent men to watch the river and to alert him of any suspicious activity. Clearly these men had been surprised by someone and had died as a result. There was evidence that horses had been in among the trees.

They flee from me that sometime did me seek
With naked foot, stalking in my chamber.
I have seen them gentle, tame, and meek,
That now are wild and do not remember
That sometime they put themself in danger

—Sir Thomas Wyatt

Chapter 31

The Quarry

After a frustrating day of casting about looking for any sign or word of his quarry, Captain Kanaan felt that he might, just might be on the right trail this time. People questioned at the well had seen some riders heading this way and they had seemed to be in a hurry.

In his desperation for results he had interrogated a luckless witness to the point of torture. The portly bearded old man had been riding a camel away from the city in an easterly direction when Kanaan and his men had come upon him and asked the usual questions. Had a party of ten or more people on horseback ridden past him at any time?

As it happened he had been on the road in the early hours on that particular day heading for Shiraz when he had heard drumming hooves; being a prudent man he had pulled the camel off the road and waited in the darkness of a copse of willow trees until the party had passed.

"They were in a hurry, Gorban," the old man had quavered, "but I was afraid to call out or enquire where they were going. There are many bandits on the roads these days and I am but one old man. God protect you, Gorban."

"How many were there?" Kanaan had asked sharply.

"There were at least ten of them, Gorban Sarvan." The plump old man with huge whiskers had wiped his face with a rag. He was sweating profusely under his turban in the hot morning sun and his expression was one of servility and apprehension. Clearly he was afraid of these mounted men with cold stares and long gleaming lances.

"Did one look like a woman? Was there a woman with them?" the captain had demanded.

The old man hesitated as though giving it some thought. He looked up at the captain and said a trifle uncertainly. "That is a possibility, Gorban. One was covered from head to foot in what might have been a chador. But...in that light... it was difficult to see."

Kanaan had walked off a short distance to evaluate the information but it made sense. There might only be ten people... if that were the case it made the task all the more easy. He had a large party and they could catch up with the fugitives with some hard riding and see for themselves if indeed the princess was with them. In sha'Allah he was on the right track at last.

He made his decision and called out to his men. "Mount up! We are following these people."

"What about the old man, Genab Sarvan?" enquired one of his men as he mounted his horse.

"Leave him. He was on his way home in any case."

They had left the old man on his knees, his hands clasped to his chest praying with his eyes shut. The camel was squatting on the ground about ten feet away chewing its cud. It had been with the old man long enough to know when to take advantage of a break and to take a rest.

Al Tayyub waited until the troop was well gone, then scrambled to his feet and hurried over to the camel. He climbed onto its back and then shouted and beat the barking and grumbling animal to its feet. He headed for the city of Shiraz as fast as he could drive the shambling animal. He needed to disappear as quickly as he could before the captain came charging back along the road and decided to punish him.

Kanaan and his men galloped along the road that led east and south for another ten miles and saw ahead of them a small train of camels lumbering along the road. They rode up to them at a good pace and found that it was a small group of Quashgai tribal people.

The women were seated on the swaying backs of the camels holding their babies or even some small goat kids that were too young to keep up with the herd that was moving slowly along the side of the road, bleating noisily and eating what could be found of the sun burned grass. The red hair and grey eyes of the women would normally have drawn the attention of a less preoccupied man than the captain.

Small children herded the goats while the men led the camels and drove heavily laden donkeys ahead of them.

When the horsemen came up to them the whole train slowed to a halt and observed the troop impassively as though they had had this kind of encounter before and were waiting for the newcomers to demand payment of some kind.

Instead Kanaan rode up to a man who had grey hair and who led the foremost camel, assuming him to be the Rais of the tribe. Wary of the camel that threatened to snap and spit at his horse, Kanaan demanded whether he had seen riders going past earlier that day.

The old man stared back at him, his glance covering the men on horses who were clustered behind the captain and then nodded his head.

"Yes, three riders came through early in the morning and did not stop."

"Three? Only three? How far ahead of you are they?" the Captain demanded.

"Not so far, the sun was there when they went by."

The old man indicated where the sun had been in the sky. The sun was almost overhead by now. That meant at least an hour, perhaps two. The Captain nodded and then without another word turned his horse and cantered off in the direction they had been following formerly. They caught up with the three riders early that afternoon. The riders were trotting along the road in the distance when the captain drew rein on a rise in the road where he could see them clearly a mile off.

He drew his sword and put spurs to his sweating horse. His men raised their lances and the whole squad of men galloped their horses hard down the slope to the three as yet unsuspecting riders. They were surrounded before they could react in a swirl of dust and horsemen. The three stopped immediately and appeared to be looking about fearfully. They were all wearing cloths wrapped around their faces that left only their eyes visible.

One called out, "Have mercy, Sirs! We are only poor travelers." The voice was muffled by the cloth so Kanaan could not tell whether it came from a female or a man.

"Get off your horses and take off your face coverings!" he shouted. The three muttered to one another but complied; dismounting slowly and removing their shemaghs to expose their faces. They looked surprised and frightened, but their faces were undoubtedly those of young men with beards and mustaches.

One of them seemed so frightened that he went to his knees and begged for mercy. He held out a small leather bag that jingled. "This is all we have, sirs. Please do not harm us!"

He began to babble with fear while his companions began to wail and wring their hands. All three were now on their knees although they still held their horses' reins in the one hand while their other arm waved in the air.

Impatiently the captain rode his horse closer and snatched the bag. He put it away in his robes but did not dismount. He said, "Where are you from, and where are you going?"

"We are students of Poetry, Firdausi, and we are from the north, my Lord. We are going to see my father, who is very sick in Kerman. It is a very long way and we are afraid that we will be too late."

The captain agreed that it was a very long way to Kerman. "Why did you leave at night?" he demanded, but he already knew. People who wanted to cover distances did so in the early hours because it was so much cooler.

The youth did not disappoint him. "We thought to make good time in the morning hours, my Lord. I hurry because I do not know if my father will live much longer. I pray to God that he will live long enough to bless me."

The captain dismounted and threw his reins at one of the soldiers then strode close to each one of the men, observing them closely. But he could find no hint that one of them might be a woman. He even tugged none too gently at the light beard of the youngest of them, eliciting a yell of pain.

He tried one last question. "Do you have a woman with you?"

"A woman? No my Lord." The young man looked around stupidly as though to say, where would we have a woman hidden? "Why in the Prophet's name would I take a woman with me in this country? It is too dangerous for that!" the leader of the three frightened young men exclaimed. The others shook their heads incredulously, staring at him as though the captain had asked a really stupid question.

His own anger barely under control now that he realized that he had lost vital time, the captain seized the reins of his horse from the trooper and remounted. He turned his horse back in the direction of Shiraz.

He wanted to strike out at something, anyone or anything he was so enraged.

"He is going to roast the old man when he catches up with him. Allah protect the old fart because our captain will not," one of his men muttered to his companion as they galloped after their captain.

Captain Kanaan certainly wanted to find the old man and thrash him within an inch of his life for misleading him either intentionally or unintentionally. He decided to keep the money anyway, small comfort though that might be. He set a grueling pace back towards Shiraz.

*****

As the troops left in a cloud of dust the three riders watched them intently, and when they had gone over the rise in the road the three then mounted up and rode casually into the low hills seeking the cover of some trees.

Kemal the leader said, "Phew, that man is angry. Talon and Reza must have succeeded or he would not be out searching, Allah protect them from this man's wrath. I am glad that he did not take our lives just for the sake of it. But now our task is done. Now it is up to Yousef and our brothers to see the lady Rav'an safe through the mountains. May God protect them, for they will need it with that man on their trail. We will go north to Isfahan in a day or so but now we should hide."

*****

The captain and his men rode hard, hoping to find the old man along the road, but he had disappeared, which did not improve the captain's temper. Stopping that afternoon in Shiraz to pick up fresh horses and some remounts and to snatch a meal, he ordered his tired men back into the saddle within the hour and left the city by the south western gate to follow the only other road out of town. They rode all night and only stopped when dawn was showing in the east and he had to water the tired horses.

Despite his desire to hasten along the road and catch up with the fugitives, the captain had no choice but to rest the horses that were drenched in sweat and beginning to flag. They had made up a lot of miles but now they would lose time while the horses recovered. The men rested in what shade they could, as there was not much this far from the river and the city, while the captain strode up and down slapping at his boot with his fly whisk with poorly controlled impatience. He slapped at the persistent flies that circled his head as he thought about his chances of capturing the Princess. He might even avail himself of her if the opportunity arose.

He had lost a day in any event and worried that he might not make the distance in time. The road that he was following was headed for Bushehr, a port on the south coast. The people of the town of Chukak confirmed that in the early hours of the morning before a small party of riders had ridden through and left by way of the mountain trail, a difficult road that was known for bandits, but still a road that led over the passes to Bushehr. The Captain was now confident that these were the ones he was looking for and that they were headed for the port. He had to stop them before they could catch a ship. However, he was at least a day behind them and needed to make up the time lost any way he could.

*****

Well ahead of Kanaan and his determined troops the four fugitives loped their horses steadily up the well worn track that represented the main road from Shiraz to the port town of Bushehr. Talon eyed the way ahead with apprehension. They were in the area he had been told was called Banal, a series of switchback climbs that the track made over the first of two high passes. He had seen no sign of Youssef and wondered if he might not have made it into these mountains yet, or worse, if he had become lost and could not find his way here. Everything depended upon Youssef being where he was expected. Talon looked back over his shoulder and thought he could see a distant dust haze to mark the passage of the sultan's men. He wondered at the speed with which they had found the trail.

The four of them could not outrun that kind of pace, nor could they hold off what must be the twenty or more men who were in pursuit. He did not relish a game of hide and seek in these hills.

They were now riding up into the higher hills over stony dry ground with poor grazing and only a few stunted trees on the slopes above and the occasional jumble of boulders wedged in the defiles they rode past. There were places where the rains had washed the boulders into gullies, and here also small sturdy trees grew.

His experienced eye told him of many potentially good ambush spots, but the way out was never good. Their path became steeper and he could see what looked like a small copse of trees ahead which the track passed through. He became alert, as did Reza. This was a perfect place for someone to ambush the unwary and Talon hoped that it would not be them.

He need not have worried; as they came to the narrow part of the track with large boulders on either side of them they were hailed. It was one of the villainous men who were attached to Youssef. Standing with him was Youssef himself, beaming happily at them. There were joyful greetings all round.

"I have to confess that I was worried that you might not have succeeded, my bothers!" he exclaimed after he had kissed them both on the cheeks and bowed low to Rav'an, who was delighted to see him. He smiled his pleasure at seeing Rav'an, and eyed the girl with her. Reza made haste to introduce Jannat. Youssef was very polite after that.

"You are welcome, my Ladies. My lady Rav'an, I thank God for your deliverance!"

"It would take more than the defenses of Shiraz to stop my two protectors," Rav'an laughed. Her relief at seeing reinforcements was matched by that of Reza and Talon, who were both grinning with pleasure at seeing Youssef.

"Your uncle Al Tayyub and Kemal did their work well, Youssef. We gained some time, but now they are hot on our trail," Reza said when they had all dismounted.

"My guess is that they have fresh horses, whereas we do not. Somehow we have to slow them down so that we can get over the passes and gain entry to the city of Bushehr and have time to get onto a ship," Talon remarked.

Youssef waved his arm around him. "This is a good place for an ambush, my friends. What do you think?"

Talon and Reza looked around them. It was true. The road narrowed at this point to become almost a gorge. Whomsoever came up the track had to pass through this very narrow defile. There did not seem to be any other way around that would allow their pursuers to get behind them.

Talon looked up at the slopes above and was frustrated at something that kept nagging at his mind. He continued to stare up at the steep slopes above. Reza and Youssef walked up to him and Reza asked, "What are you staring at, Talon? What is bothering you?"

Then Talon had it. He turned to them and smacked his fist into his palm. "I was in the battle of Myriokephalon when the Turks ambushed the huge Greek army."

What in God's name are you talking about, Talon?" Reza asked, but he turned to Youssef and said, "Beware, he is thinking again."

Youssef grinned but said nothing.

"They nearly destroyed us with rocks that they rolled down the hills at us. I have never been so terrified. They almost destroyed our whole army. We could do much the same."

Youssef snapped his head up and stared at the slopes. "What do you want me to do, Talon?"

*****

The small defile provided perfect cover for a hit and run fight, and that was precisely why Youssef had chosen it. He sent several of his friends up the very steep incline to gather rocks for a landslide. Talon went with them to prepare the ground carefully. His experience in the dreadful gorge of Myriokephalon had taught him much. When satisfied, he told two of the men to remain up in their aerie and to remain out of sight at all times. When it was time he would signal, and then they were to start the rocks on their way. He rejoined Youssef and Reza after a good hour of work.

"How many men do you have, Youssef?" Reza asked.

"I have fifteen in all, with the two you have left on that hill, Talon. If well placed, we can hold off a strong attack from the front. They will be riding uphill and we will have the advantage of cover and some bows."

Reza, the more demonstrative of the two, slapped Youssef on the back and told him, "You will make a good general one day, Youssef." They all laughed.

They knew they had only hours before their pursuers arrived and surprise was essential, so Talon and Reza, with help from Youssef, determined the best places to have men either with a javelin or with a bow. Both Reza and Talon would be using their bows to support the effort.

"I suppose we could have continued to run and hoped that we could make the gates of Bushehr before these men," suggested Reza, gazing down the pass towards the place where they expected to see the enemy.

"We might have, perhaps, but I doubt we could have outrun them, Reza. Look at how quickly they came after us despite the delay Al Tayyub and the others gave us," Talon said with a glance at Rav'an, who was hovering nearby. "If not for their help we would have been caught on the plain and that would have been the end of us."

"One of us could take Rav'an and continue down the pass while the rest of us hold them off," Reza said.

Rav'an put a hand on his arm. "Reza, my ever faithful protector, I will not leave any of you behind. You cannot drive me away as long as you are here."

Reza smiled, then shrugged in resignation. "Well, I did try, my Lady, but I shall not go against your wishes."

"We must leave during the night when we have bloodied them. We cannot stay here, as sooner or later they will overcome us or find a way around," Talon said.

"I agree, my brother. We have perhaps four more hours of daylight and then it will be dark. " Reza smiled at Rav'an and left.

Rav'an turned and moved towards Talon. He encircled her within his arms and held her while she put her head on his shoulder.

"We have not been able to talk much since we left Shiraz, my Talon. I am still astonished to see you and almost cannot believe it, but here we are together with Reza and Jannat as though we have never been separated." She smiled up at him. "Ah, how I have missed you, my Talon!"

He grinned down at her. "And I you, my Love. It is a long journey from Jerusalem to here and there were many adventures on the way." They kissed then, a long gentle kiss that left them both staring at one another when they pulled apart, Rav'an still within the circle of Talon's arms. The magic between them was still very much there.

Rav'an shook her lustrous black hair and smiled up at him. "I want to hear everything that happened to you since you first left me, my warrior. Indeed you look so different, my Talon. Life has been hard on you I think, but it has made you very strong. We are going to need your strength very soon I fear," she said tentatively.

He pulled her closer. "Courage, my Lady. I shall not let them have you back at any cost. We stay together now."

"My protector," she whispered almost to herself.

They were interrupted by a tense call from one of the sentries posted by Youssef who came running down from his lookout on the hill. "They are here!" he gasped in a low voice.

There was instant activity as those men who were not already in position on either side of the narrow defile that marked the neck of the pass dived for cover. Talon glanced up at the sun; he noted that it had moved a long way towards the west.

"Rav'an my love, please go and stay with the horses; take Jannat with you. If they break through you must ride for your life to Bushehr. The servants are there, so if you can get to the port and the quayside they will be looking for you."

"Be careful, Talon." she said, and placed a kiss on his lips that burned.

By our camp-fires rose a murmur
At the dawning of the day,
And the tread of many footsteps
Spoke the advent of the fray;
And as we took our places,
Few and stern were our words,
While some were tightening horse-girths,
And some were girding swords.

—B. Dowling

Chapter 32

Ambush

Talon let her go reluctantly and then ran to his position, which was almost opposite that of Reza's so that the two of them could create a cross fire.

"I pray to God that this is our last hurdle before we catch a boat," he said to Reza as he prepared his bow and set his arrows against a rock. His companion nodded grim agreement.

Except for the occasional rustle in the dry leaves underfoot as a lizard scuttled across them, total silence descended upon the whole area. Not even a bird flew in among the trees.

As Talon crouched among the boulders he had a good view of the track so he could see for about sixty paces down the slope. The leading horseman rode into his line of sight and walked his horse warily up the incline towards the rocks. He was watchful but not tense. There was a gap before the main party showed itself on the track as they came round a bend. They were surely the Sultan's men: their clothing, fine chain, and the trappings on their horses bespoke a rich patron, and each man was armed with a well made lance, sword and shield.

Talon could see Youssef just forward of him and saw him tense. But Youssef had been instructed by both Reza and Talon to allow the scout to come forward undisturbed so that the rest of the following party would come deep into the ambush before they closed the trap and started the killing.

What surprised Talon and evidently Youssef was the size of the party that had been following them. There had to be about twenty five men!

But suddenly the scout seemed to sense that something was not quite right and stopped. He was almost directly in front of Youssef and not at all where they wanted him. He looked to the left and the right very carefully as though he might have heard something suspicious. A man called to him from behind.

"What is it? Why are you stopping?"

The scout turned in the saddle and shouted back. "I see many footprints here, Genab Sarvan, as though a large party has been here before us."

He got no further. A javelin flew out of the bushes on the other side of the pathway from Talon and buried itself in his back.

The man choked and began to topple off his horse. There was instant pandemonium down the pathway as the sultan's men reacted. Talon was furious. One of the inexperienced men had not waited and now they would have to fight a lot more men than they had anticipated who knew exactly where they were. He shot a man out of the saddle at extreme range and had the satisfaction of seeing another topple as Reza's arrow went true.

"Youssef, get your men up here and hurry!" he shouted. There was no point in their remaining in the bushes if the enemy was going to charge them and break through. They had to stop that at all costs.

Youssef shouted for his men to close on him and then ran back to where Talon and Reza were now standing. They regrouped on either side of the narrowest part, placing spear men ready to jump out and stab at horses while the archers were told to shoot as many horses as they could. Reza and Talon would bring down riders as fast as they were able to. He glanced up at the hillside above but there was no sign of the men stationed up there. The boulders would have to wait until a better moment.

Reza was shouting angrily at the men, demanding to know who the idiot was who had thrown the javelin, but Talon put a hand on his shoulder and told him, "It is done now, Reza. We simply have to stop them as best we can."

Reza glared at the cowering men but then said loudly, "Make sure they do not get through, as that will be the end of us all if you do!"

They heard his words in chagrined silence and then they waited. They did not have long to do so, as the enemy had decided to strike while there was some confusion. The commander was a bold man, Talon realized. There was a yell and the clatter of hooves on the stones and the enemy charged up the path heading straight for them. The men had their lances down and their round shields up, screaming their battle songs as they spurred their horses into the confined space ahead.

"Get out in front!" Youssef yelled at the spearmen. They ran into place and set their long spears in the ground and crouched fearfully, awaiting the impact of the horses. Talon and Reza stepped into the path right behind them along with the three other archers and paused with their bows taut.

The ground shook as the horses pounded towards them with their yelling riders waving lances and swords. "Now!" Reza shouted.

Five bowstrings twanged and five arrows leapt away traversing the thirty paces to strike hard into the massed horses.

They all struck true and created the chaos that Talon had wanted. Men and horses went down to create a tangle of struggling bodies. A horse screamed and a man shouted with pain as he was wounded. Another flurry of arrows whispered towards them and stuck more men and horses.

It was enough for the moment. The commander pulled up his men with a shouted command and they galloped back out of range leaving dead and wounded behind.

"If they had pressed the charge they would have broken through! They will come on foot the next time," Talon said. He glanced behind him as he said this, hoping for a glimpse of Rav'an, but she was hidden by the short trees over the rise, having taken Jannat with her. He turned his attention back to the scene in front of them.

"How many did we kill?" asked Youssef of no one in particular.

"I count four killed and one wounded, and four horses are down," one of his men said.

"Do we have enough water for a long wait?" Talon asked with a glance at the sun, which was already well on its way across the western sky.

"Only if we are careful," Youssef stated. "We found a trickle down the other side of the pass but it is too far to go to now."

"Try to get the dead horses into the space where they block the road," Talon suggested. But before they could begin the work one glanced up and called out, "They are coming again!"

Indeed they were. This time the enemy came on foot and at the run. Dodging from rock to rock and tree to tree they came silently this time but full of purpose.

Talon and Reza loosed arrows at them but stopped when it became evident that they were wasting arrows.

No young recruits these, but battle hardened men who knew how to fight. Talon wondered how Youssef's men would manage against this kind of warrior.

The enemy dodged between tree and rock until they were almost within spear range and then charged in one concerted rush for the opening. Talon and Reza only had time to get one arrow off each at close range before they had to draw their swords and run into the melee that was developing in front of them. The other three archers who had been placed on rocks overlooking the attackers continued to shoot arrows at the mass of men below them.

Talon joined the press with his small metal shield firmly held across his chest and his sword stabbing forward. There was little room for slashing but he found that as long as the spear men held he could inflict telling damage. A dark bearded face appeared right in front of him so he stabbed it and the man screamed as his eye was taken out. He fell back with blood pumping out of the gaping hole with both hands raised to protect it. Someone else stabbed the same man in the chest, causing him to fall in front of his comrades, who trampled him in their eagerness to get at the defenders.

The men screamed at one another and banged their shields into each other's faces, using the edge to inflict bruising blows to chin and face, then stabbing at anything in front of them. It was not long before a low barrier of bodies, dead and wounded alike, grew at the feet of the defenders. Now the attackers had to stumble over their dead comrades to get at them.

The assault could not last. The enemy could not get enough men through the gap to drive a wedge into the defenders ranks and the archers were inflicting a lot of injuries and some deaths from their position above the fray. Talon was impressed with the way Youssef and his men fought. No one attempted to turn back and run even though several were dead already and many lightly wounded.

Talon heard a shouted command and the attackers began to pull back. "Do not follow them!" Talon called to Youssef. "They will trap you and kill you!"

Youssef merely nodded and licked his dry lips. They were all thirsty, so one of them was sent off for a goatskin of water.

Talon and Reza counted their arrows and then stepped back from the position. "We will have to recover the ones we have used from the bodies or we will run out soon," Reza suggested.

Youssef detailed two men to collect as many as it was safe to do so and they went off to perform the gristly task. One of the enemy was not dead and rolled over to beg for water but he was dispatched immediately by one of the men. Talon nodded silently when he observed this; this was no occasion for mercy. He was very thirsty, as was Reza by the sound of his voice. Neither was hurt, Talon noted with relief.

"If we can hold them off for another hour we might be able to slip away," Reza croaked. He wiped his sweating face with the tail end of his turban.

*****

Captain Kanaan peered around the rock up the trail at the wreckage of his company of men. The bodies of men and horses were clustered at the entrance to that hated ravine where the enemy was holding out. He stared around the area for the hundredth time seeking a way round but could see nothing that would allow his men to enfilade the defender's position. The one time he had sent two of his men to seek a route they had both been shot from above by bowmen who dominated the area. It had been particularly galling to see the bowmen jump down and retrieve their own arrows while the captain and his men watched seething. They sent some arrows up the hill but this didn't stop the men, who jeered and waved their arrows at them.

The survivors were clustered behind him, binding their wounds and drinking from their depleted supply of water. His men were muttering among themselves, eyeing him resentfully but too afraid to say anything. They knew the Captain would execute any one of them who went against his orders. They had not expected this kind of resistance; they were now sure they were fighting the dreaded 'Assassins. Who knew what might happen once darkness came.

Meanwhile Kanaan was pondering what he could do to settle the problem he faced. He had been as surprised and shocked as his men to find that there was a strong defense waiting for him at this pass. He had thought he was chasing only a few people, but it was clear that there were many more at this place. It confirmed his thinking that these were Ismaili and hence fanatics who would rather die than surrender, but he had to break the impasse somehow. There was no going back unless he had the princess with him.

He beckoned to one of the men squatting under the meager shade of a boulder. The man got to his feet and shambled over. His body language and his expression made it clear that he resented the captain and the situation. Abruptly the captain stepped forward and slapped the man hard on his face. He was not going to tolerate insubordination of any kind at this crucial stage.

"Wake up and come to me faster the next time, you scab. If we do not go home with the woman we all decorate the walls of the city with our heads, and that includes yours," he roared, glaring at the suddenly cowed man.

The man snapped to attention, his face going red where the captain had struck him.

"You will walk up that road and offer terms. All I want is the woman. I will let the others go if she is given up at once. Leave your weapons behind to show that you only want to talk to them. Tell them that we do not need any more bloodshed, just the woman."

The soldier would have argued but the captain seized his shoulder and pushed him out onto the road and then drew his sword. "Go!" he commanded.

*****

Talon looked up at the sky again. The sun was almost setting, having dropped behind the mountain while they fought. He agreed with Reza that they should leave when it was dark but feared that when that time came the men attacking might pursue and overtake them.

Suddenly Reza pointed down the track. A man was coming towards them. He was unarmed and held his hands away from his body with the palms open towards them.

"They want a truce?" Talon was skeptical.

"It would seem that they want to talk," Reza observed.

"Perhaps they want to surrender," Talon mused.

"What terms should we give them?" Reza snickered.

"Let him come close so that we don't have to go to him," Talon ordered.

The soldier walked slowly and carefully towards them and stopped about twenty paces away.

"What do you want?" Reza demanded.

"My Captain says that too much blood has been shed for one woman. He asks that you give her to him, then we shall leave you alone."

"She is not for bargaining," Reza called back.

"My Captain told me to tell you that we will eventually take this place and then all your heads will come back with us to Shiraz to grace the walls of the sultan's palace if you do not give up the woman."

"Tell your captain that we will not bargain with him and he is to do his worst. Allah will protect us from harm."

"You are heretics and therefore do not have the protection of God," the man replied.

He turned and walked slowly down the road towards his waiting captain.

"They think we are Ismaili! Somehow we have to delay them so that we can get away," Talon said.

Then he noticed a battle axe that had been left on the ground nearby. One of the dead men had carried it and it had been tossed into the rocks.

"Reza, if we can block the path here then they will have to clear it first. It might give us a small lead."

Reza grinned. "It is time to cut down a tree or two," he said.

They had swords and the axe with which to complete the work, all the while watching the pathway for another attack. In fact an attack came just as the sun set and they all had to man the opening again. The enemy repeated the tactics they had used before but this time they formed a sort of column, trying to drive their way through by weight of numbers. Talon and Reza threw themselves into the press to hold the line. Men could only stab at one another at very close range now and more fell sobbing or screaming to the ground as they were pierced or carved up.

The press of fighting men moved slowly back as the Sultan's men exerted their superior weight. Talon and Reza used their own fighting skills where they could best have an effect, but even so they were relentlessly pushed back. The men on both sides were just grunting and sucking at breath, they were too out of wind to shout at one another. Occasionally a man would fall wounded or dead with barely a cry. Talon looked over at Reza, who stared back.

"One of us will have to tell Rav'an to leave soon," he told Reza.

Reza only nodded tiredly, and then went back to stabbing and pushing.

The sultan's men would have succeeded had it not been for a determined counter from one of Youssef's men. This man was taller than Talon and very strong. He wielded the axe easily and in his hands it became deadly. With a mighty yell he roared into the fray, leaning over his comrades and striking at the heads of the men pushing against them. He cleared a little space and then set about him to the left and the right, decapitating one man and carving up another with one swipe so that the man's body tumbled to the ground almost cut in half.

It was too much for the enemy; they tumbled over themselves to get out of the way of this mad man whom they could not stop, and despite the screamed commands of their captain they fled.

*****

As they stumbled back to the shelter of their base the captain heard his name called. Two of his men were supporting another who hung in their arms loosely.

"We have one of them, Captain. Allah be praised, we have one!"

He turned swiftly and peered at the man they were holding up. It looked as though the man was wounded and semi-conscious.

"Get him on the ground; I want to talk to him," The captain ordered. He suddenly felt elated. Now at least they had one of the cursed Ismaili and he would extract all manner of things from him before he died. He wanted to vent his frustration on the hapless victim and this he now did.

The men dropped the inert body onto the stony ground, eliciting a cry of pain as the wounded Ismaili hit the ground. The captain found the wound, a hole in his lower chest that was still bleeding. He slammed his fist into the wound.

The man screamed with pain, his whole body jack-knifed, his legs jerked into the air before he fell back sobbing and clutching the now profusely bleeding opening in his chest.

The captain repeated the blow again and then again before his victim passed out.

Using a little water they revived the man and then the questioning began. The captain could hardly believe what he was hearing. These were not Ismaili but men from Isfahan who had made the daring attack on the palace. One of them was Ismaili, he was told, but the others were simply friends.

After the third time the prisoner had been revived the captain decided that there was nothing more to be gained from the interrogation.

Hope is a bird
With wonderful feathers
Sits on the boughs of the soul
And sings the song of how to remain alive.

—Abdul Wahab

Chapter 33

Bushire

During the respite as dusk settled in, some more of the vital arrows were recovered. Talon ran to the rise and called down to Rav'an, who was next to Jannat.

"Be ready to leave! We depart as soon as it is dark!" he called. "Youssef, now is the time to tell the men on the hill to prepare the rock slide."

Youssef whirled and called out to one of his men to prepare a torch with his flint. Within seconds they had a small torch burning.

Rav'an wanted to say something but Talon merely waved a bloody arm and turned back. He was covered in other men's blood.

He returned to find Youssef weeping over yet another of his friends who had died. They now had only five of the original ten men standing and most of them were wounded. One was missing. Reza was limping from a stab in the upper thigh but brushed it off as being of no consequence. Talon insisted upon binding it up tight to stop the flow of blood.

But then they heard a shriek followed by more screams from down the pathway. Every one stopped what they were doing to listen. The hair on Talon's neck rose. They were screams of pure agony and terror.

"That is Ardshir! They have Ardshir!" Youssef shouted. "I cannot leave him with them!"

"What happened? How did they capture him?" Talon demanded.

"He was wounded and I thought he had been helped out of the fight, but they must have seized him without us realizing it!" Youssef yelled distractedly. Talon was not surprised; in the dusk and the chaos of the fighting that could happen.

Reza leapt to Youssef's side and seized his shoulder in an iron grip. "You cannot go, Youssef. Think of all that your men have achieved. Would you throw it all away on a mad attempt to save him? By God, if I knew how I would go myself!"

Youssef leaned against Reza's chest and wept. Reza turned a bleak look on Talon and shook his head. This was the first time Youssef had lost comrades so close to him and it was hard.

The sound of chopping came to his ears and Talon blessed the man with the axe. Two of the spearmen went to help and they soon heard the unmistakable sound of a tree falling.

There was a yell and two more rushed to help pull the tree down the pathway towards the opening. They wedged the gnarled old tree into the opening right on top of the corpses of men and horses that had been dragged to form a barrier. But it was clear it would not be enough. The men rushed back to cut down another one, but even as they did so the enemy troops came running up the hill again shouting and banging on their shields. They had noticed and knew they had to stop the building of the barricade.

Then began a protracted skirmish as the sultan's troops played tug with the tree, chopping at the branches with their swords and trying to pull it out of the way, while the defenders stabbed at anyone who came near and hung onto their end of it. Talon and Reza shot arrows into anyone within range.

Suddenly he was aware of someone else with a bow nearby who had not been there before. He turned and gaped. Rav'an had a bow and was preparing to shoot into the enemy ahead of them.

He shook his head and turned back to doing the same, but he shouted at her. "Do not stay when I tell you to leave, my Rav'an. Where is Jannat?"

"She is holding all our horses and is safe. I will do as you say, Talon," she replied as she loosed another arrow.

Knowing the effect it might have if he could kill the leader, Talon searched the dusk for the man who might be in charge but could not get a good enough shot with his bow. He lost two arrows in the attempt and finally gave up to join the ferocious fight for the tree.

During a brief pause an object was thrown over the branches of the tree and landed with a soggy thump near to Youssef. Then another smaller thing was tossed over at them to land not far from the first, and cruel laughter followed. Talon and Youssef leaned down to look but then he gagged. There was no mistaking the two objects lying in the dust.

Youssef screamed then, a long and enraged scream, and seemed about to charge recklessly over the tree to attack his now hidden enemy. Only by seizing him around the chest and holding him tight did Talon succeed in preventing him for committing suicide. Finally when Youssef calmed down enough he seized Rav'an by the arm, who looked sick, and led her and the shaking youth up the slope to the horses, accompanied by Reza, where he left Youssef with Rav'an.

"Keep him here with you," he said tersely. She nodded, the whites of her eyes showing in the darkness. Jannat was already mounted and holding the other horses. She looked frightened but determined to be brave. Reza smacked her on the thigh and grinned. "My lady, be safe," he said, and left them. Rav'an mounted shakily and sat looked back to where the battle was still taking place.

Reza ran back to the crowd and seized the torch, then waved it towards the hillside. Nothing happened for a long few minutes so he continued to wave it. Then there was a distant shout and a low rumble.

"Run! Run for your lives!" Talon shouted and charged up the hill as fast as his legs could carry him. The rumble changed to a roar almost above them, men were scrambling for the safety of the rise as fast as their legs could carry them. A lone rock the size of a goat bounced onto the road just behind the last of the runners and crashed into the other hillside before rolling back to fall onto the path among other rocks that had landed there. Right behind it came an avalanche of rocks and debris that had been swept up with the onrushing boulders to tumble into the small gorge with a huge crash. The avalanche did not quite strike where Talon would have liked but it sufficed to block the road to anyone on a horse for hours to come. The dust that rose from the aftermath hid the rest of the scene from them but it was enough for the moment.

"We must hurry, there is not going to be much time. They will clear the road and keep coming!" Talon shouted.

The survivors raced over the rise to the dimly seen horses held by Rav'an and Jannat. The two men on the hill rushed down to join Youssef, who was already mounted; he only had four men left. The whole party rode as fast as they could out of the pass and headed down into the small valley ahead. There were more passes to negotiate, but this one had been the highest.

Only stopping for water where it was available, and then only for the horses while they filled their goatskins with water to drink along the way, they maintained a constant pace that ate up the miles. Reza would not allow them to stop even when one of the horses foundered. The man just left his horse on the ground and mounted one of the spares, riderless because of the men who had died. Youssef rode near to Talon but he was clearly still in shock and needed to be left alone for a while. Talon rode alongside him in silence. The women were silent, as they knew that the men were exhausted, but they stayed close to Talon and Reza. His throat was so dry he doubted that he could have talked even if he had wanted to.

But later, after many miles of riding during the long night, Youssef seemed to wake up, for he turned to Talon and asked, “You have been a warrior for many years, Talon. Have you lost many friends?”

“More than I care to count, Youssef. You will never get used to that. But you must continue to live, that much you owe the comrades who do not live.”

Youssef nodded and lapsed into silence again.

Rav’an leaned over and put her hand on Talon’s and squeezed it without a word.

“We must keep going along this road all night, as it is certain our pursuers will.” Reza gestured to the rear with his thumb. “The stars will light our way.” Jannat moved her horse closer as though this would keep here safe. Reza touched her on the arm to reassure her and said in a low voice, “We will protect you, my lady. In shah’Allah we will be able to reach the sea by morning.”

She looked at him in the dark, her eyes huge with fear and fatigue, and nodded silently.

The sky was clearing in the east with streaks of light to herald the dawn when they crested a low hill and saw the unmistakable flat dark shadow of the sea some ten miles ahead.

Talon gave a great sigh of relief when he saw the glimmer of water and pointed. He did not speak, his throat was too dry. They needed water badly, as they had not stopped for many hours. Their horses were almost blown and all of them knew that if they had had many more miles to ride their horses would not have been able to last. They paused for only a minute before plunging down the slope to continue their steady pace towards the coast and the relative safety of Bushehr.

Talon had told the others that he expected to find Alia and Rostam waiting for them in the port with some servants who were charged with the task of hiring a ship to take them away.

"Why are we going to sea?" Reza and Rav'an had both asked at the same time when he told them.

"Because none of us can stay here in Persia after this. Not even Youssef now. Think, my friends... if we went back to Isfahan what danger we would draw down upon Doctor Haddad and Fariba. We cannot do this to them. Neither the sultan's men nor your brother's people, Rav'an, would believe that they had nothing to do with this."

Rav'an had nodded, but had turned away fighting tears as she realized that she would never see Fariba or the doctor again.

Talon had leaned over to her on his horse and put his arm around her.

"I am sorry, my Rav'an, I too will miss them dreadfully. They are our family."

She had sobbed then, leaning into his arm as they rode.

"I find you and now I lose them. It is so unjust, Talon. God is so cruel."

Talon had said nothing, his heart heavy. He glanced over at Reza, who nodded his understanding. He too loved Fariba and the doctor.

They rode along the well worn road that followed the north coast of the fat peninsular leading towards the port of Bushehr as the sun was climbing towards its zenith and noonday prayers were being called from the mezzanine deep inside the walled town. Despite the fact that they were riding along the coastline with the sea to their right hand it was scorching hot. The horses were almost done and the people who rode them were in little better shape.

The approaches to the gates had the usual camel encampment, the black tents of a tribe that was passing through with their camels and goats tethered to posts between the tents. Those of the tribe who were out stood and watched in silence as the party of ragged and wounded men rode by. Talon's nostrils twitched at the familiar smell of old cloth material, camel dung and wool that seemed to accompany any tribe.

The exhausted group of riders rode their sweating horses down the dusty road as fast as they dared without alarming the guards on the tall walls of the fortified town. As this was one of the best harbors in the sea of Persia, it was a well protected city. The various Attabegs who had been given charge by the Seljuks took care to ensure that this town was well maintained; this brought more ships and thus more revenue.

Nearly all the men were wounded and wore bloody strips of cloth over their injuries. Talon had a cut on his forearm from one of the lances that had slipped past his guard, while Reza sported the cut on his thigh.

Youssef wore a bandage around his head that had been placed there by Rav'an after she noticed a cut on his forehead that would not stop bleeding. The screams of the wounded man who had been captured still reverberated in Talon's ears as he remembered the savage way the boy had been butchered by the sultan's men. He glanced over at Youssef to see how he was doing. He looked more haunted than the others.

Their approach to the city was observed by the guards on the walls and at the gates. Trying to look nonchalant the survivors of the battle in the passes rode up to the gates and Reza shouted that they wanted entrance. He had to repeat himself as his mouth was bone dry. None of them had had any water for hours now.

"We are from Shiraz and have come to meet an important merchant who is arrived by ship from the north," he called up. Then, as if to answer the curious looks from the guards, he said, "We were attacked by bandits in the hills. They may still be after us. They killed many of us and we lost all our goods. Allah be praised we kept our lives."

Talon flicked a gold coin high into the air where one of the guards caught it and laughed. The guards shouted down to the men who were by the gates.

"Open up, I don't care where he comes from; he has gold. You!" The man pointed down at Talon, "I hope there is more in your purse than just one."

"One for each of you!" Talon called up and flicked another coin towards them; he was trying to grin cheerfully, and he waved a small bag that jingled. He was dead tired but forced himself to remain alert as he wanted them all safely in the city before the sultan's men came boiling down from the hills. They could not be far behind.

In fact just as the gates opened and the first of their group were walking their horses into the gloom of the gateway tunnel Reza whispered to him, "They are here, move quickly!"

Rav'an heard him and spurred her horse alongside and the three of them jostled with the other riders to get well beyond the gates and into the town.

There was a shout from the parapet above the gates as the guards noticed the plume of dust rising from the road behind the fugitives, but Reza shouted up to them.

"Those are the bandits who attacked us while we were on the road! Close the gates! Do not let them in! They are bandits!"

Incredibly and to their delight the guards complied and the gates creaked round to close with a crash.

The group did not wait but rode forward at a deliberate pace so as not to alarm the guards and the attendant soldiers clustered about the gates, but their tension was nonetheless somehow transmitted to the men lounging nearby. Talon sensed that the town might be busier than on a normal day, as there seemed to be a lot of people heading in what he thought might be the direction of the center of the town. But he did not have time to think about that for long.

A man strode out of a doorway nearby; he seemed to be an officer of some kind. "Hey you!" he pointed at Talon. "Are you merchants ? By the Prophet's beard, if you are the Sultan is a poor man these days. Who let you in? There is a tax to pay!"

He reached forward to arrest Talon's progress by snatching at the reins of his horse, but Reza leaned down and struck him with his whip shouting, "We are soldiers of the sultan and you have no right to stop us!" He was trying to bluff it out. The officer staggered back, his hand holding his shoulder where Reza had struck him and shouted for his men, glaring back up at Talon and Reza.

"You will pay for that!" he yelled.

Just as he said this they heard a lot of shouting at the gates and then insistent pounding. It sounded as though the spearmen were using their lance hafts to make their point.

"Open up in the name of the Sultan of Shriaz. I am Captain Kanaan here on the Sultan's business! There are fugitives within your walls who have just arrived. They are to be stopped at all costs and arrested." The voice was commanding and insistent.

That was enough for the men near nearby. They were galvanized into action. Some of them had already jumped to their feet when they noticed the altercation between Reza and the officer, but now they were all on their feet and running towards the group. Reza shouted. "Go, Youssef! Lead the way! We must make for the harbor; the others have arrived at the gates. Go!"

They put spurs to their horses and opened the gap between the men chasing them on foot, but Talon also noticed that not only were the gates being opened but there were men boiling out of an opening in a high wall ahead of them. These men were also armed and looked as though they were about to try to stop them.

Youssef hauled his horse to a stop in a flurry of dust and then plunged into a nearby lane on the left; the others followed him but it was a narrow street and they were forced to go in single file. The lane was dimly lit even at this time of day, not permitting much light to filter down from the roofs and clothing that hung from the various balconies above them. To make matters worse there were people and donkeys using the street, and although they ran for the sides and doorways, cursing and shouting at the riders, they still slowed them down. Nonetheless they moved as quickly as they could along the narrow route, occasionally upsetting a basket in the middle or barging into a donkey with a large load, slamming it against the walls, leaving the driver screaming insults after them.

The donkeys objected to the rough treatment and added their braying to the general noise.

Youssef was all the while searching for another route that would take them down to the harbor.

The nine riders drove their horses out of the street into a small but crowded Maidan and were slowed almost to a stop by the density of the people crowded around stalls. It was the center of the town and it was market day. Youssef cursed, he wanted them to veer right down hill; he shouted and pointed over the crowd and the houses. Talon could see what he meant. There were masts showing above the roofs of the houses, showing the direction they had to go.

With Youssef leading, the group of riders began to push their way through the unaccommodating crowd of people who were beginning to shout up at them and wave their fists as stalls were jostled and bales of merchandise were trampled. But as they were only half way towards the exit, another group of armed men ran out of the street they had just vacated and were so close that the riders had no choice but to turn and face them or receive spears in their backs. As though to emphasize the situation a javelin, thrown hard and well, struck one of the horses just behind its ribs, going in deep. The agonized horse screamed and toppled forward, throwing its rider onto the hard packed earth of the maidan among the stalls.

Pandemonium erupted as the crowd realized that a battle was shaping up and they were right in the middle of it. Men, women and children ran in every direction, shrieking and crying as they fell over one another and brought down some stalls with them in a tangle of canvas, sticks and fruit or other merchandise. Goats and wooly sheep scattered among the wreckage and camels got to their feet and lumbered about roaring with excitement. Melons and other fruit rolled under foot, to be squashed into bright red slippery pieces, and the dust of spices and other seeds flew in all directions.

After a moment of hesitation as he considered the chaos and how it might be to their advantage, Talon realized that it was not enough. Reza wasted no further time. With a shout he spurred his horse straight at the running men. His horse jumped one of the fallen stalls and landed among some sacks of colored substance that flew up in a cloud around him. His horse stumbled and for a moment it looked as though it might go down, but kicking and scrambling among the sacks full of colored dust it recovered and Reza drove it on, his sword pointed forward at the footmen in front of him.

With barely a moment's hesitation Talon, Youssef and the other mounted men followed suit, crashing through the remaining flimsy tented stalls as they headed for their enemy. Talon just had time to shout.

"Go, Rav'an! Take the road to the port! Jannat, go with her! We will follow as soon as we can!" He did not check to see if they had done so. A large sack slid off a nearby heap right in his path and broke open. A cloud of yellow dust flew into the air and almost covered him and his horse in something sharp and smelling like spice. Youssef coughed and shook his head as he rode alongside.

They careered into the spearmen and laid about them with the ferocious desperation of men who are at their limit. The spear men were quite unprepared for the savagery of the counter attack. Talon ran his horse hard into one man, having the satisfaction of hearing him scream as he went under his horse's hooves, but he had no time to give it any further thought. On his right, shouting insults and laying about him with lightning fast strokes, was Reza, while Youssef acquitted himself well on the left.

Talon smacked a spear aside and drove his sword into the face of the spearman who stood his ground in front of him. The man fell away with a scream clutching his face, blood spurting. Another drove his spear up at Talon from the right front but Talon managed to deflect the clumsy thrust before he rose in the stirrups and hacked his blade down on the cringing turbaned head in front of him. He felt he sharp blade cut through the cloth and bite deep into the man's skull. There was no cry as the body fell away.

He was through and out the other side, hauling on the reins with his left hand, his sword bloody, looking back over his shoulder as his horse sat on its haunches and tried to turn on a pin. Reza was doing the same, his sword bloody to the hilt with new blood spraying off it. For some reason he and his mount had turned almost completely blue!

They turned together and then knee to knee they drove their horses the very short distance into the three remaining men who were standing on their feet. The men were so bewildered at the ferocity of the first charge that they were even less prepared for the two brightly colored killers who struck them from behind. The whole skirmish was over in a matter of long seconds. The maidan looked as though it had been struck by a tempest. The wreckage of the market was everywhere, nothing remained of the original temporary structures. Bales of merchandise were strewn about and among them little piles of dust indicating the former presence of spices and dyes. There was no sign of the people who had originally been there and only a few animals. A lamb was bleating in a corner and a donkey stood stoically in another. A couple of camels wandered about roaring, but their owners were keeping their distance. Frightened faces peered out at them from dark recesses in the walls and doorways but no one moved.

There were five dead men lying in their own blood on the hard packed mud of the Maidan and two wounded. But one of the wounded was Youssef's man. Youssef had garnered another wound in the leg but he shrugged it off when Talon pointed at it.

"We must get to the harbor!" he croaked. Then he leaned down and asked his man who was huddled in a heap on the ground, "Can you walk or ride, Salim?"

The man rolled over and they all gasped. He had the head of a spear sticking out of his chest. "I am on my way to meet God," he rasped; his teeth clenched in a bloody grin of death, his eyes rolling with pain.

"Leave me! I am a dead man. You cannot wait..." He choked on his own blood and his voice trailed off as he sank back, his bloody hands clutching at the broken haft of the spear. His feet drummed on the ground, his whole body shuddered and then he was dead.

"We must leave, Youssef," Reza said gently to his friend. "He was a brave man and has gone the way of a warrior."

Youssef nodded, but his face was ashen and twisted with grief. Talon now had time to look around and noticed to his consternation that Rav'an was still with them, although she was near to the street they would have to take.

He waved furiously at her and indicated that she should lead the way. They trotted their horses after her but just as they were leaving another group of men on horses entered the Maidan.

"Hurry! They are upon us!" Talon shouted. His companions needed no encouragement. He spurred his horse forward and down the steep slope towards the harbor.

The newcomers to the Maidan halted in some confusion as they saw the destruction in the middle, but then their leader shouted and pointed.

"After them! They are going to the harbor!" he yelled.

Talon realized that they could not possibly make the port without this group catching up with them so he called to Reza, "We need arrows, my brother!"

Reza turned and nodded. "Why have you turned all yellow?" he asked, but he took out his bow as they cantered down the short street and then, at a sharp turn to the right where the street narrowed, he turned his horse to face back the way they had come.

"I am yellow?" asked Talon, shaking his head and sneezing violently. "But you my brother are blue, like a Djinn! You and your horse, if that is a horse you are riding !"

Reza laughed and shook his head. His hair was spiked in all directions making him look like some crazed Djinn on a horse. The laugh broke the tension, but now they had to stop the charging men, so they turned their attention to their front. The others, led by Rav'an, drove their horses for the port which was only a couple of streets away.

Talon had also pulled his bow from its sheath. Their bows taut with an arrow knocked, the two of them urged their horses forward to the point where they could see up the street they had just taken, and there they saw the enemy charging down towards them. There had to be at least twelve men on horses jostling for room in the narrow street, hemmed in by mud brick walls on either side the street which gave only room for two horsemen side by side.

Two arrows flew and then two more quickly followed, creating chaos. The arrows were aimed at the horses and the two in front came down, tumbling their riders under the hooves of their companions who, trying to avoid them, came down themselves in a pile of struggling, kicking horses and yelling men who were trying to avoid being killed by the flailing hooves. The road in front of the body of the horsemen was well blocked for a few precious minutes.

"We must be gone," Talon told Reza, who needed no persuasion. They both sneezed at the same time.

Making their way directly to the port on their exhausted horses they looked for a likely ship that might have been chosen for their purposes. The quay was almost deserted at this time, although there was a small cargo boat tied up alongside the thick poles that looked as though it was about to leave.

They trotted alongside the stone-walled quayside, their horses' hooves clicking on the stone surface, to join the others who were still mounted but staring out towards the ships in the harbor.

"Where are these servants you talked about Talon? I see no one!" There was real alarm in Reza's voice.

Talon looked out at the other ships in the small bay and wondered which one was supposed to be theirs. He began to know despair when there came a shout from across the water. They stared out to the middle of the bay where the shout had come from. It seemed to have come from a boat that was larger than the others and anchored further out than most. It was difficult to see, for even at this early hour there was a heat haze on the water, but soon after a boat was dropped into the sea with a splash and some men piled into it and began to pull hard for the shore heading in their direction. Talon and Reza cast nervous looks behind them as they had no idea as to how close the pursuers might be.

But something else bothered Talon as he looked along the quay seeking points of trouble. He thought he recognized a man standing watching them, but he had no idea as to where he might have seen him before. The individual was showing a lot of interest for a casual watcher as he stood near the large boat tied to the quayside. Talon turned an anxious look back to the entrance of the street they had exited, half expecting men to come boiling out and attack them before they could depart. He spoke to the others.

"We should stay mounted in case there is trouble and the boat cannot reach us in time. We can escape in that direction if we have to."

He pointed to the end of the quay that merged with a sandy beach where they could just jump the horses and try to make an escape.

He glanced at Rav'an and Jannat. They looked bedraggled and exhausted. Rav'an's face was drawn and white but she noticed his look and managed a tense smile. He could see in the clear light of day just how perfect were her features even when she was exhausted; his heart went out to her and his pulse beat a little faster. He sent her a smile of encouragement.

The boat was close now, however; they could make out the people in it as the sweating men rowed it hard towards them. Standing in the thwarts was someone they all knew.

"That is the Doctor!" cried Rav'an excitedly. Talon and Reza realized at the same time that she was right and shouted greetings. The man waved and shouted something back. They could not hear clearly what he said, but by this time the boat was almost alongside the quay and it was time to dismount and hurry down the wooden steps.

They reluctantly let the horses go; they were committed to the sea now. Youssef and his remaining companions dismounted and chased their mounts away. The bewildered animals did not go far but wandered off down the quay.

"Youssef, take Rav'an and Jannat to the stairs and see them onto the boat. Reza and I will watch our back," Talon told him.

Youssef nodded and his men helped Rav'an and Jannat to the edge of the steps and then hurried them down towards the water. Reza and Talon retrieved their bows and quivers, then gave their animals a slap on their rumps to get them to depart at a trot back the way they had come. They had just done this when horsemen appeared at the far end of the quay at the street entrance they themselves had just exited.

The sultan's men saw the fugitives as they were about to disappear down the steps to the water where the boat was now bumping against the pilings, rising and falling with the low swell of the sea. They shouted and put spurs to their horses, galloping hard down the length of the stone built rampart towards Reza and Talon.

"They are here! Hurry!" shouted Reza, and he knelt on the stones, his bow at the ready.

Rav'an turned and called to Talon, "You have to come with me! You cannot leave me now!" But the doctor and the boat's oarsmen were already yelling at her and the others to get on the boat, their arms outstretched to receive them.

Looking back over her shoulder she clambered into the rocking boat, assisted by the turbaned sailors and the doctor. Then Jannat was almost thrown onto the boat into a crewman's arms. Youssef and his companions scrambled aboard.

Talon had followed Reza's example, setting an arrow in his bow. He said, "We need to kill the leaders and then leave, my brother."

Reza merely nodded. They both pulled back at the same time and sent an arrow each whispering towards the galloping horsemen. The arrows found their marks. Two men choked and fell with noisy thumps on the stones, their bodies loose in death, and their horses veered off. The other riders hauled their horses to a stop in surprise, but they were only forty yards away and perfect targets for the two skilled archers facing them. Two more arrows flew and two more men tumbled to the ground.

The remaining horsemen's courage failed them; they turned their mounts then fled to the end of the quay. One man lying on the ground wounded yelled after them that they were cowards and should be attacking, but he was badly wounded and soon fell back gasping; an arrow was jutting out of his chest and his life blood was flowing onto the stones.

Talon guessed that the man had been the leader and hoped that the others might lose heart.

Both he and Reza leapt to their feet and ran down the slippery steps to scramble onto the rocking boat. Without a word the oarsmen pulled away rowing furiously.

Talon and Reza stood in the narrow confines of the crowded boat and kept their bows high with an arrow seated, their strings taut. They were soon fifty paces out into the harbor when the men came galloping back along the quay. Several dismounted and ran over to the man who had shouted at them; he pointed from his prone position on the ground. They appeared to be discussing the situation, for some got up and ran towards the large boat, shouting and gesticulating, while a couple ran to the edge of the quay and shot arrows towards the boat. But it was pulling away too fast and far for the weak cavalry bows the men used and their arrows dropped into the water well behind it.

Talon knew his arrows could reach the quay so he sent a couple towards the men and managed to hit one in the leg, which made the others run back towards some shelter, the wounded man limping hastily after them, calling for help.

Then he decided to send and arrow in the direction of the boat to discourage the men there. The men cowered as two arrows thudded into the side of the boat, but soon after they were again remonstrating with the crew of the ship and pointing at the small overcrowded boat rowing hard for the large ship anchored out in the bay.

"They are going to come after us with that ship over there," the doctor remarked to the world at large while pointing at the ship and the activity going on around it. After settling down on a bench facing the steersman and the doctor, Rav'an demanded an explanation.

"Doctor Haddad, God be praised it is you, but how and why are you here?"

"Greetings, my children!" said the doctor; he was tense with concern but somehow seemed to be enjoying the situation. "I decided that I could not leave such an important task to my servants no matter how much I trusted them, so I came myself to ensure you got away safely." He beamed at them while they stared at him, still getting over their surprise.

Bird in a cage
Set free
Soaring in the sky...
Freedom
All cherish
Reaching a new high

—Tirupathi Chanduppatla

Chapter 34

A Falcon Flies Free

They were half way across the clear sunlit waters of the harbor and closing in on their destination, all talking at once, when one of the oarsmen grunted and pointed back the way they had come. Talon and Reza got to their feet despite the rocking of the boat and stared back at the quayside, which was now several hundred yards away. It was full of people now in among the soldiers and horses, and they were gesticulating wildly, shouting and pointing as they saw their quarry escaping off to sea.

But there was also a flurry of activity on the ship that had been moored alongside the quay, and it now seemed that it was full of men. Its sail was unfurled and quickly tightened and then they could see men pushing the boat free of the quayside with long poles.

"Hurry! We must get to the ship at once!" Reza exclaimed. "They will be on our tail before we know it."

The oarsmen bent to the task willingly, their muscles straining at the oars while the steersman shouted at the large ship ahead and exchanged words with men on board who were leaning over the high stern looking down at them. He pointed back towards the quay and told them to prepare for sea immediately. The men glanced at the activity on the distant quay and ran off, calling out to the crew.

The oarsmen accomplished their task well and within minutes they were alongside a very large ship that was full of activity as men hurriedly prepared it to sail. Men were straining at the winch to bring the anchor up while others were in the rigging unlashing the main sail and tightening the slightly smaller sail towards the rear of the ship. Others were poised to haul the to main sails tight as soon as they were released.

They clambered aboard in a rush. Youssef and the others climbed the side first to allow Rav'an to be helped up the side by both Reza and Talon. There they were met with another surprise.

Rav'an cried out as her son rushed out of the small group waiting to greet them and wrapped his arms around her waist. She knelt on the wooden deck with tears flowing freely as she hugged him and murmured endearments into his hair while stroking his neck and shoulders. But Talon and Reza were gaping at another person who stepped forward to be greeted.

"Auntie Fariba!" exclaimed Talon, and he seized her in a tight embrace.

"How did... how did you get here and why are you here?"

"That will take a little while to explain. My dear Talon, I cannot breathe! But I see you were successful and God be praised, you even have Reza with you! Why are you covered in this yellow stuff?" She sneezed and waved her hand in the air.

"I could not have done it alone, Auntie," Talon said with a grin at the bizarrely blue Reza, who was now being embraced by Fariba. "My brother was there before me and nearly killed me when I came along to help him! Also we all owe our lives to Youssef and his band of men who gave their lives for us. We could not have made it without their help, Auntie." Talon smiled at Youssef and his tattered companions. Youssef ducked his head in embarrassment but he was very pleased with the praise.

"Reza!" exclaimed Fariba, "How could you! What happened? I want to know every detail of the rescue." She disengaged herself, laughing, just in time to be enveloped in a tight embrace by a tearful Rav'an who threw herself at her and buried her face in Fariba's neck, weeping with joy. They stayed like that for a long moment, two lovely women murmuring to one another unwilling to let each other go. Finally Rav'an spoke. "Fariba, we brought someone with us. This is the princess, Jannat."

Talon and Reza gaped.

Talon noticed Dar'an in among the other servants and waved to him, relieved that the boy had made it and seemed at home with the people from Isfahan. He could be sure that the boy had brought all their baggage and the money.

Dar'an hurried forward, ready to kneel in front of him, but Talon seized him before he could and gave him a brief embrace. "I am glad to see you, Dar'an. God has seen fit that we are safe and sound."

Dar'an bobbed his head and said happily, "God has been kind again, my Lord. I am right glad to see you safe. I have prepared your cabin for you and brought everything with us." He was grinning from ear to ear with pleasure at seeing Talon again.

Talon had difficulty swallowing he was so thirsty. He coughed then said, "Good lad, go and stay with the others and I will be down presently." He pushed the boy gently back towards the assembled servants.

"Is there anything to drink?" Reza asked the world at large.

"Everyone must go below to allow the crew to do their work!" shouted an irritable voice from above in the quarterdeck. People immediately hurried towards the stern of the large ship and began to disappear below decks.

Someone provided a water skin, which Talon and the others drank from thirstily, then Talon and Reza, with Youssef in attendance, left the excited chatter of the women and the servants and climbed the stairs to the top rear deck to join the doctor and a man who was apparently the skipper. Both men were peering back towards the quay and the frenzy of activity taking place there.

The men turned as they heard them come onto the deck and after brief but heartfelt embraces the doctor introduced the man with him.

"This is Captain Ghanem, the skipper of this ship. He has agreed to take us to Muscat in Oman. He comes from there so he is going home. I have paid him handsomely with the gold you gave me for this purpose, Talon."

Reza stared at Talon. "Oman? Why there, Talon?"

"Where else can we go, Reza? We cannot stay in this land any more. They will seek us wherever we go, but there I have a friend who owes me a great deal."

The skipper turned away from the men on the quarterdeck and began shouting commands; clearly he was impatient to get his ship under way.

"That boat will be upon us before we can get going," Reza muttered apprehensively.

Talon was inclined to agree; the other boat, although laden with men, was now surging towards them with its lateen sail taut to the breeze. The men on the boat were shouting and brandishing weapons.

Finally the great sails of their own ship dropped, then flapped idly, but were quickly hauled in tight as the light breeze from the shore filled them. It was but a matter of moments before the ship was in motion, slipping silently through the clear waters of the deep bay, gaining speed with every moment.

Talon and Reza stood with their bows ready, looking back at the onrushing pursuit boat, trying to make out the distance and calculating the time when they would have to use their bows again. Its waist was full of armed men and on the quarterdeck they could see a small huddle of men on the bows pointing at them.

"It is much smaller than our ship and could be a lot faster," Reza observed quietly.

"I was thinking the same thing, my brother; but I know of one very good way to deal with another ship that is coming after me."

"Oh, so you have sailed before and you have been chased before, my brother? What adventures are these, Talon?"

Talon grinned. "I have, yes, and I have managed on both occasions to get away. We shall discuss our adventures later, but now we shall use fire, Reza."

"I must hear all about this one day," Reza laughed. "But for now tell us what you need."

Talon explained the situation to the others, including the captain, who at first looked alarmed at the idea of fire being used on his decks, but then calmed down when Talon explained how it could be done. There was of course fire on the ship, very carefully contained, but it could be used.

"You should wait a while before you worry about fire, Sirs. In shah'Allah there will be no need today," he addressed them respectfully.

"Why do you say that, Captain?" asked the doctor.

"Because their ship is heavily laden with far too many men and has but one sail. It is only an *al badan*, but this ship is a *ghanjah* and has two sails, and see how large they are. Once we are clear of that headland," he pointed, "we can show almost any boat on this sea a clean pair of heels. Not only that, this ship sails better than most in rough weather, and I think we are in for some by early afternoon and tonight. I am confident that we will lose them before dark."

As if to make the point he captain shouted an order and the second stern sail was hauled in; it bellied full and the crew lashed it tight. Talon and Reza looked skeptical but agreed to hold off until the situation got worse, if indeed it did.

At the mention of rough weather Talon felt a bit nervous; the memories of his shipwreck in the Mediterranean and another storm outside Abydos were still very fresh in his mind. As for

Youssef, he was clearly at the end of his tether, as he was shivering in the cool sea air.

"Youssef," Reza said, "go below with your brave companions and get some sleep. Everything will be all right now, and if not we will wake you. Go to sleep."

Youssef yawned and nodded silently, but he embraced the two of them and went below with his companions. Talon and Reza turned to scrutinize the oncoming vessel. They unslung their bows and laid some arrows agains the side of the ship and began to estimate the distances. They were sure there was going to be an uneven fight if the men on the following vessel managed to board them.

But the captain was right; as they neared the headland the wind changed and came from a more northerly quarter. Hitherto the men had been watching the other ship gain on them to the point where they could clearly make out the men on board as it ploughed through the light swell of the sheltered waters of the bay. But as soon as their ship cleared the bay it heeled and then steadied as the Captain called a heading to the two steersmen, and then they began to fly through the now choppy seas heading due west.

Spray flew back all the way to the high stern deck as the bow rose and fell, shouldering the seas aside.

Staring back at the other boat Talon and Reza laughed together. That boat was now wallowing in and out of the swells making heavy weather of the changed sea and stiffer wind. It began to drop behind perceptibly. Within an hour all they could see of it was the top of its sail. The land they had left was shortly only a slim bluish line on the eastern horizon.

Talon clapped Reza on the shoulder and said, "Seems the captain was right, my brother. Let's go below and get an explanation as to what the doctor and Auntie Fariba are doing on this ship!"

As they passed the captain he nodded to the north east, where there were dark gathering clouds and said, "There is going to be a blow tonight if I am not mistaken, so make sure everyone stays below tonight, Sirs. I shall continue in a westerly direction to keep them guessing," he jerked his thumb at the ship behind them, "then we will turn south in the middle of the night."

Talon and Reza nodded in unison and then headed down the ladders to the enclosed deck below the quarter deck. Here they found the others comfortably seated on cushions in a large cabin that had several now shuttered windows that opened out over the stern of the ship.

"This is a big boat, Uncle," said Reza to the doctor. "How did you find it?"

"I had hoped that there might be a large enough boat in the port; they come here regularly at this time of year so it was a fair chance we would find one," Haddad returned. "Luckily this captain is from Oman too. He knows the family of your friend whom you saved from the prison. After I told him about that he was willing... with the help of the gold, of course." He chuckled.

Talon seated himself next to Rav'an and she leaned over and kissed him as he settled in.

"My protectors," she purred, and Fariba laughed delightedly. "I remember you calling these two that long ago, my dear! Even then they were a dangerous pair of boys!" she said.

The doctor agreed with her and smiled. "I have never seen a more villainous pair of men if my life, my Dear. And now they are covered in strange colors! I pity the people in Shiraz when you two came to visit them," he laughed at Reza and Talon, who grinned back.

"We want to know how you saved these two ladies and managed to escape!" Fariba cried.

"Only after you have explained what you are doing here, Auntie," countered Talon. "I had expected Rostam and Alehla, but not you two! What happened to make you change your minds?"

Fariba sat up a little straighter and looked over at the doctor, who was seated near the doorway.

"We talked, Talon, and decided to come along for a variety of reasons. Not least being that we were afraid of the Master and the Sultan of Shiraz's vengeance; they might have sent men to our house regardless of the fact that we were not supposed to know anything. In these times it is sensible to be careful, so we locked the house up and left as though going on a visit to the north." She paused as the others nodded understanding.

"But then I could not bring myself to be parted from my darling Rav'an anymore, and that includes you, Talon and Reza, and of course my sweet Rostam here!" She patted the boy on the arm as she spoke and smiled down at him.

Rostam regarded the assembly with wide eyes from the arms of his mother, who held him as though she was afraid he might disappear.

"Where are we going, Auntie?" he piped.

"We are going to Oman, my little man, with your long lost father," Rav'an said, gently rocking him. The boy turned uncertain eyes upon his father, regarding him solemnly. Talon smiled at him encouragingly. They had not spent much time together in Isfahan but long enough, he hoped, to ensure the boy knew him and was not afraid of him.

Talon looked at Reza and then said, "Auntie Fariba, Uncle, I am in agreement that the anger of the Khan, or even more of the Sultan, could be bad for you had you stayed in Isfahan, and I am very happy you are with us, but it will be dangerous and I have little idea as to what we shall do when we get there."

He was not worried about the gold he had, there was enough for a while at least; but all the same they were now responsible for not only themselves and Rav'an and the child but also for their beloved friends from Isfahan and many more servants than before.

The doctor put him right on this.

"Talon, in time this will blow over as long as we leave with no trace, and the men on that other boat have no idea where we are going. I also want to travel and have heard exciting things about Oman. They are the finest sailors in the world and ship builders without peer. If we are lucky we will become merchants, and then what riches will we find in the kingdom of Oman, or from far off lands where they trade?

"Besides, it is not as though I am a poor man either, so we should manage well enough until we find out what we want to do."

"Uncle, you are a remarkable man," said Talon and he meant it. Fariba placed a hand on Haddad's arm, smiling up at the doctor as she did so. "You are right, Talon. My husband is a brave and adventurous man."

Haddad beamed at all of them while going quite red with pleased embarrassment in the process.

They called for some tea and drank it from small porcelain cups while the ship rose and fell in the light swell as it sailed westward. It was now late in the afternoon; a cold meal was served and as they ate they talked. There was no escaping the curiosity of the doctor and Fariba.

"Now you must tell us about the escape and how you found Rav'an and Jannat, my dear boys," Fariba insisted.

*****

Many sea miles behind them, the boat commandeered by Captain Kanaan's men turned back. The Captain had died gasping for air in the stuffy rear cabin of the boat, bleeding to death despite the best efforts of his men to staunch the blood that flowed from his chest wound.

His now leaderless men disobeyed his command to continue to follow the fugitives because they were exhausted and frightened, and now most were sea-sick, hanging over the lee side of the corkscrewing boat retching into the sea.

The skipper of the boat, angry at the fact that his boat was full of men instead of cargo, pointed out with some relish that his ship could not match the one they followed in this kind of sea. Not only that, although their quarry was going in a westerly direction now, they could alter their course at any time during the night and they would never know which way to follow.

None of the men on the ship knew who the luckless man was going to be who would have to carry the news of the failure back to the sultan of Shiraz but they were sure of one thing: they did not want to continue in this pitching and rolling hell any longer than it took to sail back to port.

*****

Several hours later, on their own ship, now steering towards the south and Oman, Talon and Rav'an stood in the shelter of the ship's side on the windward side listening to the hiss and slap of the waves. It was dark but they could quite easily make out the masts, the pale form of the sails and the deeper shadows of the ship against the starlit night. Above and behind them they could hear the murmur of the ship's captain and the steersmen as they guided the vessel towards Oman.

He held Rostam in the crook of his right arm; the sleepy boy had his arms around Talon's neck and Rav'an was within the curve of his other arm. She had pulled Talon's cloak around them, enclosing all three within its warmth. It also helped to ward off some of the light spray occasionally flying in from the sea.

Rostam pointed up at the sky, which although dark to the north was still clear above them.

"Alia calls them the jewels of heaven," he piped.

"They are indeed jewels, Rostam. Without their guidance I could not have found you and your mother,"said Talon.

"How can that be?" Rostam asked. Rav'an's hand tightened on his forearm as she listened. He knew she was smiling.

"One day, soon, you and I will learn all about the heavens and what they can tell us, but first we must go to Oman to see a friend," Talon told his son.

The End

Author's Note

I hope you enjoyed this book but...
If you think that Talon's life story is over you might be wrong. In going to Oman he has inadvertently opened many doors to future adventures, perhaps in Zanzibar and Africa, India.... But let's not forget the assassins who are still on his and Rav'an's trail, with even more cause for vengeance now. In the year of 1179 and onward for the next ten years, so very much happens in the Eastern Mediterranean world that it is tempting to think that he might have a part in that too.

About The Author

James Boschert

James Boschert grew up in the then colony of Malaya in the early fifties. He learned first hand about terrorism while there as the Communist insurgency was in full swing. His school was burnt down and the family, while traveling, narrowly survived an ambush, saved by a Gurkha patrol, which drove off the insurgents.

He went on to join the British army serving in remote places like Borneo and Oman. Later he spent five years in Iran before the revolution, where he played polo with the Iranian Army, developed a passion for the remote Assassin castles found in the high mountains to the north, and learned to understand and speak the Farsi language.

Escaping Iran during the revolution, he went on to become an engineer and now lives in Arizona on a small ranch with his family and animals.

If You Enjoyed This Book,
Visit

FIRESHIP PRESS
www.fireshippress.com

All Fireship Press books are available directly through our website, amazon.com, Barnes and Noble and Nook, Sony Reader, Apple iTunes, Kobo books and via leading bookshops across the United States, Canada, the UK, Australia and Europe.

The Talon Series by James Boschert

ASSASSINS OF ALAMUT
BY
JAMES BOSCHERT

An Epic Novel of Persia and Palestine in the Time of the Crusades

Knight Assassin
The Second Book of Talon
by
James Boschert

A joyous homecoming turns into a nightmare as a Talon must do the one thing that he didn't want to - become an assassin again.

Assassination in Al-Qahirah
James Boschert

GREEK FIRE
BY
JAMES BOSCHERT

In the fourth book of Talon, James Boschert delivers fast-paced adventures, packed with violent confrontations and intrepid heroes up against hard odds.

FORCE 12 IN GERMAN BIGHT

BY

JAMES BOSCHERT

Considering that oil and gas have been flowing from under the North Sea for the best part of half a century, it is perhaps surprising that more writers have not taken the uncompromising conditions that are experienced in this area – which extends from the north of Scotland to the coasts of Norway and Germany – for the setting of a novel. James Boschert's latest redresses the balance.

The book takes its title from the name of an area regularly referred to in the legendary BBC Shipping Forecast and one which experiences some of the worst weather conditions around the British Isles. It is a fast-paced story which smacks of authenticity in every line. A world of hard men, hard liquor, hard drugs and cold-blooded murder. The reality of the setting and the characters , ex-military men from both sides of the Atlantic, crooked wheeler-dealers, and Danish detectives, male and female, are all in on the action.

This is not story telling akin to a latter day Bulldog Drummond, or even a James Bond, but simply a snortingly good yarn which will jangle the nerve ends, fill your nose with the smell of salt and diesel oil, your ears with the deafening sound of machinery aboard a monster pipe-dredging ship and, above all, make you remember never to underestimate the power of the sea.

'Roger Paine, former Commander, Royal Navy'.

JACK MARTIN : THE ALPHONSO CLAY SERIES

THE BATTLE HYMN
OF THE REPUBLIC

AN ALPHONSO CLAY MYSTERY
OF THE CIVIL WAR

BY JACK MARTIN

Hail Columbia

by

Jack Martin

In 1869, four years after the Civil War has ended, Southerners bristle under the authority of a military government.

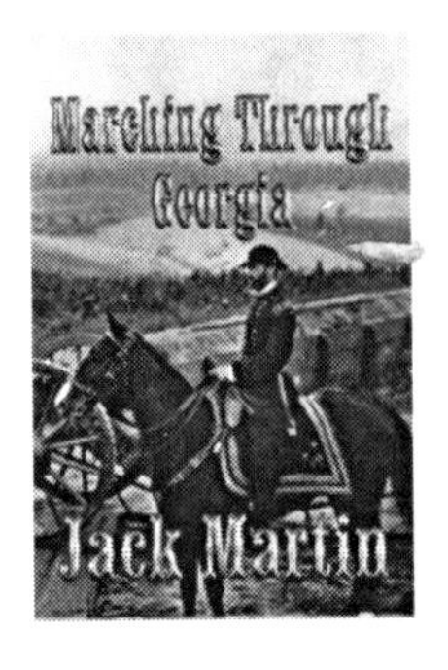

MARCHING THROUGH GEORGIA

BY

JACK MARTIN

The Eastern Door

by

David More

Immigrating from 18th century rural Ireland, Billy Smithyman builds a new life in the New York frontier, where Billy's honesty stands out in the corrupt fur trade, and where he earns the trust of formidable Mohawk war chief Emperor Marten. Smithyman becomes a Mohawk warrior and captures the love of Marten's niece, the fierce Laura Silverbirch. But Smithyman's success makes murderous enemies in the colonial establishment and leads him into his greatest challenge. In the midst of the French and Indian War, he is appointed the amateur commander of an untrained, civilian militia and ordered to capture a powerful French fort and its garrison. Smithyman and his ragtag army must quickly learn to outmaneuver a veteran French general, his well-trained army, and overcome colonial traitors if they are to survive. *The Eastern Door* is the first novel in the stunning American Colonial History series.

Lieutenant and Mrs. Lockwood

by

Mark Bois

"Captain Barr desperately wanted to kill Lieutenant Lockwood. He thought constantly of doing so, though he had long since given up any consideration of a formal duel. Lockwood, after all, was a good shot and a fine swordsman; a knife in the back would do. And then Barr dreamt of going back to Ireland, and of taking Brigid Lockwood for his own."

So begins the story of Lieutenant James Lockwood, his wife Brigid, and his deadly rivalry – professional and romantic – with Charles Barr. Lockwood and Barr hold each other's honor hostage, at a time when a man's honor meant more than his life. But can a man as treacherous as Charles Barr be trusted to keep secret the disgrace that could irrevocably ruin Lockwood and his family?

Against a backdrop of famine and uprising in Ireland, and the war between Napoleon and Wellington, showing the famous Inniskilling Regiment in historically accurate detail, here is a romance for the ages, and for all time.

"… Bois' meticulous research and command of historical detail makes this novel a must read. He sets the standard for research and understanding… and the audience will demand more novels from this new author. Historical fiction welcomes Mark Bois with open arms." – Lt. Col. Brad Luebbert, US Army.

Close to the Sun

by

Donald Michael Platt

Close to the Sun follows the lives of fighter pilots during the Second World War. As a boy, Hank Milroy from Wyoming idealized the gallant exploits of WWI fighter aces. Karl, Fürst von Pfalz-Teuffelreich, aspires to surpass his father's 49 Luftsiegen. Seth Braham falls in love with flying during an air show at San Francisco's Chrissy Field.
The young men encounter friends, rivals, and exceptional women. Braxton Mobley, the hotshot, wants to outscore every man in the air force. Texas tomboy Catherine "Winty" McCabe is as good a flyer as any man. Princess Maria-Xenia, a stateless White Russian, works for the Abwehr, German Intelligence. Elfriede Wohlman is a frontline nurse with a dangerous secret. Miriam Keramopoulos is the girl from Brooklyn with a voice that will take her places.

Once the United States enter the war, Hank, Brax, and Seth experience the exhilaration of aerial combat and acedom during the unromantic reality of combat losses, tedious bomber escort, strafing runs, and the firebombing of entire cities. As one of the hated aristocrats, Karl is in as much danger from Nazis as he is from enemy fighter pilots, as he and his colleagues desperately try to stem the overwhelming tide as the war turns against Germany. Callous political decisions, disastrous mistakes, and horrific atrocities they witness at the end of WWII put a dark spin on all their dreams of glory.

www.Fireshippress.com
Found in all leading Booksellers and on line eBook distributors

CPSIA information can be obtained at www.ICGtesting.com
Printed in the USA
BVOW04s0635020714

357993BV00010B/907/P

9 781611 792850